SCARE TACTICS

SCARE TACTICS

Michael Raff

Other books written by Michael Raff

Special

&

Seven: Tales of Terror

May be purchased online at mraffbooks.com

ACKNOWLEDGEMENTS

Since joining the High Desert Branch of the California Writers Club in 2011, my writing skills have improved considerably. So I would like to thank the entire branch, (about 105 members) for their support, advice and inspiration. In particular, I would like to thank my fellow writers in the three critique groups I have participated in. Without their input, this book would not have been as imaginative or as well-written as the material turned out to be. Therefore, I'm thanking the following individuals, in no particular order: The Electica group: Jenny Margotta, Virginia Hall, Diane Neil, Barbara (Rusty) LaGrange, Linda Cooper, and Anthony Enriquez. The Dark Side group: Curt James, Steven Marin, John (Rocky) McAlister, F. L. Gold, and Roberta L. Smith. The Genre Gurus group: Jeanie Newcomer, Katherine Hamor, Monica Edwards and Elizabeth Paine. I have thoroughly enjoyed my collaboration with each and every one of these dedicated writers.

Also, I thank my good friends, Joe and Cam Gonzalez, who have encouraged and supported me on my various writing projects. Another vote of thanks to Roberta L. Smith for her formatting skills. An enormous thank you to Jenny Margotta, my talented editor. Every writer needs a good editor, but I'm lucky, I have a great one.

A special thank you to my extremely wonderful and understanding wife, Joyce, for putting up with my long hours at the computer, my endless drivel about writing, rewriting, and even more rewriting, my countless book-related activities, and her many hours of proofreading my material. Thank you, honey.

To my beloved Aunt Betty, whom I miss dearly.

And to my wife, Joyce, whom I love dearly.

"Are you ready for your next go 'round?" - Marcus Croft, president and founder of Croft International.

Illustration by: John Margotta Ferrara
Cover graphics by Jenny Margotta

CONTENTS

FORWARD

Move over, Stephen King. Michael Raff has done it again.

Mr. Raff first appeared on the horror story scene in 2013 with his book, *Seven: Tales of Terror,* which featured such memorable characters as Melissa with her very strange brood of cats, Father Manacheck hearing the last confession of an avowed vampire, and Nurse Mary Dawson dealing with the terrors of the night shift on an isolated hospital ward. Now he has surpassed that memorable cast with the introduction of his second anthology, *Scare Tactics.*

Michael has the uncanny ability to take every day, common situations and turn them into deliciously chilling episodes of fear and terror. What could possibly go wrong at a neighborhood pizza place? Or what could anyone have to fear during an innocent morning jog? In another story, a horseback ride turns into a frightening experience when the rider is threatened by an unexpected presence. Then there's the guy trying to rid his garage of a single rat. An easy solution, right? Think again!

You won't be able to put the book down until you've read it from first page to last. But once you've read it, beware. You just might find yourself viewing the familiar, commonplace world around you from a totally different perspective. Or find yourself lying awake late at night asking, "Am I next?"

Michael Raff is a relatively new voice on the horror story stage – but he's definitely here to stay.

March, 2014. Jenny Margotta, editor, author

A WORD ABOUT HORROR

Ah, horror! How I love the sound of it . . . the sight of it . . . the thrill of it! But why? Or should I ask, why do millions of us love to be scared out of our cotton-picking minds? Why do we buy dozens of books by writers such as Stephen King and Dean Koontz, or go to the movies and nearly choke on our popcorn . . . just to be terrorized? Well, I can only guess why *you* love it so much, but as for me, I can explain the true nitty-gritty as to why I'm so attracted to those hidden, unspeakable things that go bump in the night.

It all started with two zany guys – a famous comedy team of long ago. I was in the first grade, a scant seven years old, and discovered that the movie, "Abbott and Costello Meets Frankenstein," was going to be broadcast on television at 10:00 PM. Too late to stay up for such a young lad, you ask? Perhaps, but it was a Friday night with no school the following morning. So I pleaded, promised, and totally humbled myself in order to persuade my extremely conservative mother to allow my brother, Eddie, and me to stay up and watch something that might very well give us all kinds of blood-curdling nightmares. After much debate, browbeating, and bickering, our mother finally relented. It was a stunning victory, nothing short of a *bona fide* miracle.

I had tried talking her into allowing us to stay up late on Saturday nights countless times before to catch one of the many old monster movies that were, at the time, haunting the entire metropolis of Chicago. The defining difference was that the Saturday night films were aired at midnight, much too late for a pair of respectable schoolboys. Besides, on Sundays we had to rise early and attend Catholic Mass.

When the grand hour finally arrived that Friday night, misinformation abounded regarding the proper station and we ended up tuning in late. I was panic-stricken, frustrated, horrified (pun intended), and going out of my ever-loving mind. How much of this wondrous event had we missed? Life was so cruel, so hideously unfair! Fortunately, only a few minutes had aired, and in my very first excursion into the realm of horror, Lou Costello was opening a coffin where a nefarious Count Dracula resided. Before long both the famous vampire and the Frankenstein Monster were creating spine-tingling havoc.

Shortly thereafter, things became really hairy when the Wolf Man jumped in. That's when my brother and I began watching the remainder of the film from behind the couch. There were several scenes that scared me senseless, not that I had a whole lot of sense to begin with. For many a day thereafter, that's all I talked about – that wild and scary movie. My fate had been sealed. At the tender age of seven, I was irrevocably hooked on horror.

Now you're probably thinking that I didn't even answer my own question of why so many of us, me in particular, take such inane pleasure at being scared. Or why we just seem to naturally gravitate to the dark, mysterious world of horror. Well, in a sort of roundabout manner, my little anecdote does answer those very questions.

We all start out as innocent children with an incredible sense of curiosity. When we're terrorized, whether in the guise of a book, cartoon, or movie, it gives us a thrill, or more specifically, a *vicarious* rush, which, quite fortuitously, is not an *actual* threat to our own safety. We don't have to climb onto a rollercoaster ride, or jump out of an airplane and pray that our parachute opens. In our cozy little scenario, all we have to do is sit there and take it. It's easy, fun, and most importantly, no one gets hurt. And as the years go by, many of us, yours truly included, never actually grow up, at least not when it comes to the horror genre.

Now let's flash forward fifty years, and guess what? I outgrew Abbott and Costello. Nothing against them, they're perfectly fine, but they don't entertain me like they used to. Now, on the other hand, I still *love* the Frankenstein Monster, the Wolf Man, and Dracula. They truly have a special, yet admittedly depraved, place in my heart. To me, they are the epitome of the horror genre.

Make no mistake about it, there are thousands of lousy "horror" movies, television shows, and to a lesser degree, books. Creating horror, at least the style I'm driven to, is no easy task. Back in the 1930s when Universal Studios released, or should I say unleashed, the film, "Frankenstein," it created quite a stir, and grown moviegoers actually ran screaming from the theaters. Many a person who saw that particular film lost a considerable amount of sleep. Nowadays, that type of horror spectacle appears exceedingly tame and, sadly enough, outdated. Too bad. We've upped the ante. Today's patrons are bombarded with scads of gore and special effects, far greater than in the days of the Great Depression or even when I was growing up in the '50s and '60s.

Gore and special effects don't necessarily make a good movie, television show, or book. Many horror excursions these days lack an important ingredient or, more accurately, a certain *emotion*. It's an emotion we frequently thrive on, one to which we can easily become addicted to, and one which dwells at the very core of the horror genre. It's called *suspense*, otherwise known as the anticipation of things to come. It's great stuff, but to create it, to mold it into something tangible, takes considerable, sometimes painstaking effort. Yet sheer, pulse-pounding suspense is the *essence* of horror.

In summary, that's what I've tried to accomplish regarding these selected tales of terror – to create an enormous amount of suspense, so much so that it will entice you into reading one page after another. I hope I'm successful. The truth is, I've scared myself more than a few times.

So, dear reader, sit back, prop your legs up, make sure your reading light shines brightly upon the pages, and without further ado or actual risk, brace yourself to be frightened. Just like when I peered out from behind that couch so many years ago and gazed with great enthusiasm at my maiden venture into the world of horror, I suspect you will also become so wonderfully captivated.

Michael Raff, May 21, 2014

BARKING DOGS

Rialto, California, 2003

The Corman's radio alarm struck 3:45 AM, and the tune "Cherish" by The Association resonated from the speaker. Debbie rolled over and elbowed her husband in the ribs. Bruce sat up, glanced around, and eyed his radio on the nightstand. *Yeah,* he thought, *Cherish, good song, but I sure don't cherish getting up this early!* He switched off the alarm and tossed his bedding aside. The fifty-two-year-old financial adviser struggled to his feet, and in the process nearly threw out his sacroiliac. He grunted and glared at his wife. *Yeah, go ahead and sleep. Five o'clock will come soon enough!*

With the help of two separate nightlights, Bruce stumbled toward the bathroom. During the night he had traveled this way before, three times to be exact. Even his urologist had mentioned there was nothing else he could do. "Just avoid drinking fluids at night, and take your medications before going to bed," the doctor had advised him.

Rounding the corner, Bruce stubbed his toe, cursed, and staggered on. After he was finished in the bathroom, he ambled over to the closet and removed his pajamas. *Wish I could go back to sleeping naked. Now that was comfortable!* But the pajamas were from Debbie, which made them a mandate. He slipped into his sweats, snatched up his Nikes and, sitting on the edge of the bathtub, laced up his tired, old shoes.

Bruce rolled his head from one side to the other and, on his way to the stairs, passed Mandy, their mixed Spaniel. She gave him a warm gaze and a wag of her tail.

"Good morning, girl. What a life, huh?" As he descended the staircase, he added, "Just make sure the old Arctic Queen gets up on time."

The house had grown dark and decidedly cold. Pausing at the thermostat, Bruce turned up the heat, being mindful not to go over sixty-five degrees. With his arms held over his head, he positioned himself face forward against the entrance wall. Rising up and down on his toes, he began his back exercises. He would complete six sets of thirty by the time he was through. A few years earlier, he completed ten sets of forty, but times had changed.

Bruce scooped up his house key, fanny pack, and his tried-and-true cassette player. He paused and frowned at the golf club propped against the wall. He had started carrying the thing on his walks to discourage the occasional stray dog. *Aw, the hell with it!* As the front door closed, a nearby wall clock chimed 4:00 AM.

There was a time when Bruce had enjoyed his early morning walks. Listening to a variety of old rock classics on his Walkman cassette player, he had felt a natural high by pushing himself to just the right degree. And when it was clear outside, he had relished the sight of the glistening stars. But thanks to one of his neighbors, that enjoyment had soured considerably.

Bruce hurried down the driveway. Entering the street, he continued his warm-ups by positioning his right foot on the curb and placing both hands on that knee. He quickly stretched thirty times, then rotated his feet and completed thirty more.

When he finished, Bruce fastened the fanny pack around his waist and dropped the cassette player inside. He placed the earphones on and started the cassette. "Gloria" by The Shadows of Knight suddenly roared in his ears. He smiled contentedly. "Nothing but the best."

Bruce turned to his right and ambled down the street. He braced himself as a gust of wind knifed through him. He shivered and felt his face turn red. For the most part, he remained on the street, roughly four feet from the curb, close enough to give traffic plenty of room.

Just as he was picking up his stride, he remembered his glasses. It was the second time this week he'd forgotten them. Once he started walking, he hated to go back, especially if Debbie woke up. After his heart attack, his cardiologist informed him that exercise, particularly a vigorous walk, was just what he needed.

"But I've been doing exercises!" Bruce had exclaimed. "I've been working out for years now!"

The doctor's unusually large eyebrows had arched above his glasses. He was one of the top heart specialists in the entire state of California, and there he was, picking his nose. "Oh, really? What type of exercise?"

"Some back stretches, but mostly calisthenics."

The man stopped picking his nose and banged on the desk. "Wrong type! You must walk. A brisk walk every day, no exceptions!"

Frustrated, Bruce wanted to strangle the guy. "Great, I've wasted all those years working my ass off, for what?"

Bruce's thoughts were suddenly wrenched back to reality. Just past the mailboxes, the Becks' wrought iron gate stood wide open. Most nights they kept "Killer" locked in their house. No doubt about it, their Rottweiler craved a nice, big, juicy pound of flesh, and if Killer had his way, that flesh would be located in a painfully vulnerable area. Every time Bruce retrieved his mail, the canine would come slamming into that gate like a runaway train. That's why the Becks started storing their trash cans against it, to discourage the beast.

Come to think of it, he once had a nightmare that the gate had popped open, leaving nothing between him and that four-legged demon from the depths of hell.

"Why didn't I bring that damn golf club?" Bruce moaned. Hopefully, Killer was in the Becks' house and not out roaming the streets. Actually, he didn't know the dog's name, so he just called him "Killer." After all, the name suited him well.

Bruce swallowed and reminded himself, *Breathe through your nose.* He rounded the corner and put some distance between himself and the Becks'. He looked up and spotted a full moon gliding in and out of the clouds. Almost immediately his thoughts drifted to Marilyn. If only he could have married her, instead of old razor-mouth. Marilyn had always been the love of his life, and because of her, he considered himself to be the luckiest guy alive. She was the world's most perfect woman, and in all the years he'd known her, she had not aged a day. She was the ideal woman, companion, lover, you name it. And to think she would have given up a movie career just to be with him.

The song "Gloria" was followed by the tune "I Got a Line on You" by the group, Spirit, another one of Bruce's all-time favorites. *Yep, they sure don't make songs like that anymore.*

As he rounded the next corner, Bruce had to push himself harder. To control water drainage, his neighborhood had been built with slight inclines, and he'd just reached one of the steeper ones. Not only was he climbing, but it seemed as if the wind was trying to demoralize him. The area had been nicknamed "the wind tunnel" because, in winter months, the airstreams blasted through the south end of the Cajon Pass. It was nearly unbearable during the early morning hours before warming up.

Just make the sign of the cross and deal with it, snapped a voice that sounded like Sister Mary Himmlerschmidt's, Stuart's hair-pulling, face-slapping, sixth grade nun, who should have been wearing a swastika instead of a crucifix. *And don't forget to breathe through your stupid little nose!*

Bruce approached Terra Vista Boulevard, the main drag through the neighborhood. The world's most despicable tree was located just across the street. He tried not to look at it, but like the proverbial accident at the side of the road, his resistance would wane every time.

Swallowing, Bruce raised his head and peered at the tree. It wasn't tall, wide, or even intimidating. In fact, it looked normal in every respect. But just behind it, on the brick wall, it cast a shadow that resembled a man. Even without his glasses, Bruce could see the "Shadow Man" holding his arms up. But the horrifying part was that the shadowy arms ended at the top of the wall, thus creating the effect they were cut off at the wrists. He shuddered from one end of his spine to the other. *Good God, it has no hands! Why did I have to see that?*

Bruce bore right, staying inside the crosswalk, but he was at the nearest point to the "Shadow Man." He increased his speed, wiped his brow, and turned down the street. Once again, he managed to slip by. Between that handless fiend and Killer the Wonder Dog, it was a miracle he was still walking.

If only he didn't have to commute all the way to Los Angeles, he wouldn't have to walk so early. At this time of the morning it was easy to imagine stuff. Like they say, "It's darkest before dawn," and more often than not, he spotted things lurking in the shadows. He wasn't sure what they were, but they were certainly out to get him. It reminded him of countless zombie movies, of how those dead, decaying creatures crept out of the woodwork and ate people alive. Those films had haunted him for years and inspired the majority of his nightmares, starting back in 1968 after he had fidgeted his way through the movie, "Night of the Living Dead." It never mattered how his dream began. He could be in high school taking a math test, but somehow he'd wind up being chased by those flesh-eating creatures.

They're coming to get you, my boy! taunted a voice that sounded exactly like Boris Karloff's. *They're coming to get you!*

Bruce glanced over a shoulder, and like always, there was nothing behind him. He couldn't hear a thing, not with the classic garage song, "I Confess," by The New Colony Six, pounding in his ears. Yet he kept thinking something was back there, and just because he couldn't see it, didn't mean it wasn't there. He swallowed, smiled and shook his head. *Aw, you dummy, it's just your imagination!*

As Bruce approached the McGriffs' house, he rolled his eyes. Here it was, the middle of February, and they still hadn't taken their Christmas lights down. Everyone else in the neighborhood had removed their decorations just after the New Year, but not these idiots. Of course he didn't actually know the McGriffs, or their real names, either. He just made the name up. The only people in the neighborhood Bruce actually knew by name were the folks on either side of his house, plus the guy across the street.

They're probably psychos, he concluded, *every single one of them.* As a matter of fact, he suspected Lawrence, the guy across the street, was a *bona fide* serial killer. Never mind the fact that he was a God-fearing preacher with his own congregation. Hell, you couldn't ask for a better cover than that! Deep down, the guy was a cold-blooded murderer. You could see it in his eyes.

Concentrating on his breathing, Bruce shoved Killer, the "Shadow Man," the zombies, and even his neighbors out of his mind. He was traveling downhill now and had to watch his speed. He liked the lyrics to "I Confess," but just as he began singing along, the tape started dragging.

Damn batteries! I hate when they run low!

Bruce turned off the cassette player and shoved the earphones back into his fanny pack. The whole time he kept reminding himself,

Maintain your speed, it's important. But it was becoming harder and harder for him to keep the same pace. Walking for at least an hour seven mornings a week was beginning to take its toll on his knees.

Of course, Bruce realized that his knees were the least of his problems. Sure, they wanted to buckle every now and then, but his bum ticker took full priority.

"The main problem with your heart," the nose-picking cardiologist had informed him, "are your genes." Guess the guy was right. Bruce's father had died of a heart attack at just sixty-one. Both his uncles also had heart problems, but at least they lived longer. Even his mother ended up having cardio-vascular issues.

So what chance do I have? a frustrated Bruce wondered.

"Well, at least there's one good thing," the cardiologist had gone on to say. "Since it was a mild heart attack, perhaps it's not too late to change."

Bruce had sat beside his doctor, watching a video of his own heart. It was the weirdest experience seeing your ticker pounding away on a computer screen.

Especially since your arteries are half the size they're supposed to be! Sister Mary Himmlerschmidt butted in. *So you'd better start listening to your doctor . . . you bold creature!*

Bruce had cringed and given the cardiologist his undivided attention. "What kind of change do you mean, doctor?"

"Reduce your stress, eat a healthy diet, take your medications, but most of all . . . walk! That's the *best* thing. You must *walk* as much and as often as possible!"

Bruce's thoughts were interrupted when he rounded another corner and, out of nowhere, a black Explorer came at him. He jumped toward the curb and barely avoided being pulverized.

"You idiot! What are ya trying to do? Kill me?" It was probably Patterson, or at least the guy he called Patterson. Among the world of idiots, he ruled as the alpha moron. Bruce would never forget his early morning walk about a month ago when the guy, still dressed in his pajamas, came shuffling out of his house.

"Excuse me," Patterson had uttered, "but do you *have* to walk in front of my place?"

Bruce came to a stop, had taken his earphones off and talked to the guy.

"You pass by my house at four-thirty every morning. It disturbs my dogs and their barking wakes up my family."

Bruce felt some momentary embarrassment, but it quickly dissipated. "Your dogs? You mean the ones that charged out of your yard and attacked me a couple of weeks ago?"

Now it was Patterson's turn to look embarrassed. Bruce had never mentioned the incident, only because he scared off the dogs by faking some bogus karate moves. True, it was an act of desperation, but it spared him from being mauled.

The guy flinched then sighed. "Well, the wind must have blown the gate open. It won't happen again. So what do you say? Will you take your route elsewhere?"

Bruce nodded and slapped on his earphones. So began his alienation with his early morning walks. It was also the start of his alternate route, avoiding Patterson's house entirely. Then again, perhaps he shouldn't have bothered, because a few nights later, Debbie gave him a sharp jab to his chest, rousing him at 1:00 AM. At first he thought the music was playing from his radio. But instead of the usual rock and roll, there was the sharp twang of country-western. *Damn, since when did this neighborhood get so rowdy?* He jumped up and followed the music to its source. He didn't have far to go. It was Patterson's house. Luckily, the idiot's wife answered the door. Otherwise there would have been another embarrassing confrontation.

Bruce shook his head and glared at the taillights of the Explorer. *So now he's trying to run me over?* No way did he want to spend another night at a hospital. Not that he'd had a choice when his ticker misfired. And it wasn't as if he'd been exerting himself or anything. While he was watching TV and nibbling on some caramel popcorn, something had pierced his heart like an ice pick; then the pain gradually radiated to his left shoulder. The whole thing couldn't have lasted more than ten seconds, and what to do about it kept eluding him. He'd rather be castrated with a pair of dull tweezers than wake Debbie up for a ride to the emergency room. And since the whole thing was already over with, calling for an ambulance had seemed pointless.

It's just another one of those trivial pains, declared the nun inside his head. *You have them all the time.*

But since the previous episodes had never traveled to his shoulder before, Bruce had decided to compromise.

When morning came, he had informed Debbie about the whole affair. "Just to play it safe, I think we should go to the hospital."

An unmistakable narcissistic expression had crept into his wife's eyes just then. "I'd take you if I could, but I can't miss Shannon's visit." Her rebellious granddaughter, Shannon, just happened to be the only person who Debbie actually cared about.

So Bruce had driven himself to the emergency room. In keeping with his HMO, that particular drive was a good twenty-five miles away. After a ten-hour wait, the blood enzymes results had finally come back. Needless to say, the nose-picking cardiologist admitted Bruce. He had to stay the night and endure an angiogram the next morning. There were forms and consents to sign, an educational video to watch, and an unmentionable area of his had to be shaved. His roommate snored incessantly and the staff kept waking him to take his blood pressure. It proved to be the worst night of his life. Even after suffering a heart attack, he had still been deprived of sleep.

What had really galled Bruce was Debbie's absence. The name of the hospital had slipped her mind, and by the time he was able to call her, she was too tired to drive over. And even though she was there the following day, it was during the night that he'd *really* needed her. When the nurses began mentioning the possibilities of implanting balloons or aluminum devices inside him, he had nearly freaked out.

Face it, you're a wimp, a real embarrassment, snarled a new but familiar voice.

That night would have been a whole lot easier if Debbie had shown up. *Marilyn would have been there,* Bruce realized. *She would have driven me to the emergency room and stayed the entire time.*

A trickle of sweat made itself known along the side of Bruce's face. The wind had settled down to an occasional gust. It was then that he heard what chilled his blood. Most likely the sound had been present the entire time, but Bruce was so lost in thought he hadn't noticed it. There had to be at least three dogs barking nearby. *What the hell? Are they barking at me?* He shook his head. *I guess so, because there's no one else out here.* Just as he reached the end of the block, one of the dogs began to howl.

Hell, I've never noticed that before! He grinned and rolled his eyes. *That's because you've always had your earphones blasting, you idiot! No wonder Patterson came out to complain.*

Bruce finally reached the former model homes. When he first moved to the neighborhood, they were in pristine condition, but now, after all this time, the owners had let them deteriorate. Even the largest, most expensive lots had weeds thriving in them.

While he was gazing at the homes, he noticed something strange. A dim light in the backyard of the third house revealed a long, murky shadow.

Just some guy taking out the trash, Bruce surmised.

Yeah, right! the new voice exclaimed, a voice that bore a suspicious similarity to his late business partner, Ray Huntley. *Taking out the trash at the butt crack of dawn?*

Why not? shrieked the nun. *We're out here!*

Yeah, but we're exercising, Ray argued. *That guy's cramming something huge into his trash. It's probably his wife's dismembered body. Or maybe it's one of those door-to-door Jehovah's Witnesses.*

Bruce shuddered. All this obsessing was wreaking havoc on his already battered nerves. *Breathe through your nose, for crying out loud! Through your damn nose!*

He was now approaching the halfway point of his new route, further out than ever. It was also the darkest area in the entire neighborhood. *Yeah, plenty dark, so you'd better pay attention!*

To forget about dismembered bodies in trash cans, Bruce thought about his job, particularly Ray Huntley, the same louse who had been so fixated on Debbie.

First thing in the morning, instead of "Hello" or "How's it going?" Ray always asked "How's Debbie?" The more the conniving embezzler inquired about her, the more Bruce suspected there was something funny going on. Instead of "How's Debbie?" maybe Ray should have been boasting, "Hey, your wife was a real peach last night. The best I've ever had!" It was more than possible they were sleeping together, especially since Debbie had that affair two years ago.

Bruce sighed and decided not to think about work either. He veered to the right and barely missed the pothole that remained so well-hidden in the dark.

When are they going to fix that? the nun asked.

When pigs fly, Ray fired back.

Bruce pushed on. He kept hearing more and more dogs out there, barking in what was beginning to sound like the theme from the movie, "The Magnificent Seven." You'd think he was some type of threat to them or that they had something against him.

They do have something against you, Ray mocked. *They want to chew you up into a nice, big, tasty . . . idiot burger!*

Bruce's heartbeat suddenly shot up a notch. With all the barking going on, it reminded him about a particular cold and cloudy morning when he was a kid.

A neighbor down the street had owned a pair of dachshunds. Bruce had always considered them to be the meanest curs around and they absolutely despised him. All he had to do was walk by and they would hit the front gate, yapping their little snouts off. It was like Killer all over again, except in miniature. One particular morning, the neighbor's front gate had been left open. Bruce couldn't just turn around because he was already late for school, so he tried to sneak by. At first, he thought he would be all right, as there wasn't a wiener dog in sight. Then, suddenly, he'd heard an unmistakable yapping. With their fat little bellies dragging on the ground, both dogs had chased him as fast as their tiny wiener legs would go. Bruce had taken off with his heart pounding harder than a thoroughbred's. By the time he had reached the end of the block, the dogs had vanished.

That was a long time ago, Sister Himmlerschmidt interjected.

Yeah, but it's a lot like now, taunted Ray. *Except Killer has about a hundred pounds over those little wieners! Hell, his fangs alone could tear your guts out!*

Shut up! the nun barked. *You're creeping me out!*

Bruce was now approaching the homes that were built during the neighborhood's final building phase. Due to rising construction costs, they had been designed smaller, and just like the former model homes, the owners had let the yards deteriorate.

As Bruce hurried along, he noticed the barking had died down. *Thank God Almighty!* the nun rejoiced.

Yeah, they've stopped yapping, murmured Ray, *but do you know why?*

It was then that Bruce spotted what unleashed a river of ice through his veins. Killer was just three houses away squirting a tree in front of the Dudley house, or at least the people Bruce called Dudley.

Wandering around and lifting his leg wherever he pleased was all probably a part of the Rottweiler's escape plan.

Without missing a beat, Bruce swung around and picked up his speed. As strange as it seemed, it felt as if he was floating above the asphalt.

Don't make a sound, the nun advised. *And keep those feet moving! Yes, let them float. That way Killer can't hear you.*

But Ray disagreed. *Ya haven't got a chance! Ya shoulda bought that life insurance policy, because when that dog's done with you, they'll be scraping you up with a shovel!*

Bruce doubled his speed. His side ached and his hamstrings gave him fair warning. But it was his heart that worried him. It was getting a workout all right, but he hadn't counted on running for his life. A lot of good avoiding Killer would do him, only to suffer a heart attack.

Or worse, Ray added, *getting your guts torn out and then having a heart attack!*

Bruce wanted to look over his shoulder, but knew it would slow him down. He also thought about unfastening his fanny pack. It didn't weigh all that much, but letting it go might increase his speed.

If it comes to that, go ahead, Sister Himmlerschmidt agreed.

Oh, yeah? challenged Ray. *Then you'll lose your cassette player and end up buying one of those CD Walkmans . . . with all those damn little buttons!*

Bruce thought he would burst at the seams. "Shut up, the both of you!"

Sprinting his way through the darkest sector, Bruce ignored the nun's demands to slow down, and when he leaped over the pothole, a bolt of pain shot through his right ankle. He lost his balance and landed on his hands and knees. He moaned and fought off the pain. He had to get up and, this time, defend himself, because his bogus karate moves would never impress a brute like Killer.

Bruce staggered to his feet but, after glancing around, realized the dog had disappeared. He brushed himself off and decided to head for home before his ankle swelled. Although his palms and knees stung, there were no abrasions. He sighed and struggled forward. He kept looking around, wondering about the Rottweiler.

So where is he? the nun inquired. *And why didn't he attack us?*

Maybe he's toying with us, Ray suggested. *Maybe he's behind that bush over there, or around the next corner.*

"Shut the hell up!" Bruce hollered. Everything inside his head was about to self-destruct. Hopefully, by now Debbie would be awake. If she wasn't in too bitchy of a mood, maybe she would take a look at his ankle.

As he rounded another bend, Bruce suddenly halted. It felt as if every hair on the back of his neck stood at attention. Killer was trotting down the street just like he owned the entire neighborhood.

Turning around, Bruce tried to appear as casual as possible. From what he recalled, when dogs sensed fear, they often attacked. He gradually began accelerating, but his injured ankle tweaked, throbbed, and held him back.

Fly like an angel! the nun urged. *It's our only chance!*

Don't listen to that old Nazi bat! Ray shouted. *We have to make a stand and kick ass!*

The perspiration poured off Bruce's face, and not only was his side hurting, but his heart felt as if it was about to burst.

For the love of God! the nun bellowed. *Never mind breathing through your stupid, little nose! Breath through your mouth, you moron! Through your mouth!*

Despite his pain, Bruce moved at a decent clip. Still, he could never hope to outrun a dog. And making matters worse, he could hear Killer's metal tags jangling behind him.

He's gaining! Sister Himmlerschmidt screeched.

Yeah, Ray added, *but he could've already nailed us. He's probably stalling for the rest of the goon squad.*

"Goon squad?" Bruce croaked. "What do you mean, goon squad?"

Ray laughed. *Go ahead, take a look behind ya, because it just might be the last thing you'll ever see . . . and oh, by the way, how's Debbie?*

Breathing through his mouth, Bruce gazed over a shoulder. What he discovered caused his heart to pound double-time. They were all back there, every one of them. The "Shadow Man" was near the front, still flaunting his handless arms over his head. Just behind him, waving a huge machete like a battle flag, was the neighbor who stuffed bodies into trash cans. Then directly behind him were dozens of zombies, and for decaying cadavers, they were traveling at an impressive speed. Leading the entire pack and wearing a rather toothy snarl was, of course, Killer. And scurrying just behind him were the two wiener dogs, yapping like a pair of surly phantoms out of a blood-curling hallucination.

I don't believe it! the nun screamed. *We must be having a nightmare!*

Ray roared with laughter. *What a dummkopf! This whole thing's real all right, and before ya know it . . . that mob's gonna tear our guts out!*

Bruce kept glancing over his shoulder. No matter how hard he tried, he could not outrun his pursuers. When he rounded a corner, he failed to see the van that passed him every morning, the very vehicle that delivered his newspaper. As he turned, he found himself trapped within its headlights. There was a squeal of tires and a ghastly thud. Bruce flew backward as pain bolted through his body. He hit the asphalt, landing on his left shoulder. As he lay motionless, stunned and gasping, the van pulled to the curb.

Struggling onto his side, Bruce gazed down the street. When everything came into focus, even Killer had disappeared.

* * *

Limping into his house, Bruce slammed the front door shut. The driver of the van wanted to take him to the hospital, but Bruce refused and accepted a ride home instead. Just the walk from the driveway to his door became a punishing ordeal. He lumbered into the kitchen and found Debbie, clad in her bathrobe, pouring herself a cup of coffee.

"Good grief, what happened to you?"

Bruce hobbled to the sink and rinsed his face. "I got run over by our newspaper man."

"You idiot!" she shrieked. "Weren't you paying attention?"

Bruce shook his head and dried his face with a paper towel. "Naw, I was too busy being chased."

"Chased? Chased by what?"

"By the Rottweiler from across the street."

Debbie rolled her eyes. "When are you going to learn? That's the third time you've been attacked by a dog."

"Yeah, I know." He limped toward the table. "As soon as you're ready, I need a ride to the emergency room."

"What? You want *me* to drive you?"

Trying not to twist his neck, Bruce turned toward her. "Yeah, if that's not *too* much to ask."

Debbie slammed her coffee cup down. "Fine, I'll be ready in ten minutes!" She took off, but over her shoulder she snarled, "And you'd better not bleed in my car!"

Bruce clenched his fists and then cringed when something rubbed against his knee. It was Mandy. She was staring at him as if he was the Father, Son and Holy Ghost all rolled into one.

"Hey, girl." He bent down and patted her. "And to think people call *you* a bitch!"

***

Bruce's alarm clock struck 3:45 AM, and the song "Happy Together" by The Turtles resonated from the radio. He opened his eyes and peered at the other side of the bed. Mandy crawled over and licked his face.

"Easy girl," he croaked. "You ready for another day?"

Wagging her tail, she gave him a bark and jumped off the bed.

After going to the bathroom, Bruce slipped into his shorts and T-shirt. It was summer now and his sweats were on vacation. Mandy watched his every move with her usual eagerness.

"Time's a wasting, girl!"

She gave him another bark and raced off.

Bruce grabbed a towel from the linen closet, and with his dog leading the way, hurried down the stairs. He let her out through the patio door and retrieved a bottle of water from the refrigerator. He completed his back exercises then secured the fanny pack to his waist. Dropping his new CD Walkman inside the pack, he hummed the tune "Happy Together." He placed the earphones on and stepped into the garage.

After letting Mandy in through the yard door, Bruce began his stretches. His dog trotted over and guzzled from her water dish. While he stretched, he glanced at the stack of cardboard boxes near the far corner. It was the last of Debbie's belongings and would be gone by tonight. Finally, she was out of his life; this time for good.

Bruce turned and smiled at his treadmill. It was a long time in coming, but it was definitely worth the wait. Even in the dim light, the machine seemed to sparkle.

After finishing his warm-ups, Bruce turned on the CD player. "Hello, I Love You" by The Doors blared through the earphones. He smiled again. Life was never better. And to top it off, ever since things were settled with Debbie, his relationship with Marilyn had flourished.

Placing his water bottle into the cup holder, Bruce hopped onto the treadmill. He draped the towel across his shoulders and adjusted the machine's settings. "Let's see now, how about an even four miles? What do you think, girl?"

This time Mandy did not respond. She kept sniffing around Debbie's boxes.

"Four miles it is," he confirmed. With the treadmill facing his favorite poster of Marilyn, the one in which the subway breeze raised her billowing white skirt, Bruce grinned and began walking. But when "I Put a Spell on You" by Creedence Clearwater Revival came on, the disc started skipping.

Cursing, he shut off the Walkman, removed the earphones, and heard a scratching sound by the boxes. Mandy was still over there, barking and prancing around.

Bruce paused the treadmill and peered over his shoulder. Carrying a human finger in its mouth, a rat scampered out from the boxes. "Damn, is that what I think it is?"

Yes, Sister Himmlerschmidt barged in. *That's a very bold creature!*

Don't listen to her, advised Ray. *Where there's one rat, there's more.*

Bruce moaned and rolled his eyes. Ever since his "divorce," the voices had grown unbearable.

And when those rats are done with me, cried Debbie, *they'll sneak into the house . . .*

Then, in perfect harmony, his wife, the nun, Ray, and the rest of Bruce's dismembered victims shrieked . . . *AND EAT YOUR GUTS OUT!*

DIRTY, STINKING RAT

Paul Donovan entered his garage and flipped on the light switch. Lady and Mister Jiggers followed him. Lady was a black, long-haired spaniel. Jiggers was a tan, chubby, mixed-terrier with the most abrasive fur imaginable.

Paul hurried toward his treadmill while the dogs guzzled from their water dish. Stepping onto the machine's conveyor belt, Paul checked his watch. He had just enough time to jog thirty-five minutes.

As the treadmill clicked on, Lady and the older Jiggers leaped through the doggie door that led to the backyard. Their tails were wagging the entire time. Paul didn't know why they loved their morning routine so much, but their enjoyment appeared quite evident.

The treadmill gradually accelerated to the preset speed of 3.5 miles per hour. Just as Paul fell into his stride, he caught a glimpse of a small, shadowy figure scurrying out from under his car. Before he could react, it disappeared beneath his workbench.

Was that a mouse . . . he cringed and shook his head *. . . or a rat?*

Despite his uneasiness Paul continued his workout, but he didn't like the idea of sharing his garage with an unknown creature. Both Lady and Mister Jiggers returned through the doggie door and Jiggers trotted over to their water dish. Lady, however, stopped, glanced around and, with her nose to the floor, inched toward the workbench. Paul moaned and turned off his treadmill. In her own unique manner, Lady had just confirmed the problem.

Good God! Not another infestation!

***

Jimmy Bentz stuck his head into Paul's office. Both his chef's hat and apron appeared as if he had been pelted with tomato paste. *He looks like an inkblot test gone berserk,* Paul mused.

"Line one for you, sir," the teenager announced.

Paul nodded and picked up the telephone as Jimmy rushed back to work.

"Paul Donovan here."

"Hello," came the voice on the other end. To Paul it was the most engaging voice ever, and the owner just happened to be his future wife. "How's life in the restaurant business, honey?"

Paul chuckled. "Not bad, except Jimmy keeps eating up the profits."

Janice laughed. "Are you coming over later?"

"Sure. I'll call you when I'm on my way." Paul settled back into his seat and recalled the mysterious creature he had spotted in his garage. "Hey, do you know a good exterminator?"

"Don't tell me you've got ants! Summer's terrible. I can never get rid of them."

"No, it's not ants. I'm not sure *what* it is, but there's something sneaking around in my garage."

"Could it be a rat?"

"I dunno for sure."

"Well, why don't you take care of it yourself? Exterminators can be expensive."

"How expensive?"

"About a hundred dollars."

"Just for a couple of rodents?"

"One or a dozen, it doesn't matter."

"Okay, I'll see what I can do."

"All right, I have to go. I'll see you tonight. I love you."

"I love you, too."

They hung up. Paul leaned back and thought about his situation. He never liked the idea of killing things. Coping with a mouse outbreak about a year before, he had hidden some "snap" traps in his garage and must have killed a dozen mice in all. Thankfully, they never found their way into his house. Two years ago he had used several "glue" traps to eradicate what was probably a family of rats. Then, back when he was living in Chino, he poisoned at least five gophers through the years. So, when he had to, he would defend his property. But, for some strange reason, the thought of once again killing an unsuspecting creature – or more likely, *creatures* – made him feel uneasy.

***

Paul stepped into his garage and tossed a plastic bag on the workbench. Lady and Mister Jiggers rushed over and greeted him. He bent down and gave them both a rubdown. "Hey, guys, I'm glad to see you, too. Wanna go out?"

Paul raised the plastic insert and both pets hurried toward the doggie door. Lady was always the first through, followed by the older Jiggers. Paul hated the idea of his dogs sharing the garage with an unknown animal whenever he was away, but due to Jigger's weak bladder, he couldn't just leave them in the house. The backyard was also taboo because his dogs tended to rearrange the flower beds. So, by default, the garage turned out to be his sole option.

Reaching into the bag, Paul removed three packages of rat traps. They were of the glue variety, two traps per container. He had to locate six areas in the garage that were inaccessible to his dogs. He decided on beneath the workbench, one on each side, stashed safely behind a stack of boxes. He glanced at his long-neglected liquor bar. He could hide another trap beneath it and the fourth in the storage loft, just below the garage's ceiling. Finally, he could place the last two traps on each side of the length of the garage, also behind some boxes.

While he was working, Paul discovered a forgotten mousetrap he had hidden last year behind a pair of paint cans. It was also of the glue variety, which he had placed as a backup in case the snap traps failed. Surprisingly, its corners were still quite sticky. *Great! Now I have seven traps!*

Paul brushed off his hands and raised the doggie door. Entering the garage, both dogs gazed at him intently. "Well, guys, how about some chow?"

Lady all but ignored him. With her head hung low, she glanced around, curled her lips, and growled.

***

After he had ushered his dogs out through their doggie door and pulled his Grand Am into the garage, Paul began checking the rat traps. It had been three days since he last checked. When he first hid them two months ago, he checked every day, but they had always turned up empty. He kept thinking, *Did I really see that thing?* Surely, he should have caught it by now. And why wasn't there some type of evidence that the creature existed – like droppings, chew marks, or a nest?

Using a flashlight, Paul stooped down and peered beneath the workbench. All he found was a dead spider in the trap on the right. Because of their proximity to where he had spotted the creature, he was hoping that one of these two traps would come through.

The trap under the bar turned up negative, as well. But when Paul checked on the right side of the garage, to his bewilderment, that trap had disappeared. A moment later he discovered the mousetrap had also vanished. Jiggers must have been up to his old tricks again, because as far as he knew, rats weren't known for rearranging traps. A thorough search of his garage, however, proved wasted. Of course, when his dogs returned through the doggie door, they followed him the entire time. Taking a weary breath, Paul confronted Jiggers. "Okay, I give up. What did you do with those traps?"

The dog turned, hopped through the doggie door then quickly hopped back carrying a rubber ball in his mouth.

Paul rolled his eyes and shook his head. "You old fart. You're no help at all."

***

Later that night Janice came over and Paul cooked dinner. They were just finishing when Janice asked, "Whatever happened to that critter you saw in your garage?"

"The traps keep coming up empty," he answered.

Janice set her fork down. "That's strange. You should have caught it by now."

"I know. I've never had this problem before. But do you know what's really weird?"

"What?"

"Two of the traps have disappeared."

"How can that be? It must have been Jiggers. He probably moved them."

"Well, if it was him, then he's a world-class magician."

Janice dabbed her mouth with a napkin. "They have to be around. Let's go take a look."

Paul retrieved a pair of flashlights and they stepped into the garage. He opened the overhead door and backed out his car. Returning from the driveway, he aimed his flashlight to the right side of the garage. "They were both over there, behind those boxes."

"Did you look under the workbench?"

"Yep, and behind the bar, too."

"What about under that chest over there?"

Paul stared at his old wooden trunk. He had bought it over twenty years ago, filled it with scads of unwanted items, and kept it in the garage. "Well, Jiggers could never get behind that."

Janice smiled and her dimples flourished. "Let's just take a look, shall we?"

They rolled the trunk out together and it squeaked along on its rusty casters. Sure enough, amongst the dust and dog hair were the two missing devices, with the mousetrap stuck on top of the larger rat trap.

"What the . . .?"

Janice shrugged her shoulders. "Jiggers couldn't have done this."

"Don't tell me you think a rat did it?"

"Yes, I'm certain of it."

"You're telling me that a rodent moved these two traps across a three car garage then stashed them under my trunk?"

"Well, something like that." She frowned and turned toward the right. "It must have been caught by the mousetrap first, probably on a hind leg. Then, while it was trying to free itself, it picked up the rat trap with the bottom of the first trap."

Paul scratched his head. "Are you serious?"

"I don't think there's any other explanation. After it got caught, it must have dragged both traps across the garage."

"And then what?"

"I guess it crawled under the chest and caught the traps along the bottom edge, giving it enough leverage to pry itself loose."

"But what about my dogs? They would've ripped the stupid thing apart."

Janice chuckled. "The whole thing happened at night. That's when rats are active and when your dogs are in the house."

Paul switched off his flashlight and sighed. "Well, I guess you're right. It seems like the only possibility."

Janice leaned forward and kissed him on the cheek. "I don't know if it *actually* figured out how to remove those traps, but from what I've heard about rats, I wouldn't doubt it." She smiled and took his hand. "Let's just hope it hasn't learned to avoid your traps. Rats aren't stupid like you said, they're quite clever . . . sometimes even *devious*. That's why scientists use them so much for their experiments, because they're so smart."

"Great," Paul moaned. "Enough bad news. Let's move on to more important things, like who does the dishes."

***

Paul never replaced the wasted traps, as he decided five would be more than enough. Three days later he noticed one of the traps lying face down in the middle of the garage floor. He hurried over and pulled it loose. *Glue's ruined, damn it! Now I'm down to four traps.* Frowning, he gazed upward. *It's from the loft and it just didn't fall down here by itself!*

The old, dusty cardboard boxes stored in the opened loft were packed with Christmas decorations and a variety of other miscellaneous items. Janice had warned Paul that the rat might be smart, so was it possible that it *deliberately* shoved the trap down? More importantly, could it still be up there, doing whatever rats do during the daytime? He sighed. Despite his lifelong distrust of heights, there was only one way to find out.

Paul carefully positioned his ladder below the loft, then exercising an extreme amount of caution, he began climbing. His memory of falling out of a tree at the age of eight kept flashing through his mind. When he reached his destination, he discovered tiny bits of cardboard scattered haphazardly along the ledge. On the front of the nearest box he found a ragged hole roughly two inches in diameter. Finally, at long last, he had some tangible evidence. Until now all he'd had to go on was that brief sighting over two months ago and, of course, the relocated traps.

Just in case it's still in there, I'd better find something to kill it with. He groaned and, wrestling with his dwindling courage, inched down the ladder.

Paul removed a hammer from his toolbox and glanced at his wristwatch. His grocery shopping would just have to wait. Once again he cautiously scaled his way up. Since there was no room for him on the loft, he had no choice but to remain on the ladder. *To open the box I either have let go of the ladder or set the hammer down . . . but if the rat's still inside, I won't have time to pick up the hammer.* He didn't like the decision, but he had to be prepared.

As Paul released the ladder, he raised the hammer and slowly pried open the box's flaps. There was no rodent inside, but something had been around. The rear of the box contained some old photographs, cassette tapes, letters, and a pair of beer mugs wrapped in newspaper. At the front of the box, however, was a custom-made, state-of-the-art, rat nest. Scraps of newspaper, cardboard, and Paul's letters and photos made up the miniature habitat. Of course there were rat droppings all along the perimeter. What really captured Paul's amazement was what had been so intricately laced into the nest. Apparently, for some additional padding, the creature had managed to unravel one of the cassette tapes.

Paul rolled his eyes, and just as he was about to descend the ladder, he halted, gasped and sneezed. It was just enough movement to cause him to lose his balance. Swaying back and forth, he lost the hammer and his legs slipped off the ladder. Before Paul knew it, he was hanging by his elbows from the edge of the loft. He tried to anchor his forearms along the ledge, but the weight of his own body undermined him. Before he had a chance to holler, he hit the floor with a tremendous thud.

***

Janice opened Paul's front door and stepped into the entryway. With his left arm suspended in a sling, Paul followed her, hobbled over to his couch and flopped down. He winced as a bolt of pain shot through him.

Janice placed Paul's house keys on the coffee table and noticed his agonized expression. "Are you okay?"

He took an uneasy breath and sighed, "Never better."

She stepped over to the sliding patio door and drew open the vertical blind. "What can I do for you? How about some dinner?"

"No, thanks, I left my appetite in the garage."

"Well, there must be something I can do."

"Believe me, a ride to the hospital was more than enough." He smiled placidly. "Besides, a few more pain killers and I won't have a care in the world."

Janice sat next to Paul and kissed him. "I'm just glad nothing was broken. Overall, I'd say you were pretty lucky."

"Yep, just a few bruises and a shattered ego."

Smiling, she held his hand. "In a couple of days you'll be as good as new. Just take care of yourself . . . and no more chasing after that rat."

A somber expression crept into Paul's eyes. "So . . . you're *sure* it's a rat?"

"It has to be. Using a cassette tape for a nest? Only a rat would think of that." She kissed him again. "I'll bring Lady and Jiggers in before I go." She paused and softly gazed at him. "What about work? Are you going to take some time off?"

Paul shook his head. "There's no one else to take my place."

"Well, I wish you had more time to recuperate. Try to get some rest and I'll see you soon."

With that, she opened the sliding door, prompted Lady and Jiggers into the house, then kissed Paul goodbye. Much to Paul's grief, the minute Jiggers made his way into the living room, he threw up a huge pile of undigested food.

***

Stumbling out of bed, Paul groaned and slowly straightened himself. He felt as if he'd been tied to a car bumper and dragged along the Interstate. From their padded bed, Lady and Jiggers stared at him in what could only be described as utmost wonder.

"Whatever you do," he advised them, "don't *ever* fall off a ladder."

Both dogs appeared to understand his every word. Jiggers seemed somewhat better. Paul had no idea what the old boy had scarfed up, but whatever it was, it had turned three shades of green inside his stomach.

After tossing the cumbersome arm sling into a dresser drawer, he approached his pets. "Well, what're you waiting for?"

They jumped out of their bed and followed him. Of course, Jiggers fell behind. Even when he was younger, he could never keep up with Lady.

Paul opened the door to the garage and Jiggers rushed to their water dish. He drank as if he had just trotted his way through Death Valley.

"What's the matter, boy? All that puking make ya thirsty?"

As soon as Jiggers had guzzled his fill, Paul headed toward the backyard door. As he walked along, he heard a faint scratching sound. He glanced to his right and spotted something moving on top of the water heater. When he realized what it was, he nearly jumped out of his slippers. "Holy shit!"

Standing upright on its hind legs was a rat the size of a small cat. Before Paul could recover, it leaped onto the wall and scrambled down to the floor. It moved so quickly it turned into a blur and disappeared behind the water heater.

Clutching his chest, Paul gazed at his dogs. "Mother of God! Did you guys see that?"

From his blank expression, Jiggers seemed to have missed the entire affair. But slinking close to the floor, Lady peered at the water heater and softly whimpered.

***

When Paul returned from work, he couldn't help but notice how sluggish Jiggers had become. As he urged his dogs into the backyard, he decided not to park his car in the garage. "Rats love to chew electrical wiring," Janice had mentioned. Reaching into the passenger seat, he pulled out a white, plastic bag. In doing so he bumped his sore shoulder on the steering wheel. His whole left side, from the base of his neck to his waist, ached. Most of his upper arm had turned purple, and now his ribcage was starting to catch up.

Paul removed the three rat traps from the plastic bag. They were of the "snap" variety and, in comparison to the smaller mousetraps, looked positively gigantic. When he held them in his hands, their size and lethalness repulsed him. Thankfully, the rat wouldn't know what they were. After the fiasco with the glue traps, he knew if the creature managed to escape its first encounter, he could write off these devices as well.

It took Paul some time to situate the traps, mostly due to their delicate handling and the daunting possibility that he could injure himself. The first of the sites would be under the work bench, close to where he had initially seen the creature. Next would be along the right side of the garage where the glue traps had nearly caught it. Finally, he chose underneath his old liquor bar. Such a nice, dark corner seemed a likely place for a rat to hang out. As Paul rolled the bar forward, he discovered just how active the rat had been.

Among his beer mugs and wine glasses he found an appalling mixture of dry dog food and rat droppings. There was even more rat waste scattered among his surplus dishes and liquor bottles. The thing had even defiled his favorite shot glass by using it as a toilet.

A sharp, burning sensation suddenly ignited in Paul's stomach. Kicking the side of the bar, his face turned beet red.

"Why, you dirty, stinking rat!"

Tormented by his sore left shoulder and ribcage, he hauled out his belongings. After such a nauseating debasement, he flung everything into the trash. He swept out the dog food and rat waste and scrubbed the bar with disinfectant.

After an hour Paul was finally ready to set the last trap. To his amazement he had worked up a profuse sweat. It took him awhile to situate the mechanism, as the bait refused to stay in place. When the trap was finally ready, he rolled the bar back. Dusting off his hands, he confidently murmured, "One dead rat coming up."

***

After letting his dogs out the next morning, Paul checked the rat traps. The thought of the creature waltzing around in his garage, chewing up his belongings and defecating wherever it liked, had kept him awake most the night, that plus Mister Jiggers. More sluggish than ever, the old, reliable chowhound, had declined his dinner. Something was wrong and a trip to the vet seemed likely.

The first two traps appeared untouched, no big surprise. Paul knelt down to check beneath his bar for the third device. It was lying face down, empty, and of course, the bait had disappeared. He wiped the sleep from his eyes and shook his head. All three snap traps were useless now, as the rat would certainly avoid them.

Shaking his head, Paul tossed the device into the trash. It made a dull clank as it struck the defiled dishes. He prompted his dogs back inside the garage and discovered that Jiggers was drooling. The more Paul looked the old guy over, the worse he appeared. There was a lump about an inch in diameter between his shoulder blades. Paul's heart sank even further. Gazing around like he had lost his way, Jigger's normally cheerful eyes looked dull and confused.

Paul tried giving the old boy a dog biscuit, but he merely lumbered off and flopped down into his bed. Lady hurried over and gobbled up the treat.

So now what should I do? I have to go to work, but I can't just leave him like that.

Paul patted his elderly canine goodbye, hurried through the house, and headed toward his car. He would leave work early and then rush Jiggers to the vet's. Hopefully, after the poor guy was feeling better, Paul could settle things with his dear little pal, the crafty rat.

***

Opening a fresh can of Budweiser, Paul staggered to the phone. Perhaps he was a bit tipsy, but nevertheless, each time it rang it sent electric shock waves through his skull.

"Hello?"

"Hi!" Janice greeted. "How did it go at the vet's?"

Taking the cordless phone to his recliner, Paul flopped down. A gush of beer shot from the can and soaked his groin. *Man, oh man, it's just not my day!* "It's worse than I thought," he finally answered.

"Oh, no, what's wrong?"

Paul glanced over at Jiggers. The ailing dog was stretched out and sleeping on a blanket. Relaxing in the family room had always been his favorite pastime. "The results of the tests indicate cancer."

"Oh, no," Janice repeated.

"Yeah, not only that, he probably had a stroke."

Janice's voice sounded choked. "That would explain his confusion."

As if he were agreeing, Jiggers moaned from his corner of the room.

"And the growth between his shoulders," Paul added, "when the vet lanced it, all kinds of fluid came out. More than you can imagine."

"Did he say where the lump came from?"

Paul glared at the garage entrance. "He didn't know. But if you ask me, I think it came from a rat."

"A rat bite? No, honey, I don't think that's possible. But I'm sorry about Jiggers. He's such a good boy, too. Do you want me to come over?"

Paul swallowed and struggled with his emotions. *That rat must have bitten him! How else could he get so damn sick?* "No, I'll be okay."

"You sure? I don't mind."

"No, that's all right. I just want to spend some time with Jiggers. The vet says he's suffering . . ." Paul hesitated and swallowed ". . . so I'll stay home tomorrow and if he doesn't get better by then . . ." His voice trailed off. He couldn't bear to finish.

On the other end of the line, Janice whispered, "I understand."

Sipping his beer, Paul's features darkened as a vexing anger rushed through him. "And besides, tonight a sneaky, filthy, little rat is going down, and this time . . . for good."

***

Paul opened the sliding door to the family room and urged his dogs out. Naturally, Lady led the way. Jiggers was moving slightly better, which wasn't saying much. Paul proceeded to the garage and flipped on the light. By the time his plans were carried out, it would be well after dark.

Slipping on a pair of work gloves, he began rearranging the garage. "They like to run along the walls," Janice had mentioned. Boxes, paint cans, the wooden trunk, everything Paul could move, were relocated to the center of the garage. Only the wooden cabinet, the bar, a set of metal shelves, and a cardboard box containing a torn bag of potting soil were left by the walls. After a short while Paul's left side began to throb. The entire time he labored, he felt tired and dizzy.

After he had situated the last box, Paul glanced around. Smiling, he picked up an old coffee can filled with small rocks. He studied the distance from the shelves to both sides of the garage. For the most part, he could see quite well along the walls. Satisfied, he placed the can on one of the shelves, looked at his watch, and stepped into the house.

***

Paul had muted the volume to his television long before he nodded out. Just as he began dreaming about an army of goose-stepping rats invading his bedroom, he sprang up. *Did I just hear a noise from the garage?* He glanced at his watch. It was ten o'clock. He hopped off the recliner and his shoulder wrenched violently. Wincing, he gazed at his pets sprawled in front of the fireplace. "You'd better go outside, you two. Things are about to get ugly."

Both dogs leaped to their feet and Lady rushed out the sliding door, followed by a slightly improved Jiggers who was intermittently wagging his tail. As Paul slid the door shut, he heard a distant thud from the garage. Perhaps the wily, little varmint was inspecting its altered surroundings. According to Janice, they were extremely curious. Taking a breath, he rolled up his sleeves.

Easing the garage door open, Paul stepped inside. Everything seemed unnaturally quiet. Picking up the can of rocks, he removed just one. His heart pounded. His mouth dried out.

I can't see it or hear it . . . but it's here somewhere.

Just as Paul began wondering if he'd been mistaken about the noise, he heard a scratching sound from behind the cabinet. Entirely self-contained, the wooden fixture featured double doors and stood six feet tall by four feet wide. He stretched to his left and retrieved a flashlight.

As Paul approached the far end of the cabinet, the scratching halted. *What in the world is it doing back there?* He raised the flashlight and readied the rock. The space between the wall and the cabinet was only about three inches wide. He had a better chance at winning the state lottery than throwing a rock through such a narrow gap, yet it still might be worth the effort. He inched closer until the side of his face touched the wall. Holding his breath, he positioned the flashlight.

At first Paul didn't know if he was still tipsy or had lost what was left of his mind. Either way, he thought he was seeing things, because the rat had twisted itself upside down between the wall and the cabinet. The outrageous position made the thing look like a furry corkscrew. *Whoa! How weird! He's got himself trapped. Now, if I can just clear the cabinet . . .*

As Paul raised the rock, the rat stared at him, twitching its nose. They both stood motionless, looking at each other for a long, daunting moment. When the creature finally blinked, Paul flung the rock as hard as he could. For as long as he could remember, he'd always been surprisingly accurate at throwing things, especially when his blood was up. Nevertheless, the rock ricocheted off the cabinet, and Paul had to duck to avoid it.

Hell! I'm going to lose him!

But, incredibly, the rat remained twisted in that peculiar position, twitching its nose as if it was posing for pictures.

Well, maybe he's not so smart after all.

Looking over his shoulder, Paul eyed the push broom he had placed on top of the trunk. It had a handle long enough to prod the rat out into the open. But when he glanced back at the space between the wall and the cabinet, the sneaky little Houdini was nowhere in sight.

A distinctive rattling suddenly erupted from the metal shelves. Paul glanced over at a trash bag sitting below the can of rocks. The bag was stuffed with plastic, two-liter soda bottles earmarked for the recycling center. Evidently, the rat was moving around between the bag and the wall, causing the empty bottles to shift around.

Taking a hesitant breath, Paul retrieved the push broom. He would select a second rock from the coffee can and then nudge the bag with the broom. When the rat took off, he'd hit it with the rock. Fast or not, he was confident that this time he'd nail it. Then, while it was lying stunned and helpless, he'd finish it off with the broom.

The closer Paul came to the bag, the more his stomach tightened. His heart still pounded rapidly and his mouth had grown drier. Ever-so-slowly, he reached into the can and removed a smooth, evenly curved rock. Then, unable to stand the tension any longer, he lunged forward and screamed so loudly his lungs strained. Instead of a nudge, he slammed the bag with the broom. The rattling halted and the bag stopped moving, but no rat came flying out. Not to be discouraged, he struck the bag again.

Paul heard a muffled thud on the floor, but the creature was so quick, by the time he threw the rock, it had rounded past the bar and was already behind the cardboard box. The rock struck the garage wall with a powerful thud, leaving a perfectly circular and conspicuous hole in the drywall.

"Damn it all!" Paul screamed.

Thinking his blood was about to boil, he heard Lady howling from the backyard. That wasn't like her. Something was wrong. He'd investigate as soon as the rat met its painful and gruesome death.

As Paul focused on the box, he wiped the sweat from his brow. With his eyes locked on his target, he inched closer. Once again there was plenty of activity going on. Packed with a torn bag of potting soil, the box's contents also appeared to be shifting around. And just as before, there was another noise. *What's it doing now? Digging through the dirt?*

Paul raised the broom and kicked the side of the box. As he waited, an anxious grin stretched its way across his drenched face. But, after a while, he realized the little monster was not about to cooperate. He could still hear it digging around like a renegade gopher, strung out on uppers. He had no desire to start digging through the soil, so he gave the box another kick.

Paul stood stationary. His left shoulder and arm ached. Once again he heard Lady howling from the backyard. Then, to his shock, there was another noise, barely audible over his dog. It was a scampering sound, like tiny claws racing across concrete.

Is that coming from . . . my driveway?

Lowering the broom, Paul inspected the box. Nothing, no sound, no activity. The little escape artist had somehow vanished. Placing his free hand on his hip, he stared at the nearby gap between the wall and the overhead door. Without some type of space separating them, the door would scrape against the wall every time it was used.

"Don't tell me it squeezed through that!"

Feeling utterly demoralized, Paul threw the broom down and proceeded toward the backyard door. It seemed inconceivable that something that large could fit through such a small opening. The rat had disappeared for now, but it would be back. Janice was right; this little monstrosity was a downright mastermind.

Paul flung the door open and found Lady prancing about. The second she spotted him, she backtracked along the side of the house toward the patio. As Paul followed her around the corner, he discovered the reason for all the commotion. And when he did, his heart sank.

***

As Paul pulled his car into the driveway, he turned off his cell phone. He had just told Janice the bad news. She would be over as soon as she could.

Paul's eyes were still tearing as he removed his sunglasses. He took a breath and turned off the engine. Shifting to his right, he placed the cell phone down and picked up Jigger's collar. He kept remembering how he had found him, panting feverishly and unresponsive. "It was probably another stroke," the vet had concluded. Of course that was only a guess, but when it came down to it, nothing else mattered. Jigger's suffering had to end.

Using the remote, Paul opened the garage door. As he stepped out of his car, Lady came trotting over. She seemed reluctant to greet him. With her tail hanging limp, she sniffed at Jigger's collar. Paul had to clear his throat. "You know . . . don't you?"

Just as Lady hopped through the doggie door, a white van parked in front of Paul's house. Printed on the van's side in large lettering it read, "Evans' Exterminators." Under the name there was a drawing of a rat lying face up in an opened coffin, holding a flower on its chest. "Hell, wish that was *my* rat," Paul muttered.

A middle-aged man with a full head of white hair climbed out of the van. He was dressed in dark jeans and a blue denim shirt. Paul set the dog collar on the workbench and headed down the driveway.

The man pulled out a clipboard. "You called for an exterminator?"

"Yep, sure did."

He stretched out a hand. "I'm Don Evans." There was a faint scent of liquor on his breath.

Paul shook his hand. "Paul Donovan. Thanks for coming."

Evans must have been around Paul's age but had dark creases below a pair of wary blue eyes. And despite his own recent problems, Paul could see that there was something in the man's gaze. He could not put his finger on it, but behind those eyes was an extremely unhappy person.

"So you have some rats in your garage?"

"Yeah, just one, but it's given me a lot of trouble."

The man nodded. "Yeah, they're good at that."

"How much will it cost to get rid of it?"

"A hundred and fifty."

"For just one?"

"One or twenty, it doesn't matter."

Paul shrugged. He was past caring. "So, how are you going to kill it?"

The man opened the side of his van and handed Paul a dark, green object. Other than its color, it looked like a small Bundt cake. "Poisonous," he murmured, "with peanut butter inside."

Paul shook his head. He had considered using poison but decided otherwise because of Lady and Jiggers. "What if my dog eats it?"

Sliding the van's door shut, the man smiled halfheartedly. "I can hide them in places where your dog will never get to."

Nodding, Paul handed the poison back. "Okay, let's do it."

And from that moment on, he never saw the rat again.

* * *

There wasn't anything in Paul's refrigerator except for a pair of dried up pork chops, but that was okay. He wasn't hungry. Hopefully, when Janice arrived, she wouldn't mind skipping dinner.

Paul glanced at the TV Guide then tossed it aside. He didn't feel like watching television either. As he eased down in his recliner, a lackluster Lady slinked over.

"Still upset, huh? Well, aren't we the pair?" She obviously took some comfort, though, when he started rubbing her behind an ear. *Wish I hadn't gone so berserk last night. I should have spent more time with Jiggers.*

When the doorbell rang Paul struggled to his feet. His left shoulder and side were still sore. Even though he sensed the rat had been taken care of, the repercussions from his fall would probably last for weeks. Lady jump up and followed him. "That'll be Janice," he informed her. "So let's put on a happy face, shall we?"

When Paul opened the door, Janice handed him a puppy with the bluest eyes he'd ever seen. "What this?"

She smiled brightly. "He's a Siberian Husky."

Lady rose up on her hind legs and gave the boy a thorough once over.

"I heard you had a vacancy. So why don't we just call him an early wedding present?"

Paul held the pup up to his face and it licked him on the nose. He turned to Janice. "My God, thank you! You shouldn't have!"

"So what do you want to call him?"

Paul gave her a kiss. "Why don't we name him . . . Mister Jangles?"

"After Mister Jiggers?" she inquired.

He nodded and for the first time in several days, smiled.

Name: Federal Research Facility #98
Location: Inland Empire, California

Wearing his white lab coat over his uniform and carrying his ever-present clipboard, Captain Adrian Myers, PhD, slid his ID badge through the door's metal receptor. Entering the office, he approached the heavy-set, middle-aged, and often intimidating, administrator. A name plaque on the man's desk read, "Colonel Edward Remington."

Engrossed in paperwork, the commanding officer bellowed, "What is it now, Captain?"

The research scientist gave his superior a compulsory salute. "Sir, there's been another escape attempt in Sector 17."

Remington gazed up. His eyes brimmed with annoyance. "Again?"

"Yes, another male and female, working together, sir, but we trapped them just outside the perimeter." Meyers lowered his voice, "But if any more escape . . ."

The Colonel leaned forward. "What's the genetic code at 17?"

The scientist swallowed. "I-21."

Remington rose to his feet. "Very well. Discontinue all tests, except for I-21 and place Sector 17 under maximum security." He paused, frowned, and stared at a form on his desk. "Any word on the escapees? Subjects, 84 and 85?"

"No, sir," Meyers responded tentatively. "We can only hope they won't breed, sir. If they do . . ."

The Colonel motioned toward the door. "Our reports indicate they're sterile, Captain. Just stand down and proceed with your orders."

As Meyers hurried out into the hallway, he removed a handkerchief from his lab coat and wiped his forehead. "Sterile, yeah, right! What do you wanna bet those little suckers will bury us?"

***

By midnight Paul and Janice were sound asleep. Lady had curled up in her padded bed, and Mister Jangles slept in his very own dog carrier. Not even Lady suspected that inside the garage wall just behind the water heater, a female rat, formerly known as Subject 85, had gone into labor. The process wouldn't take long, and the entire liter would remain hidden until they were fully grown. Genetically enhanced prenatally, each of them would prove to be healthy, intelligent, and especially, devious.

AMBER'S CORNER

As I drove down Allen Street it began to rain. I guess you could call it rain, at least folks here in California call it that. Born and raised in Chicago, I would call it a drizzle or just enough moisture to get whatever you're driving nice and dirty. So I reached over and turned on my van's windshield wipers. They began making those swishing sounds that get on your nerves after awhile.

I sped through the green light at Spruce Avenue and approached my destination. It was dark and the asphalt looked slick, so I eased up on the gas. Then, about forty feet before Carmel Boulevard, I pulled over and parked. I took out my best buddy, Jackie, who's actually a metal flask that once belonged to my old man. I cleared my throat and chugged down a nice, hardy gulp. Then, a little late, I looked around. Fortunately, no one was watching.

I'm a burnt-out alcoholic, no doubt about it, but no way do I want any more trouble with the law. I had a DUI five months ago and I've been paranoid ever since. I need another charge on my record like I need another blood-sucking addiction.

People often tell me I'm a "warmhearted" guy. As a matter of fact, I was on the wagon for over eleven years. Then, about six months ago, I had a particularly nasty setback that really floored me. I would tell you about it, but for now, I'd rather not. When the setback happened, Jackie and I became reacquainted. I know people say it all the time, but I could quit drinking whenever I'm ready. I did eleven years ago, so naturally I can do it again. I guess when it comes down to it, I just don't have the proper motivation for now.

By the way, my name is Don Evans. I run my own business, which is to say I exterminate pesky little creatures. I don't have to pay a lease for a store or anything like that. There's just my van, my business phone, and a bunch of toxic chemicals stored in my garage. You can recognize my van easily enough. On both sides there are drawings of a rat inside an opened coffin with a flower lying on its chest. It's my very own logo and I'm quite happy with it.

My old man started the business, must have been nearly fifty years ago. When he died thirty years later, I sort of inherited the job by default. My one and only brother wanted no part of it. Like Robert always said, "I'm a high school economics teacher trained and educated to make a *difference,* so I'm not about to start killing rats for a living."

I wasn't doing much at the time, just a couple of odd jobs, so I took over my old man's line of work. It was an easy enough transition, because I had filled in a few times when Pop's health gave out. Guess you could say I was a natural, right from the start. Of course, killing rats is just a small part of the business. I kill every type of insect you can imagine, too, including wasps, which I hate like nothing else. I also eliminate mice, gophers, snakes, and so on. Once I even got a call to terminate a nest of rabbits. They had taken over some guy's ranch in the Cajon Pass, but I turned the job down flat. That's where I draw the line. No killing bunny rabbits, although I did trap a family of raccoons one time. I drove the whole bunch all the way to Lake Arrowhead and turned them loose up there. It's a nice locale, especially if you're a raccoon.

I took another hit off Jackie, killed the engine, and turned off the headlights. It would have been pitch black if not for the lone streetlight across the way. Between the rain, the darkness, and my foggy windshield, everything looked kind of hazy – surreal-like, you might say. It was almost like a scene from a gloomy black and white horror movie. Not one of those new flicks with all that fancy editing and camera work that after awhile makes you crazy, but the kind of horror films they used to shoot back in the 1920s before sound kicked in. But, anyhow, even with all the lousy conditions, I could still see the northwest corner of Allen and Carmel just fine.

Sometimes I wish I never saw this damn intersection with all the flowers and stuff. There's even a poster on the electrical box that has an eight by ten photo of a girl on it. I guess one of her relatives must have printed it up. The picture has long since faded, and tonight it's probably soggy as well. I think it's been up there for about a year now, but I just noticed it seven months ago. The girl was attractive, a real heartbreaker, that was for sure. In the photo she must have been around nineteen or so, with long, dark hair, big brown eyes, and a knockout smile to die for. I didn't mean to make a pun just now, but that's the gist of it. She died here, at this very corner, on this very spot, where the candles and flowers are. And it all happened just over a year ago.

I shook my head and took another belt off Jackie, a little more this time. My old pal doesn't make me forget, but as the guys like to say at our weekly poker game, he sure makes remembering easier. I glanced at my watch. It was only ten to twelve. Hell, how did that happen? Normally, I'm never early, except on Saturday nights when I'm headed for this specific location, which I've already nicknamed, "Amber's Corner."

Yep, Amber was her name. I know that because it's written all over the poster. It also mentions the name of the website her family keeps up. I never knew her myself, at least not when she was alive. Kind of confusing, isn't it? Well, I have to warn you, this little story will get a whole lot *more* confusing. If anyone ever told me what I'm about to tell you, I'd call them either crazy or a liar. But yeah, it *is* confusing and downright unbelievable, as well. So I'd better start explaining the whole disaster right from the start.

It was just three weeks ago, on a Saturday night. I was coming home from my weekly poker game with the guys. Some of them I've known since high school, if you can imagine that. We just play this one game called Texas Hold 'Em. It's fun, and at least half the time I come home with extra money in my wallet. I can't recall if I won anything on that particular night. Of course, I was drinking, just like any other time. But us poker rats always down a few pints when we're tossing around the cards. In fact, all that booze is probably the reason why I tend to win. There isn't a single brand of liquor known to man that I can't handle better than any one of those pirates.

On the way home after the game, I ran into some stalled traffic on Sierra Avenue. *It's probably another fender bender*, I decided. So rather than just sit there, I turned around and took an alternate route, namely Carmel Boulevard. I had to drive a little further east and the streets were darker there, but that was no big deal. I could find my way home blindfolded, with one arm tied behind my back.

So there I was, driving up Carmel with my friend, Jackie, and I caught the light at Allen Street. As I was waiting for it to change, I noticed there wasn't anyone else around, probably because the area was smack-dab in the center of No-Man's-Land. Not only that, but it was midnight and pretty dark, except for that streetlight I mentioned before.

My radio was playing the song, "Get Ready." Not the version by the Temptations, but by the group called Rare Earth. I'm the kind of guy who likes to listen to the good old stuff from way back when, not the crap they play nowadays. Then, right in the middle of the song, the radio went on the fritz, and nothing came through but static. I looked across the street and there was this girl, around eighteen or nineteen, standing in front of all those flowers and the poster. I thought, *Where did she come from? She wasn't there a second ago.* I looked around and couldn't see a car, bicycle, or any mode of transportation whatsoever.

Now this was basically an industrial area, not a residential neighborhood. Plus it's not the greatest place in the world to wander around in the middle of the night. I was beginning to think that this girl must be either stupid or crazy.

I turned my radio down because all the static was getting on my nerves. I watched the girl the whole time, but she never moved or looked over. When the light finally changed, I turned left on Allen Street but kept an eye on the young lady. She was still standing there, gazing at the poster, and I started wondering what to do. Should I warn her about the neighborhood? Maybe I ought to offer her a ride. Of course she might mistake me for a pervert or maybe something worse. But still, I was concerned enough to consider some kind of action.

Since I'd been driving north on Allen, I pulled over just across the street from her. She more or less had her back to me and didn't notice my van. So I honked my horn and rolled down a window, but she just kept staring at the poster. Then I called out, "Hey, Miss!" But she still didn't seem to hear me. So I slammed on my horn and yelled, "Hey, you over there!" That was when she finally turned around.

"Are you okay?" I asked.

I could see her rather well because of that streetlight I told you about. She was around five feet, five inches tall, had long dark hair, and wore jeans and a maroon blouse. Her face was clear, not a flaw or blemish anywhere. Like I said, she was real young, too, and for some strange reason, she looked familiar. She gazed my way for a second and then, at long last, she answered, "I don't understand."

I looked at her for a while, probably with a funny expression on my face, and finally I asked, "What do you mean, you don't understand?"

She glanced at the electrical box then turned toward me. "The girl on the poster," she answered.

I rolled my eyes and looked over. It was too dark to make out the details, but I'd seen it about a hundred times before. So I hollered, "What about her?"

I will *never* forget what happened next. She answered, "That's me on the poster and it says I died in a car accident!" Then, as she stepped off the curb and into the street, she vanished before my eyes.

"Holy crap!" I shrieked, as my heart damn near blew a gasket. I just sat there, bug-eyed and trying to catch my breath. I couldn't believe it. Where did she go? Then, suddenly, my van's radio flipped back to normal. A cold shudder ran down my spine. I kid you not, the hair on my arms stood at attention.

Well, I got the hell out of there. I must have peeled rubber half the way home. No doubt about it, I took a few hits off Jackie, as well. I can tell you this much: I didn't get a whole lot of sleep that night.

Day after day I kept thinking about the girl, trying to figure her out, but after a while I said the hell with it. I decided, after all the years of drinking, then quitting for eleven years, and falling off the wagon these last six months, I was entitled to at least one hallucination. So I put the whole thing on a back burner and, to the best of my abilities, kept the girl out of my head.

When the next poker night arrived, I still managed to win a couple of bucks. Around eleven-thirty, I got really tired, but the guys didn't want me to leave. Of course, it wasn't because of my dazzling companionship; they just wanted a chance to win their money back. I ended up telling them some lame story I made up on the spot. Something about visiting a sick aunt first thing in the morning. Otherwise, if I didn't give them some type of excuse, I'd be playing poker until all hours of the night.

As I drove up Sierra Avenue, I was daydreaming, and before long I remembered the girl. It was just about the same time a week ago that I spotted her. So I did a really stupid thing and turned east down Carmel. I guess you could say my curiosity got the better of me.

I turned left on Allen Street around eleven-fifty. I did a U-turn and parked exactly where I'm sitting now. I took a nip off Jackie and relaxed. It was a clear night and the stars were bright, but after a while I began to nod out. You know, the kind of sleep where you can still hear things? I left my radio on low, thinking it would help keep me awake. Well, the song, "For What It's Worth," by Buffalo Springfield, came on. Before I knew it, a sudden burst of static nearly blew out my eardrums, and I shot up like some over-the-hill jack-in-the-box.

I looked around, wondering what the hell I'd gotten into. It took me awhile to focus, as my eyes aren't what they used to be. That's when I saw her, the same exact girl. Because I was looking south on Allen Street, she was more or less facing me, and just like the last time, she kept eyeing the poster on the electrical box.

I tried swallowing, but my mouth needed a kick start. I reached for Jackie, but he came up empty. "Thanks, old pal," I muttered. "Just when I needed ya."

I started the van but didn't turn on the headlights because I was afraid of scaring Amber. I inched up, pulled over, and lowered the passenger's window. This time she was aware of me and looked over. Right away I could tell she'd been crying.

"Hey, kid," I squealed, sounding like I'd been snorting a load of helium. "Are you okay?"

She seemed to remember me from a week ago. She started to step closer but then stopped. Instead, she bent down so she could see me better and again answered, "I don't understand."

I cleared my throat and tried another approach. "Can you tell me what's wrong?"

"That's me in the poster," she insisted, "and it says I'm dead. But I'm not dead. You can see that, can't you?"

I nodded. "Yeah, you seem pretty lively to me." I didn't know what else to say, so I asked, "Are you sure that's you in the poster?"

This time she did the nodding. "It has my name and everything."

Then I got down to some pretty tough questions. "So what are you doing out here?"

She folded her arms across her chest and glanced around. "I don't know. I can't remember."

I figured she was gearing up to cry again. In both my deranged marriages, I never had children, much less teenagers, but I still can tell when a kid is about to turn on the waterworks. So I asked, "Look, why don't you let me drive you home? Do you live far from here?"

She frowned and gave me a serious once over. "You're a stranger. How can I trust you? I don't know who you are or what you might do."

"Well, I'm Don Evans," I enlightened her, "just like it says on my van. I'm an exterminator and I live about two miles from here. So there you go. Now you know me."

She just looked my way with the saddest expression that ever existed.

"I'd like to help ya," I added, "if you'd let me."

She glanced southeast and answered, "I live by Riverside and Dudley."

I felt myself smiling, a major accomplishment, considering everything. "That's not far. Why don't ya hop in?"

She wiped her eyes and nodded. "Okay, but please don't tell me I'm dead."

"You got it," I promised, "my lips are sealed."

Then, as she reached for the door, a frightened expression suddenly crossed her face. When I thought about it later, I realized what had happened, but I just couldn't see it from where I sat. When she tried to open the door, her fingers went straight through the handle. Then, as she started to cry out, she again disappeared right in front of me.

I just sat there with my mouth hanging open. Of course, my radio came back on, and once again I found myself blown away. But I think I was more frustrated than anything because I really wanted to help her, to make a *difference*, as my brother always liked to say. But I messed up. She couldn't open the door because . . .

And then it hit me. I finally knew what was going on. The poster was right. The whole thing just hadn't sunk in with her yet. I started the van and drove home but not as fast as the time before. I was pretty sure I had another week to mull things over, and then again I would try to do something to help her. Hell, now more than ever I really wanted to make a difference.

When the next poker night came along, all I could think about was that kid, Amber. I was thinking about her so much, I wound up losing over forty bucks. The guys couldn't believe it. In fact, one of them said, "Don, you're not yourself tonight. Maybe your luck's finally run out." At around eleven forty-five, I headed for the door. They tried to talk me out of leaving, probably wanting to take advantage of my losing streak, but I did some fast talking and left anyway.

This time I drove straight up Allen Street. Some fog had rolled in and everything looked murky and damp. I had to admit, I was nervous. Once, while I was taking a hit off Jackie, I drove right through a red light. Lucky for me there were no cops around. In fact, no one was around. Just like every night, the streets in this part of town were deserted.

I crossed Carmel and made the U-turn. I parked, turned off the headlights, and then the engine. But like before, I left the radio on. It was three minutes to midnight. The fog was getting worse, but I could still see the corner of Allen and Carmel. I spotted some fresh flowers beneath the poster and shook my head. After all this time, too.

When the clock on my radio turned to midnight, the commercial that was on burst into static. I lowered the volume and when I glanced up, there was Amber. I gave her a minute to look at the poster and to think about what it said. Then I turned my engine over and pulled up beside her.

"Hey, kiddo," I greeted. My voice sounded a lot less screwy than the last time.

She turned toward me and bent down. Once again, her eyes were puffy and her cheeks looked moist. "What's happening to me, Mister Evans?"

Although I figured she couldn't recall the accident, she somehow remembered me. I didn't want to be the one to break the bad news, at least not if I could help it. I thought it might be better for her if she could recall the details on her own. "I'm not sure what's going on," I lied. "Why don't ya tell me the last thing ya remember?"

"I don't know," she answered. "I think I was on my way home." She turned and glanced over her shoulder. "But that poster says I was in a car accident. That I'm dead!"

I could tell she was getting worked up again. Who could blame her? So I said, "Maybe the poster's wrong. Maybe it's just a sick joke." But in my head I was thinking, *I have to be here for a reason. If for nothing else, to help her . . . but how can I help someone who's already dead?* I cleared my throat and asked, "Do you need a ride somewhere?"

She wiped a tear from her face. Although her eyes still looked frightened, for the first time I spotted a glimmer of hope in them. "I just want to go home. I miss my parents. I miss my whole family."

I nodded and offered her a lousy excuse for a smile. She reached for the van's door and this time I waved my hands and shouted, "Wait a second!" It gave her a bit of a start, so I lowered my voice and added, "I'll get the door."

I climbed out of the van and rushed over. She gave me a strange look, like I was from the planet Mars or something. Even though she remembered me, she didn't seem to recall what had happened when she had tried to touch the door handle. I opened it, and looking unsure of herself, she slid in. I slammed the door shut, hurried around the van, and jumped in. Once again she looked at me with one of her really sad expressions. I didn't know what to say, and I couldn't even begin to comfort her. I was afraid if I mentioned the wrong thing she might vanish like before. So I kept to myself. Better safe than sorry.

After a long and awkward silence, she finally asked, "Do you really think the poster's a prank?"

I gazed at her for a second. I've always hated being less than honest, but I was stuck between a rock and a hard place. "Yeah, it's possible," I answered. "I've seen people do stuff a whole lot worse than that," but I had the feeling she didn't believe me.

Taking a deep breath, she slumped back into the shadows. Looking more scared than ever, she whispered, "I can't be dead. A person would remember something like that, wouldn't they?"

I nodded. "Sure, especially since it's so . . . god-awful."

I hurried down Carmel and the lights kept with me. I turned south on Riverside Drive and we were almost there. She had been fighting back her tears the whole time, constantly sniffing and wiping her eyes. She told me to turn east on Dudley, and before long we were pulling in front of her folks' home. The whole ride took only about ten minutes, but to me it seemed like ten hours.

Her parents lived in a small, one-story house with wood siding and shutters alongside the windows. It had a grassy front yard with an overturned tricycle sitting beside the porch. A big maple tree stood off to the left. To my surprise, there was a light coming from a front window.

"Oh, look!" she cried. "They're awake!"

I switched off the engine and turned toward her. "Let me get that door for ya. It jams all the time."

As soon as I let her out, Amber bolted from the van and rushed toward the house. I wanted to shout, "You'd better let me knock on that door!" But I just clammed up because, once again, I didn't know what to say or what to do. After I thought about it later, I realized that maybe, deep down, I figured nature would just have to take its course. She wanted to come home and be with her folks, but what could they *possibly* do to help her? Something told me they would never be able to *see* her, much less lend a hand.

Amber halted on the porch and reached inside one of her pockets. I assumed she was searching for her keys. When she came up empty-handed, she tried turning the doorknob. I just shook my head. Even though I couldn't see the results, I knew her hand went straight through. I don't know why, but this time she didn't disappear.

More determined than ever, she tried knocking. Of course the outcome was the same, and although I expected her to vanish by then, she hung in there. Maybe her sense of resolve made the difference. Maybe, when she had something really important to do, she was able to stay in this world a little while longer.

Amber turned toward me. I knew what she was going to do next, so I nodded. She turned and, clenching her fists, stepped straight through the door. I just smiled and muttered, "That a way, kid. Nice going."

I hung around, waiting to see what would happen next. After a while, I started pacing back and forth. I kept wishing I could just snap out of this entire mess and everything would be all right. It was really quiet on that street, so I pulled Jackie out of my van. I took a hefty swig and he didn't seem to mind. Then, leaning against my vehicle, I whispered, "Sure hope she's not *too* disappointed."

No sooner had I said that, Amber shuffled back through the door. She had that scared look on her face and I realized what had happened. Of course, I was tongue-tied. Me, Don Evans, the guy who just wanted to make a difference. I wish I could have given her some moral support right about then, but just like before, I didn't know what to say. Then, as I watched, she once again disappeared. That's when my heart broke into a thousand pieces.

The look on Amber's face touched off a new low for me. I kept failing because I was out of my league — about a hundred miles over my head. So I said the hell with it and gave up completely. I was a guy making a living at killing things, a guy with no prospects for the future. A fifty-year-old alcoholic whose best friend's a metal flask. I had racked up two bum marriages and lived alone. Maybe my brother was right. Maybe I *was* a big, fat nothing and would never make the slightest difference at anything.

For the next week, I did my best to keep Amber out of my head. It was business as usual. There was plenty of work to be done, that was for sure. And at night, Jackie and I stayed home and partied together. Of course, during the daytime I'd still be reeking of alcohol. Some of my customers would give me a weird look, the one where they were probably thinking, *Gee, that guy must be plastered. What a loser!* Then, more often than not, they would change their minds about hiring me.

My miserable life dragged on. Monday became Tuesday and Tuesday became Wednesday. I kept as busy as possible and avoided the intersection at Allen and Carmel.

When Saturday night rolled around, the guys phoned me and wanted to know why I wasn't at the game. I coughed a couple of times and claimed I had come down with the flu. The truth was I didn't want to take any chances. On the way home I might get curious, then that would lead to Amber and me being shot down all over again. She was like a drowning victim I was incapable of saving. It was a lot like that setback six months ago that kicked my ass. I failed then, too, and naturally, that was when my good buddy Jackie came back into my life.

Flopping down on my couch, I kept checking the time. The television was on, but I couldn't watch it. As hard as I'd been resisting, Amber had been haunting my every thought. Her gut-wrenching eyes would turn up every time I blinked.

Then, suddenly, it felt like a lightning bolt hit me square between the eyes. I jumped off the couch and rushed to my computer. Before I knew it, I was on Amber's website. There were plenty of photos of her starting from the day she was born to well past her high school graduation. Even as a baby she had those big, brown eyes, but they looked different back then. In those photos her eyes never appeared sad or helpless. They were bright and beaming and she was happy and confident. Her relatives did a great job on the site, but I thought they should have skipped the part about the accident.

It seemed that Amber was driving home around midnight from a girlfriend's house. At the corner of Allen and Carmel, some drunk ran a red light. The impact was horrible and Amber broke her neck. She probably never knew what hit her and she died where all the flowers and candles are. She had always been popular and had a lot of friends. There was a packed funeral, and later her old high school held a memorial. The website didn't make Amber into a saint; it made her *incredibly* real.

Once I finished reading the material, I read it again. My eyes kept watering and I couldn't see straight. Hell, why should any of this get to me? The name of the funeral parlor was mentioned more than once, and it was a place I knew all too well. The site even named the cemetery and the location of her burial plot. In fact, it was just a couple of rows down from my old man's grave.

Then something occurred to me that blew away what was left of my pickled brain. Finally, for the first time in my life, I knew what to do. I shot to my feet and checked my watch. It was eleven-forty. I could still make it to Allen and Carmel in plenty of time. Grabbing my coat, hat, and, of course, Jackie, I was out the door. I didn't want to think about my previous failures. There would be plenty of time for that later.

So that's the whole story, as crazy as it sounds. I've been sitting here, on Allen Street facing Carmel, just a matter of yards from all the flowers, candles, and the poster. It's now midnight, but nothing's going on. Maybe something's wrong. The radio's playing "Kind Of a Drag" by a group from Chicago, my old hometown, but there's no static or interference. It's a Saturday night and now it's *after* midnight.

I shook my head and took a hit off Jackie. He was a very obliging fellow, that Jackie. That was when my radio went ballistic. I lowered the volume and glanced out the window beside me. I jumped from the shock and nearly choked on my tongue. Amber was standing next to my van, already bent over so she could see me.

"Holy crap!" I shouted. "What are ya trying to do? Give me a frickin' heart attack?"

"I'm sorry," she said. "I didn't mean to frighten you."

"That's okay," I managed to croak. "Believe you me, I've had worse scares than that."

"Thank you," she whispered.

"For what?" I asked.

"For coming here," she answered. "You're very kind for trying to help me, but I guess I know the truth now. I don't understand it, but I have to accept it."

I nodded and took another swig off Jackie. The hell with discretion. It's overrated anyway.

"But I'm still scared," she added. "I don't know what to do or where to go. Why am I still at this place? I hate it here!" She glanced around, looking anxious and upset. "Is this where I'm supposed to be from now on? Can you please tell me, Mr. Evans? It would help me out a lot."

I shook my head, climbed out of the van, and opened the door for her. "Get in," I said.

We drove east on Carmel. Of course, I never told her to buckle her seatbelt. I took a little nip off Jackie. Out of the corner of my eye, I saw her horrified expression.

"I wish you wouldn't do that," she murmured. Then, all of a sudden, I remembered a drunk driver had killed her.

That was when I flashed back to the worst day of my life, that day six months ago and the setback that brought Jackie back into my life. I was driving south on Oak Street and noticed the congested traffic two blocks ahead. There were lots of people running around, so I figured something awful had just gone down. By the time I got there, traffic was barely crawling along.

As I drove by, there was a white car in the middle of the street. I don't recall the make, but the windshield was all busted up. There was stuff spread out all over the place, mostly groceries and things. As I passed by, I saw a woman lying on the street. Some guy had propped her up and they were talking back and forth. The woman was pretty beaten up, but I figured she was going to be all right. As I moved on, I noticed a boy, probably around nine-years-old, lying face-up on the concrete. I tried not to stare at the puddle of blood near his head. Then, as I drove a few yards further, I saw the toddler. Hell, he couldn't have been much more than a year old. He was just lying there on his back like he was taking a nap.

I had to pass some parked cars and when I did, I pulled over, jumped out and ran toward the scene. There was a lot of chaos going on, like being stuck in the middle of a war zone. Even though there were all kinds of people standing around, no one was helping the two small boys. So I ran over to the toddler. Both his overturned stroller and baby bottle were lying nearby. He was so still, he reminded me of a toy doll. His eyes were open, but I realized he wasn't seeing a thing. I knelt down and started CPR. I gave him two quick breaths and checked his pulse. *God, no, there's nothing!* I hollered inside my head. I began the chest compressions just like I had learned in my old life guard days. I gave him two more puffs of air, being careful not to over-inflate his lungs. I could hear the air going in, because of a gurgling sound, and I kept giving compressions using just three fingers of my right hand. Any more pressure than that, I could break his ribs. During this entire time I was thinking, *Come on, breathe! I can't let this kid die!* But there wasn't even a hint of life. There were just those two tiny, sightless dark eyes.

I kept giving CPR until the paramedics took over. As they placed the toddler, the nine-year-old, and the woman into three separate ambulances, my knees just sort of gave out and I dropped to the street gutter.

While I was sitting there wiping my eyes, I shouted, "They're not going to make it, damn it! Dear God, why the hell did this have to happen?" Some snooty-looking lady came by and stared down her nose at me like I was a piece of slime. So I told her, "I just wanted to make a difference, that's all. Just some kind of difference!"

I let go of a huge shudder and pushed that miserable, messed-up day back to where it had come from. Right now it was the last thing I wanted to be thinking about.

After a while I turned on a street called Willow and headed south. Amber was sitting quietly in the passenger's seat, gazing out the window. If I hadn't known better, I'd say she was almost relaxed. "Aren't you going to tell me where we're going?" she asked.

I shrugged and answered, "You'll see."

I pulled up to the east side of Saint Christopher's Cemetery. The smaller auxiliary gate had a big padlock hanging from its hasp.

She looked out the window for what seemed like forever. "I thought so," was all she said.

"Don't look so sad," I told her. "I know you were taken at a young age, but I just happen to know a lot about you, like how wonderful everything was in your life and what a great family you had. But I still have to tell you, you're going to a much better place now. And in a few more minutes, I think all your regrets and problems will be forgotten. You'll be happy and trouble-free for longer than either of us could ever imagine." There, I finally said something. It had been years since I'd talked so much. Just hope I didn't blow it.

She smiled but still looked a little scared. I hurried out of the van and opened the door for her. As she climbed out, her eyes fixed themselves on the locked gate. "How do we get in?" she asked.

"The same way you did at your folks' house," I answered. "I'll wait here and make sure you're okay. Just head for the fifth row, seventh headstone down."

Amber crept forward and passed through the gate like she'd been doing such stuff for years. It appeared to me she didn't need to count the rows or even the burial plots. I think by then she was drawn to this particular location. She took a final look at me then stepped on top of her grave. She gazed at the headstone as I leaned against the gate. I could see her really well because of a streetlight just behind me. Her eyes were glistening, and she looked nervous and uncertain. Of course, I could still hear the static from my van's radio. I took a long hit off Jackie and wiped my mouth.

What happened next is *beyond* fantastic, and I still find it hard to believe. I've never even told the guys at our poker games about it. Most people with any common sense would never believe it anyway. Instead of being laughed at, or sent to the local funny farm, I've written down every last detail. Hopefully that will help, because if I don't vent about what happened that night, I just might go out of my ever-loving mind.

As I stood there, I noticed everything looked a whole lot brighter. I glanced over and in front of Amber there was this nearly indescribable sight. It looked like a rain cloud had dropped from the sky. It emitted a blinding light, forcing me to shade my eyes. The cloud – or whatever it was – was whirling around like a huge tornado, forming what resembled a long tunnel. It was round at the opening and its far end was hidden by the stormy sky. There was a pretty stiff wind coming from it, too, more than enough to blow my hat off.

Staggering backward, I almost dropped Jackie. I peered over at Amber and she smiled at me. This time she looked like those photos on her website, happy and sure of herself. Suddenly, Amber, the tunnel, the wind, the light, all of them were gone, just like they had never been there. I rubbed my eyes and stared at Jackie. Somehow, even after all that, I was surprised to find my van's radio playing again.

It took me quite a while to recuperate. Can't say I was paralyzed, but it was pretty darn close. My heart felt like a bass drum and I was breathing like a winded greyhound after a championship race. But most of all, I had this strange mixture of feelings bouncing around inside me. I was happy for Amber because I really meant what I said about her going to a better place. But most of all, I was feeling really *lonely*. I know it sounds crazy, but I was already missing her.

As I walked around the van, low and behold my radio went on the blink again. I also heard that wind from the tunnel, but this time it was much calmer. Inside my head, along with a warm, tingling sensation, there was this strange commotion going on. Just over the wind I heard a soft voice. Of course, I recognized her right away. In Amber's own gentle manner she whispered, "You've made a *huge* difference to me, Mr. Evans. Thank you so very much."

Well, I nearly keeled over right then and there. After that, the night became quiet once again. Of course, the static from my van's radio halted, exactly like those other times. That was when I noticed Jackie clutched in the palm of my hand. In spite of everything, I still managed to hold on to the guy. But then, suddenly, I found myself not needing him anymore. I poured out the remaining contents and left him laying there in the street gutter right next to the cemetery.

I climbed into my van and, taking my sweet time, drove home. I have to admit, I haven't felt this good for a *very* long time.

INSIDE THE BOX

Chicago, February, 1983

A black, four-door BMW sedan pulled in front of the snow-covered house on Maxwell Street. The engine idled for a moment before it was turned off. Behind the steering wheel sat a young man of twenty-five. He wore dark sunglasses and a gray wool suit. Next to him was a thirty-five-year-old woman dressed in black leather boots, a suede jacket, and a blouse buttoned to her neck. A social worker's ID badge hung on the lapel of her jacket.

While brushing her hair, the woman glanced over her shoulder at the young boy in the rear seat. "Now . . . he sleeps," she whispered.

"That's weird," her companion replied. "His file says he's a borderline insomniac."

The social worker grinned and chuckled. "Don't believe everything you read." She rummaged through her purse and removed a roll of breath mints. "Then, again, his file says his IQ registered off the charts, and he can read at an eighth-grade level . . . unlike his mother – or father – from what I've heard." She placed the breath mint in her mouth before continuing. "He seems more like his aunt to me, but since he doesn't even know her, I guess that's just a coincidence." She turned to her companion. "You ready?"

The man removed his sunglasses and motioned toward the house. "The question is, is *she* ready?"

The social worker laughed. "That's not a problem. I've met the woman." She turned and glanced at the boy. "Trust me, *he's* the one who needs to be ready. His Aunt Rosalie's *quite* the eccentric, to say the least. A real force of nature." She cleared her throat and leaned toward the boy. "Joshua, wake up. We're here."

Opening his eyes, the nine-year-old blinked before peering out the window. "We're here?" He frowned and murmured, "I don't remember this place."

"Yes," the woman responded. "This is your new home. At least for now."

Josh's eyes widened as he stared at the house. The gold-colored, two-story brick building featured a single front window and no porch, just a concrete step half-buried in the snow. The discolored wooden door was enhanced by a colorful, stained-glass window dominated by the letter "N" at its center.

The woman bit down on her mint and climbed out of the sedan. The young man rushed around the car, slipping on the ice in his haste. Recovering quickly, he opened the rear door.

As Josh stepped out, a gust of wind turned his cheeks scarlet and ruffled his hair. In his hands he carried a small, tan suitcase crammed with all that remained of his belongings.

"Now, remember what you've learned at the center," the woman insisted. "Mind your manners and don't tell *lies*."

Biting on his lower lip, Josh peered at his feet and nodded.

The boy turned toward the house and followed the two officials as they trudged through the snow. Still chewing the mint, the woman gazed at Josh while ringing the doorbell. "And don't forget . . . I'll be checking on you."

After she rang the bell a fourth time, the door opened to reveal a tall, slender woman with dark, curly hair standing in the entryway. She wore a lavender sweater, black pants, and a pair of house slippers. "May I help you?" she asked, with a faint Italian accent. She appeared somewhat groggy, as if she had just awakened.

Despite the cold, the social worker's face turned pale. "Don't you remember, Miss Naples? I'm Martha Coyne from the Cook County Child Care Center. And this is my intern, Eric Lance."

The woman waved a hand and laughed. "Oh, yes, of course! Maybe I should change my name to Rosalie *Alzheimer*." She stared at them intently. Her eyes appeared exceptionally dark. "So where's Josh?"

The boy stepped out from behind the social worker. The breeze continued to mess his hair and his cheeks remained red. Gazing at the woman vacantly, he swayed his suitcase back and forth.

The woman shrieked, "I'm your Aunt Rosalie!" She bent down and hugged him. "Don't you remember me?"

The boy stiffened, took an anxious breath, and shook his head.

"Well, I'm not surprised. I haven't seen you in a *very* long time. I'm your mom's older sister and I taught her everything she knows." She kissed Josh on the forehead, leaving a red smudge below his hairline. Straightening, she turned toward the two officials. "How about some coffee?"

The social worker still hadn't recovered her facial color. "That'll be fine, but we can't stay for long."

Rosalie smiled as she took the boy's hand. "You're going to love it here, Josh," she informed him. "We'll get along fabulously."

They followed Rosalie into the front entrance, which was little more than four dark walls and a dingy tile floor leading to a flight of stairs. The cramped area was surprisingly humid; it was the first time Josh had ever breathed such a musty odor. "Watch your step," his aunt advised the boy.

She guided them up a staircase to the second floor and opened the door to an entryway that seemed to face every room in the apartment. From left to right were the two bedrooms, then what appeared to be a rather small bathroom, followed by the kitchen and, on the immediate right, the living room.

"Have a seat," Rosalie suggested, "and I'll get the coffee."

Josh started toward the recliner but stopped short when he discovered the English bulldog sleeping on the floor. Covered in short brown and white fur, the animal snored and drooled simultaneously. Its protruding bottom jaw exhibited a formidable set of teeth. The boy cowered behind his suitcase and inched away.

Sitting on the couch next to Miss Coyne, the intern uttered, "Wow! That is one *ugly* dog."

"Quiet," the social worker scolded, "she'll hear you."

"Oh, that's just C-Note," Rosalie mentioned from the kitchen. "He actually belongs to my ex-husband. He won't bother you. He wasn't ugly until he ran into a tree and knocked out an eye."

The young man grinned and whispered, "Gee, ugly and dimwitted. Maybe we should notify animal control."

Inching away from the dog, Josh chose the loveseat instead and, along with the two officials, glanced around the room. The wall above the couch exhibited six dark, abstract oil paintings that were signed "R. Naples." The far wall displayed a large Egyptian mural. In the foreground stood a golden casket and an opened scroll of strange writings. The background featured a camel, two pyramids and what the boy believed was a structure called a sphinx. Both ceramic table lamps were figures of African natives carrying hunting spears, shields, and feather headdresses. Mounted on a shelf above the recliner nested a stuffed hawk with huge talons and an opened beak.

The intern turned and clutched Miss Coyne's arm. "Are you nuts? We can't leave the boy here!"

The woman cringed. "Lower your voice!"

"Look at this place. Something's not right with this woman!"

"It's already a done deal," she hissed. "Besides she's his next of kin."

Rosalie entered the room carrying a wooden tray consisting of two cups of coffee and a glass half-filled with a thick, green substance. "You don't have to worry, Mister Lance," she stated. "I'll take good care of Josh." She lowered the tray and the two guests helped themselves.

"Aren't you going to have some coffee, Miss Naples?" the intern asked.

Rosalie handed her nephew the strange-looking drink. "No, to tell you the truth, caffeine makes me crazy."

The two officials exchanged uneasy glances. The social worker stood, flashed a smile, and handed Rosalie a file folder. "Would you please sign these papers?" Her smile faltered as she returned to her seat. "Like I said before, your responsibility for Joshua has been approved for *six* months. If it becomes necessary, the length of his placement can always be renewed."

"Miss Naples, exactly how many children have you raised?" inquired the intern.

"I haven't raised any," Rosalie answered. She gave the sleeping canine a prod with her foot. The dog groaned and struggled to its feet. With scarcely a hint of surprise, it glanced at the guests with its single, bloodshot eye then quietly lumbered off.

The boy's aunt eased into the recliner. "I kept busy and never had time for kids."

The young man scooted away from the social worker's nudging elbow. Arching his eyebrows, he asked, "Why not?"

Rosalie sighed and answered, "You could say I'm a professional student. I've taken years of college courses to advance my career, and now, at forty-three, I feel it's too late to have babies. Besides, decent husbands are hard to find. But I'll take good care of Josh. He can stay with me until Luciana recovers." She paused and took a heavy breath, "Or if his father *ever* comes back."

She glanced over and noticed her nephew's bewildered reaction. "Sorry, Josh. I meant *when* your father comes back." She rolled her eyes and quickly signed the papers.

The intern glared at Miss Coyne, who appeared to be doing her best to ignore him. When Rosalie returned the folder, the social worker rose to her feet. "I'm sure you'll be a wonderful guardian for the boy, Miss Naples." She turned toward Josh and gave him a weary grin. "You're so lucky to have such a smart and terrific aunt, Joshua. I'm sure you'll be *much* better off living with her."

***

Standing inside the entryway, Josh listened as his aunt locked the downstairs front door. When she stepped into the apartment, he maintained a guarded distance. Even though his arms had grown tired, he still carried the suitcase.

"Well, that's that," Rosalie announced, shutting the front door. "Have you eaten yet?"

The boy shook his head while staring at the floor.

She motioned toward the kitchen. "Come, I'll make you a feast."

Josh sat at a table covered with a black and white checkered cloth. On the wall overlooking him hung a clock modeled after a cat. The head, legs, and tail were black in color, but its eyes and bowtie were a stark white. The cat possessed a clock's face instead of a torso, which it held in its chubby paws. The tail acted as the pendulum, swaying back and forth. Its eyes were huge and it wore the distinctive grin of a trickster.

"You like my clock?" Rosalie asked.

Josh shrugged. "It's okay."

"Wait until you meet Felicia, my Persian cat. She's pretty, but she's also a snotty little bitch."

The boy flinched. He hadn't heard such language since his father had vanished. He kept staring at his suitcase, sitting on the floor.

Rosalie sighed and rolled her eyes. "Sorry, Josh. I've never been a role model before."

"That's okay." He gazed at the clock again. He didn't know why, but for some reason, it bothered him.

Rosalie removed a plastic container from the refrigerator. Josh noticed the small, free-standing cage by the window. Inside, a green and yellow bird sat on a perch. "*Buono sera*," it squawked.

"What's that?" Josh asked.

"Oh, that's Figueroa, my parakeet." His aunt placed the container into the microwave and pressed a series of buttons.

Josh peered at the birdcage, but he also kept an eye on the clock. "What language was that?"

"Italian," she answered. "He belonged to your grandmother and when she passed on, I took him home. He's very clever and speaks both Italian and English, with a combined vocabulary of nearly sixty words." She removed the container from the microwave. "Figueroa, what do you like to eat?"

"Pizza pie," squawked the bird.

"And who do you love?"

"Momma Mia!" it answered.

A frail grin crept across Josh's face. It felt good to smile after such a long time. But when his aunt placed the lunch in front of him, all traces of his contentment disappeared.

"Soybean casserole!" she announced sitting beside him. "I made it just for you."

Josh thought he was going to throw up. "I've never heard of it."

"Well, it tastes better than it looks and it's good for you, too. I don't know if you've heard, but I gave up eating meat quite some time ago."

The boy pushed the meal away. "No, thank you. I'm not hungry."

His aunt stood and removed the plate. "Let's try some peanut butter and jelly, shall we? Who knows? Your appetite might come back."

Josh suddenly jumped in his chair. Something enormous had just brushed against his leg. A moment later, C-Note, stumbled out from beneath the table. The boy took a breath and glanced at his aunt. "Mister Lance thinks your dog is dimwitted."

Rosalie returned to the table and placed a sandwich in front of Josh. She clapped her hands and called the canine over. "C-Note, how much is this?"

She held up a pair of fingers as the dog sat down. Drooling, the animal studied her hand with his single, watery eye. With what appeared to be a broad smile spreading across his craggy face, he threw back his head and barked twice.

Josh's mouth dropped open and his eyes widened.

"And how much is this?" Rosalie grinned and this time raised four fingers. The dog peered at her while his stubby tail twirled about. Licking his chops, he threw back his head and barked four more times.

Rosalie's dark eyes glistened. "C-Note is *very* smart. All my animals are. I trained them myself."

The boy gazed at her in amazement. "How did you do that?"

"It takes time and practice." She smiled and sat next to him. "But if you're patient, you can train an animal to do almost anything."

Josh scrutinized the dog as it lumbered away. "What kind of name is C-Note?"

Rosalie laughed and leaned toward him. "Your ex-uncle came up with that bit of nonsense. It's what he paid for him, a C-Note . . . a hundred dollar bill." When she smiled and touched his shoulder, Josh flinched and drew back. Then, appearing embarrassed, he gazed at his sandwich.

Caught off guard, Rosalie lowered her hand. "Go ahead and finish eating," she stated, as if nothing had happened. "When you're done, I'll give you the grand tour of my modest little abode."

***

The majority of Rosalie's apartment had been decorated in the same fashion as her living room. It seemed everything she owned was either very dark or black in color. The furniture appeared ornate; the knickknacks were all African, Egyptian, or Asian. Josh's bedroom, however, was all but bare. There was only a standard-sized bed, a small dresser, and a familiar looking souvenir tacked on a wall.

"Wow!" Josh exclaimed while admiring the Chicago Cub's baseball banner.

His aunt beamed. "I thought you would like that."

They entered her bedroom, and again, everything appeared dark, including the furniture and bedspread. Even the drapes were a mixture of black and brown colors. Smiling proudly, she handed Josh a wooden figure of a bald man with a huge stomach.

"Who's this?"

"That's Buddha," she answered. "He was a religious leader who lived in India. I carved him myself."

The boy inspected the piece and handed it back. "Cool," he murmured. He turned and noticed the large glass enclosure on top of a metal stand. "What's in there?"

"Medusa, my python."

"A snake?"

"Of course, they make *great* pets."

Josh peered inside the container. "Where is it?"

"You see that log? During the day, she sleeps inside it. She's only active at night."

"Hey, what's that mouse doing in there?" Josh asked, spotting the creature scurrying around inside the enclosure.

Rosalie shook her head. "As much as I dislike eating meat, I can't convince Medusa to modify her diet."

He turned and gazed at her. "You mean she's gonna eat him?"

"I'm afraid so."

The boy stepped away. "That's gross!" His gaze then fell upon a free-standing birdcage, much larger than the one in the kitchen. He hurried over and looked inside.

"That's my cockatiel condo," Rosalie boasted. "I used to have two beautiful specimens, Romeo and Juliet."

Inside the cage were several objects, including a food container and various bird toys, but there wasn't a cockatiel in sight. "Where are they?" Josh asked.

Rosalie frowned and her dark eyes became even darker. "I gave them away."

At a far corner of the cage stood the ugliest wooden box Josh had ever seen. Approximately twelve inches by twelve inches in size, the relic appeared ancient. The various shades of its dark grain ran in jagged, horizontal patterns and were accompanied by several surface cracks. It was clearly lopsided, as the left side was higher than the right. Strange lettering, resembling the writings on the Egyptian mural in the living room, slanted downward. A round, uneven hole at the front appeared to be about three inches in diameter. "What kind of box is that?"

"I used it as a nesting box for my cockatiels when they mated," Rosalie answered.

"How come it's still in there?"

His aunt hesitated before answering. "I just haven't had the chance to get rid of it." She reached forward to touch his shoulder, but apparently recalling what had happened earlier, she halted. "Come, let's get you unpacked. I'll show you around some more then I'll have to leave for work."

Josh's expression suddenly turned grim. "You work . . . at night?"

She nodded. "Yes, I have to. My schedule's pretty set, five days a week, from four in the afternoon to midnight."

"What kind of job is it?"

"I work in a laboratory."

"You mean with blood and stuff?"

Rosalie laughed. "No, I'm a scientist and I work with different types of chemicals and formulas. Mostly government stuff." She motioned toward the doorway. "Come, let's get you unpacked, and then I'll make dinner. I have a new recipe I've been dying to try. It's called Spinach Soufflé."

***

Josh woke with a start. His urge to go to the bathroom could not wait until morning. He glanced around and discovered he was back home in his old bedroom. Everything looked the same, from his dresser to his toy dinosaurs on the nightstand. *What happened to Aunt Rosalie?* he wondered.

The boy climbed out of bed and heard his parents' voices from the kitchen. He knew he could be punished for leaving his room, but if he didn't get to the bathroom soon, he would wet himself.

As he crept toward the door, his parents began arguing. Ever so cautiously, he nudged the door open. The bathroom lay directly across the hallway from his bedroom, merely a few steps away. *If I could just sneak out . . . Dad might not see me.*

"You're crazy, you know that?" his father bellowed.

"Yeah, and you're drunk," his mother snapped.

"Don't you talk to me like that!"

Josh heard a chair scrape against the kitchen floor. That meant Dad had jumped to his feet. The boy still wanted to race to the bathroom, but an all-consuming fear held him back.

"Get your hands off me!" his mother cried. "You make me sick, you know that?"

The boy then heard the most dreadful sound – the sound of his mother being slapped – followed by her sobbing, his father's cursing, and the shattering of glass.

Josh remained frozen by the doorway. He kept reminding himself that his dad was a good man, but when he drank . . . he became scary. He was still trying to decide what to do when a towering shadow closed in on him.

"What did I tell you about getting up in the middle of the night?" his father growled. "Why do you always make me have to punish you?"

***

Josh shot up in bed. His heart pounded and his bladder ached. He glanced around. It took him a moment to realize he was not at home, or at the children's center, but had been sleeping in his aunt's spare bedroom. It was dark, but apparently, Rosalie had left a light on somewhere near the rear of the apartment. Throwing his blankets back, he hurried toward the bathroom.

After flushing the toilet, Josh washed his hands, and searching for a towel, he opened the linen closet. As he dried his hands with a washcloth, he noticed a small door built into the closet floor. Framed in dark wood, it appeared to be about fourteen by fourteen inches in size.

Josh dropped to his knees and opened the door. Four metal walls plunged into what appeared to be an endless blackness. As he gazed downward, an inexplicable feeling suddenly struck him. It felt as if something hidden below was trying to lure him into the darkness.

It's gotta be my imagination, Josh decided. Closing the door, he headed toward the kitchen. He missed his dad, but it was nice being free from all his rules, threats and, especially, punishments.

As the boy neared the sink, he heard a grunt from behind. His heart leaped as he swung around. To the right, Figueroa's cage had been covered by a towel. Everything seemed quiet there. He heard another grunt, followed by what sounded like a snore. He peered under the table and discovered the elderly bulldog, C-Note, soundly sleeping. Despite his aunt's assurances that the animal just looked scary and would never hurt anyone, his menacing appearance still frightened the boy.

Josh stepped over to the sink and drank some water. He placed the glass on the counter, turned, and gazed at the clock. As the cat's tail swung back and forth, its round center read 10:45. Its ticking not only sounded louder but had become faster, as well. The boy fought off a shiver. The cat's eyes seemed to be watching him, carefully following his every move. He did not know why it appeared to take so much pleasure in scaring him, but he sensed if he glanced away even for a moment, it was liable to pounce on him.

"If you need anything, let Mrs. Wellington know," his aunt had suggested over dinner.

"Who's Mrs. Wellington?" he had asked.

"She's my landlord, or perhaps I should say my *landlady*. She lives downstairs on the first floor. She's getting on in years, but she's still pretty sharp. Her phone number's on the bulletin board. You can either call her or just knock on her door."

The cat's expression became so disturbing that Josh considered calling Mrs. Wellington. *But what would I tell her?* he asked himself. *That I was scared of a clock? No, that would be way too embarrassing and make me look like a little kid. I'd better go back to bed and forget about that stupid, old clock.*

When Josh returned to his room, he found Felicia sprawled across his mattress. Earlier, Rosalie had tried introducing him to her skittish cat, but refusing to make friends, the animal howled, spat, and then raced off.

Josh gritted his teeth and tried to shoo Felicia away, but glaring at him, she held her ground. When he inched closer, she hissed and arched her back. *You can do this,* he told himself. *You're bigger than she is!* He cautiously reached down, gave the bedding a tug, and the animal scrambled out of the room.

The boy crawled under the covers, but he kept tossing and turning. His aunt had mentioned if he couldn't sleep, he could always try watching TV.

As soon as Josh entered the living room, some of the furnishings began intimidating him. The African lamps with their spears held high appeared as if they were hunting for their next victim. Flaunting its sharp beak and claws, the stuffed hawk looked even more threatening.

Using the remote control, Josh flipped through the stations until he found a program called "The Twilight Zone." It featured two miniature spacemen from a flying saucer shooting tiny ray guns at a terrified woman. Josh plopped down on the floor and immediately became mesmerized. But a far-off tapping sound from one of the bedrooms kept distracting him. He tried to ignore it, but after a while it became a complete and utter nuisance. During the commercial break, he decided to take a look.

Josh crept into the entryway and discovered the door to his aunt's bedroom had somehow swung open. *That's not right,* he recalled. *It was closed before.*

Taking a breath, he murmured, "Aunt Rosalie?"

The only response was the same tapping sound, a little louder this time.

"Aunt Rosalie?" he repeated.

When there was still no answer, he inched closer to his aunt's room. "Don't be nervous," he whispered. "That noise . . . it's gotta be one of the animals."

Josh slowly crept through the doorway. To the right stood the cockatiel's cage. On the left a heat lamp had been attached to the snake's enclosure, illuminating the room with a murky, red glow. He stood motionless and listened for a long, uneasy moment. Other than the monotonous ticking from the kitchen clock, everything remained hushed. But after a while he heard a thud from the snake's enclosure. Medusa had curled herself into a large, muscular knot. It was impossible to tell for sure, but the reptile appeared to be at least four feet long. When Josh inched closer and searched for the mouse, his heart sank. Little by little, the snake was devouring the rodent whole.

"Yuck!" he cried. "Wish I didn't see that."

When the boy turned toward the doorway, the noise resumed, sounding as if something was tapping on a wooden surface. *It's coming from the birdcage*, he realized. *I don't want to look . . . but if I don't find out what's going on, it'll keep bothering me.*

Taking his time, Josh approached the cage and gazed inside. Everything looked perfectly normal and harmless. He stepped to the left for a better view of the nesting box. Even with the reddish hue from the snake's enclosure, it remained cloaked in darkness. He thought about flipping on the ceiling light, but now that he had finally become sleepy, all he could think about was going back to bed.

Just as Josh neared the door, he heard another sound, an audible gasp, followed by an indistinct utterance. He turned and, with his heart pounding, peered at the front of the box. What appeared to be blood trickled from the opening.

Josh whirled around and dashed out of the room. After jumping into bed and pulling the covers over his head, he heard some eerie music from the living room. He moaned and realized he had forgotten to turn off the television. Any further ventures out of bed seemed like a horrible idea, but what would his aunt think? If he had ever left the TV on at home, his father would have certainly punished him.

The boy took a determined breath and yanked off the covers. As he passed his aunt's bedroom, he kept his eyes focused ahead. He hurried to the living room and snatched up the remote control. Quivering, he pressed the OFF button; the room became so dark he thought he would never find his way back. When he turned around, however, he discovered the reddish glow from the snake's enclosure had permeated into the entryway.

All I gotta do is get in bed and everything will be okay, he told himself. He set the remote down and crept forward. As he progressed, a loud banging suddenly erupted from the kitchen.

Josh ran to his room and again buried himself under the covers. He kept listening, but all he heard was the kitchen clock. *That banging must have been the ice maker,* he decided. He shook his head and bit down on his lower lip. *How can this be? Am I going crazy?* Along with tears, he fought back feelings of sorrow and abandonment. Memories of the dreary place Miss Coyne had called a "psychiatric hospital" returned to him. *Will they lock me up like my mom?*

He thought he would never fall asleep. Everything seemed so dark and . . .

Josh's breath caught in his throat. The clock's ticking had grown louder. He cringed as the cat's ever-watchful eyes flashed through his mind. *When will my aunt get home? She should be here any minute now.* He kept waiting for the sound of a door opening or his aunt's footsteps walking across the floor.

Then Josh did hear footsteps as they trudged into his room. Thinking his heart would burst, he remained frozen, unable to bring himself to glance out from beneath the covers. A moment later he heard a groan followed by a solid bump against the bed.

Josh held his breath and forced himself to peer out from his bedding. He gazed toward a shadowy figure that circled awkwardly about before dropping to the floor. When he realized it was only C-

Note, a wave of relief swept through him. No matter what else happened, deep down inside, he knew the dog would protect him.

At long last, a much needed sense of security drifted through the boy. He smiled and after a short while, fell into a deep slumber.

***

Josh yawned and stepped out from the bathroom. He glanced around and once again found himself back at his parents' house. *What am I doing here? Miss Coyne said I have to live with Aunt Rosalie.*

The boy turned and spotted his mother sitting at the kitchen table. She was staring vacantly at the oven; her eyes looked red and swollen. As he started to approach her, he halted and shuddered. The room reeked of burnt turkey.

His mother glanced over. "Josh, what are you doing out of your room?"

He tried to answer but couldn't find his voice.

Luciana's eyes grew huge. "Get to bed, hurry!"

Josh tried rushing back to his room, but for some reason found himself helpless to escape. Knowing what was about to happen, his heart quickened.

The kitchen door flew open and Josh's father swaggered in. It took only a moment for Dan Tyler to realize the outcome of their Thanksgiving dinner. "Luciana, did you burn the god-damned turkey?"

Josh's mother lit a cigarette and looked away from her husband.

Say something! the boy wanted to scream

Exhaling a long stream of smoke, Luciana merely shrugged her shoulders.

Josh's father glared at the stove. The huge bird sat on top, scorched beyond recognition. "You did! You burned the hell out of it! Do you know how much that thing cost?"

He cursed, hollered, then suddenly lunged at his wife, slapping her while Josh begged him to stop. When Luciana tried to reason with the man, he backhanded her, grabbed her hair, and dragged her to the stove. "Do you see what you did?" He shoved her face into the burnt turkey. "Do you see?" He kept swearing and shoving her into the bird.

"No, stop it, Dad! Stop it!" Josh grew desperate. He wanted to help his mother, but an overwhelming terror held him back. "Don't hurt her! Please, don't hurt her!"

His cries were drowned out by his father's rage. Dan's entire attention remained fixated on Luciana. Clutching her by the throat, he threw her to the floor and punched her repeatedly.

***

Josh shot up in bed. His eyes darted about. He was back in his aunt's spare bedroom. *It was just a nightmare,* he reminded himself, *just a terrible, terrible nightmare.* But his parents *did* have a fight on Thanksgiving. The next day his mother admitted herself to a psychiatric hospital. After that his father disappeared without a word.

The boy rubbed his eyes. He missed his mom and wished he could be with her. He cleared his throat and tried to ignore his thirst, but it was no use. If he wanted to sleep, he had to leave the safety of his bed and make his way to the kitchen sink.

Aided by the red glow from the snake's enclosure, Josh crept toward his destination. He retrieved a glass from the counter, filled it with water and, as he raised it to his mouth, realized there was something different about the room, something that wasn't right.

The clock! I can't hear it! He turned and scanned the wall over the table. His stomach sank. His heart pounded. The cat with the body of a clock was nowhere in sight.

Josh set the glass down and inched toward his room. Once he was inside, he was certain C-Note would protect him. But as he moved forward, a blurry shadow suddenly sprang out from beneath the kitchen table. Shrieking, it raced across the floor and disappeared into the entryway.

The boy halted and gritted his teeth. *That was a cat.* He paused and wrestled with his own perceptions. *But it wasn't long or skinny like Felicia. It's gotta be the clock . . . it must have come off the wall and . . .*

Josh stood motionless, wondering about the clock's whereabouts. The image of the cat – with its watchful eyes and knowing smirk – kept flashing through his mind. From the moment he had first encountered it, he sensed how badly it wanted to hurt him.

When the boy took a step forward, a low, guttural howl resonated from inside the entryway. He stopped and wiped a lone tear from his cheek. *It's by my bedroom, waiting for me . . . I'll never get past it.*

An angry growl then pierced the night, followed by a high-pitched scream. He spotted a pair of entangled shadows slamming into a wall. As he stood frozen, unable to grasp what was happening, a silhouette rushed past him, followed by a second shadowy figure. He staggered back and realized Felicia had attacked the intruder and they were now both under the kitchen table, screeching and hissing.

Josh raced through the entryway and leaped into bed. He buried himself under the covers, held his breath, and listened carefully. A moment later, more relief drifted through him. The shrieking and howling had stopped; everything in the apartment sounded calm, peaceful, and most of all, quiet.

The boy rolled over and closed his eyes. A frail smile crossed his lips. Despite Felicia's hostile manner, she had come to his aid and saved him from the clock.

***

When Josh opened his eyes, he was surprised to see daylight. His mind seemed to race in all directions. He wanted to tell his aunt about the box and the clock, and how it was unsafe for him to stay with her. Hopefully, she would believe him, even though Miss Coyne had never believed anything he'd told her, especially about his father.

The boy flinched and sprang up in bed. He felt something moving by his foot. He threw back the covers and his heart nearly jumped into his throat. A huge snake was slithering its way up his leg. When Josh flinched again, the creature stopped, flicked its tongue, and gazed at him.

"Aunt Rosalie!" he hollered. "Hurry, Medusa's gonna *eat* me!"

Appearing undaunted by the snake, his aunt stepped into the room. She handed the boy a glass of what looked like orange juice then tightened the sash to her bathrobe. "Good morning," she greeted. "Let's get dressed, shall we? It's Sunday, and we have a busy agenda ahead of us."

The boy found himself unable to take his eyes off the reptile as it curled into a huge mound on his stomach. "But, Aunt Rosalie, what about the snake?"

His aunt laughed. "Medusa, what on earth are you doing?" She scooped up the creature as if it was a frisky puppy. "You're such an escape artist!" She sighed and turned toward the door. "Drink your carrot juice, Josh, and get ready. You're in for a treat! We're having egg foo yung for breakfast!"

***

Throughout their meal, Josh kept staring at the clock. It was back on the wall just as if it had never left. Had he been dreaming? Had it *actually* come alive? He didn't know why, but it was becoming harder for him to distinguish between his dreams and reality. He wanted to tell Rosalie about his ordeal, but the clock kept watching him as if it was spying on his every move, or more importantly, every word. *Maybe I'd better wait,* he decided.

As soon as Rosalie and the boy had finished eating, they were on their way. Climbing into her Chevrolet SUV, she hopped onto the expressway, and before long they were touring the downtown Chicago area.

"This is the John Hancock Building, and back that way is the Sears Tower," Rosalie mentioned.

Josh had never seen so many tall buildings. They drove down Michigan Avenue, State Street, and Lake Shore Drive. Even though there wasn't time to stop, they drove by an attraction called Navy Pier.

They arrived at the Field Museum shortly before the doors opened. Inside were ancient mummies, early man exhibits, and replicas of saber tooth tigers. But Josh's all-time favorites were the dinosaurs. "Look, Aunt Rosalie, a Tyrannosaurus!"

His aunt had to catch up to him. "So I take it you like dinosaurs?"

The nine-year-old stood in awe beneath the towering skeleton. "Yeah, they're really cool!"

She smiled and her dark eyes softened. "Remind me when we get home to show you something."

Josh discovered some more dinosaur exhibits, along with several ancient civilizations and a life-sized model of a blue whale that hung from the ceiling.

"Thank you for taking me," he stated on the way out.

She laughed and took him by the hand. "Your day's just beginning."

As Rosalie's boots clattered on the sidewalk, she led the boy to Shedds Aquarium, located just behind the museum. Inside, he observed everything from sharks to angel fish. There was a reddish octopus and a huge fish called a grouper. Plus there were several strange creatures he had never seen before, such as moray eels and trigger fish.

Josh still wanted to tell his aunt about the events from the previous night, but she was in such a wonderful mood, talkative, and showing him so many things, that he decided the time wasn't right.

When they returned to her SUV, she asked him what else he'd like to do.

"Well, I'm kinda hungry . . ."

"Good. Me, too. So where would you like to eat?"

The boy shrugged. "Can we go to where Mom and Dad used to take me?"

Rosalie appeared dubious. "You mean Tasty Hasty?"

Josh nodded. "But they won't have anything you'd like."

She laughed and shifted her vehicle in gear. "Well, we'll see about that."

Rosalie and the boy stood in line just outside the yellow brick building known as Tasty Hasty. When they reached the order window, a large, unshaven man waited on them. He wore a greasy paper hat and he dangled a toothpick from his mouth. "What'll it be, lady?"

"One hot dog and small Pepsi for my nephew, and I'll have a medium salad."

Rolling the toothpick around in his mouth, the man stared at Rosalie. "We don't have any salads here, lady. All we got are hot dogs, burgers, and sodas."

"You have lettuce, don't you?"

"Sure, they go on the burgers."

"And I see you have tomatoes and cucumbers. Just put them on a plate and we'll call it a salad."

The man burped and shook his head. "Yeah, well, okay, lady, but don't expect me to cough up any salad dressing."

Rosalie reached into her purse and pulled out a packet of low-calorie ranch dressing. "You don't have to. It pays to be prepared, especially when it comes to eating right."

They ate their lunch outside on an old wooden picnic table. Josh had been craving a nice, juicy Tasty Hasty hot dog for months.

Rosalie watched the boy as he devoured his meal. Even in the late afternoon sun her dark eyes sparkled. "I hope you won't mind going back to a healthier diet."

Josh nodded. "It's okay. I won't mind. Thank you, Aunt Rosalie. It's been a *great* day."

She smiled and pushed away her salad. "Your day's not over yet. I have *another* surprise for you."

The boy stopped eating and gazed at her. "Don't ya have to work tonight?"

She shook her head. "I told them I'd be late."

Josh hurried and finished his hot dog. He could not imagine what else his aunt had in mind, but his enthusiasm was soon tempered by her changing mood. As soon as they climbed into her SUV, she became unusually quiet. Even a nine-year-old could tell something was about to happen.

***

Josh glanced around. They were alone in the psychiatric hospital's visiting room. With tile floors, vacant walls, and fluorescent lights, the huge room resembled an old, run-down cafeteria. Rosalie sat across the table from her nephew. She kept chewing gum and rummaging through her purse. The boy had a hard time sitting still. He had not seen his mother since Thanksgiving.

"How are you feeling, Josh? Are you nervous?"

The boy shrugged. "Naw, I'm okay."

She nodded and whispered, "Good."

A door opened and Josh glanced over. Wearing a plain beige dress, and with her dark hair hanging limply at her shoulders, his mother had just stepped into the room. He could not help but notice how gloomy and tired her eyes appeared.

Josh jumped from his chair and hurried over. He grabbed Luciana by the waist and held her tight. He thought his heart would explode.

"Oh, Josh," his mother sighed. "I'm so sorry . . . for everything."

Rosalie sat motionless. Her eyes narrowed as she carefully watched them. When they joined her at the table, she stood and hugged her sister. "You're looking better," she murmured.

Luciana pulled away and laughed. "If only that were true."

They sat down and for a long, lingering moment, the two women stared at each other. Josh glanced back and forth, thinking there was something very wrong between them. Luciana finally broke the silence. "You know, *Dan's* the one who belongs in here."

Rosalie nodded. She appeared reluctant to make eye contact. "I know."

"Have you heard from him?"

"No, have you?"

"Nope, and I don't care anymore." Luciana tapped her fingers on the table, then appearing to catch herself, stopped. "He's taken off before. I'm just gonna have to forget about him and move on." Leaning over, she kissed Josh on his cheek. "I feel so much better knowing you're okay." She turned to Rosalie and again sighed. "Thank you, Sis. I owe you. Maybe we can forget about the past or at least . . . put it behind us."

Rosalie smiled and handed Luciana a paper cup. "Here, have some coffee."

Josh's eyes widened. He had been surprised earlier when his aunt had purchased the drink from a vending machine. "Caffeine makes me crazy," she had mentioned before. Sometime later, he had wandered over to a window and, when he turned around, had spotted his aunt pouring a yellow powder into the coffee.

Luciana gazed at her sister. "You're buying me *caffeine*? You of all people?"

Rosalie nodded; her dark eyes became even darker. "Consider it . . . a peace offering."

Over the next half hour, Josh's mother sipped her drink. The boy told her about his fun day and, listening carefully, she smiled appreciatively. Shortly thereafter, a man in a white uniform announced, "Visiting hours are over."

There were tears from Josh and Luciana as they hugged goodbye. "I'll be home soon," she promised. "So be good, and mind your Aunt Rosalie."

Within minutes, Josh and his aunt had returned to her SUV. The boy had been wrestling with his courage for some time. He didn't want to upset Rosalie, but suspicious feelings plagued him and he wanted to know the truth. While she checked his seatbelt, he asked, "What did you put in my mom's coffee?"

Holding her head back, she studied him cautiously. Her eyes never looked darker. Then leaning forward, she whispered in his ear, "Something to make her better."

***

During the ride home, Rosalie, again remained unusually quiet. When she pulled into her garage, however, she turned to Josh and smiled. "Hungry? How does a vegetable casserole sound?" And just like that, she was back to her old self.

As Rosalie and Josh climbed the rear staircase, Mrs. Wellington shuffled out of her apartment. She was dressed in an olive-green bathrobe, and there were beads of perspiration clinging to her forehead. "He was here," she uttered in a thick, Slovak accent.

Rosalie stopped beside her. The boy could not help but notice how his aunt towered over the elderly woman. "Who was here, Loretta?"

Mrs. Wellington pulled out a wrinkled handkerchief from her pocket and wiped her forehead. "Joe. I could not stop him. He took the dog."

Even in the darkness, Josh could see the surprise in his aunt's eyes. "Who's Joe?" he asked. "Did he take C-Note?"

Ignoring Josh's questions, Rosalie nodded and thanked Mrs. Wellington. Turning, she led the boy up the second flight of stairs. "Joe's my philandering ex-husband," she finally explained, "the most disagreeable man since Attila the Hun. But I have to admit, he loves that dog."

"He stole him?"

"No, not really. C-Note belongs to him, but he should have called first."

"But how did he get inside your apartment?" Josh asked.

She rolled her eyes and shook her head. "As long as I kept his dog, I thought he was entitled to a key."

While Rosalie unlocked the door, a grim apprehension gripped the boy. Both C-Note and his aunt would gone tonight. With only a skittish cat around, who was going to protect him?

***

"You're going back to school tomorrow," Rosalie announced over dinner. "So tonight I want you to get plenty of sleep."

Josh frowned and finally confessed. "I kinda had some trouble last night."

His aunt sat at the kitchen table beside him. She was wearing her white laboratory jacket with her name badge clipped to the front pocket. They were eating her homemade vegetable casserole. Josh thought it tasted absolutely horrible, but he didn't have the heart to tell her.

"Trouble? What kind of trouble?"

The boy took a breath and told Rosalie how the kitchen clock had come to life and fought with Felicia. He went on to describe the strange sound he had heard from the nesting box. By the time he brought up the blood, his aunt's concerned expression had changed to complete exasperation. "Josh, why didn't you tell me about this before?"

Unable to explain himself, he merely shrugged.

Rosalie set her fork aside. "Come, let's take a look."

Josh reluctantly followed his aunt to her bedroom. She opened the door to the cockatiel cage, reached in, and removed the lid from the box. Bracing himself, the boy stepped over and looked inside.

Rosalie appeared unimpressed. "It's empty, Josh."

He took a step back and shook his head. "But what about all those noises I heard?"

His aunt smiled and glanced at the window. "Well, even this neighborhood can get a little unruly on a Saturday night. Don't you think it's possible those sounds came from outside?"

Josh sighed and stared at his feet. "Well, maybe . . ."

Rosalie slid the box cover into place and closed the cage. "I have to leave, Josh. If you have any more problems, don't bother with Mrs. Wellington. Just give me a call and I'll come home right away. My work number's on the bulletin board. I want you to feel safe, so don't hesitate to use it."

"But what about the blood I saw . . . and that stupid clock?"

"You must have been dreaming, Josh. You saw for yourself the box was empty . . . and a plastic clock *cannot* come to life."

Frustrated, the boy followed her into the entryway. An assortment of feelings raced through him. He wanted to believe his aunt, but a wary sensation kept haunting him.

***

Josh opened his eyes and glanced about the room. He had fallen asleep, but the constant ticking from the kitchen clock kept waking him. He rolled over and shut his eyes. As hard as it was, he had to stop thinking about the box. *If only C-Note was here . . .*

Suddenly, his bowels roared with dire urgency. He shot out of bed and rushed to the bathroom. His aunt's casserole was about to make *another* appearance.

Once again Josh had to retrieve a towel from the linen closet. While drying his hands, he stared at the mysterious door in the closet floor.

"Oh, that's just the laundry chute," his aunt had explained over dinner. "It goes all the way down to the basement, by the washer and dryer. It's a lot easier than lugging a clothes hamper up and down two flights of stairs."

Josh had taken a nibble of her casserole and somehow managed not to gag. "I never heard of a laundry chute."

"You have to remember," Rosalie had answered, "these homes were built back in the 1920s when laundry chutes were common."

The boy finished drying his hands and dropped the towel into the chute. It plunged downward, spiraling from side to side before vanishing.

Josh returned to bed, but as the minutes ticked by, he remained wide awake. *Maybe some TV might help me sleep.*

He threw back his covers and glanced at the photo of his parents on top of the dresser. In his aunt's old black and white picture, his father had one arm wrapped around his mother and was waving with his free hand. His mom was smiling and appeared uncommonly happy. *That was before I was born . . . before . . .* he paused and struggled for the exact word he had heard from his mother . . . *before their . . . separation.*

As he stepped into the entryway, Josh gazed at the open door to his aunt's bedroom. He took a breath, closed it, and hurried to the living room. He picked up the remote, turned on the TV, and began flipping through the stations. He stopped when "The Twilight Zone" again came on. A man and a woman were boarding an airplane. The man acted extremely nervous. "Hey, that's Captain Kirk!" Josh exclaimed.

The boy nestled himself on the couch as the brave and daring man he had often seen piloting a space ship . . . grew hysterical with fear. After considerable torment, the man flung open his window curtain. Plastered against the glass lurked the most hideous creature with a misshapen face, bulging eyes, and thick, matted fur.

The nine-year-old watched in morbid fascination, intermittently peeking through his fingers, until the TV clicked off and everything around him turned black. He leaned forward and swallowed. Not even the streetlights were shining through the windows.

Waiting for the electricity to turn back on, Josh sat in the darkest room he had ever known, a darkness that seemed endless. When he finally rose to his feet and inched toward the entryway, a mysterious sound emerged. He stopped and took a tentative breath. *It's coming from Aunt Rosalie's bedroom.*

Gradually, the noise grew louder and more persistent. This time it was *not* a tapping sound. Listening for what seemed like hours, he thought it sounded like a pair of scissors, with the blades snapping rapidly. *Oh, no, not again! It has to be coming from the box!*

Then, as suddenly as it started, the sound halted. Josh stood motionless between the couch and coffee table. He didn't know why, but the silence seemed more frightening than the noise itself.

The moment he was able to find his way, Josh crept forward. Fearing he might trip, he took small, deliberate steps. Once he approached the entryway, a wave of bewilderment raced through him. The door to his aunt's bedroom had once again opened on its own.

Josh swallowed and inched into the kitchen. Reaching the counter, he opened the drawer next to the sink and removed the flashlight his aunt had told him to use in case of an emergency. He pressed the "ON" button and, to his relief, a bright beam of light appeared.

Turning, he carefully scrutinized the clock. The cat's ticking had fallen into an eerie silence, but even in the darkness, those large, mischievous eyes seemed to be watching him.

Josh progressed to the entryway then, peering at Rosalie's bedroom, wondered how Medusa would manage without the heat lamp. He took a long, unsteady breath. *I hope she's okay. Since that sound's gone, maybe I should check on her.*

The boy entered his aunt's room but averted his eyes from the cockatiel cage. He moved to his left and approached the snake's enclosure. Medusa had risen to an upright position and was trying to push the lid open. As Rosalie had promised, a huge dictionary sat on top. The boy cracked a triumphant grin. *Looks like the little escape artist is busted for good!*

Josh turned to his right and peered at the curio cabinet next to the enclosure. Earlier that evening, his aunt had asked "Remember when we were at the museum and I mentioned I wanted to show you something?"

"Yes," he had answered, "when we were by the Tyrannosaurus."

"Well, I think you're going to like this."

She had opened the door to the cabinet and handed him an object from the center shelf. It was a tan, kidney-shaped rock the size of a grapefruit. Protruding from its jagged surface were several small, white fragments.

"What are these?" he had asked.

"They're fossils," she had answered. "Bones of a dinosaur that existed millions of years ago."

Josh's mouth had dropped open. Holding the relic in his left hand, he had taken his right index finger and gently caressed several of the bone fragments. They had felt much smoother than the rock. "What kind of dinosaur was this?"

His aunt's eyes had beamed. "I can't say for sure, but judging from the region where I found them, I think the fragments belonged to a small herbivore."

Josh smiled just thinking about the fossil. Since he was already in his aunt's bedroom, it felt like the perfect time to take another look. He opened the cabinet door and carefully removed the relic. Holding it in his left hand, he placed the flashlight under his arm. *This belonged to a real dinosaur!* he reminded himself.

Suddenly the snapping sound returned. Josh leaped backward and the fossil and flashlight flew from his hands. Once again he found himself stranded in the dark. *The flashlight! It went out! Where did it go?*

The boy dropped to his knees and groped about. The room had become so dark he thought he would never find it. *It has to be close by! It has to be!* Fanning his arms out further, his left hand brushed against metal. He snatched up the light and pressed its button. There was an agonizing delay before the light appeared.

Holding his breath, Josh turned and peered at the box. Again the sound had stopped. *I can't just go away and not look. Maybe nothing will happen, then I can forget about the stupid thing and go back to sleep.*

But you won't sleep, something inside him whispered. *You might never . . . ever sleep again!*

Josh wiped the perspiration from his forehead and crept toward the cage. *The electricity will come on any second now,* he assured himself, *and then I'll be able to see . . .*

Grasping the flashlight firmly, the boy bent forward. As he inspected the cage's interior, the sound returned with renewed intensity. Catching him off guard, he stumbled backward and had to clutch the flashlight with both hands. No longer did the sound resemble the snapping of scissors. It had changed to something quite different — something similar to what a rattlesnake would make. While Josh watched in mounting dread, the front of the box shifted. Then, at the opening, he detected movement.

What appeared to be two, long, slender feelers glided forward in a concise, concurrent fashion. Extending upward, they slithered along the front of the box.

Attached to antenna-like appendages, a pair of ruddy, oval-shaped eyes followed. Methodically searching back and forth, they steadily gravitated toward the boy.

A pair of serrated claws then squeezed through the narrow opening, snapping at the air. Josh shuddered as he perceived an emerging creature with a sharp beak and a long, flicking tongue. Its limbs and body appeared muscular and coated with a dark, moist substance. The tail flaunted a bulb-like rattle amongst several barbed stingers.

The instant the creature cleared the opening, it lunged forward. Screeching and snapping its claws, it hurled itself against the cage's door.

Josh stared in stunned amazement. He knew the wire door could not withstand such punishment for long. Forcing his legs into action, he inched away. *It wants to hurt me! I have to keep it inside this room! I can't let it out!*

The boy slammed the bedroom door shut then hurried to the kitchen. He grabbed a chair and dragged it into the entryway. After two failed attempts, he wedged it firmly beneath the doorknob. He wiped his forehead and clutched his chest. He felt winded and lightheaded. *What was that thing? How could something that big get through such a small hole?*

As Josh stepped back, something slammed into his ankle. He heard an ear-piercing howl, lost his balance, and fell to the floor. He peered toward the kitchen and caught a glimpse of Felicia as she raced away. "Thanks a lot, you stupid cat!"

Josh snatched up the flashlight, sped to his room, and quickly closed the door. Glancing about, he realized there was just the bed and dresser to barricade the room with, and he would never be able to move the dresser.

Inching the bed away from the wall, he kept pushing until it was flush against the entrance. *That should do it! No way can it get passed two blocked doors!*

The boy climbed into bed and pulled the covers over his head. He felt exhausted, but the image of the creature with its sharp claws and multiple stingers kept racing through his mind. He was certain his aunt knew more about the box than what she had said. Since there wasn't a phone in his room, he wished he had taken the time to call her from the kitchen.

Just as he started to drift off, Josh remembered he had dropped the fossil in his aunt's bedroom. He sat up, groaned, and wrestled with his emotions. Trying to sneak by the creature was, no doubt, foolish, maybe even stupid, but those were *dinosaur* bones for goodness sake! How could he possibly abandon something so valuable? What would his aunt think? And how would his father react? He had to get up, remove the barricades, and search for the relic. Hopefully the creature was still locked in the cage or, better yet, had gone back into the box.

Everything will be all right, he promised himself. *I'll go in, grab the fossil, and get out. I can do it!*

***

Josh slowly crept into his aunt's bedroom. He turned to his right and aimed the flashlight at the birdcage. The contents inside – the food container, toys, and nesting box – seemed like gloomy images from a nightmare. Each item appeared murky, strangely out of proportion. Dreary shades of gray were ever-present, but above all, it remained unnaturally quiet.

When Josh spotted the open cage door, panic gripped him. He flinched and scanned the room. *Where is it? Did it go back inside the box?*

The beam from the flashlight ran across the fossil partially hidden beneath the cabinet. Josh rushed over and scooped up the relic. Upon inspecting it, he discovered it had broken into two separate fragments. *Oh, no!* he groaned. *What have I done?*

A loud metallic thud suddenly diverted the boy's attention. He turned and spotted the creature perched on top of the cage. Twice its original size, its eyes roved erratically on their appendages, its claws and stingers raised to strike.

Josh uttered a gasp and peered at the doorway. *Can I make it?* He tightened his grip on the flashlight and held the fossil halves to his chest. *I gotta try . . .*

The boy took a deep breath but before he had a chance to move, the sound of a fierce wind swept through the room. He turned and gazed at the box. *It's coming from inside.* Yet for some reason, the wind was not propelling outwardly but was pulling *inwardly* into the box.

Thrust against the cage's bars, the creature squirmed about, snapping its claws and screeching, trying to free itself from the wind.

Josh inched backward as the window drapes were pulled toward the box. The intensity of the wind escalated; a ceramic vase flew from the dresser and struck the cage. The free-standing enclosure swayed precariously back and forth for a long, unsettling moment.

The creature's screaming suddenly fell silent as portions of its belly were whisked through the bars and into the box. A pair of its legs and additional particles of its underside tore away. A claw buckled and wrenched from its socket. It mashed through the bars, as the tail and the last remnants of the stingers broke off, followed by the spine and surrounding tissue. Moments later, nothing remained. As far as the boy could see, there wasn't even the slightest blemish on the cage.

Josh swallowed and, keeping his eyes focused on the box, slipped through the doorway. He held the flashlight and still cradled the fossil halves. As he closed the door, the wind faded to a gentle whisper, followed by a bleak, unnerving stillness.

After the boy settled into bed, the living room television came back to life. *Electricity's on,* he realized, *but no way am I gonna get up. From now on, I'm staying in bed!* He lay silent, with the fossils halves wrapped within his arms, but the constant ticking from the kitchen clock kept him awake.

The seconds yielded to minutes and the minutes yielded to what felt like hours, but after his trembling subsided, Josh fell into a deep, yet restless, sleep.

***

Once again, the boy found himself back at home, kneeling on his bedroom floor. He had just finished straightening his room exactly like his father had wanted. He still had a few minutes before lunch, so he played with his two favorite toy dinosaurs. Mr. T Rex was trying to eat Mr. Brontosaurus and the outcome had not yet been decided.

On top of the dresser, Herbert, his pet hamster, climbed into the wheel inside his cage. Herbert could run all afternoon on that squeaky, old contraption.

"Josh!" Dan Tyler bellowed from the living room. "Get in here!"

The boy scrambled to his feet and hurried toward his father, who was lounging on his recliner, reading the newspaper. As usual, he still hadn't shaved or combed his hair. "Did you clean your room?" he asked.

"Yes, Dad," Josh responded.

His father lowered the paper and glared at the boy. His eyes appeared piercing and dark, and even when he was calm and contented, they typically looked suspicious. "Ya sure?"

Josh nodded, but something inside him grew nervous. "It's all picked up, Dad, honest."

Dan Tyler tossed the newspaper aside. "It better be." He grabbed his son by a shoulder and led him to his room.

Both Josh and his father peered inside the doorway, inspecting the boy's dresser, bed, and floor. Everything had been picked up, except for the two dinosaurs Josh had been playing with.

"Get your hamster and bring him to me," his dad demanded as he hurried back to the living room.

Josh reached into the cage and carefully scooped up Herbert. He liked holding the furry animal because he was so soft and warm. What really amazed him was how completely his pet trusted him. When his mother had first purchased the hamster, they named him Heidi, because the store owner had told Luciana it was a female. But after a while, his mom insisted something was wrong. "Josh, we'd better take Heidi to a vet. It looks like she has some tumors by her tail."

"Those aren't tumors," his father scolded. "They're called testicles, you dumb wop!" He proceeded to taunt and torment his wife for the rest of the day.

Josh headed toward the living room with Herbert cuddled in his hands. He felt extremely anxious about bringing his pet to his dad. *He hasn't been drinking,* he reminded himself, *so he should be okay.*

The boy entered the living room and approached the imposing figure in the recliner. Dan Tyler leaned forward and held out his hand. Josh swallowed and relinquished his beloved pet. His father never even glanced at it. He stood, drew back his arm, and threw the hamster across the room. It struck the far wall with a decisive thud.

"You lied!" he hollered. "Two toys were lying out."

Picking up the newspaper, Dan Tyler eased back into his recliner and, without saying another word, continued reading.

***

When Josh woke up, it was already daylight and Rosalie had just stepped into his room. "It's time to get ready for school," she announced.

The boy grimly recalled the events of the previous night. This time he would tell his aunt right away. "I . . . I gotta talk to you about something . . ."

"Sure, get dressed and we'll chat over breakfast."

After going to the bathroom, Josh struggled into his clothes. He felt achy and hot all over. While making his bed, he found the broken fossil. "Sixty-five million years down the drain," he moaned.

Josh sat at the kitchen table while his aunt prepared something called "millet waffles." He kept glancing at the clock. The cat still looked wild and sinister, always watching with those large, devious eyes.

Rosalie placed the breakfast in front of the nine-year-old. Holding his stomach, he groaned, "I'm not feeling so good . . ."

His aunt leaned forward and felt his forehead. "Josh, you're burning up!"

Rosalie hurried to the bathroom to retrieve a thermometer. Covered with an assortment of fresh fruits, the boy's meal appeared to be floating around in nearly every direction. Before he knew it, the contents of his stomach came hurling out. By the time he was done vomiting, he could no longer see his waffles.

***

Josh had dozed off briefly, and when he opened his eyes, it took him awhile to gather his thoughts. After he had thrown up, his aunt had guided him back to bed. His temperature had been a whopping 104. While applying a cold compress to his forehead, Rosalie had mentioned she used to be a nurse. "You don't have to worry," she had assured him, "you're in capable hands."

The boy's aunt telephoned the school and when she returned, a remorseful Josh showed her the broken fossil. With tears in his eyes, he told her everything, from the electricity going out, to the strange noises he'd heard from the box. He went on to describe the creature and the wind that had destroyed it. He finished by explaining how he had discovered the broken fragments.

His aunt sat quietly on his bed. She never interrupted or asked any questions. When he finished, she stood, and although her manner appeared calm, he could see a sad but guarded expression in her eyes. "There's no need to feel bad about this, Josh. The fossil was broken a long time ago. In fact, it's the same, *exact* break. If you look close enough, you can still see the glue."

The boy peered at the dried substance and breathed a sigh of relief. Yet he still remained concerned about Rosalie's guarded expression. "But what about the box?"

"You don't have to worry, Josh. I'll get rid of it. I'm sorry, I should have done it before." She sighed and the guardedness within her eyes dissipated. "I just want you to feel better." She glanced at the water pitcher she had placed by his bed. "For starters, you have to drink plenty of fluids."

Josh sat up. "Don't you believe me?"

Rosalie stood and stared out the window. "I know you've been through a lot already . . ." She shook her head and took a heavy breath. "Sometimes I just don't know what to do. I thought I would catch on faster, but I'm afraid I have a lot to learn about being a guardian." She stepped over and kissed him softly on the forehead. "Get some rest and I'll take care of the box." She smiled, turned, and left the room.

***

Much to Josh's relief, Rosalie's days off from work had finally arrived. Except for his trips to the bathroom, however, he was confined to bed. Although he still felt feverish, by mid-afternoon he'd become increasingly bored. His aunt took his temperature and gave him plenty of aspirin.

"I just want to run downstairs for something," she said, straightening his blanket.

When Rosalie returned a few minutes later, she carried a portable television set into his room. "Compliments of Mrs. Wellington," she announced.

Two hours later, Rosalie told Josh she had an important errand to run. He stayed in bed and this time she was gone for an hour. When she returned, she brought in a sack of groceries and a brightly wrapped package. "Open it," she urged.

Wrapped inside the parcel were two dinosaur books, complete with colorful illustrations and abundant text. Josh gazed at his aunt in astonishment. Other than his mother, no one had ever done anything like this for him before. "Thank you, Aunt Rosalie," he croaked.

"Well, they're not as unique as a sixty-five-million-year-old relic, but they'll help pass the time."

The boy nodded and smiled. "I'm sorry . . . I didn't mean to break it."

"Josh, please, don't worry, it's fine. The pieces are downstairs on my work bench. As soon as I pick up some glue, the fossil's yours. I want you to have it, because I know how much it means to you."

Josh's eyes welled up. First the books and now the fossil. "Thank you," he uttered.

Between watching television and reading his books, the boy kept busy. Rosalie prepared meals she thought would be easy on his stomach. But when she placed the bean sprout soup in front of him, he flew out of his chair and made a beeline to the bathroom. Yet his aunt seemed to take it all in stride. Without saying a word, she replaced the meal with a peanut butter and jelly sandwich.

By the next day Josh was feeling less feverish. The telephone rang while they were eating breakfast. After Rosalie answered it, she returned to the kitchen table.

"That was Miss Coyne, your social worker. She's having a meeting today with your mom's doctor. She asked if I could be there. Would you stay in bed if I left?"

"Sure, I can read my books and watch TV."

His aunt smiled, but when she tried to brush the boy's hair, he nearly jumped out of his chair. Seeing her distraught expression, he felt guilty and embarrassed. "Sorry, I-I don't know why I do that."

Rosalie offered a halfhearted smile. "That's okay, Josh, I understand." She took a breath and glanced at her watch. "I'll ask Mrs. Wellington to check on you. I shouldn't be long, but if you need anything, just let her know."

Josh sighed. He didn't mean to overreact. *I jump like that because of Dad.* Frowning, he pushed away his soy pancakes. They didn't taste any better than the wheat germ muffins. Slouching back, he wondered what Miss Coyne would have to say about his mom, and how long he would have to wait to see her.

***

Josh closed his dinosaur book. He was finished reading and there wasn't anything interesting on TV. He was feeling much more energetic and it was becoming harder for him to stay in bed. Picking up the empty water pitcher, he headed for the kitchen.

As Josh filled the container, he glanced at the clock. It was almost five and it would be dark soon. Mrs. Wellington had checked on him twice, but it seemed like forever since his aunt had left.

The boy fought back a shudder. Of course the cat was still staring at him. But for some reason its expression had changed. Instead of that wily smirk on its face, the animal appeared to be nervous.

Turning off the faucet, Josh carried the pitcher to his bedroom. He set the container on his tray and remembered the nesting box. Since it was gone, he could safely check his aunt's cabinet for another fossil. After all, it seemed likely she would have at least one more.

Josh opened the door to his aunt's bedroom. He paused and stared at the birdcage. It was empty, just as if the box had never been there. Satisfied, he turned toward the cabinet. There were all types of items on display, including photographs, a pair of porcelain dolls, a wooden African mask, and a purple Easter egg that had the name "Anna" written on it. But there wasn't anything inside the cabinet that resembled a fossil.

Josh sighed and, making sure his aunt's door was shut tight, headed toward the bathroom. After he washed and dried his hands, he opened the linen closet and peered down the laundry chute. His aunt had told him that it led to the basement, but more importantly, she had also mentioned that the fossil halves were downstairs on the workbench.

The boy folded the towel in half and dropped it down the chute. Almost immediately, it disappeared. The nine-year-old shrugged and hurried to his room. He picked up a penny he had left on the dresser next to the photo of his parents. He returned to the bathroom and, holding the coin over the chute, dropped it. He listened carefully, but he couldn't hear it land.

Josh didn't know what to do. He wanted to see the fossil but hated the thought of going down the chute. Then, as a new idea occurred to him, he smiled and hurried to the entryway.

The boy opened the apartment's front door and, before easing it shut, made sure it was left unlocked. He tip-toed down the stairway to prevent Mrs. Wellington from hearing him. He continued until he approached the basement door. When he tried turning the knob, he discovered it was locked. He groaned, shook his head, and slowly plodded his way back to his aunt's apartment.

Turning off the television, Josh decided to take a nap and crawled under the bed covers. Except for the kitchen clock, everything remained quiet, but that didn't matter. This time his preoccupation with the fossil kept him awake. After tossing and turning, he threw back his blankets and headed for the bathroom.

Josh stepped into the linen closet, stood over the chute, and peered into the darkness. *It's gotta be a long way down,* he surmised.

I sure hope the fossil's still there. Dropping to the floor, he positioned himself by scooting toward the opening. Using his arms as supports, he eased his lower body into the chute. He took a breath and unlocked his elbows.

At first the boy descended so swiftly his stomach lurched, then tightened. All he could see were glimpses of the chute's interior flying by. When he tried to glance down, he bumped his forehead on the wall in front of him. Just when he thought he was nearing the basement, his descent halted.

Oh, no! I'm stuck!

Panic erupted inside Josh. He could not perceive anything except for the metal walls that held him in place. His body felt on fire, his breathing grew shallow, and the walls appeared to be closing in on him.

I have to get out of here!

He banged his hands and feet against the walls, sending deafening booms through the enclosure. His panic grew intolerable and the belief he was about to die consumed him. When he finally felt the wall to his right buckle, he was able to jar himself loose. Slowly at first, but rapidly picking up momentum, his descent continued.

A moment later a light broke through the darkness. The boy plunged from an opening in the basement's ceiling and landed in a laundry basket on top of a table. Before he could move, the basket toppled over, and along with an assortment of linen, he tumbled to the floor.

Josh rose to his feet. A strange mixture of relief and uncertainty surged through him. His breathing, body temperature, and heartbeat gradually returned to normal. He straightened his shoulders and, filling his lungs with musty air, glanced about the room.

A scant amount of light drifted through the window above him. To his right stood a discolored washing machine and dryer. A large, imposing furnace seemed to be hiding in the far corner. When he turned to his left, he discovered four, separate black curtains which appeared to be concealing large portions of the basement.

I don't understand . . . what could be behind those drapes? His eyes suddenly gleamed with anticipation. *Maybe the fossil's behind one of them! It's gotta be here somewhere.*

Josh approached the nearest curtain, gazed upward, and discovered it was suspended from the ceiling by thin, beaded chains attached inside a metal track. He took a breath, gripped the drape, and yanked it open. The chains unleashed a metallic rattling and a cloud of dust filled the air. He shielded his eyes and fanned away the particles. Towering above him stood an enormous, wooden case laden with dozens of books. He inched closer, and because of his advanced reading ability, he was able to sound out the titles. "Mood Disorders and Treatments," he whispered, then added, "The Post Trau-matic Patient." He paused and glanced at another shelf. "Pharm-a-ceutical Interventions," and continuing, he murmured, "Natural Remedies for the Psych-i-a-tric Patient." From an upper shelf he read, "Theories into Other Di-men-sions," followed by "Discovering Alternate Worlds."

The boy's mouth had dried out. Although he could read the titles, for the most part he had little idea of their meaning. He shrugged, stepped over to the next curtain, and cautiously drew it back. After the dust had cleared, he discovered a long, narrow table that housed glass test tubes and small, plastic bottles. He inched closer and tried to read the labels, but the lengthy names were beyond his ability to pronounce. He picked up a bottle lying on its side; on the label he recognized his aunt's distinctive handwriting. "Integrated Mellaril, Valium, and Herbal Extracts," he read aloud.

Josh wiped away a trickle of sweat from his face. *They're medications . . . every one of them.* He drew a cheerless breath and recalled his visit to the psychiatric hospital and all the tension he had felt between his mother and aunt. When he had asked Rosalie what she had poured into his mom's coffee, she had answered, "Something to make her better."

A nagging anxiety rippled through the boy. Everything appeared hazy and doubts about Aunt Rosalie crept through his mind. *She made the yellow powder right here . . . on this table.* He frowned and rubbed his eyes. *But was it really supposed to make Mom better?*

Deciding to move on, Josh inched to the third curtain and eased it back. Along a dusty wall stood an old workbench with a hutch and shelves crammed with containers of watercolors, brushes, and unused canvases. A red metal vice had been bolted to the front of the bench, and what he spotted beside it sent his heart soaring.

Josh rushed over and scooped up the fossil halves. *I found them! I finally found them!*

Then, within an instant, his jubilation vanished. From behind the fourth curtain came a tapping sound, the same noise he had heard a few nights earlier from his aunt's bedroom. It was scarcely audible one second, then the next it grew louder. A moment later the sound halted and the boy's surroundings fell into a grim stillness.

Holding the fossil halves to his chest, Josh stared at the curtain. There was no sound, no movement, just the musty scent of the basement air. Afraid he might drop the relics, he cautiously placed them on the workbench. As he crept toward the curtain, he decided if something should happen, he could always grab the fragments and run up the stairs.

The boy paused and struggled with his anxiety. *I gotta do this. I gotta find out what that noise is.* Reaching for the curtain, he flung it back.

Standing before him was an old, decrepit, wooden shelf packed with cardboard boxes. Written in bold, red ink across their sides was, once again, his aunt's handwriting.

Before he had a chance to make out the lettering, the tapping resumed, immersing the room with the same random sound. Startled, he peered at the center shelf, and scanning through the shadows, he discovered the noise's source – the seemingly ever-present nesting box.

The boy staggered backward, feeling stunned and betrayed. *No! No! She promised to get rid of it!* He couldn't breathe; he grew lightheaded and sick to his stomach – yet his entire attention remained focused on the box. Then, after a brief moment, again the tapping ceased.

I didn't mean to find it! I just wanted to see the fossil, that's all! Just the fossil!

Josh shuddered, and as he turned to retrieve the relic halves, he heard another sound, one that released an unsettling fear within him. From inside the box came a distant voice.

No! This can't be! I gotta be crazy!

The voice grew louder and repeated the same phrase over and over. Although he was unable to understand what it was saying, its pleading tone could not be denied.

Taking a step backward, Josh's knees nearly buckled. *Am I dreaming? How can this happen?* But he suspected there were many things about the box he would never understand. *That voice, it sounds human. I don't want to . . . but I have to look. I have to see what's inside.*

The boy stood beside the curtain and again wrestled with his fears and misgivings. He never thought he would see the box again, but like some recurring nightmare, it refused to go away.

The voice grew louder, faster, and more intense. Still, he could not understand a single word. Then, seemingly for no reason, it stopped.

Josh bit down on his lower lip and inched closer. His stomach shriveled and his heart raced. The box was positioned at eye level but turned slightly to the left. The area around it looked uninviting and exceptionally murky. Maintaining a reasonable distance, he leaned forward and peered at the opening. *It's just too dark . . .* He crept forward and raised his right hand. *I'll turn it toward me . . . so I can see better.*

When the boy touched the box, a strange iciness chilled his fingers. A gust of air rushed across his face and before he could react, something lunged through the opening and grabbed him by the wrist.

A choking fear staggered Josh. He slid on the floor and his heart spun out of control. For an instant he wanted to deny everything; the box, the voice, and especially the hand that held him so determinedly.

At last he screamed, "No! No! Let me go!" The more he struggled, the tighter the grip became.

He punched the hand repeatedly. His mind burst into fragments and perspiration dripped from his brow. If he didn't break free quickly, he thought would be dragged into the box forever.

He then spotted what terrified him beyond all endurance. The hand's third finger lacked its tip from just below the first joint. *No! It can't be! I have to get away! I have to right now!*

Josh braced his foot against the bottom shelf and pushed with all his might. Yet the hand held him in place. As his strength diminished, he heard the sound of the wind, the same inverted wind that had destroyed the creature with the sharp claws and deadly stingers.

Almost instantly, Josh felt the hand's grip weaken. He broke away, fell backward, and struck the concrete floor. He propped himself on his elbows and watched as the hand thrashed about. The wind would not relent. It howled and roared, forcing the struggling appendage back into the box.

Yet still the inverted wind raged, building into what sounded like a violent crescendo. The boy winced, doubled up, and held his ears. Suddenly, in a matter of a heartbeat, the room fell silent.

Josh leaped to his feet and fled up the stairs. Reaching the top, he clutched the doorknob, but it refused to budge. With tears flowing from his eyes, he recalled the basement door being locked from the outside as well. He took a breath and began pounding with his fists. "Let me out!" he screamed. "Mrs. Wellington, help me!"

He continued to yell and pound until he heard a metallic click. Dressed in her bathrobe and wearing a quizzical expression, the elderly landlady cautiously opened the door.

The boy bolted past her and flew up the stairs. He never said a word or looked back until he was safely inside his aunt's apartment.

***

Folding her arms across her chest and still wearing her jacket and scarf, Rosalie entered Josh's bedroom. Her face appeared pale and drawn. Her eyes looked anxious and remorseful.

Josh sat at the center of his bed. He was facing the window, watching the snow as it drifted downward. His aunt suspected the boy had fallen into a state of shock. She sighed and wondered if he would ever speak to her again.

She stepped forward, slipped the scarf from her neck, and eased onto the bed. Josh remained motionless and gave nothing in the way of eye contact. Straightening her shoulders, Rosalie whispered, "I spoke with Mrs. Wellington and I can well imagine what you've been through. I don't blame you for being mad at me. I told you I would get rid of the box . . . but I couldn't bring myself to do it. I thought you'd be *safe*, but I hadn't counted on the laundry chute."

Rosalie noticed she had twisted her scarf into a tight knot. She took a weary breath and slipped it into her coat pocket.

"I'm sorry for not telling you the truth, Josh. I was wrong and thought you'd be better off not knowing. I've been studying the box for over two years now, but I still don't understand much. I discovered it seven years ago in an abandoned building while I was traveling in a country called Nepal. It was just an ordinary artifact . . .

rather strange looking, but nothing special. After I took it home, I decided my cockatiels could use it for a nesting box, and it sat dormant in their cage for *five* years. Then, one day . . . for no reason . . . it changed."

She gazed at the boy and wanted to hold him, but he was too angry, too confused. She didn't know if she could ever reach him.

"While I studied it, I developed something called a working hypothesis. Many light years from our planet there are objects known as black holes. We're still learning about them, but some people think they're doorways to other universes. That's what I believe the box has become – a doorway to another universe or, more accurately, another *dimension*. The smallness of its opening doesn't seem to matter. It's completely adaptable and could assimilate, according to most theories . . . an entire city."

Rosalie shrugged her shoulders. "Of course there's no way I can prove any of this, at least not yet. I've kept it a secret because I'm afraid if it gets into the wrong hands . . ." She sighed and shook her head. "I've been working for the government for over twenty years now, and I know what they would do with such a powerful force."

Glancing at Josh, she frowned. He was still staring out the window. His distant expression had not changed. She understood. He needed tranquility, a chance to regroup. His entire life had been a nightmare, first at home, and now here, thanks to her selfish behavior. She just wanted him to be happy, well-adjusted, but most of all, unafraid.

"From what I've seen, I think inside the box must be a *horrible* place. Some things have tried to escape, but nothing ever leaves, at least not for long. And the wind that comes from it will not take anything that's good or decent. It only takes *bad* things and will never let them go. And every now and then the box seems to alter its surroundings, creates illusions, or animates objects." She motioned toward the rear of the apartment. "Such as your malicious, little friend . . . the kitchen clock."

Josh cleared his throat and turned his head toward Rosalie. Realizing he was about to say something, she leaned forward.

Nearly gagging on his words, he whispered, "I-I saw a hand." He hesitated as his expression darkened further. "It-It was missing a . . . fingertip." He peered back at the window. A sudden breeze stirred the drifting snow.

Rosalie's eyes widened and something inside them seemed to ignite. "I love you, Josh. I would never do anything to harm you." Her voice strained while her hands trembled. "I just want to protect you, and I take full responsibility for my actions. I thought I was doing what was best for you, your mom . . . for *all* of us." She paused and sighed. "I can only hope someday, you will come to understand my actions."

Glancing at the window, Rosalie's dark eyes lightened. "Well, at least I have some positive news. The doctors at the hospital said your mom has recovered, and as soon as the legalities are completed, she'll be discharged. Everyone's amazed! Miss Coyne has confirmed . . . you're going home, Josh. By this weekend, you'll be back with your mom."

The boy turned toward his aunt with tears in his eyes; his body quivered, his face reddened. Then, much to her surprise, he held out his arms. She reached forward and tenderly embraced him, all the while fighting back surges of old and bitter emotions.

***

"You'll be leaving in just a few more days," Rosalie reminded Josh, "and from now on, you won't have to eat any more health food. You'll be enjoying lots of peanut butter and jelly sandwiches." She took a breath and cringed. "And, of course . . . plenty of *junk* food."

They sat at the kitchen table, eating what Josh had described as "the best pizza I ever tasted!" Rosalie leaned forward and, mindful of his previous reactions, brushed back his hair. To her astonishment, he did *not* flinch. He merely gazed at her and smiled appreciatively. She returned his gesture and recognized his response for what it was – a sign of healing.

"And you don't have to worry about the box, Josh. I can't bring myself to destroy it . . . it's just too valuable . . . but from now on, you'll be safe, I promise."

When he reminded Rosalie about the kitchen clock and how it still bothered him, she snatched it off the wall, smashed it with a hammer, and tossed the pieces into the trash.

* * *

The black BMW sedan pulled in front of a small brick house. It was a sunny day, but the snow still clung to the ground. The rear passenger door opened and Rosalie and Josh climbed out. In one hand the boy carried his suitcase, in the other, his beloved fossil. Martha Coyne joined them, and tossing a breath mint in her mouth, she asked, "Well, Joshua, how does it feel to be home?"

"Great!" The boy turned toward his aunt. "But I can still see you, can't I, Aunt Rosalie?"

She smiled and nodded as the door to the house opened. Josh dropped his suitcase and raced toward his mother. He slipped on the ice and nearly fell, but when he reached her, she held him tight.

Rosalie and the social worker lingered by the car. Miss Coyne appeared bewildered. "Luciana's doctors were right. Her recovery's an absolute *miracle*."

Rosalie smiled. "I'm not so sure. Given the proper medications, I think even the most traumatized people can recover."

"Well, I appreciate what you did for Joshua," the social worker stated. "In case you're interested, I can pull some strings at the Cook County Adoption Agency. A lot of single woman have been adopting lately."

Rosalie waved her hand and chuckled. "No, thank you. I've decided my lifestyle's entirely *inappropriate* for raising children."

Bidding farewell to Miss Coyne, she picked up Josh's suitcase and followed her loved ones into the house.

***

Rosalie placed the nesting box on top of her dresser then murmured into the microphone, "Seven weeks and still no activity."

She turned off the tape recorder and shook her head. "Guess the portal's closed for good."

She set down the microphone and removed a wallet-sized photograph of Josh from her pocket. She entered the guest room and peered at the picture of Luciana and Dan Tyler on top of the dresser. Her eyes darkened as she stared at her brother-in-law who, in the photograph, waved at the camera with his right hand. The ring finger of that hand was missing its tip from just below the first joint.

"I warned you to leave them alone, Dan," she whispered. "They're family and I want them safe." Walking toward the doorway, she glanced at Josh's photo in her hand. "Because of our betrayal, Joshua will never learn the truth."

She sighed and leaned against the door jamb. "You lied and convinced me you and Luciana were through . . . I was weak and naive and ended up hurting my only sister." She took an uneasy breath as her voice all but broke down. "Trying to make things right . . . I gave her an incredible gift."

Wiping away a tear, she glared at the picture on the dresser. "I've made my peace, Dan, and gave up our son. You should have listened . . . and stayed away. Now you're trapped in a hell beyond anyone's imagination . . . and there's nothing you can do about it."

EPITAPH

San Bernardino, California, July, 2008.

Warren Perry leaned back in his office chair, staring at the lanky, fifteen-year-old sitting across from him. Similar to many of his fellow students, the boy's demeanor conveyed an underlying resentment. "How long have you been feeling this way, Justin?"

The teenager shrugged. "I dunno. Quite a while, I guess."

"What about your parents? Have you told them?"

The boy's eyes flashed anger. "No, but I told *you* some time ago."

Warren scanned his notes. "No, you never brought this up before."

Justin groaned and shot to his feet. He leaned forward and slammed his fists on the guidance counselor's desk. "Yeah, I told you eleven months ago, remember? And what did you do, you sack of shit? You turned around and called my parents. My old man had a fit. I spent three damn weeks locked up in a nut house because of you!"

Warren shook his head. "I don't know what you're talking about, Justin." But for some strange reason, the incident sounded familiar.

"Yeah, the whole thing caused me all kinds of grief. Everyone got on my case. Hell, you're the reason why I slit my wrists!"

"Calm down, son. Let's go back and . . ."

"Don't tell me to calm down, and don't call me your son!" Justin brushed his blond hair away from his eyes and then held his wrists in front of Warren. "Here, take a look and see what you've done. Take a *real* good look."

Stunned, Warren gazed at the open wounds. The tissue around the lesions appeared infected and decayed. Blood trickled out the corners and dripped onto the floor. "Because of you, my life's over!"

"Now, wait a minute, Justin." Warren's stomach sank. His body felt on fire. "I don't understand why you're making all these . . . accusations."

"Because it's your *fault,* damn it! I'm dead and rotting in a grave because of you!"

***

Warren bolted up in bed. His heart raced; he felt drenched in sweat. Taking a deep breath, he assured himself, *When a teenager tells you he wants to kill himself, you do what you have to . . . there are rules . . . procedures . . .*

Yeah, sure, whispered Justin's voice. Warren peered at the boy's fading image by the bedroom door. *So what good did your rules do me?* the fifteen-year-old asked.

Hurrying toward the bathroom, Warren had just enough time to reach the toilet. Dropping to his knees, he gagged and threw up the meager contents of his stomach. When he finished, he stared into the bowl. Traces of blood were mixed into the emesis.

The former guidance counselor wiped his chin and flushed the toilet. He rinsed out his mouth and gazed at his reflection in the mirror. Admitting he looked horrible seemed like a gross understatement. He had not only lost weight, but for the last few months, people kept telling him how old he looked. His facial color resembled a fashion statement out of a mortuary. What was left of his hair had turned an ugly shade of gray. Of course, there were large bags beneath his eyes, and his medications had dilated his pupils.

"Unbelievable," he murmured. "And to think, people call these the golden years."

***

Warren showered and dressed. As he hurried toward his apartment's front door, he halted in the middle of the living room. Where did he think he was going? Off to work? He was lucky not to have been fired over the Justin Tate fiasco. When a minor tells a school official he's thinking about killing himself, that official is legally obligated to notify both the child's parents and the authorities. Not that his fellow academics and the police department, blamed him for Justin's suicide. But, then again, what about that early retirement? Why did the school district push so hard for that?

Maybe it's 'cause my grandfather's a famous California senator. Justin's ghostly image glided through the kitchen counter. *Plus, my old man's a powerful congressman.*

Warren flopped into his recliner. Perspiration and nausea beleaguered him. He had spent an entire career counseling teens at three different high schools, which amounted to thirty years of assisting kids, working after hours, driving to their homes, and even interviewing family members. Since he'd never had any children of his own, he tended to overcompensate. The truth was he would sell his soul to help a teenager. He had acquired more than twenty certificates and plaques attesting to his abilities and work ethics. Then, when Justin Tate came along, everything fell apart.

Warren returned to the bathroom. It was time to take another pill. He opened the medicine cabinet and gazed at the bottle containing the capsules known as Darvadol, the ones that knocked him out. He continued searching, found his antidepressants, and pitched two into his mouth. He didn't bother with a glass of water. *Well, enough of that. It's time to look for a job.*

***

When Warren returned to his apartment, he tossed his mail on top of the coffee table. Among the stack of bills was an envelope with the return address stamped "Royce and Davis." It was another payment demand from Margo's lawyers. She had been awarded the house, the furniture, and their bank account. Warren sighed and glanced around the living room. Somehow he'd managed to find this dreary old apartment and hold onto his retirement. Thank God he could still afford to eat, at least during those rare times when he had an appetite.

Actually, the breakup wasn't Margo's fault. She just couldn't cope with the Justin Tate debacle and living with a guilt-ridden husband who had too much time on his hands. Simple, really. If you can't stand the heat, then to hell with those twenty-four years of marriage.

Warren headed for the bathroom. So what if he was only supposed to take his pills twice a day. Because of his despondent condition, he was going to take another pill, no matter what the time. He tossed a capsule in his mouth, swallowed it, and then discovered he had just taken a Darvadol. *Woops, looks like I'm in for a nice little nap.* He studied the directions. It said to ingest with food. No wonder his stomach burned. He thought that was odd because Darvadol was a sleeper and who eats before bedtime? The pharmacist had warned him that these capsules might cause nausea and internal bleeding. *Well, that's the price I pay for a few hours of sleep.*

Doctor Ricker had also enlightened Warren about this so-called "miracle drug." It had taken over twenty years, but the FDA had finally approved it. Since everything else he'd tried never touched his insomnia, Ricker had claimed, "If these bad boys don't knock you out, nothing will." Warren cringed, swallowed another antidepressant, and headed for the bedroom.

Collapsing onto his bed, Warren whispered, "Okay, quit feeling sorry for yourself." Sure, he had to start all over again, and at fifty-eight it wasn't easy, but still he could handle it. Yet that Justin Tate thing, that was different. No matter what people told him – not Margo, Principal Webber, or Doctor Ricker – none of it made any difference. No matter what, he, Warren Perry, one-time guidance counselor beyond compare, had failed that kid.

Warren struggled to his feet, and again proceeded toward the bathroom. It occurred to him the more pills he took the better he felt. He opened the medicine cabinet and swallowed two additional Darvadols. *Jeez, I'm only supposed to take one at a time.*

Looking into the mirror, he discovered a smirking Justin standing beside him. *Go ahead, take some more,* the fifteen-year-old urged. *Take a whole bunch more so we can sit down and have a nice, long guidance session!*

As Warren peered inside the bottle, he discovered the capsules had grown arms, legs, and small, gargoyle-like faces. They bumped into each other as they frolicked about. *Take me!* they cried. *Take me, and be free from all your guilt and sorrow!*

Warren shuddered and staggered backward into a wall. He shook his head. The last few remnants of his sanity had finally slipped away. *So it all comes down to this. A few more of these babies and my troubles are over.*

It was a horrible shame to take your own life, but now he understood what Justin Tate had gone through. The minutes, the hours, the days, they simply crawled by. Eventually, you sink to a point where you just don't want to endure any more pain.

Warren inched toward the sink and stared inside the bottle. The Darvadol capsules were no longer chanting or frolicking about. He dumped the contents into his hand, nearly thirty in all. He poured himself a glass of water and, in groups of five, swallowed them. He wiped his mouth and stumbled to the bedroom. Strange, but his knees were already buckling. *Those pills can't be working that fast. It's just because I'm so tired!* Night after night he would lie awake, obsessing about his life. Then, when he finally drifted off, Justin would rouse him, snarling his accusations and rage.

Warren dropped onto his bed and turned toward the nightstand. He gazed at the photograph of Margo, the one he took when they were still passionately in love. Raising his hand, he stared at the plain, gold band on his finger. It took a hell of a lot, and it had been a long time in coming, but finally, he had reached his limit.

"Fifteen-years-old," Warren gasped, rolling onto his back. "That kid's life was just starting out. Why him? It should have been me. I should have been the one. It doesn't make any sense."

Then, as he inhaled his final breath, everything in the room disintegrated.

***

Warren found himself inside a circling tunnel. His body spun backwards at an incredible rate. He felt feverish and out of control. All around him roared a violent wind, lashing at his face, arms, and legs. An endless kaleidoscope of flashing lights rained incessantly. Panic swept through him until he realized he wasn't descending – he was spiraling horizontally. Then, quite abruptly, his momentum slowed and the lights disappeared.

The wind gradually ceased as Warren opened his eyes. Unbelievable as it seemed, he was lying in bed, still very much alive. He took a breath and glanced about. Everything appeared distant and hazy. *Probably the effects from the Darvadol,* he surmised. As his surroundings came into focus, he discovered he was no longer in his drab, little apartment. It was another room, some place that looked strangely familiar. "My God!" he cried. "This was my bedroom in Chicago!"

In front of Warren stood the tiny clothes closet his former wardrobe had been crammed into. To his right was his old dresser, complete with countless dings and a cracked mirror. Across the room and beneath the window sat the record player he'd not seen in forty years.

He sat up and everything turned gray. By all rights he should be lying in a morgue someplace, undergoing an extensive autopsy. Perhaps the Darvadol had sent him into a hallucinogenic state. Instead of stopping his heart, it had catapulted him into what could only be described as a mind-numbing flashback. But what really amazed him was how incredibly real everything looked.

Warren flung the bedding back and rose to his feet. He leaned forward and touched the mattress, sheets, and pillow. Each item felt amazingly authentic. He realized he was dressed in pajamas and shook his head. He had not worn pajamas since he was seventeen.

He stumbled toward the dresser and gazed into the mirror. His heart jumped and his eyes grew wide. No longer was there a fifty-eight-year-old relic staring back. In the reflection stood a younger, scrawnier version of himself, with a baby face and full head of hair.

Rushing to the closet, Warren rummaged through the clothing. He slid into a pair of jeans and, rubbing his eyes, hurried to the window. Stepping over a stack of vinyl records, he noticed his *Meet the Beatles* album sitting on top. *God, I bought that back in 1964.*

Warren threw back the curtain and shielded his eyes. It was a sunny day; everything in the backyard looked just the way he'd always remembered. The two metal laundry posts, the brick garage, and the tulip garden were all present and accounted for.

I'm dreaming. I have to be. He began touching objects again – the window, the stereo, the records. There was no denying it. Everything felt utterly and astonishingly real. *Okay, so I'm not dreaming . . . but this is insane! I wake up from an overdose, and I'm back in the sixties?*

Then Warren smelled something that caused him to gasp out loud – the wondrous scent of his mother's cooking. *How can this be real?* His heart pounded. *But what if it is? What if I'm young again? I can see, touch, and smell things. Doesn't all of that make it real?*

Warren hurried to the dresser and snatched a T-shirt from the top drawer. He noticed a folded paper jammed into the edge of the mirror. He swallowed and pulled it out. It was a *WLS* "Silver Dollar Survey" from a Chicago radio station that listed the latest rock hits. The number one song at top of its chart was "Satisfaction" by the Rolling Stones. He peered at the date. "Oh, God," he whispered. *It's July of 1965. That makes me just fifteen-years-old . . . the same age as Justin Tate when he committed suicide.*

Cringing, Warren gazed at himself in the mirror. *This is no coincidence. I'm here for a second chance. I don't know the reason or what I'm supposed to do . . . but it has to be something important . . . something . . . extremely important.* He took a breath and finished dressing.

***

Warren inched open the door to his bedroom. He was at the rear of his parents' old house, facing the kitchen nook. A clatter of pots and pans could be heard from around the corner. A delightful aroma enticed him further into the room.

Someone stood in front of the stove. Even with her back turned toward him, he knew the woman was his mother. Apparently, she sensed his presence and glanced over her shoulder. The mere sight of her swelled his heart with joy.

"Sit down," she urged, "before your breakfast gets cold."

Warren collapsed into a chair. His mouth had dried out, and no matter how hard he tried, he remained incapable of uttering a word.

"You slept in today," she stated while lighting a cigarette. "It's nearly ten-thirty." She set a plate of French toast in front of her son and joined him at the table. "Richie came by. You're supposed to meet the gang at Gardella's. He said to bring your baseball bat."

Warren stared at his breakfast. Sitting before him were three slices of French toast with butter, sugar, and cinnamon on top. For as long as he could remember, it had always been his favorite meal. He peered across the table at his mother as she took a long, leisurely drag from her cigarette. Kay Violet Perry had smoked her entire adult life. Her prolonged suffering and eventual death from lung cancer would devastate him, but for now she was alive and healthy. "Mom?" he croaked.

She sipped her coffee. "Yes?"

"Thanks for everything you've done for me."

She stared at him, bewildered. "Why . . . you're welcome."

Warren stood, hugged her, and whispered, "You're the best mother who ever lived." He kissed her on the cheek then returned to his breakfast.

Kay regarded her son with a shocked expression. "Warren, are you okay?"

He swallowed a hefty bite then, for perhaps the first time in months, felt a smile spread across his face. Her cooking never tasted better. "Yes, I'm feeling great, thank you."

They sat in silence, Warren eating his French toast, his mother smoking her cigarette. When he finished, he stood. "Thanks, Mom that was delicious. You need anything?"

"No," she answered. "I'm fine."

He glanced toward the front of the house. "Where's Dad?"

"He's at work," she replied frowning. "My goodness, don't you know what day it is?"

Warren paused and wrestled with his options. He wanted to tell her he was actually from the year 2008 and to describe the chain of events that led to his overdose. But why spoil this miraculous reunion with such a morbid, unbelievable story? He would just have to carry on and find the reason for his unexpected, but *exceptionally* welcomed, reincarnation. "Oh, I just forgot. What day is it?"

"Friday, the sixteenth." Her eyes reflected her concern. "Are you *sure* you're okay?"

He gave her another hug. "I'm great. I'm just happy to see you, that's all." He turned and started toward his room. "Will you be home this afternoon?"

"Of course," she answered, crushing out her cigarette. "Have a good time, but stay out of those *god-awful* woods."

Warren halted and gazed at her. He thought her request sounded peculiar but, then again, so was this entire morning. "Sure, mom, and later today I want to talk to you about your smoking."

***

Warren hurried out of his parents' house. A bright, blue sky stretched above him with hardly a cloud in sight. The air smelled fresh and he could hear a variety of birds singing. Carrying his baseball bat, he descended the stairs and journeyed down the street. He could not remember his body ever feeling so invigorated. *I'm young again. My whole life's ahead of me. I have a second chance. With what I already know, I can change my entire future.*

Reaching the end of the block, Warren turned right, and headed toward Parkside Avenue. As he crossed the street, he could see Gardella's Pharmacy just down the block. *God,* he thought, *I'll never get over this. Maybe it's true. Maybe I'm back from the dead.*

Warren stopped in front of the drug store's entrance. Just above him hung the neon sign bearing the pharmacy's name. The store stood on the corner of a short block that included a barber shop, a bakery, and a convenience store. Each of the shops exhibited the same tan brick exterior and faced Elston Avenue, a major thoroughfare.

I'm here, he realized. *I'm actually here.* He was about to enter his favorite childhood haunt. It was a place long since gone but filled with wondrous memories, a meeting place where Warren and his friends had relished their blossoming relationships. He opened the door and stepped inside.

The alluring scent of vanilla filled Warren's lungs. To his left stood the tall, red and white Coca-Cola machine where, as a boy, he had spent half his allowance. Next to the machine stood a newspaper stand housing stacks of *The Chicago Tribune* and *The Jefferson Park Press*. Behind the stand a long glass display case appeared packed with candies, gum and baseball cards. To his right sprawled a variety of metal shelves containing everything from toys to pharmaceuticals. On his immediate right stood the comic book stand where, for the most part, he had spent the remainder of his allowance.

I'm back, he kept reminding himself. *I'm back. Is this heaven? It has to be.*

Warren reached into his pocket and removed the seventy-five cents he had found on his dresser. He placed a dime in the soda machine, opened the glass door, and pulled out a bottle of Coke. He popped off the cap with the machine's opener, took a swig, and noticed the matronly woman behind the counter. Over the years, he'd forgotten how frail and tired Mrs. Gardella had appeared. A widow for as long as he could recall, she would run her late husband's business for another year before she closed the doors forever.

Warren glanced at the comic book stand. There were brand new, twelve-cent editions of *Superman, Fantastic Four,* and *Archie* comics on display. He selected the *Classics Illustrated* version of *Frankenstein*, edition number 26, and glanced through the pages. Seeking revenge for the death of his bride, Elizabeth, Victor Frankenstein relentlessly pursued his monster to the ends of the earth. *I had this one*, he remembered. *It was one of my favorites.*

As Warren flipped through the comic, he heard someone clearing their throat. He turned and could not believe his eyes. Squinting at him in a most hangdog manner slouched Ira Kowalski.

"Are ya gonna buy that or what?" Ira muttered. Of course, he was scratching his head, hence the irrefutable nickname, "Itchy." Warren had not seen his former best friend in decades. During the late sixties, they had gradually drifted apart. After the Perrys moved to California, they lost contact, which was something Warren had always regretted.

"Itchy, am I ever glad to see you!" He reached forward to hug his friend.

Ira jumped back. His eyes bulged in horror. "Hey, whatcha doin'?" he hollered.

Warren lowered his arms. *That's right, Itchy never liked being touched. In fact, he hated it.* Nevertheless, just seeing Ira delighted him immensely. With pale blue, sunken eyes, and crooked teeth, he was a strange, but gratifying, sight. "Sorry, Itchy . . . I forgot because I'm really happy to see you!"

Ira recovered quickly. "Well, then, if you're *that* happy, buy me a soda."

Warren reached in his pocket, pulled out another dime and dropped it into the Coke machine.

"Thanks," Itchy mumbled while yanking out a Cream Soda.

"You know, Ira, I hope we can always be friends. I mean, even if one of us moves away, I want to stay in touch, okay?"

Itchy popped off the bottle cap, turned toward Warren and rolled his eyes. "Sure, as long as ya don't try *hugging* me again."

The pharmacy's door swung open. Warren turned and watched as Richie Boyer and Bobby Swift hurried in. Richie, with his red hair and husky frame, and Bobby, with his thick, black-rimmed glasses, nodded at them and proceeded to the soda machine.

"You guys been here long?" Bobby asked.

Warren could only gasp. They looked so young, so full of themselves. He would stay in contact with Richie and Bobby right up to 2008.

"No," answered Ira. "We just got here."

Richie dropped a dime in the machine. "Vince and Ralph are going to meet us at Indian Hills. You guys ready?"

"I was born ready," Itchy boasted.

Stepping toward the machine, Bobby quipped, "I thought you were born naked!"

Richie sipped his drink and stared suspiciously at Warren. "You okay?"

"Yeah, sure, I'm fine. Why do you ask?"

Bobby smiled and leaned against the newsstand. "'Cause you're grinning like a freaking idiot, that's why!"

Warren scrutinized the three of them. Why shouldn't he be grinning? For some unknown, inexplicable reason, he'd been transformed into a kid again and reunited with his three best friends. "To tell you the truth," he replied, "I've never been better. Now, come on, you knuckleheads, let's play some baseball."

***

Two city blocks north of Gardella's, Indian Hills was also just how Warren had remembered. There were no hills to speak of, just a grassy plain adjacent to a forest of trees. The woods lined both sides of Central Avenue for several miles. They were the same woods Warren's mother had warned him to stay out of.

After the game, Vince and Ralph hurried off and the remaining four boys returned to Gardella's. They purchased their sodas, snacks, and baseball cards, then sat outside on the sidewalk, propped against the building.

"You need to practice your fielding more," Bobby advised Warren. "You play like a fifty-year-old man!"

Warren nearly gagged on his drink. "Yeah, guess I'm a little rusty."

"Rusty? How can you be rusty?" inquired Richie. "We play *four* times a week!"

Warren nodded and gazed at his old friend, Ira. "Well, there's nothing rusty about Itchy's playing. You should go pro, you know that? With a little more self-confidence, you could break into the majors."

Squinting at his new baseball cards, Itchy beamed with pride.

Across Elston Avenue, a city bus pulled over and a young girl stepped out. Warren noticed she was wearing a familiar-looking blouse and skirt. "Hey, that's a Cardinal Stitch uniform."

"No kidding, Sherlock," Bobby shot back.

"Yeah, good old Ann Maynard," observed Richie, "Miss Pollyanna herself. Don't look now, but I think she's putting on some weight."

Bobby grinned and pinched his friend's stomach. "Yeah, look who's talking!"

Itchy glanced up from his baseball cards. "She looks okay to me."

"Everyone looks okay to you!" laughed Bobbie. "You're blind as a bat."

Richie leaned forward and nudged Bobby's glasses. "Now look who's talking."

Ira, Richie and Bobby burst out laughing while Warren kept his eyes on the girl. "Why is she wearing a school uniform?" he asked a moment later. "It's the middle of July."

Itchy tossed a stick of gum in his mouth. "Maybe 'cause she's going to summer school?"

"What do ya wanna bet she flunked Algebra?" Bobby ventured.

Warren frowned as he watched Ann. "But she was an A student all through grammar school."

"Yeah, but algebra's algebra," chimed in Richie.

Holding a text book across her chest and toting a purse on her shoulder, Ann Maynard crossed Elston Avenue. She walked at a brisk pace, with her dark hair flowing behind. As she passed the four boys, she remained on the opposite side of Parkside Avenue. She kept her eyes lowered toward the sidewalk, appearing determined not to look their way.

Never keen on being ignored, Bobby hollered, "Hey, Ann, how's it going?"

The girl glanced at them, nodded, then quickened her pace.

Richie shrugged. "After all those years we've known her, you'd think she'd be friendlier."

Itchy popped his gum. "Maybe she's stuck on herself, you know, conceited."

"Naw." Bobby shook his head. "She's just shy, that's all. It's too bad because she's not bad looking."

"See, I told ya!" shrieked Itchy. "I said she looked okay and you said I was blind as a bat."

"But you *are* blind," Bobby retorted. He reached over and turned Ira's baseball cards right side up. "Why don't you get your folks to buy you some glasses? I don't know how you can see the ball coming, much less play like you do."

Warren shot to his feet. His eyes remained fixed on Ann Maynard, who was already half a block away. "Today's the sixteenth, right?"

Bobby turned toward him. "That's right, Einstein. Why, what's up?"

Warren set his Coke down, hurried into Gardella's, and rushed to the newsstand. He snatched up a copy of *The Chicago Tribune* and began flipping through the pages. *I hope I'm wrong*, he kept repeating to himself. On page three he found what he was searching for.

ORLANDO PARK MURDER BAFFLES INVESTIGATORS

Police authorities admitted there were no new leads to last Friday's murder of a young Orlando Park girl. Janet Riley's body was discovered

Saturday afternoon by two boys playing in the Edgebrook Woods area. The results of the autopsy confirmed she was beaten with a blunt instrument. "We have not uncovered any new clues in this case," stated an anonymous police source. "There were no fingerprints or any other evidence left at the crime scene." Miss Riley was last seen leaving a friend's house, late in the afternoon on Friday . . .

Warren returned the paper to the newsstand. *That's why Mom warned me to stay out of the woods. It's because of this murder. She thinks it may happen again.*

A flood of memories suddenly raced through Warren. They were so disturbing that his mind had long since suppressed them. His mother would tell him on Sunday that Ann's body had been discovered in the woods at Indian Hills. For weeks on end the newspapers had declared a serial killer was on the prowl. They even nicknamed the suspect "The Friday Night Stalker" due to the regularity of his crimes. Ann would be the second victim and would also be beaten to death. There would be two more fatalities before the killer was finally apprehended. *What was the guy's name?* Warren asked himself. *God, I have to remember his name!*

Turning, he rushed toward the door. His eyes burned with resolve. His heart tripled its beat. "Now I know why I'm here," he whispered. He flung the door open and stormed out.

* * *

"Hey, where ya going?" Itchy asked as he rushed up from behind.

Warren hurried faster. His every thought seemed to be caught in a whirlwind. "I have to do something."

Ira scratched his cheek. "Like what for instance?"

Warren barely slowed down. "I can't tell you, Itchy."

"How come?"

"Because it sounds crazy. Just trust me and go back."

"So now you're keeping secrets from me? Man, we used to tell each other everything!"

Warren shook his head. There was no sense in hurting Ira's feelings. "Okay, come over later and we'll talk about it."

Appearing satisfied, Itchy turned and headed back to Gardella's. Warren did not have far to go. Ann Maynard lived just down the street. He had to think fast and come up with a feasible plan. *I'll have to protect her. No matter what, tonight I'll have to keep her near me.*

Ann lived in a two-story, brown brick house, located just across the alley from Warren's home. They had been neighbors and classmates for years, yet they barely knew each other. He raced up the front porch steps and stopped at the door. He was out of breath and could feel his heart pounding. Ann was smart, attractive, and deserved a long, happy life. There would be two additional victims, both teenage girls, whose families would be devastated. Forget about telling Ann, or anyone else, the reason for his presence here, it sounded too crazy, but he had to stop the killer before he struck again. He swallowed and knocked on the door. *Stay calm. You have to appear rational. Don't mention the murders, Justin Tate, or anything about the future.*

The door opened and a man in his mid-forties appeared. He looked disoriented, with unkempt hair and an unshaven face. Even after all the years, Warren recognized him. It was Ann's father, Frank Maynard.

"Hello, sir, may I please speak with your daughter?"

There was no recognition in the man's eyes. He simply turned, left the door ajar and vanished into the house. *That's right*, Warren recalled. *His wife died from cancer about a year ago and he's still grieving.* Another memory flashed through him. *God Almighty! After they found Ann's body . . . he killed himself!*

Ann peered out from inside the doorway. When she spotted Warren, her eyes narrowed, and her expression reflected a most wary disposition. "What are you doing here?" she asked.

Warren had forgotten how brown her eyes were or that she had a cluster of freckles scattered across her nose. "I just wanted to see if you're okay."

She glared at him then folded her arms across her chest. "I'm fine! Now, please go away!"

Warren cringed. He felt as if he'd just stepped into a minefield. Why was she so hostile? So guarded? He sighed and cleared his throat. "Since you've been through so much, I was just wondering how you were." He was hoping she would invite him inside so they could talk more intimately, but she just stood in the doorway with a look of disdain cemented across her face.

Ann took a breath and appeared to brace herself. "Why are you being so nice?"

Warren shook his head. "What do you mean?"

"Don't you remember, two years ago, when you chased me on the way home from school? How you tackled me and pinned me to the ground?"

"I did?"

Her expression tensed even further and it appeared she had to force herself to look at him. "Yes, and last year you kept calling on the telephone . . . and hanging up on me."

Warren's heart sank. Of all the dumb, immature stunts, why did he have to do them to her? "I'm sorry. I-I don't know why I did all those stupid things."

Her face softened, but not by much. "Yes, they were *stupid* . . . and they really hurt me!"

More remnants of the past came flashing back to Warren. At just ten years of age, his attraction for Ann had become his most guarded secret. Yet, year after year, all he managed to do was annoy her. Then there was that dreadful shame he'd felt when the police found her body. No wonder his mind had blocked it out. He took a breath and cleared his throat.

"You know, I just realized why I did all those terrible things. I could never express myself to you – or to anyone else, for that matter." He glanced at her briefly then looked away. After all the heartaches and the Justin Tate disaster, it amazed him how he could still feel this much humiliation. "So to gain your attention, I came up with all kinds of idiotic behaviors. I never meant to hurt you. I apologize . . . and hope you can forgive me."

Warren glanced at the young girl. Her resentful expression had changed to one of astonishment and, as she spoke, the wrinkles across her brow relented. "Okay, why don't we just forget about it?" She gazed at him as if seeing someone for the very first time. "You seem so . . ." she paused and appeared to be searching for the proper word, ". . . different."

He nodded and straightened his shoulders. It was time to take the plunge and set his plan in motion. "Could you step outside for a minute?"

Her eyes again narrowed. "Why?"

She's still wary, Warren realized. *I'd better be careful.* "I was hoping we could talk."

Ann stood frozen. She was shocked by his apology; there was no doubt about that. But her suspicions, understandable as they were, would make everything he had to do extremely difficult.

She inched forward as if she were entering a lion's den. He wasn't sure, but she appeared to be trembling. "So, what do you want to talk about?" Her voice sounded frail, insecure.

Warren swallowed. In order to protect her, he had to remain in her company tonight, stay rational, and proceed with the utmost discretion. "I just wanted to know what you're doing this evening."

Again, she folded her arms across her chest, appearing flustered and confused. "Why do you ask?"

He hesitated, trying to consider every possible answer. "Just curious, I guess."

"Well, my cousin Emily's coming over . . ."

He shuddered and fought off his panic. Ann's cousin would be the last person to see her alive. There wasn't time to be subtle. He had to be decisive and act immediately. "Actually, I was hoping you and I could spend some time together."

Ann's mouth dropped open. No doubt she was finding this entire discussion full of surprises. "I-I can't. Emily and I are supposed to go out."

"Why don't you call her and cancel?"

She shook her head. "No, that wouldn't be fair."

"Well, maybe the three of us could do something together?"

Ann stared at him for the longest while. At least it appeared she was considering the possibility. She unfolded her arms and shuffled her feet. "I don't think Emily would like that. Thank you, anyway." She paused and glanced at her watch. "I'd better go now."

Warren followed her to the door. He could not give up. He had to find a way. "Ann, I don't blame you for turning me down. But I *really* would like to see you tonight."

Ann was not only trembling, but she looked enormously sad, as well. That was the way Warren had always remembered Ann Maynard, even before her mother's death.

"I'm sorry, but I can't." She started to close the door, but then she stopped and a dramatic change seemed to occur. For the first time since he could remember, she appeared composed and self-confident. "Thank you, Warren." And to his surprise, she added, "maybe some other time." Her eyes lingered on him briefly as she eased the door shut.

Warren plodded down the steps. It seemed like a long way to the sidewalk. *A near miss*, he concluded. Ann appeared much more congenial toward the end of their conversation. But even if she had changed her mind about her troublesome neighbor, a crucial task lay before him. In just a few short hours, she would be leaving with her cousin, and later tonight, Ann would end up being alone and vulnerable. Emily would arrive home safely, but Ann's broken body would be found in the woods by this time tomorrow. *If only I could remember what they're doing this evening . . .*

Out the corner of his eye, Warren noticed how the Maynard's front drapes were swaying back and forth. *Someone must have been there watching me.*

Turning north he hurried home. *It's not too late. I still have time*, he reminded himself. *I'll find a way.*

***

Warren opened his parents' basement door. He could hear his father's table saw screeching as it sliced through wood. The air smelled of fresh lumber and cherry blend tobacco. He descended the staircase while gazing at his father, John Perry. Just forty-two-years-old, he looked healthy, energetic, and strong. He wore a White Sox baseball cap perched on the back of his head.

Too engrossed in his favorite hobby to notice his son, John Perry seemed to defy gravity as he dangled his old briar pipe from his mouth. Warren's mother had mentioned he'd been building another set of bookshelves. Warren had forgotten how handy his dad had always been. "You should open up your own carpenter shop," Kay Perry had urged him, "and quit the butcher's business. It's not healthy working in a refrigerator all day." But John Perry would remain status quo while his job took a heavy toll. He would suffer a fatal heart attack, four days after his fifty-fourth birthday.

Approaching his father, Warren cleared his throat. "Hi, Dad, how are you?"

John turned and removed his safety goggles. Specks of sawdust were scattered across his face, shirt, and cap. "Hey, son, what's up?"

Warren's heart plunged. There were so many things he wanted to say to his father, starting with heartfelt thanks for all his years of devotion and hard work. Yet it was always easier talking to his mom — not that there was anything wrong with Dad. For some reason talking to him was like clearing a boulder out of your throat. Everything Warren had ever wanted to say to his parents would have to be written in a letter. "Dad, I'm going out tonight."

His father placed a freshly cut shelf on the workbench. "With Richie or Bobby?"

"No, it's with a girl."

John turned toward his son. His mouth opened and his pipe dropped out. Reacting quickly, he caught it before it struck the floor. "Y-you mean you have a date?"

Warren swallowed. "Well, sort of . . ."

His father simply stared at him. Warren wasn't sure what to make of his reaction. There was a sparkle in his eyes he'd never seen before. "Guess you'll be needing some money. Go upstairs and take a sawbuck out of my wallet." He smiled again, returned the pipe to his mouth, and picked up another shelf. "I can give you a ride, if you'd like."

Warren shook his head. "No, that's okay, Dad. We'll manage."

"Well, watch yourself, son. There's a lot of dangerous people out there."

Warren nodded. If only his father knew. "Sure, Dad, I'll be careful." He turned toward the stairs, stopped, then turned around. "Thanks, Dad, I really appreciate your help." And without looking back, he hurried to his room.

***

Warren remained seated on his bed, sealing the envelope to his second letter. Just as he stood, there was a knock on his door.

"Ira's here," his mother announced.

Opening the door, Itchy entered the room carrying a grease-stained, white paper bag. He hopped onto the bed, reached into the sack, and pulled out a French fry. "Hey, you want some?"

"No, thanks, Itchy, we've just finished dinner."

"Dinner?" His friend chuckled and pulled out another fry. "Oh yeah, dinner."

Warren shook his head. He had forgotten what a dysfunctional family Ira had come from. The poor kid had grown up never knowing concepts such as social structure and family unity.

"I have something for you, Itchy." He handed his friend the two envelopes. The first letter Warren had addressed to his parents, and the second one to Ann Maynard. "I want you to hold onto these, at least for now."

Ira gobbled down a pair of French fries. "What for?" he asked.

"Well, in case something weird happens . . . I want you to deliver them."

"Whad'ya mean, if something *weird* happens? Are ya gonna tell me what's going on, or not?"

Warren breathed a heavy sigh and sat next to his friend. "I can't just now, Itchy. But if everything goes okay, then we'll talk about it tomorrow, I promise."

"That's what you said before, remember? For me to come over and we'd talk *now*."

"I know, I'm sorry."

"So, you're *not* gonna tell me what you're up to?"

"Well, let's just say I have a date."

Ira's sunken eyes bulged nearly twice their size. "You have a date? Get out of here! With who?"

Warren cleared his throat and hesitated. He recalled how sensitive Itchy could be about such matters. He hated to be left out of anything. "You *could* say I'm going out tonight . . ." he paused and lowered his voice ". . . with Ann Maynard."

His friend's eyebrows arched and a rather impish grin flashed across his face. "Cool, man! What did ya do? Go over to her house and ask her out?"

"Yes, something like that."

Itchy glanced at the two envelopes. He had already smudged a grease stain on one of them. "So, does Ann have something to do with these?"

Warren shrugged. "Yes, and no, Itchy, but that doesn't matter. What matters is . . . will you do what I ask . . . and deliver them?"

"Yeah, okay . . . I will. In case something *weird* happens. But what do ya mean by weird?"

"Trust me, you'll know if it happens. I'm counting on you." Warren reached over to pat Ira on the back, but remembering his friend's phobia with physical contact, he glanced at his watch instead. "Now get out of here. I have to get ready."

"Well, at least tell me where you're going."

Warren rose to his feet and looked into the dresser's mirror. In the reflection stood one extremely nervous teenager. "From what I recall . . . we're going to the movies."

***

After wracking his brain all afternoon, Warren finally remembered what Ann was doing the night she was murdered; she was walking home from the Gateway Theater. He may have never remembered that vital detail if it wasn't for the fact that the Gateway was another one of his favorite haunts.

When Warren thought the time was right, he began watching Ann's home from behind a large tree. From that vantage point he was able to see her front porch. It was still hot outside and perspiration accumulated on his brow.

Warren remained hidden until Ann and Emily were well out of sight. Just as he had guessed, instead of taking a bus, they were walking to the theater. The shortest route was south on Parkside Avenue. They would zigzag along several other streets and eventually make their way to Lipton Road, the street next to the theater.

Knowing that the girls might spot him if he followed them, Warren rode the Milwaukee Avenue bus. He sat in the back and kept fidgeting in his seat. With each stop he grew increasingly impatient. He knew he would beat the girls to the theater, but for the sake of his sanity, he still wanted to get the ride over with.

Warren peered out the window, trying to distract himself. When he spotted the restaurant called Shanghai Lil's, he leaned back and smiled. He had eaten there once with his parents. Dinner included live Polynesian entertainment complete with grass skirts and hula dancers.

Next along Milwaukee Avenue Warren recognized Shoppers' World, where he had purchased his first baseball bat and many of his vinyl records. Then, finally, at Lawrence Avenue, the bus pulled over. He hopped off and walked the lone block to the movie theater.

Standing in the Gateway parking lot, Warren leaned against a wall and stared down Lipton Road. It was still light out, and except for a few parked cars, he could see quite clearly. If the girls wanted to make the 7:30 show, they should be just a few minutes away.

He kept mulling over what he would say to Ann and Emily when they arrived. Hopefully, Ann wouldn't be too suspicious. When he finally spotted the girls, he ducked behind the theater's front entrance. He glanced over a movie poster for the latest James Bond film, "Thunderball," while trying his best to appear casual.

When he thought enough time had passed, he stepped into the ticket line. As he purchased his admission, he had to struggle to keep his hands from trembling. Just as he turned from the booth, he collided with Emily, banging his chin against her forehead.

"Oww . . . oh, sorry," he muttered.

Ann halted alongside her cousin and blurted, "What are you doing here?"

Warren made sure his tone reflected the proper amount of surprise and sincerity. "Oh, I come here all the time!"

Ann glanced at her cousin, who was still rubbing her forehead. Clearing her throat and turning toward Warren, Ann introduced them. "Warren, this is my cousin, Emily." Although her voice sounded jittery, her tone remained formal and polite. "Emily, this is my neighbor, Warren Perry."

Emily merely stopped rubbing her forehead and glared at Warren. But seeking to win her approval, he shook the girl's hand. Possessing short, red hair neatly parted down the middle, she appeared somewhat thin and fragile. Evidently displeased about this "chance" encounter, she frowned, gave him a curt nod, then both girls stepped into the ticket line.

Still hoping for an invitation to tag along, Warren stayed behind them. While Ann stood in line, she kept glancing over her shoulder at him. When he decided to approach her, she blushed a pleasant shade of scarlet, then quickly turned away. Her dark hair glistened in the late day sun. "Do you go to the movies often?" he asked.

Ann inched toward the ticket booth and paid her admission. "No, just once in awhile."

Warren followed them through the front entrance. As they made their way into the lobby, the scent of fresh popcorn captivated him. Due to the lack of windows, the lighting remained exceedingly dim. The plush carpeting, along with the majority of the décor, featured a maroon color laced in a gold trim. The concession stand stood squarely at the base of a towering wall. To the right a winding staircase led to a sprawling balcony. Warren kept peering about, savoring the nostalgic wonders that surrounded him. He eventually shifted his attention back to the girls and followed them to the concession line. "May I buy you something?"

Emily turned and snapped, "No, thank you, we can take care of ourselves!"

Not about to be discouraged, Warren smiled and overlooked the response. Every time Ann glanced his way, her eyes displayed their astonishment. Perhaps she had reconsidered and wanted him to join them but was too shy to ask. Of course, there was only one way to find out. "I'd still like to join you, if that would be okay."

Ann shrugged. "Well, if Emily doesn't mind."

They turned toward the visibly dour, red-headed girl. "I guess," she groaned, "even though it's *our* night out, you can still come along if you want."

Ann flinched and her eyes never looked sadder. "Maybe we shouldn't."

Warren nodded. "Sure, that's okay." He then switched to his alternate plan. "It'll be dark soon. At least allow me to walk you home."

Ann smiled and a pair of dimples Warren had never noticed before made an appearance. "Sure, that sounds great, thank you."

"Good. I'll see you *after* the show."

Warren turned and walked away. He had to prepare himself for the longest double-feature of his life. After that, he had no idea what would happen. Originally, for some reason, Ann had left the Gateway by herself. *This time,* he affirmed, *I'll be there to protect her.*

***

Warren selected a back row aisle seat. Concealing the movie screen, a massive maroon and gold curtain hung from the ceiling. The overhead lights masqueraded as a galaxy of stars. An upstairs walkway possessed a marble banister accompanied by statues that depicted ancient nobility. There was even a modest stage built below the screen. Both flamboyant and majestic, the Gateway mesmerized him all over again.

As the curtain began to rise, Warren spotted Ann and Emily hurrying down the center aisle. They carried containers of popcorn and sodas and sat near the front.

The coming attractions included "That Darn Cat," "Crack in the World," and "The Art of Love." When the first feature started, the audience applauded. The movie, "Von Ryan's Express," starred Frank Sinatra. Warren had never seen it before, and although it seemed interesting, he could not keep his mind on the screen.

How will this turn out? he wondered. *Ann ends up alone, so what happens to Emily? Will the killer change his plans because of me? Or will there be . . . some type of confrontation?*

Fifteen minutes into the second feature, Warren noticed the girls hurrying up the aisle. Surprised, he sprang to his feet and caught up to them in the lobby.

"Hi, are you leaving?"

Ann nodded. "I'm afraid so. Emily has a headache."

"Oh, sorry. It wasn't because . . . I bumped into her, was it?"

Ann shook her head. "No, she has them every now and then."

Warren followed the girls through the front doors. Darkness had fallen, but the theater's entrance remained brightly lit. He checked his wristwatch. It was 9:45.

"My headache's getting worse," Emily murmured. "If you don't mind, I'll take a bus home." She'd been rubbing the side of her head and her face had grown pale. "I need to rest and take my pills." She glanced at Warren and offered him a brief but appreciative smile. "I'm glad you're walking Ann home."

He nodded. "What about you? Are you going to be all right?"

She motioned across the street. "Yes, I'll catch a bus over there and I should be home in ten minutes." Emily crossed at the light and hurried along the sidewalk. Just as she reached the stop, the

Lawrence Avenue bus pulled up. As she climbed on she waved good-bye.

So, that's how Ann was left on her own. Now that I'm involved, we can simply ride a bus and avoid the killer altogether.

Ann turned toward him. "I hope she's going to be okay."

"She'll be home before you know it. So, Ann, why don't we catch a bus?"

She sighed and hung her head. "To be honest with you, after all those snacks, I don't even have enough change for bus fare."

Warren laughed. "Don't worry, I'll treat. It's the least I can do after all the trouble I've been."

Ann smiled and fidgeted a bit. "All right, if you insist."

They turned and walked toward the Milwaukee Avenue bus stop. Every time their eyes met, she'd blush and look away. *I always had a crush on her and never did anything constructive about it. Now that circumstances have changed, who knows? She just might warm up to me.*

Ann adjusted her purse strap and peered down the street. There was considerable traffic but not a bus in sight.

Warren glanced over the schedule posted on the sign. "It looks like we'll be here for a while."

"That's okay. I'm in no hurry." Then, apparently gathering her courage, she established eye contact, swallowed, and he knew she was about to say something important. "You're so different . . ."

Warren smiled. "I am?"

"Yes, you've changed. I noticed it earlier."

He nodded. "In what way?"

She gazed at him intently. "You're much nicer now."

"Thank you, Ann. I hope you don't mind my saying so, but I've always thought you were smart, polite, and dare I say . . . attractive?"

Ann's face turned a glowing red before she turned away. Warren guessed that within the realm of teenage relationships, they had just experienced a groundbreaking moment. "Can I ask you something?"

"Sure."

"As smart as you are, how can you possibly be going to summer school?"

She giggled and blushed some more. "Oh, it's algebra. I never get it. It's so embarrassing."

Warren frowned as his breath caught in his throat. What was he thinking? Ever since he had spotted Ann, it felt as if his feelings for her had been brought back to life. Beneath his youthful exterior, however, he was still a fifty-eight-year-old man, so to him any notions of romance seemed highly improper. Yet, despite everything, they could still establish a long-lasting friendship, and more importantly, after surviving tonight, he was certain she'd go on to live a full and meaningful life. He smiled and shook his head. As nervous as he was, he was actually having a good time.

"Can I ask *you* something?" she inquired.

"Sure."

"You didn't follow me here, did you?"

Warren hesitated. Now, of all times, he found himself thrown into what was certainly a moral dilemma. He didn't want to lie to her, but he didn't care to take any chances either. If he told her the truth, then he would have to explain the unexplainable. Like it or not, he had to play it safe. "No, that's silly," he answered. "I would never do something like that."

The sparkle in Ann's eyes immediately vanished. "No, I think you *did* follow us." And with that, she whirled around and hurried down the street.

A torrent of stunned and frustrated feelings battered Warren, as he chased after her. "Ann, please . . . wait a second!"

She had to stop for the Lawrence Avenue light. When he caught up, she refused to make eye contact. "Emily saw you behind a tree. She thought you were spying on us."

"I'm sorry. Believe me, I wish I could tell you more, but I can't."

Ann's eyes remained fixed on the stoplight. Her body trembled. Her breathing escalated. "I can't stand being lied to. I never could!"

Warren grabbed her by the arms and stared into her eyes. "I can't explain it, Ann. But please believe me. I have my reasons."

She frowned and pried herself loose. "You should have been honest. I wouldn't have cared if you followed us." Her eyes narrowed as she glared at him. "My dad, the doctors, they all *lied* about my mom's condition. Now you've lied and I won't put up with that!"

Sensations of desperation and anguish gripped Warren. He had come so close. No way could he give up. He'd done everything in his power to save Justin Tate and he still failed. This time he held the advantage of knowledge and ability. He had to save her, not for his sake, or even hers, but for everything in the world that stood for decency and goodness. Perhaps now the truth was the only way he could convince her.

"What if I told you I'm from the year 2008?" he blurted.

Ann turned toward him. Her eyes burned with anger and distrust.

"That I committed suicide and ended up here? That I just wanted to save you from being murdered? Would you believe me then?"

Ann glared at him. Tears welled in her eyes. "You haven't changed at all. First you lie then you take me for a fool! Damn it! Just go away and leave me alone!"

The light changed and before Warren could say another word, Ann bolted away.

***

Perspiration dripped down Warren's face as he hurried along Milwaukee Avenue. He kept his distance from Ann but had no problems keeping her in sight. That was exactly what he had to do – keep her in view and, when the time came, be close enough to intervene. Fortunately, Milwaukee was well lit with plenty of traffic. At least she was not traveling on Lipton Road. With a lack of streetlights and plenty of dark alleyways, it would have been a nightmare trying to protect her.

Warren sighed and rushed across an intersection. Once again he had managed to hurt Ann's feelings. Perhaps, when this crisis was over, he could offer her a second and even more humbling, apology. Even if she never forgave him, however, at least she would survive this horrible night.

Ann passed several stores, all of which looked dark and deserted. Her pace remained brisk, extremely determined. The closer she came to where the street dipped beneath the expressway, the more anxious Warren became. He remembered the underpass well. It was dark and isolated with a variety of places for the killer to hide. He took a breath and managed a halfhearted smile. *There's just too much traffic. As long as she stays on Milwaukee, we'll be okay.* But when Ann crossed Central Avenue, she turned to the right.

Warren shuddered then wiped his forehead. She had merely chosen the fastest route to their neighborhood. Even though Central was a major street, its immediate area was predominantly residential and considerably darker.

Ann sped along. She never turned to see if Warren had followed her. At this rate he knew she would be home before long. If she would just remain on Central he thought they'd be safe. But at the first side street, Lovejoy Avenue, she turned left into what was essentially the south end of their neighborhood.

Warren hurried to close the gap. Since they were now traveling on a side street, there was hardly a streetlight to be seen. Each city block was lined with homes that featured walkways between them. There were rows of bushes and trees and even parked cars along the curbs. The killer could be hiding anywhere. *Just a few more blocks*, he reminded himself. *Just a little bit further . . .*

Ann turned right on Parkside Avenue. Warren remained approximately sixty feet behind her. A car suddenly lurched forward from the intersecting street between them. It was an ordinary looking 1955 Chevrolet, but when Warren spotted it, his insides rolled over. Something about the way it crept along appeared unnatural and sinister. As it passed in front of him, he made out the silhouette of a man sitting behind the steering wheel.

The car turned right and, taking its time, kept pace with Ann. Warren tried to read the license plate, but it was too far away. The passenger-side window must have been rolled down because Ann glanced over and said something to the driver.

A cold shudder scurried down Warren's spine. *This has to be it. That guy just offered her a ride.* He took a breath as a flurry of thoughts swept through him. Ann was not the type to jump into a stranger's car. She was too smart and reserved and would certainly know better. He groaned and, again, wiped the perspiration from his forehead. Yes, Ann would never enter a stranger's vehicle, but that particular driver just might be someone she knew.

The Chevrolet pulled to the curb and the passenger-side door swung open. The interior light never came on. A little hesitant, Ann stepped over and leaned forward.

Warren's heart nearly ruptured. Still trying to make out the license plate number, he burst into a run. "Don't get in!" he screamed. "Run away! Hurry!"

As Warren closed the gap, Ann halted and looked his way. When she recognized him, her eyes grew huge. The driver turned in his seat and also spotted Warren. Again, his face remained hidden in the darkness. Then, with incredible speed and agility, he lunged forward and grabbed Ann by her wrist.

"Fight him!" Warren shouted. "Don't let him pull you in!"

Ann shrieked, broke loose, and stumbled away. The driver slid back behind the steering wheel, jammed the car into gear, and stomped on the gas. The rear tires squealed and the passenger-side door slammed shut on its own. Ann stood motionless and stared at the screeching vehicle. As Warren caught up, she whirled toward him. "Are you crazy?" she screamed. "What are you doing?"

Grabbing Ann by her arm, Warren peered down the street. The Chevrolet completed a U-turn at the nearest intersection. "I'll tell you later. We have to run."

He pulled Ann forward and they hurried down the sidewalk. At first she resisted, but when she noticed the car closing the distance between them, she picked up her speed. "Just tell me what's going on!"

But Warren was too busy to answer. He had to weigh their options and decide what to do. There wasn't enough time to knock on doors and wait for a response. The Chevrolet was already across from them, most likely looking for a place to jump the curb.

Ann stumbled, but Warren held onto her. "How did you know?" she gasped.

He still couldn't answer. He had to stay focused. Ann must have known the driver, someone who would never let them escape. She kept glancing at the car, slowing them down.

Warren yanked her harder. "Keep up!" he demanded.

The Chevrolet's engine roared. The vehicle shot forward, leaped over the curb, and raced toward them. Running was no longer an option. If they were to survive, Warren had to act immediately.

A row of trees to the right offered little protection. The cars parked along the curb would provide enough shelter, but the nearest was too far away.

Ann glanced over her shoulder and cried out. The vehicle's headlights engulfed them. Warren's reflexes took over. He swung around and shoved Ann behind a tree. As he did, the Chevrolet slammed into him. An unbearable agony wrenched his body. He flew onto the hood and his head struck the windshield. There was the sound of shattering glass and a bolt of pain ravaged him. He bounced off the sidewalk and rolled across a lawn before coming to a stop.

Warren felt as if his entire body had been set ablaze. He could barely breathe and everything appeared blurry. *I have to get up. I have to protect Ann.* He tried lifting himself. Shattered bones in his arms and ribs erupted. *Oh God, no! I can't move . . .*

The Chevrolet halted on the sidewalk, forty feet away. Warren sensed that the killer was planning to finish what he'd started. As far as that person was concerned, he had nothing to lose. Warren fought off the pain and rolled onto his side.

Ann kept tugging his arm. "Warren, we have to run!"

"I can't . . . go . . . get help . . ."

Ann wouldn't give in. Every time she pulled his arm, his body shuddered with agony. As he pushed her away, he heard someone shout, "Hey, what's going on out there?"

Across the street, a tall, burly man stood on a front porch. Ann dropped to her knees next to Warren. "Someone is trying to kill us! Call the police. Call an ambulance!"

The Chevrolet sat immobile on the sidewalk with its engine roaring with defiance. Warren could almost hear the driver's mind spinning feverishly, wanting to back up, slam on the gas, and run them down. But he kept hesitating, fearing he didn't have enough time. All around, porch lights turned on and more and more people peered out their windows.

Suddenly, there was another squeal of tires. The Chevrolet raced forward, bounded over the curb and onto the street. A moment later, its taillights disappeared. Relieved, Warren exhaled. A trickle of blood seeped from his mouth.

"Why did you do that?" Ann gasped. "You saved me . . . but not yourself?"

It took tremendous effort, but somehow Warren managed a smile. "C-couldn't do both."

"How did you know, Warren? How could you have possibly known this was going to happen?"

"The letters . . ." It was becoming harder for him to talk. And it was strange, but his pain seemed to be dissipating.

"You wrote some letters?"

He took a breath; his lungs released an ominous rattle. "I-Itchy has them . . ." He motioned to where the Chevrolet had been. "D-do you know . . . that man?"

She shook her head. "I don't know his name, but he lives around here."

Warren frowned. The police would need more. Blood continued to seep from his mouth. "K4749," he murmured.

Ann wiped her eyes and propped Warren on her knees. He could see her better now. She still looked lovely, even with those watery eyes. "Is that the license plate number?"

He nodded. People were coming out of their homes. He could hear them talking and moving closer. It was strange, but there were all kinds of multicolored lights behind Ann – the same lights he had encountered earlier after his overdose. They were circling clockwise and forming a long, bright tunnel. "Yes, K4749."

A grim expression flashed through Ann's eyes just then. She repeated the number and sobbed, "Warren, please stay with me."

He could barely see through the lights. They were not only growing brighter but were circling just above them. He shook his head. "I-I can't."

"I'm so sorry," she cried. "Thank you for saving me, Warren. You warned me and I should have listened."

He could feel the pull of the lights. They felt warm and invigorating and he was not afraid. "The letters," he whispered. He felt something leave his body. It did not hurt. In fact, except for the lights, he could no longer see. What he wanted to say would take the remainder of his strength. "Enjoy your life . . ." His voice grew weaker. Ann bent down to hear him. "You deserve the best . . ."

He closed his eyes and found himself speeding upward inside the tunnel. It was beautiful and for the first time since he could remember, he did not regret a thing.

CHICAGO, ILLINOIS, July 2008

A black limousine pulled into Lake View Cemetery. It traveled along the road between the rows of headstones that covered the rolling acres of lawn. It pulled beside an elm tree and the chauffeur turned off the ignition. A fifty-eight-year-old female opened a rear door and stepped out. She wore a dark dress with matching shoes and purse. The woman shaded her eyes as she glanced around. The late afternoon sun warmed an amazingly youthful face. A cluster of freckles were scattered across the bridge of her nose.

The chauffeur handed the woman a bouquet of roses. "Do you need anything else while you're here, madam?"

"No, thank you," she answered. "But while I'm gone, would you mind not waking my grandson? It was a long flight from Los Angeles."

"Why, of course, madam. Do you know your way to the site?"

The woman nodded. "Yes, I know it well."

She smiled and walked along the narrow rows between the headstones. They were of various shapes and sizes. The older tombstones tended to be larger and ornate. The more recent markers were mere tablets cemented into the ground. She had not walked far when she noticed someone standing beside Warren's grave. The man spotted her, waved, and hurried over.

"Hey, Ann, how are you?" They hugged and he kissed her on a cheek.

"Hi, Itchy. Except for some jet lag, I'm fine, thank you."

Ira chuckled and scratched his head. "You know, you're the only person who still calls me that. And for the life of me, I don't understand why."

Ann laughed and her eyes came alive. "That's because some things never change. To me you'll always be Itchy Kowalski." She held onto his arm as they walked toward their destination. She smiled. Professional baseball had given Ira enough confidence to finally cure his touching phobia. She gazed at him and still couldn't get over how much better he looked since having his teeth fixed. "How are the Perrys doing?"

"Well, they're getting on in years, but they're fine. They told me to say hello and were sorry they couldn't make it. I guess these visits are still tough on them."

They stopped at the foot of Warren's grave. "It's all right. I'll be in town for a while. I'll give them a call and see if we can still get together."

Ann and Ira peered at the headstone. A mild breeze fended off the July heat. A variety of birds sang cheerfully from a nearby tree. Itchy cleared his throat. "Pretty astonishing epitaph, don't you think?"

"I'm delighted with it. I just wish it wasn't so long in coming."

"You've done Warren a remarkable service, Ann. I'm sure the Perrys appreciate it. They're just a little conservative, that's all, and didn't want people to think they're presumptuous."

"You know, Itchy, it took me ten years to convince them. And I should have done this *thirty* years ago. I just never thought 'Beloved Son' was enough. But now that it's finally completed, you know what?"

Itchy started to scratch his head again then evidently catching himself, stopped. "I don't know. What?"

Ann paused and smiled triumphantly. "It was worth the wait." She bent down and placed the flowers on the grave. Even after all the years, she still felt many of the old feelings creep back. The strange mixture of love, guilt, and the sense of loss could still affect her. She straightened and wiped away a tear. "I have something for you, Itchy. I finally remembered."

"You're kidding. It's only been forty-three years."

Ann rolled her eyes as she searched through her purse. "Jeez, don't remind me." She removed an envelope and handed it to Ira. "I know it's a little wrinkled . . . and has a grease stain on it, but other than that, it's not in bad shape."

"Grease stain, huh? Boy does that bring back some memories!" Ira put his glasses on and opened the envelope.

Ann wiped away another tear. "It still overwhelms me every time I read it. Warren had the knowledge to prosper for the rest of his life, but because of his caring nature, he sacrificed it all. Just think, Itchy. Along with the Perrys, we're the only ones who know the truth. I never even told my husband."

Ira glanced up. "I once told Richie and Bobby, but they thought I was crazy."

Ann nodded. "Well, it's quite the story, isn't it? Yet he didn't just save my life. There would have been two other victims. If Warren hadn't memorized that license plate . . ." She paused and shrugged her shoulders. "Even Warren's parents have lived longer because of what he wrote in their letter. And my father would have never survived another loss."

Itchy folded the letter and returned it. "Yeah, according to Kay Perry, she'd be dead ten years by now. And John's heart would have given out decades ago."

Ann placed the letter inside the envelope and slipped it into her purse. "It's so strange how it all turned out. Instead of the Perrys, my father and I were the ones who moved to California. And look who I ended up marrying? A prominent senator." She sighed and smiled. "Although Warren's letter mentioned *who* he was, we *still* fell in love . . . and that changed everything."

"I'm grateful, too," whispered Itchy. "Warren always nagged me about joining the majors. I think, in a lot of ways, baseball saved my bacon about a hundred times over."

They stood in silence at the foot of the grave, each of them lost in their own thoughts. Dressed in a dark suit and matching tie, a boy of fifteen approached. In one hand he carried an iPod, in the other he held a single carnation.

"Hi, Grandma, sorry I dozed off."

Ann wrapped her arm around the boy. "There's no need to apologize. But I'm glad you're awake. I want you to meet someone." She motioned toward Itchy. "This is Mister Ira Kowalski, or 'Killer' Kowalski, if you prefer, one of the greatest baseball players that ever lived. Ira, this is my one and only grandson, Justin Tate."

The boy grinned and shook hands. "Wow, glad to meet you, sir. I've heard all about you!"

Itchy flushed with pride. "I'll never get tired of hearing that."

Justin turned and peered at the headstone. "So, this is Warren's grave?"

Ann nodded.

The boy studied the epitaph and smiled. Stepping forward, he bent down and placed the carnation on the grave. "Glad I finally got to see this, Grandma. He must have been a really good person."

Trembling, Ann lowered her eyes. "Yes, he was."

"I'm still a little tired. Do you mind if I wait in the limo?"

"No, go ahead. I'll be there in a minute."

Justin waved good-bye. "It was nice meeting you, Mister Kowalski."

Itchy waved back. "Nice to meet you, too."

The boy turned on his iPod and headed toward the limousine.

"That's a fine grandson you have there, Ann."

"Yes, it's surprising what a change can do." She paused and smiled contented. "Especially a *well-informed* grandmother. Will you join us for dinner? I know a great restaurant by our hotel."

"It'll be my pleasure."

They shared a final view of Warren's epitaph.

Ann sighed. "I'm happy with the addition. It's a proper homage, don't you agree?"

Itchy nodded. "Yep, proper and well-deserved."

Beneath the original inscriptions of "Warren Perry, 1950-1965" and "Beloved Son," were the accolades, "Hero, Redeemer, Friend."

SHADY TRAILS

Jenny Trenton turned her black Dodge Ram onto Buckthorn Lane. Dust and sand filled the air. Her stereo boomed Carrie Underwood's "Cupid's Got A Shotgun" as she sang along under her breath. It felt good to get away from all the clutter of her life, and she was feeling better than she had in years.

Wearing her favorite sunglasses and black felt cowboy hat, she glanced in the rearview mirror. Of course she couldn't see Maverick standing inside her well-worn horse trailer, but most likely he would be gazing out the left window, keeping tabs on the countryside. Every now and then she heard him holler whenever they struck a pothole. She grinned and took a swig of her Pepsi. "Pipe down, old-timer. We're nearly there."

Jenny slowed as the road snaked upward toward Arlene's. The narrow curves used to intimidate her but that was during her marriage to "Chip" Darnell, the dark lord of sociopaths. She shook her head. No, she had promised herself to quit dwelling on that hateful marriage or, as Arlene had once coined it, "the disaster from the bowels of hell itself." The court battles were over and the losses were reckoned with, so why not have a fun weekend and get on with life?

Taking a deep, refreshing breath, Jenny glanced out the window and savored the endless vista of pine trees. Arlene's ranch was neatly snuggled at the foot of a mountain range, and to Jenny, the rolling hills and lush forest were a paradise unsurpassed. The locals could always use a capable veterinarian such as her, and if it weren't for her kids, Katy and Nelson, she would have moved this way long ago. Naturally, a horse corral and plenty of acreage were needed, but now that she was dirt poor, such expensive properties were beyond her means. Good old Chip walked away with nearly every dime that wasn't nailed down. She was lucky to have hung onto her three-bedroom home. In fact, if he'd been able to pull it off, Chip would have stolen Maverick just to spite her.

Jenny rolled her eyes. Getting that man out of her head wasn't so easy. If these were biblical times, he would have been right up there with the ten plagues of Egypt.

Slowing for a right, she approached the entrance to Arlene's ranch. A "Welcome" sign hung on the crest of a ten-foot-tall, split rail gate. As she pulled in, she noticed a new sign proclaiming "Solicitors Will Be Eaten." That was just like Arlene: independent, ornery and as hyper as a four-year-old maxed out on candy bars.

Pulling onto the gravel driveway, Jenny tapped her horn and drove toward the one-story cabin with the wrap-around porch and stacks of firewood. As soon as she killed the engine, Biscuit Eater hurried toward her, barking and drooling at the same time. The old, black Labrador still looked plenty intimidating. When he finally recognized her, he stopped barking and wagged his tail.

Jenny opened her door and climbed out. Her back ached and her joints had grown stiff. Biscuit Eater trotted up and appeared eager to renew their acquaintance. She stooped down and massaged his head. "Hey, big fella, nice to see ya. Where's your good buddy, the Artful Dodger?" She glanced around, but the German Shepherd was nowhere in sight.

She carefully raised both sides of the Lab's upper lip. "Well, I see your teeth are looking better, so let's concentrate on that breath of yours, okay?" She straightened and removed a dog biscuit from her coat pocket. The canine gulped down the snack and, without so much as a glance toward her, lumbered off.

"Eat and run, huh? Next time I'll give Dodger the treat." She again looked around and shrugged her shoulders. "If I can ever find him."

When Jenny turned toward the porch, a loud, metallic boom erupted from behind. The sound echoed progressively through the canyon. It gave her a start until she realized her dear, sweet boy had just kicked the inside of her trailer. "Patience, old-timer. You'll be out soon enough."

Jenny stepped onto the porch and discovered a typewritten note taped on the door. She removed her sunglasses and shaded her large, hazel eyes. She wore little makeup, and even after living through a rather turbulent forty-five years, her family and friends still insisted she possessed a teenager's face. She snatched the note off the door and read it aloud. "Jenny, Mom took sick and I had to go down the hill. I won't be able to join you today. Have a safe ride and I'll see you tomorrow. Arlene."

Frowning, Jenny folded the note and placed it in her hip pocket. Everything had been okay when they talked on the phone last night. Hopefully, Arlene's ninety-year-old mother would bounce back. Too bad, her friend's companionship would be missed. Riding alone was never a good idea, especially after that woman's body had been found not far off the trail five weeks ago.

Jenny sighed and shook her head. Having Arlene for a friend had sometimes been a mixed blessing. She couldn't ask for better company, but ever since her longtime friend moved away, their time together had suffered. At least they could still visit tomorrow after Jenny returned from the O'Dells'.

Slipping on a pair of leather gloves, Jenny opened the trailer's escape door on the driver's side. Of course Maverick was right there, wide-eyed and tossing his head.

"Okay, quit your bitching." She patted him on a shoulder. "We'll be on the trail before you can snort twice. Now let me by."

Stretching forward, she untied the lead rope from the tie bar. Maverick watched her the entire time. She hurried to the rear of the trailer, opened the loading door, and lowered the ramp. As usual, her mustang had left a rather large pile of dung on the floor. That was okay. An hour and a half in a trailer was a long time for such a hearty animal. She unfastened the safety chain, folded her arms across her chest, and stared at him. Maverick turned his head and, with his bulging eyes reflecting his amusement, watched her every move.

"Whenever you're ready, your majesty, would you mind backing out?"

The eighteen-year-old mustang nodded and inched out. As Jenny reached for the lead rope, however, he bolted back into the trailer. Cantankerous as ever, he peered over his shoulder at her, tossed his head, and snorted twice.

"You're quite the jokester, aren't you? But if you want your carrot, you'll have to come get it."

Maverick's eyes again widened as he quickly backed out. Perhaps she was biased, but to her there wasn't a more beautiful animal on the face of the earth. Rust-colored, with a broad, white forehead and a flowing mane and tail, he was perfectly proportioned. She picked up the lead rope and pulled him over. "Now that's more like it." She removed a small carrot from her coat pocket. He quickly took it in his mouth and gobbled it down. "You'll get another as soon as you're saddled."

She led the mustang to the hitching post across the yard from the corrals. Arlene's horses, Fred and Ethel, watched the entire time. Right from the start Maverick had inflicted his own vendetta against the duo. When on the trail he would take every opportunity to provoke them. Then, when riled up, the other horse would buck Arlene off. It made for a rather chaotic, if not painful, ride. So hitching

Maverick near their corral was an invitation for all types of shenanigans. Horses were like that: petty, temperamental, jealous, and they always maintained a pecking order. When trail riding, Maverick simply demanded to be in the lead, otherwise he had his own bag of tricks. Once, while passing, he grabbed Fred's reins with his teeth. It nearly sent Arlene flying. And forget about riding with a mare. Poor Ethel still had a scar on her chest from one of Maverick's more malicious kicks.

Jenny tied the mustang to the hitching post at the front of the cabin. She opened her trailer's storage door, removed the grooming bucket, and sprayed the horse with a thick coat of fly repellant. After she had brushed him thoroughly, she used a hoof pick and cleaned the bottom of his hooves, paying special attention to his "frogs," the soft area at the center. In Maverick's case they were vulnerable to thrush, a common infection. As usual, he cooperated initially, but on the last hoof, he pranced around.

"All right, hot shot. I wouldn't mind eating that carrot myself."

Maverick tossed his head and offered his final leg.

Jenny hauled out the padded blanket, flung it onto the mustang's back then returned to the trailer for the saddle. In the days before the carrots, by now her horse would have dumped the blanket. She flung the saddle onto his back and cinched it. Maverick behaved but kept glaring at Fred and Ethel.

She placed the bit in the mustang's mouth and fastened the bridal onto his head, then retrieved her saddlebags from the trailer. They were stuffed with bottled water, a flashlight, an emergency kit, a Swiss army knife, and plenty of snacks for both of them. She fastened the bags onto the saddle and removed a carrot. "Now was that so bad?"

Maverick shook his head.

"Are you going to behave?"

He nodded.

Jenny gave him the treat, and chewing around the bit, he munched it down. "There's plenty more, but you'll have to earn them."

Swallowing, he gave her a most angelic look. She laughed and rubbed him behind an ear.

Untying her horse from the hitching post, Jenny climbed into the saddle. She tugged the reins and they sauntered past Fred and Ethel. Maverick snorted and folded back his ears.

"Now be polite. Remember, you're a guest here."

As they rode, Jenny checked both corrals, making sure Arlene's horses had enough water. Maverick picked up his pace and hurried past Biscuit Eater. The Lab was hunkered down, enjoying a rather mangled-looking bone. A mother hen rushed by, leading her brood of chicks, but the mustang ignored them. He rarely spooked and was surprisingly tolerant about such creatures.

Jenny glanced around, but there was no sign of Artful Dodger, Arlene's German Shepherd. Hopefully, he hadn't taken off again. As tough as he could be, he was still no match for a pack of coyotes.

A huge, aluminum shed with steel braces stood at the rear of the property. Stacked within it were roughly thirty bales of Bermuda hay. The start of the trail was just beyond the shed. A large split rail gate extended across its width. At the gate's crest hung another sign. Carved by Arlene in black lettering, it read, "WELCOME TO SHADY TRAILS" and beneath that, "BEWARE OF SNAKES."

***

Jenny rode along a trail well known for its twists and turns. The sun broke through the clouds and its warmth penetrated her clothing. Tugging the reins briskly, she ordered, "Ho," and the mustang halted. She slipped out of her denim jacket, tied the arms around her waist, then removed a water bottle from her saddlebag. She took a swig and gazed at her horse. "We'll stop by the creek so you can have a drink, too."

Grazing on some weeds, Maverick ignored her.

Jenny tugged the reins and they continued. Other than an occasional bird, the trail remained quiet. All the noise, smog, and congestion down the hill seemed like a dreary memory. Everything here was so serene, so peaceful.

Unfortunately, the last six years had been far from peaceful, thanks to good old Chip Darnell. It was funny, but the harder she tried to keep him from renting space inside her head, the more he did just that. Perhaps six months wasn't enough time after all, not when she and her children's lives had been turned upside down.

As corny as it sounded, when Jenny first met Chip, she thought she had finally found a healthy relationship. Both her former marriages had bellied up, and her other relationships had never come close to going the distance. She knew she had her own share of flaws, but evidently many men could not handle her profession. At first the long school hours had discouraged her suitors, then there was her internship and, after that, her practice, which consisted of even longer hours. It had not only been hard on her intimate relationships but hard on her kids, Katy and Nelson, as well. On top of everything, through the years, three of her significant others had admitted to having issues being with someone who earned more money than they did.

Jenny spotted a hawk gliding across the sky. Maverick poked along, appearing to take everything in. He had always been a smooth ride and undemanding on her sensitive spine.

Feeling alive and rejuvenated, Jenny pulled her cell phone out of a hip pocket. She frowned and shook her head. *Crap! The battery's dead!* Of course she could always recharge it when she arrived at the O'Dells', but for the time being, she'd better stay the hell out of harm's way. She returned the phone to her hip pocket and her mind wandered back to the cradle of her regrets.

***

Jenny would never forget the first time she had met Norman "Chip" Darnell. After not dating for over two years, she had joined an online dating club. She searched the website for weeks before discovering Chip's profile. It appeared concise, well-written but, oddly enough, hadn't included his photograph.

When they first talked on the telephone, Chip came across as soft-spoken and easy-going. When they met the next evening at a local restaurant, she arrived first and had been seated in the middle of the room. While she waited, she grew anxious and uncertain. *What am I doing here? Meeting a man from a dating service? This is crazy!* After waiting thirty minutes she started to leave. That was when a man carrying a red rose approached her.

"Hi, I'm Chip. You must be Jenny."

They shook hands. He wasn't particularly good-looking, but he was tall and solidly built. Dressed in jeans and a flannel shirt, he sported a well-trimmed beard and a full head of gray hair. His voice was soft, his manners polite. After divorcing Nelson's father, Jenny had grown indifferent to handsome men with their frail egos. An easy-going, plain-looking person like Chip just might be the kind of man she had needed all along.

Insisting on picking up the check, Chip paid cash and left a generous tip. While he walked Jenny out, he invited her over for an upcoming barbecue and added, "You can bring your kids, if you'd like." That particular gesture impressed her more than anything else. They did not kiss goodnight; instead they merely shook hands.

The following Saturday, Jenny drove to Chip's house, a mere five miles away. She had decided not to bring her children, because it seemed much too early for that sort of thing. Katy had just turned seventeen and was responsible enough to look after Nelson.

Chip lived in a newer home in a rather older, rundown neighborhood. Another couple, Dennis and Celeste, were lounging by the pool. She thought it sounded peculiar at the time, but Chip kept referring to Dennis as his "business associate" rather than a friend. All three of them drank gin and tonics excessively, but as far as she could tell, Chip remained surprisingly sober. If he hadn't, their relationship would have been over before it started.

Brimming with enthusiasm Chip gave Jenny a tour of his home. A large, four bedroom, featuring fireplaces and skylights, he professed he had designed and built the house himself. Everything appeared clean and well-organized. Displayed on a wall in his office were several real estate and public accountant licenses. When she asked him about his career, he admitted he had been permanently disabled. He went on to describe how he had taken a fall while showing a home, injured his back, and filed a lawsuit against his former employer. Curious, she asked him how he could afford such an extravagant lifestyle while remaining virtually unemployed. He grinned and a rather contented expression crept into his eyes. "I negotiate all types of business investments," he answered.

Of course, not a word of these particulars were mentioned in Chip's dating profile. She should have smelled a rat that very second, but looking back on it, she realized how desperate she had become. Katy was older and never figured in the equation. But Nelson, on the other hand, was just six and, with his father moving out of state, needed a man to relate to. Judging from Chip's credentials, he appeared to be a legitimate businessman, and considering his house and comfortable lifestyle, it seemed unlikely he would be intimidated by her professional status.

***

Maverick stalled, let out a holler, and Jenny's attention jumped back to the present. She discovered they were approaching the stronghold of pine trees that lined both sides of the path, hence the name, "Shady Trails." As far as she could see, there were no rattlers or coyotes in the area, so she gave Maverick a brisk kick and he lurched forward. The mustang's shoulders remained tense, however, and he kept searching around. Jenny sighed and her mind drifted back to her former marriage.

***

Chip would come over twice a week and Jenny would spend the weekends at his house. He seemed uncomfortable while visiting, especially with Katy. For some reason they never gelled. But he became friends with Nelson and would bring him a toy every time he came over. Before long, her youngest had grown attached to the man. This, more than anything else, remained crucial to Jenny. Nelson needed this relationship much more than she ever did.

Looking back on their courtship, there were several hints of a pending disaster. They rarely went out together, and Chip didn't seem to have any actual friends, just some people he did business with. His older sister, who lived in Redding, wanted nothing to do with him. All of his other relatives lived in either Iowa, or Kansas. With the exception of Nelson, he never took the slightest interest in her social circle. He clashed with Arlene, much more than he ever did with Katy. He often grumbled about Arlene being too loud and full of herself. Arlene rarely complained about Chip, but during their long, drawn-out divorce, her friend finally confessed, "I could never get along with the bastard, but hell, that's just me. Besides, what right do I have to push my opinions on other people?"

After Jenny had enlightened her friend about some of the more grisly details of her marriage, however, Arlene changed her mind. "Maybe I *should've* said something," she admitted, "but I just wanted you to be happy. So I kept my big trap shut and hoped for the best." Later, she added, "He's a Chip all right . . . a chip off the old buttocks."

Even when they were dating, Jenny thought there was something odd about the man. All of his money transactions were paid in cash. He had even asked her if he could deposit five thousand dollars into her checking account. Then, down the line, he talked her into writing several checks for his various business transactions.

When she questioned this, he claimed he had poor credit due to a "misunderstanding." Most revealing, however, were his constant legal battles, as he was forever representing himself in lawsuits. Whether he was suing a private party, a real estate agency, or a construction company, Chip kept the California courts overloaded.

***

Jenny pulled the reins toward the sound of the creek. Maverick obliged and followed a side path to the water. As they approached the bank, she noticed the yellow tape attached to a circle of trees. It took her a moment to realize that the police had sealed off the area. *Good, God! This is where they found that woman's body!*

Cringing, Jenny felt as if a long, icy finger had just meandered its way down her spine. Her little paradise had been violated in the worst possible manner. Even out here, in all the peace and quiet, violence could still lash out. There were no suspects to speak of and the killer remained at large. The newspapers mentioned the victim had lived down the hill in San Bernardino. It had taken the authorities some time to discover her identity, but the woman had been an exotic dancer and part-time prostitute. So perhaps one of her "customers" had murdered her, dismembered the body, and dumped it out here.

That's so horrible . . . the poor woman . . . but at least she wasn't killed in these parts. It would be unthinkable if the killer had been some transient or homeless person who might be lurking around the next bend.

Maverick bent down and drank eagerly. The creek's water rippled serenely as it sped amongst the rocks. Jenny frowned and stared at the crime scene. The wind had thrashed the tape, but it still clung to the trees. Perhaps she should have kept better track of the investigation, as there may have been some new developments. *That woman must have been murdered elsewhere. Otherwise Arlene would have cancelled our ride.*

After drinking his fill, Maverick appeared raring to go, but just like before, he kept glancing around. Horses, just like most intelligent animals, were extremely sensitive to their environment. Even though the murder had occurred five weeks ago, he still might be sensing something disturbing.

Jenny shuddered and looked over her shoulder. She could have sworn someone had been watching her through the trees. Perhaps seeing the crime scene had roused her imagination. She retrieved her water bottle, took a swig, and wiped her mouth. *Stop it, Jenny. There's no one else around here.*

She tugged Maverick's reins and they resumed their journey. It was still six more miles to the O'Dells'. She and Maverick should arrive around dinnertime and, hopefully, well before dark.

***

Maverick labored his way along the trail as it gradually climbed upward. After two miles, the thick growth of trees yielded to scattered clearings. The O'Dells' cabin lay just beyond the hills to the left. Marvin and Joan were true rarities, a pair of modern day hermits, living on the backside of nowhere.

***

Jenny had to admit that right up to the time they were married, Chip remained extremely kind to both Nelson and her. For the first time ever, she had not been attracted by a man's appearance, but by his intelligence and easy-going manner.

With the exception of Dennis and Celeste, Jenny's wedding turned out to be an informal gathering of her many friends and relatives. As for Chip, his family never even answered their invitations. Arlene later informed Jenny of how Celeste kept chugging down the martinis, and "Stared at ya like she wanted to say something important." As for Dennis, she described him as, "A klutz who could shoot both his feet with one bullet."

Due to some unexpected real estate ventures, Chip delayed their honeymoon. When they were finally able to spend a weekend in Las Vegas, he disappeared for three hours. When he returned he explained, "I had to collect some debts," and tossed four thousand dollars in front of her. Jenny found out later the cash came from a retired couple who thought they were investing in the stock market. Needless to say, they would never see their money again.

One evening a man called on the phone and asked for "Steve." Jenny informed him he had the wrong number and hung up. When Chip found out about it, he flew into a rage and broke everything he could get his hands on. She had no idea he'd been using the name "Steve" as an alias for one of his business deals. Of course, he denied any wrongdoing. "I switch names to keep track of my transactions," he had claimed. He must have thought she was three notches below stupid to believe such a boldfaced lie.

While Jenny worked nearly sixty hours a week, Chip neglected his own home, where they were living, and tried manipulating Katy into being his personal housekeeper. She turned him down and, much to Jenny's anguish, moved to her father's after turning nineteen.

At nearly eight, Nelson was placed in charge of washing clothes, scrubbing floors, and mowing the lawn. Chip would pick up the boy at school and put him to work the minute they pulled into the driveway. Nelson's homework began to suffer, but since her son was so delighted at being paid a whopping five dollars a week, Jenny held her tongue. Unable to play with his friends, and falling even further behind at school, Nelson finally rebelled. In no uncertain terms, Jenny told Chip to get off his lazy ass and clean the house himself, which, of course, he never did.

After much debate, Jenny leased her vacant home to a young newlywed couple and naturally, Chip collected the rent himself. If they didn't pay promptly on the first of the month, by the end of that day he would have their water and electricity turned off. Then as soon as the couple came up with the money, he would charge them an added fee for being late and another fee for turning the utilities back on.

Chip claimed he was depositing the additional funds into their joint savings account. Instead, he was investing everything into his financial schemes. When her house needed a new roof, he hired Hispanic illegals as laborers. He often coerced them into working twelve hour shifts then, on payday, he would short-change them. One haggard, elderly man turned up at their front door pleading to be paid. Chip scared him off by threatening to turn him over to the immigration authorities.

Then there were the animals. Chip would buy a pure bred dog that lacked papers and, by the next day, sell it for a profit. They were never pets to him, merely a means to make money. He even told one buyer, "I've raised that dog since it was a puppy." When Jenny later confronted her husband about his dishonesty, he told her to keep her mouth shut and mind her own business.

Since Chip's home sat on five acres, he purchased several horses, goats, and even a nasty, old llama. The yard behind the swimming pool became something of a menagerie. Occasionally, he would wait a few weeks until Nelson had become attached to an animal . . . and then he would turn around and sell it.

Three of the meanest varmints that ever walked on hooves were Chip's Shetland ponies. Because Jenny loved animals so much, he managed to con her into hauling them to the local carnivals and charging kids seven dollars for a five minute ride. While loading the ponies into the trailer, they sometimes attacked Jenny and even fought amongst themselves. Every now and then, one of them would buck or rear, sending both the child and parent into a frenzy.

Of course these unruly behaviors managed to provoke Chip's ever-increasing wrath, and he demanded that Jenny beat the ponies into submission. When she refused he threatened to do it himself, so she lied and promised she would. After two more bucking episodes, however, she finally quit and told Chip he would have to do the rides himself. He flew into another one of his tirades and broke nearly every coffee mug they owned. The next day he sold all three ponies but still managed a tidy profit.

***

Jenny didn't want to think about her ex-husband anymore. She would clean horse corrals until doomsday to forget him, if only she could. Katy moved away in time, but after six grueling years, she and Nelson had become emotionally scarred. A person did not have to travel all the way to Iraq to suffer from post-traumatic stress. They simply had to deal with Chip Darnell.

Retrieving a water bottle from her saddlebag, Jenny commanded Maverick to "Ho." As she drank, the mustang began prancing back and forth, his ears turning in every direction. She patted his neck, peered ahead, and spotted a dark substance on the ground. "So, that's the big deal? What's wrong with you today?"

Jenny gave Maverick a kick and he inched forward. As they approached she leaned back in her saddle and groaned. The substance appeared to be a trail of blood that led to the brush. *Damn! It's probably a coyote victim.* She sighed and reined the mustang toward the right. *I'd better take a look. If it's not too bad off, maybe I can help it.*

Maverick's edginess appeared to dissipate as they journeyed into the brush. She was by no means a tracker, but there was enough blood to show her the way. After roughly fifty yards she could hear the familiar sound of the creek. It made sense. Other than hiding, an injured animal would most likely seek the nearest water supply.

As they advanced Jenny spotted a large dog lying on the ground. Just before they reached it, she recognized its coloring. She cringed and wiped her forehead. It was Arlene's German Shepherd, Artful Dodger.

***

Jenny placed the last of the river rocks on the grave. Since she didn't have anything to dig with, she had to bury the dog under a bed of stones. Burying him at the O'Dells' seemed like the proper thing to do, but quite understandably, Maverick wanted nothing to do with hauling a dead animal on his back.

Climbing onto the mustang, Jenny peered at the grave. She would borrow a shovel from the O'Dells and give Dodger a decent burial tomorrow. Hopefully, the coyotes would not discover the body. Jenny shook her head. She had not found a single bite or claw mark on the dog. What she had discovered, however, was a telltale bullet hole in his neck. She glanced around. Who could have done such a thing? She sighed and shrugged. She was not looking forward to telling Arlene about her favorite pet.

Maverick trotted up a gradual slope, and before long, they were back on the trail. Jenny again glanced around and found herself shuddering. First it was the dead woman and now Dodger. Both bodies had been near the creek with just three miles separating them. Was it possible that the deaths were related? She adjusted the brim of her hat. No, she didn't think so. Someone had murdered the woman five weeks ago and dumped her body near the creek. By Dodger's appearance, he had died within the last twenty-four hours.

Jenny kept glancing around. *I just can't shake the feeling I'm being watched.* There were no other homes between Arlene's ranch and the O'Dells'. She rubbed the hard muscle at the base of her neck. She considered heading back to Arlene's, just to play it safe. *But I'm much closer to the O'Dells' . . . a couple of miles past the point of no return.* She cursed and rolled her eyes. Like it or not, she was better off continuing.

The base of a steep mountain stood before them. The sun had lost its warmth and was creeping toward the west. Burying Dodger had put Jenny behind, but she still could make it to the O'Dells' before dark.

She didn't want to think about Chip anymore, but what else could she do? She loved everything about riding, but once in the saddle, her mind simply wandered. Even thoughts about her screwed-up marriage seemed better than dwelling on poor old Dodger.

***

After a horrific year and a half, Jenny decided to put the marriage out of its misery. There would be no counselors or second chances because she knew Chip would never change. Besides, Nelson had started suffering bouts of insomnia and had been in and out of trouble at school. Chip had not only caused her son all kinds of psychological grief – but had actually intimidated the boy. To hell with caution; her son's welfare came first.

While they were eating breakfast one Sunday morning, she decided to break the news. Chip was reading the newspaper and Nelson had just been excused. Of course, he had to ask Chip's permission first. Jenny had been thinking of what she was going to say. She knew her safest bet was a straightforward approach and not let any of her emotions get in the way.

Jenny cleared her throat and calmly informed Chip that their marriage wasn't working out, and she was planning on moving back to her old house. She didn't want anything from him, only to be left alone. She felt it would be best for everyone and hoped that when the divorce came through it would be fair and amicable.

Eating his eggs just the way he liked them, soggy and under-cooked, Chip's eyes never left the sports section. "Is that so?" A speck of yoke hung from his beard. "You want a fair and amicable divorce?"

She nodded and braced herself.

His face remained expressionless. His silence grew unbearable. Finally, he murmured, "There won't be a divorce. You made a vow when we married and I expect you to keep it."

Jenny could not believe what she was hearing. "My mind's made up, Chip. I have Nelson to consider." She paused and swallowed. "You just don't have any say in this."

Chip rolled his eyes and belched. "As usual you don't know what you're talking about." Looking up from his newspaper, he stared at Jenny; his eyes reflected his cold and arrogant mentality. "In case you've forgotten, it's my marriage, too, so I have plenty of *say* in it."

Jenny felt another migraine coming on. She started having them just after their honeymoon. Rubbing her temples, she gazed at her untouched bowl of cereal. "Why bother? You know perfectly well we can't stand each other."

He dipped a half slice of toast in his eggs and shoved it in his mouth. "How we feel about each other doesn't matter."

She placed her hands on her hips and counted to ten. She knew at this point Chip might take anything she said as a challenge. It seemed imperative to keep her tone as neutral as possible. The last thing she wanted to do was to set him off. "What if I don't stay? What if Nelson and I just packed up and left?"

"You can't," he retorted with a smirk, "not until *death* does us part."

She jumped to her feet. Her neutral tone took a sudden hike south of the border. "Are you threatening me?"

He turned a page of the newspaper. Perhaps it was better he was focused on something else. That way she didn't have to look into those condescending eyes of his. "Let's not call it a threat, shall we? Let's just say it's a warning . . . to you *and* your son."

She shuddered. "W-what did you say?"

He looked at her as if she was something nasty he'd just stepped on. "If you're so concerned about his welfare, then you'd better consider what would happen to *him* if you left."

At that precise second, their conversation came to an abrupt end. Before she knew it a year and a half of misery turned into six years of hell.

***

Maverick came to one of his more dramatic stops, with his leg shooting out sideways. It was a rare behavior that only occurred when he spotted something that frightened him. Jenny jerked forward and grabbed the saddle horn just in time. She searched around but couldn't see anything out of the ordinary. There was just a gradual slope that led to the mountainside, plus the pine trees and brush that dominated the area. So what was wrong? Maverick had been acting skittish all day. When she tugged his reins, he started moving, but with great reluctance.

"Come on, boy. Would you stop imagining things?"

She leaned back. *Maybe I should quit feeding him that alfalfa supplement. It's making him nervous.*

Approximately twenty yards off the trail, Jenny spotted a man watching her from beside a tree. He was wearing a baseball cap, sunglasses, and sported a long, scraggly beard. Even from that distance, she could see the dirt smudged on his jacket. As she moved along, the man looked over his sunglasses at her. *Why is he watching me? What does he want?*

The closer she came, the more nervous she grew. *Stay calm; don't let him see you sweat.* When she glanced his way, he merely folded his arms across his chest and kept staring.

Jenny gave Maverick a kick and he hurried along. *A homeless man,* she concluded. She knew they were around but had never seen any of them this far up the mountain before. She stifled another shudder. *Could he be the one who shot Dodger . . . or killed that woman?* Gritting her teeth, she shook her head. Just because he was in the area didn't make him guilty. Most likely, he was just passing through. Besides, if he was the killer, why would he be hanging around just a few miles from the scene of the crime?

She gave Maverick another kick and he seemed happy to oblige. They were at a near gallop now, as fast as she would allow on such rocky terrain. She leaned forward and patted the mustang on his shoulder. "I'm sorry boy, you were right." His ears turned toward her. "You knew he was around and I should have listened."

The O'Dells' cabin was just a little more than a mile away. She wondered if they knew about the homeless man. Then it struck her. *Good, God! Could he be one who's been watching us? Following our trail this whole time?*

She rubbed her left temple. All these uncertainties were giving her a migraine. She gave Maverick another kick and, as they hurried along, she once again allowed her mind to recall old – and mostly bitter – memories.

***

Jenny had cut back on her work hours and, as a result, lost much of her clientele. She had no choice but to take her husband's threats seriously. She avoided Chip whenever possible, but surprisingly enough, he didn't seem to mind. By then he was taking business trips to Iowa twice a month. She realized the safest time for her to leave him would be during one of those trips. Unfortunately, to pull it off, she would need more than just a few days.

During those dark times a bright spot enriched her life considerably. Arlene called one morning and asked her to come over. Jenny had been borrowing either Fred or Ethel and riding in the hills behind her friend's ranch. When the terrain was just right, they would cut their horses loose on a full gallop. Feeling the wind against her face and saddled on all that power felt like a rollercoaster ride, but more personal and natural. It brought to mind a sense of liberation, not only from the drab realities of Jenny's existence, but from the harsher ones as well. And when they slowed for a walk, it would help her sort through her problems and regrets.

When Jenny arrived at Arlene's, her friend led her to the corrals. In the first pen stood a mustang like no other. He looked so majestic and handsome, with vibrant colors, intelligent eyes, and a flowing mane.

"He's gorgeous! What's his name?"

"Whatever you'd like, honey," Arlene replied. "He's all yours. Just don't let that Chip get his hooks on him."

That was when the perfect name came to Jenny. "Maverick," she whispered. "I'll call him Maverick."

The mustang's eyes never left Jenny as she approached. She sensed an instant bond and the feeling that, in some mysterious way, they had always been connected. When she later rode him along the trail, his gait proved flawless, and a comfort on her much abused back. Of course he behaved magnificently, a true gentleman. She laughed. Horses were not that much different than most men, perfect in the beginning, with their faults surfacing later. Maverick's shortcomings were insignificant, however. He was smart, loyal, and very sweet. That was why Jenny often preferred animals over people. Dogs, cats, horses, goats, they were more forthright and loved unconditionally. But most of all they never engaged in power plays, financial schemes, or hidden agendas.

Naturally, Chip and Maverick flat-out hated each other. You could feel the tension the second they met. It only grew worse over time. No doubt Arlene's generosity had struck an unfamiliar chord with the conniving huckster. "She *gave* you that animal?"

Jenny nodded. "Yep, that's right."

Grappling with this outrageous concept, his expression turned vacant. "Why would she do that?"

"Out of friendship, of course."

He sized up Maverick with a trace of greed creeping into his eyes. Turning, he gave Jenny his most loathsome wink. "Not bad. Once I've trained him, we'll make a killing."

She winced and shook her head. "No, he's not for sale . . . he's mine, and I'll be doing the training."

He laughed and she wanted to slap his pompous face. "You train him? You gotta be kidding."

"Like I said . . . he's my horse."

Chip tried time and again to undermine Maverick's training. Whether it was saddling, working the commands, or running the mustang in the round pen, he watched their every move.

"Use the whip, damn it!" became his signature phrase. "Don't let him get away with that! Beat his ass!"

But Jenny remained adamant in her refusals. Eventually, Chip's inability to control the situation seemed to get the better of him. Cursing, he would storm off, red-faced, kicking the dirt with the toes of his boots.

Jenny would only laugh and feel good about her modest victories. How could she not treat her mischievous, but loyal, horse with kindness and affection? Her avoidance of discipline was probably the reason why Maverick retained so many quirks. But the more kindness and affection she lavished upon him, the more he loved her.

One morning a few weeks later she was lying in bed suffering with a migraine. It was no coincidence that her headaches occurred more often during those turbulent years. Just as she was about to fall asleep, Nelson came bolting into her room, announcing Chip was at the corrals, saddling Maverick.

Forcing herself out of bed while her migraine punished her, Jenny arrived just in time to witness Maverick send Chip flying. The cad hit the pipe corral and landed on the ground head first. From his arrogant face to his plumb belly, he was covered in blood, dirt, and horse dung. It took him quite a while to find his feet. His nose had been bloodied, a tooth was chipped, plus a sizable knot and laceration adorned his forehead. The cut would leave a scar, something, no doubt, that would remind him of this painful event. "You bastard! Now you're gonna pay!"

Jenny beat her husband to the whip. Off in the distance, Maverick carefully watched them.

Chip stretched out his hand. "Let me have it."

No doubt about it, she felt no shame, as the most deliberately sarcastic grin swept across her face. "I'd *love* to let you have it . . . really . . . I would." She paused and tapped the whip against her palm. An all-out confrontation had been *long* overdue. "But you're not going to touch Maverick. He's my horse and I'll do the disciplining."

Chip's eyes burned like steel rivets. "You saw what he did!"

"Yeah, and you had it coming. If you don't like it, then stay the hell away from him!"

She didn't think it was possible, but his staring intensified. "And what if I don't?"

Jenny turned toward the house, and to her surprise, all the pain from her migraine disappeared. She had reached a turning point. From that moment on she would stand her ground. "Well, then, I can always borrow that shotgun of yours."

That was the last time Chip ever tried riding Maverick. And whenever her husband came near the corrals, the mustang would holler his head off.

Later that week Chip started receiving letters from a "J. Candle" in Anderson, Iowa. The handwriting on the envelopes appeared quite elegant, not to mention feminine. When Jenny confronted her husband over the matter, he confirmed it was a woman. "She's just a business associate," he claimed. Although Jenny had been tempted, she never opened any of the letters. *I can't stand the sight of him, so why should I care?* But it added another grievance to her already overwhelming stockpile. Meanwhile, his business trips escalated.

As the weeks rolled by, Jenny grew desperate. Although Chip's cruelties remained entirely psychological, there were no guarantees he wouldn't eventually resort to violence. Even though she had been protecting Nelson, he still suffered with insomnia and remained wary of Chip. For her son's sake, she had to take a chance and not wait until her husband took an unusually long business trip.

Jenny gave the couple renting her house a thirty-day notice to vacate and free rent during the interim. She reserved a moving van and hired a divorce lawyer. Her property was not zoned for horses, but Arlene had no problems boarding Maverick. With each accomplishment, Jenny's confidence soared. This time she would succeed. She even waited until the day before her move date to drop the bomb on Chip.

"I told you before," he uttered from his recliner. "You're not going anywhere."

"You can't stop me," she returned. "And keep your threats to yourself. I'll slap a restraining order on you faster than Maverick can buck you off."

He laughed in his usual arrogant manner. He always laughed whenever he wanted to degrade her. "Restraining orders aren't worth squat." His eyes remained fixed on the television set. "Quit your bellyaching . . . and just deal with it."

"Why should I?"

He flashed that look again, that infuriating leer of superiority. "Let me put it this way. I have plenty of experience in courtrooms and know how the system works. By the time I'm done with you, everything of yours will belong to me, including that damn horse."

"No, you're bluffing." She clenched her fists. "He was a gift from Arlene."

He smiled and shook his head. "Legally, I'm disabled. I have no job and no documented income, but you own a lucrative business. So who do you think the court will side with? When I'm through with you, you won't have a nickel left to your name. And when I'm awarded your horse, I'll sell that lousy bastard for dog food!"

He smiled again and gave her a spiteful wink. "Just remember the poor schmuck the next time you open a can of Alpo."

Long after Jenny had left the room, Chip howled and barked like a dog.

***

Jenny rolled her eyes and sighed. Dwelling on such atrocities seemed ludicrous and counterproductive, but each time she drudged up Chip, she purged a little more poison from her system. Six months after the last of the court battles, her emotional state had improved, and sooner or later she would *fully* recover. But for now she would just have to sort through the past and work her way back.

Maverick snorted as they rounded a sharp bend and approached the clearing. For the next hundred yards, the path meandered along the bottom of a wide valley. Countless pine trees lined the surrounding mountain tops. It was Jenny's favorite view along the trail. Just the sight of the mountain crest reminded her of how beautiful nature could be. Their ride was nearly complete. The O'Dells' cabin was just a half mile away.

As they progressed, she gazed upward. The sky was as blue as she could remember. The sun had entered the west and was about to start its descent. She took a long, leisurely breath. The fresh air invigorated her. She heard a distinctive cawing and spotted a crow taking advantage of a mild breeze, gliding effortlessly across the sky.

As she watched, the bird appeared to slam into an invisible wall. It wasn't until it began plunging downward that she heard a sharp, cracking sound. Maverick whinnied and halted. The crow continued to plummet, feathers and bits of its body drifting behind. It struck the ground thirty feet in front of them.

Jenny turned toward the mountaintops. Whoever shot the bird had to be hidden somewhere in trees. *God, from that distance they could have killed me.*

Just as she was about to shout some choice obscenities, something hit the ground in front of her horse. Another cracking sound followed. Maverick hollered, reared, then bolted. Before she knew it they were charging toward the woods at the opposite side of the clearing.

Everything happened so fast, Jenny's mind had to catch up. Someone had taken a shot at her. The crow might have been an accident, but that last bullet was meant for her.

Maverick galloped at top speed. His panting and thundering hooves pounded in her ears. She yanked the reins hard, but the mustang shook it off. The end of the clearing loomed closer. She was certain once they entered the woods, he would slow down.

Suddenly there was another discharge. Jenny only heard it after Maverick screamed. His legs buckled and she tumbled forward.

***

When Jenny opened her eyes, she discovered she was lying on the ground, facing a darkening horizon. Everything appeared gloomy and out of focus. She propped herself on an elbow and realized she had taken a fall. Her eyes stung; her head, back, and left ankle hurt. She sat up but, for the time being, felt too weak and disoriented to stand.

She glanced around. Where was Maverick? If he'd been injured, he would have remained by her side. Since he was well-acquainted with the O'Dells', perhaps he had sought the protection of familiar surroundings.

As Jenny took a flustered breath, her eyes grew wide. Memories of the crow dropping from the sky sent chills down her spine. There wasn't time to lie around in the dirt and feel dizzy.

Someone wants me dead and they could be anywhere.

Using her arms for leverage, Jenny struggled to her feet. Her head and legs throbbed, but she forced herself along. She glanced at the sky. She must have been out for some time because the sun had descended just above the horizon.

Damn it! I'd better make it to the O'Dells' before dark.

When she entered the forest, she noticed a set of hoof prints and drops of blood along the trail. She groaned and fought off tears. Maverick had taken a bullet. She bent down and ran her fingers across the droplets. *It's fresh.* She shivered. *Don't panic. Whatever you do, stay calm.*

Jenny brushed back her hair and discovered she was missing her hat and jacket. She thought for a moment and remembered tying the coat to her waist. *Guess I lost them back at the clearing.*

The increasing pain in Jenny's ankle kept slowing her down. But what about Maverick? She had stashed her medical kit in the saddlebag and could stop his bleeding once she found him. Occasional drops of blood kept appearing through the growing darkness. *Calm down! Keep it together. He'll be all right.*

The O'Dells' cabin lay just up the trail. Twilight quickly slipped into night, making it impossible for her to see any more blood or hoof prints.

Out of the corner of her eye, she spotted movement off to her left. She swallowed and pushed herself harder.

I'm still being followed. When the hell am I going to listen to my instincts? Even Maverick warned me.

She heard something snap. Whirling left, she caught a glimpse of a shadow half-hidden behind a tree. It was hard to see in the fading light, but the figure appeared to be nearly sixty feet away. She turned and hurried as fast as she could. The trail climbed uphill toward the O'Dells' cabin. She felt lightheaded. Perspiration trickled down her face. The faster she moved, the more her ankle throbbed. She shook her head. *I can't believe this. Someone's following me . . . hunting me down.*

After rounding the final bend, she veered left and reached the O'Dells' driveway. The trail had merged onto a dirt road which would wind its way downward, ending at Longhorn Drive. Of course there were no other homes in that direction, not for miles.

Rushing up the porch steps, Jenny stumbled and landed on her hands and knees. She crawled forward, flipped over the welcome mat, and scooped up the house key. Swallowing, she clutched the doorknob and struggled to her feet. Her hands refused to steady themselves. Holding her right wrist, she inserted the key into the deadbolt.

More terror unnerved her. She cringed and peered over her shoulder. Was that the sound of footsteps behind her? She could barely think or hear over her own breathing. She unlocked the deadbolt then placed the key in the brass doorknob. Seconds felt like hours. *God, no! The handle's not budging!*

A noise from behind nearly stopped her heart. A barrage of shudders overwhelmed her. It seemed as if she would never contain her panic. *Think, Jenny, think!*

A glimmer of hope rushed through her. Joan had mentioned the front door had been sticking. Grimacing, Jenny jiggled the key up and down then back and forth. She took a wary breath and rammed the door with her hip. A chafing sound followed as the door flew open.

Stepping inside, she turned back toward the woods. A rising wind stirred the trees; darkness had closed in on the last remnants of light. She was stranded in the middle of an isolated region, without a hint of moonlight. It would grow darker – much darker – beyond anything she'd been accustomed to. She shuddered and slammed the door shut.

***

Jenny flipped on the light switch. Curio cabinets, an aquarium, and an oversized fireplace garnished the living room. The cabin appeared similar to Arlene's, except the O'Dells had installed an enclosed rear patio and a well-stocked wine cellar, extremely unusual for homes in California.

She caught her breath and stared out the front window. Everything looked dark but peaceful enough. She slipped the house key into her back pocket and hurried to the kitchen. It would take the police some time to travel up the mountain, but they just might send a forest ranger first. There had to be at least one station on Longhorn Drive.

Jenny leaned over the breakfast bar and discovered the exposed phone jack on the kitchen wall. *Okay, why would the O'Dells move their telephone?* She turned toward the master bedroom. Again feeling lightheaded, she suspected her fall had given her a concussion.

Entering the bedroom, she flipped on the light. The phone on the O'Dells' nightstand had also disappeared. *My God! I just called Joan three days ago. They couldn't have taken their phones out since then.*

Sure, the O'Dells were a bit eccentric. Marvin collected all types of toy soldiers from the 'fifties and 'sixties, and Joan liked to talk to her tropical fish. Neither of them believed in televisions, microwaves, or computers. But people just don't pack up their phones and take them to Las Vegas!

Jenny checked the guest bedroom and double-checked the living room. There were no telephones, but she discovered a message from Joan on the kitchen table. Addressed to both Arlene and her, it was a thank you note for taking care of Joan's fish. Strange, but elderly woman's handwriting appeared legible for a change.

She dropped the note on the table and started to chuckle. Oh, yes, Joan's tropical fish, the reason for her monthly excursions. She was supposed to feed them tonight and again tomorrow. But that could wait. Right now she'd feel better if she had something to defend herself with.

Rushing across the kitchen, she opened a utensil drawer and removed a large carving knife. She gazed at it and whispered, "Okay, you and I are hanging out tonight."

Jenny braced herself against the breakfast bar. She could no longer hold back her emotions. Covering her mouth, she doubled up and laughed. The whole thing seemed so outrageous. She had ridden all the way up here just to feed some fish. She could be lying on the trail with a bullet in her head, because of those stupid fish! Collapsing into Marvin's recliner, Jenny's laughter turned to sobs. Perhaps it wasn't so outrageous after all. Feeding Joan's fish was just an excuse for Arlene and her to ride together. Her tears started to flow harder now. She had no idea if Maverick was still alive. He could be lost, scared out of his mind, and bleeding to death.

Wiping her eyes, Jenny pulled her dead cell phone from her hip pocket. Of course she had stashed the charging cord in her saddlebag. Her stomach growled, and yet she had no appetite. Someone had followed her, tried to kill her and, in all probability, was still out there. Who could it be? The homeless man? It seemed unlikely he could afford a rifle. She cringed. Could it have been Chip? He had owned several guns at one time or another. Since he had never tried to physically harm either Nelson or her, was he capable of such a thing? As cruel as he could be, traveling all the way from Iowa to take a shot at her sounded utterly insane. She massaged her throbbing forehead. The more she worried, the more her head ached. A single, morbid thought managed to work its way through her growing pain. *Don't forget about that dismembered woman they found by the creek . . .*

Jenny hurried through the cabin, closed the window drapes, double-checked the locks on the front and rear doors, then wedged the backs of two kitchen chairs beneath their knobs. All she could do now was hope her attacker would move on. She again collapsed into Marvin's recliner. To be safe she would have to stay awake. Gazing at the knife, she recalled how she was finally able to leave Chip and start what had to be one of the wildest, nastiest divorces in state history.

***

Just over two years ago, Chip announced he was taking another trip to Iowa. In addition to his usual business, this time he wanted to see if he could make amends with his mother and siblings. He expected to be away for at least two weeks altogether. Jenny listened, nodded her head, and held her tongue. Two weeks would be cutting it close, but if she hurried, she and Nelson would be free of him for good.

As soon as Chip walked out the door, Jenny called and asked her renters to vacate. She apologized for the short notice and promised to refund a full month's rent. To her surprise, the young couple readily accepted. "We're more than happy to be rid of that greedy husband of yours," the man confessed.

Jenny hired another lawyer and another moving company. She took time off work, hitched up her trailer and hauled both Maverick and her newest horse, Laramie, to Arlene's ranch. Naturally, Maverick bit the Palomino before the trip was over. After that, she and Nelson started packing.

During that time, Chip's so-called business associate, Dennis Conway, showed up unannounced. Jenny tried to turn him away, but he pushed himself inside. His breath reeked of alcohol and his eyes looked blurry and red. He handed her a small check from one of their business ventures, something that could have waited. More than likely, Chip had enlisted him to spy on her.

After helping himself to a gin and tonic, Dennis glanced at the stack of boxes in the kitchen. "Are you going somewhere?"

"No, I'm just storing a few things," she lied.

He smiled and sipped his drink. "Come on, Jenny, I wasn't born yesterday."

She leaned against the kitchen counter and stared at him. A wave of goose bumps crept over her. She had never trusted Dennis and there was no sense in starting now.

"Chip's been telling me you want out. Not that I give a damn, but I'm supposed to let him know what's going on around here."

Jenny sighed. "I thought so." But being right about her suspicions didn't make her feel any better.

"Well, your secret's safe with me."

She had to stifle a laugh. Nothing could ever be safe when it came to either Chip or Dennis.

"A little surprise won't hurt him." He chuckled and stirred his drink. "I'll let you in on another secret. He won't be back for at least a month. He's looking around for some investments all right, but he's also searching for a place to live."

Jenny all but keeled over. "Are you telling me he's moving to Iowa?"

Dennis sipped his drink. "Well, yes and no, but mostly yes."

She could not believe what she was hearing. She should have been relieved, jumping for joy. Yet, despite everything, she felt guarded and deceived.

"Eventually, he'll leave you . . . if you don't leave him first. What he's actually doing back there is setting up another life. He'll return here on occasion, but he'll mostly live in Iowa. He's done it before. This will be the third time, as a matter of fact."

"You're not serious?" She knew Chip was a slick con artist, but this was a new low, even for him.

"I'm afraid so." He strolled past her and sat at the kitchen table. "I'm not one to talk; I've done some questionable things myself. But Chip, he's the demigod of double-dealers and predators. Believe me . . . I know." He took another sip of his drink. A hint of regret crept through his eyes. "I know him better than you — or better than anyone else."

As he sipped his drink, Dennis divulged enough trash to write a tell-all biography. Chip had been married not just once before, like he claimed, but three times. The first divorce wiped him out financially, but after that no one could touch him. When the next two wives came along, they paid dearly for marrying him. Dennis told her about several scams, including the Las Vegas venture, the one that Chip initiated when he had disappeared during their honeymoon. He had been investigated by the IRS, and that was the real reason behind his aliases. Naturally, he fooled around on the side, but according to Dennis, Chip wasn't interested in sex. Nice, fat, bank accounts were the only thing that attracted him. After an hour of listening, Jenny mentioned the letters from the mysterious "J. Candle."

Dennis poured himself another drink. "Yes, that's Jackie, his next mark. She's just a grammar school teacher, and a little older, but her late husband left her a small fortune. As a matter of fact, Chip's already got his hands on some of it. He called yesterday and told me she invested three grand in one of our real estate deals."

Jenny flopped into a chair. She kept thinking, *What have I done to myself?* She knew Chip was a clever snake, but she'd had no idea of the magnitude.

Dennis tossed some ice in his drink and joined her at the table. Feeling stupid and overwhelmed, she stared at him. "Why are you telling me this?"

He smiled and leaned toward her. "Because I like you, that's why. You're a good person and deserve better." He reached over and took her hand. "Screw the degenerate bastard. Maybe you and I can make a go of it. What do you think?"

Jenny jerked her hand away. She didn't mean to overreact, but Dennis was nothing more than a cheap imitation of Chip. "No, that's impossible."

The expression in Dennis' bloodshot eyes appeared stunned. "How come?"

She stood and moved away. She didn't want him to ever touch her again. "I don't care to be with anyone right now. Besides, you're married."

He laughed and waved a hand. "Yes, I'm married . . . to good old Celeste, who's a dishonest drunk. Hell, everyone knows she's a lush. As long as she's good and liquored up, she won't care *who* I sleep with."

Jenny hid her revulsion the best she could. What kind of hypocrite was this guy? He had the nerve to call his wife a dishonest drunk, while he boozed it up over here? She folded her arms across her chest and kept her emotions in check. "I think you'd better go now. Thank you for your help. I appreciate it."

Dennis nodded and rose to his feet. Jenny thought by now he'd be staggering around, passing out, or at least slurring his words. Apparently, just like Chip, he could handle his liquor better than most men. "Okay, have it your way. But I think you're making a *huge* mistake."

She walked Dennis to the door then quickly shut it before he had a chance to say another word. *Goodbye and good riddance*, she thought. *Hope I never see you again.*

It took her the entire month, but before Chip returned she and Nelson were living comfortably in her old home.

***

Jenny jumped out of the recliner. She thought she heard a noise outside. She raised the knife and limped toward the front window. Her left ankle still ached and kept throwing her off balance. She pulled back a drape and peered out. The porch light lit the immediate area and everything looked perfectly normal. *So far, so good.* She made her way to the bedrooms. The cabin felt chilly and she missed her jacket.

In each of the bedrooms, Jenny peered out the windows. There was nothing to see but a few towering trees. She limped toward the kitchen. Her back ached and her ankle throbbed. She took a long look out the rear door window. The O'Dells had cluttered their enclosed patio with furniture, bookshelves, and all kinds of other junk. There were just too many hiding places and she could not be certain if the room was safe or not. She rolled her eyes and groaned. *Oh, great! I forgot to check that exterior door.* Clutching the knife, she took a deep, wary breath. *If I don't take a look . . . I might end up wishing I had.*

Opening the door, Jenny inched through the maze of furnishings. Her heart pounded as she checked behind the larger items. Everything was covered with a thick layer of dust. As she progressed she questioned if all this effort was worth the risk. When she reached the door, she tried turning the handle. *Good, it's locked.* After studying the door, however, she felt little relief. Made of flimsy aluminum, a child could kick it in. She cursed then flipped on the porch light.

Across the yard stood a large wooden storage shed. A glaring light shined above its door. The O'Dells' entire property appeared to be a mere clearing surrounded by the never-ending forest. Weeds, brush, and pine needles littered the ground. At the left side of the shed Jenny spotted an ax and a hatchet propped against a stack of logs. She frowned. *All I have to do is run out there and grab one.* She shook her head and turned off the light. *Yeah, if I want to commit suicide. Besides, could I actually use such messy weapons?*

Jenny's eyes widened as she backed away from the window. She just remembered a phone conversation she'd had with Joan about a year ago, something to do with Marvin bringing home a handgun. *Crap! What's the matter with me? Why didn't I think of that before!*

Relocking the rear interior door, Jenny hurried toward the master bedroom. She paused and, once again, fought off her lightheadedness. *Get your act together, Jenny, before it's too late.*

She hobbled into the O'Dells' bedroom and searched through the nightstands. Her ankle had swelled and she wanted to take her boot off to relieve the pressure, but most likely she would never be able to get it back on.

After a thorough search of the nightstands, she checked the closet. She removed three shoeboxes from the top shelf. They were stuffed with old, plastic toy soldiers. Marvin had always fancied himself an avid collector but was normally so tightfisted that Arlene had dubbed him "Mingy Marvin."

Jenny looked through a dozen shoe boxes in all. Besides toy soldiers she found Marvin's collections of eight track tapes, comic books, and photographs. He had even saved some old, decrepit Blue Chip stamps. She shook her head then removed a wooden box. It seemed heavier than the rest. The lid resisted, but when it opened, she felt as if she had discovered a goldmine. She knew nothing about guns, hated the sight of them, but felt thankful nevertheless. The weapon appeared to be a small caliber, snub nose revolver.

She fumbled with the cylinder; it opened and her stomach dropped. *Just my luck, empty.* She searched the remainder of the closet but could not find the bullets. What was Marvin thinking? When buying a revolver, why not keep the bullets with it?

Jenny hurried to the dresser and checked each drawer. When she came up empty-handed, she fought back a flood of tears. What good was an unloaded gun? She would hold onto it for now, and perhaps it might serve some type of purpose, but more urgently, her energy level had dropped to a dangerous low, and the effects of her fall were slowing her down. She would take a break then resume her search as soon as she felt better.

Taking both the gun and knife, Jenny hurried to the bathroom. She needed to take a shower, but after sitting through too many movies like "Psycho," she simply rinsed her face and neck. She searched the medicine cabinet and helped herself to four Tylenols.

After checking the area outside the front window, Jenny limped to the kitchen. She had grown weaker and needed to eat. She halted by the back window and stared at the ax and hatchet propped against the woodpile. They still looked sharp and, she had to admit, more than a tad inviting. *Thanks just the same, but I prefer the gun . . . if I can ever find the bullets.*

As she peered through the window, a nagging sensation gripped her. *Someone's out there. I can feel him!* She swallowed and closed the drape. *Maybe I should turn off the lights so he can't see me.* She glanced about the kitchen. *But if I turn them off . . . I'll never find the bullets.* Her stomach rumbled and she stepped away from the window. *I'll eat first; then I can grab the flashlight under the sink.*

When Jenny opened the refrigerator, she discovered a note printed on copy paper. She picked it up and read it aloud. "Jenny, I left something special for you in the downstairs freezer." There was no signature. The word "special" had been underlined.

Why would Joan write a second note? Why wouldn't she just add this message to the first? Besides, the truth was the O'Dells took pride in evading technology. Since they had never owned a computer, or a printer, how could they have possibly printed this note? She stood motionless and wiped her forehead. Someone *else* had printed it, brought it to the cabin, and left it in the refrigerator for her to find.

A sense of panic gnawed deep inside Jenny's stomach. *I never checked the cellar.* She dropped the note and rushed to the living room. She thought she could use the fireplace poker for an additional weapon. To her alarm she discovered both the poker and shovel were missing from their caddy.

She gazed at the revolver in her hand. *Okay, if anyone's downstairs, they would have to assume this gun's loaded. But shouldn't I stay up here where it's safe?* She straightened her shoulders and glanced about the room. *Because it's not safe, that's why. If someone's in the cellar, they could attack me at any time.* She wiped her upper lip and raised the gun. It sounded reckless on the surface, but it just *might* be to her advantage to initiate a confrontation. She didn't know if her attacker was still around, but someone had been inside the cabin. The missing poker, shovel, and telephones were all part of it. Perhaps he had even taken the bullets.

Jenny swallowed and slowly crossed the living room toward the entrance to the cellar. She opened its door and flipped on the light. A ceiling bulb hanging from the rafters barely lit the staircase. She hesitated and again convinced herself to proceed. As she descended, her ankle sent a bolt of pain up her leg. *Shit! It's getting worse. I'll just have to rest it later.*

To her right a washer and dryer stood against the wall. Piles of clothing lay everywhere. She flipped on the fluorescent light over the dryer. Even with the added voltage, the majority of the room remained dim and murky. She paused, took a breath, and a musty scent nauseated her. She exhaled and turned left.

Towering before her were six wine shelves – three on each side – which formed a short, narrow aisle. Against a wall at the far end stood the white, standard-sized, horizontal freezer that Marvin had purchased from a flea market. Dating back several decades, it featured a cockeyed Nixon/Agnew bumper sticker pasted on the front.

Jenny inched down the aisle, cautiously checking between each row of shelves. Raising the knife, she paused, held her breath, and listened. Except for the hum of the freezer's compressor, the cellar remained hushed. As she studied the appliance, she noticed the latch that Marvin had installed on its door had been broken off and was lying on the floor.

Taking a deep breath, Jenny lowered the knife, leaned forward, and gripped the freezer's handle. Her hands were shaking; her throat had dried out. She slowly lifted the door and stepped back. A vapor cloud appeared then dissipated. A layer of frost covered the inside portion of the lid. There were several items stacked to the top, wrapped in a hazy plastic. It all appeared perfectly harmless and ordinary.

Jenny chuckled and shook her head. *Well, what did you expect? That a polar bear would come flying out?*

Exhaling, she felt a tremendous weight leave her body. *Thank God, this whole thing's nothing but a hoax. Someone may have been here, but as far as I can tell . . .*

Jenny froze. Her eyes grew huge. A reddish substance had been splattered across the items in the freezer. Her heart pounded harder than she thought possible. There was no denying it. The substance resembled blood, not just a few drops but more than she could count.

Again Jenny felt lightheaded. Placing the knife on the edge of the freezer, she wedged the gun under her belt. She held her breath and picked up the top item. It was oval-shaped, surprisingly heavy, and roughly the size of a soccer ball. Condensation and the hazy plastic distorted the contents. As irrational as it seemed, the more she inspected it, the more the item looked like a large ball of dark, wavy hair. *God Almighty, what the hell is this?*

Ever so cautiously, Jenny turned the object around and wiped away the outside moisture. It felt like an eternity had passed before she realized what she was seeing. And when everything fell into place, when she finally discovered what she was looking at, her body temperature plunged and her heart leaped. Wrapped inside the plastic was the bloated face of her friend, Arlene.

Jenny screamed and her body reacted with a massive jolt. The room spun out of control. She tried to steady herself, but her injured ankle sent her stumbling backward. The side of her head slammed into a wine shelf. It toppled over, struck the middle shelf, then the third. The sound of shattering bottles resonated through the cellar. Half of Marvin's wine collection had been destroyed in an instant.

A sudden, blinding pain made Jenny gasp. Sprawled on top of the shelf, her entire existence spiraled into a mass of confusion, grief, and denial. Her surroundings grew dark and she barely clung onto consciousness. *No, that was not Arlene! It couldn't be! She's out of town taking care of her mother! She's . . .*

***

Jenny blinked and opened her eyes. Lifting her head, she glanced about the cellar. The room looked unfamiliar, off kilter. *What happened? I must have blacked out.*

Leaning forward, she used the shelf for leverage and struggled to her feet. As she gazed at the open freezer, the unthinkable tore through her. She clutched her chest and groaned. *Oh God, there's probably . . . there has to be . . .*

Jenny didn't want to look inside, but she had to. She owed Arlene that much and more.

Holding her breath, she crept forward. Tears trickled down her face. *She was my best friend. A smart and wonderful person. How could this happen?*

As Jenny stood over the freezer, its compressor hummed a low, monotonous lullaby. She bent forward and stared at the items wrapped in plastic. *What about the O'Dells? Were they murdered too?*

To her right a window shattered. Glass flew everywhere. A rock the size of a tennis ball bounced, then rolled across the floor. She glanced toward the broken window and spotted a fleeting shadow.

Fear engulfed her. Turning, she hurried toward the staircase. A glistening pool of wine had drenched the floor; the sound of broken glass crackled beneath her boots. As she passed another window, a second rock crashed through. She ducked, covered her face, then hurried toward the stairs.

Clutching the wooden banister, she rushed up the steps, then slammed the cellar door shut. With her heart pounding, she gazed at the light switch beside the front door. *He can't see me in the dark.*

Another rock hurled through a window. It struck Jenny's left shoulder, knocking her backward to the floor. The impact against her spine and ribcage purged her lungs of air. Pain and spasms ravaged her. She curled into a fetal position, taking shallow, erratic breaths through her mouth. *I can't lie here! I have to get up!*

She opened her mouth wider, inhaled, exhaled, again and again, every breath a little fuller. Slowly, deliberately, she repeated the sequence, fighting for every gain. Gradually, her lungs filled with the most precious air she had ever known. She waited until at long last she was able to move. *Don't stand . . . stay low . . .*

Jenny rolled onto her stomach. Determination consumed her. Using her elbows, she slowly crawled toward the front door. Inching her arm up the wall, she turned off the light, then realized she had left a bedroom and kitchen light on as well.

As Jenny crawled forward, she recalled the broken window downstairs. She dragged an armchair toward the cellar door, braced it beneath the knob, then peered to her right. *He can still come through that front window.* She paused, shook her head, then crawled toward the bedroom. The living room window was within hearing distance; she could defend herself if he came through.

Jenny worked her way into the spare bedroom, stretched up the wall, and switched off the light. She moved across the floor toward the rear of the cabin; her progress sluggish and painful.

As she entered the kitchen, another rock shattered the back window. Glass burst into the sink and onto the floor. Flinching, she covered her face. *Damn it! He knows my every move.*

Silently, cautiously, she scooted toward the interior wall. Taking a sated breath, she peered above her head. The light switch appeared miles away. *Come on, just one last time!* She stretched upward. Her body felt on fire. Her lungs ached. She kept stretching until she reached the switch.

Total blackness immersed the cabin. Jenny waited, and after a long, grueling moment, her eyes adjusted as well as she thought possible. *Now what? Oh, yeah . . . the flashlight.*

A solitary groan escaped her lips as she struggled to her feet. She would just have to adapt to her ankle pain, ignore it the best she could. She took a breath and crept toward the cabinet beneath the sink. Again, broken glass crackled beneath her boots.

Jenny bent down and opened the cabinet door. She had to feel her way through dozens of items but could not find anything that felt like a flashlight. She leaned against the counter and cursed. Missing flashlights, fireplace tools, even telephones. She wanted to scream, cry, anything to relieve her frustration. *Pull yourself together! Think! You can't end up like Arlene!*

Straining, she stared at the living room's dark outline. *I might have a chance if I barricade myself in the bathroom.* She pushed onward. As she neared the hallway, there was another crash, this time to her right. Something had shattered the south window. Turning, she froze and shuddered at the sight.

A fiery object rolled across the floor and landed on the throw rug in front of the fireplace. The flames quickly spread to the wooden floor. She bolted forward, dropped to her knees, and smothered the blaze with the rug.

As soon as the object had cooled, she held it up, and inspected it with both hands. It was a rock that had been wrapped in a material that felt like denim. *Oh, God, no.* She sighed and fought back tears. The material had been doused in gasoline.

Another crash exploded through the cabin. A second fiery rock bounded across the living room. Clutching the rug, she hurried over, dropped to the floor, and smothered the flames. Again, as soon as the rock cooled, she felt what was left of the material. *It's denim . . . there's a brass button . . .* She shivered and softly whimpered. It was her jacket, the one she had lost on the trail.

Suddenly the front window shattered. The cabin lit up as the living room burst into flames. Jenny gasped and shuddered. This was no rock wrapped in denim, but a glass bottle filled with gasoline. The air temperature skyrocketed; the floor and drapes caught fire. In a matter of seconds, Marvin's recliner, the couch, and one of the curio cabinets were set ablaze. Smoke burned her eyes and she could barely breathe. *I have to get out. It's too late, there's nothing I can do.*

Jenny hurried to the back door, her ankle throbbed with every step. Her attacker had won for now. But if she could make it to the woodpile, she could grab the ax or hatchet, then barricade herself inside the shed.

As she rushed to the kitchen, her lungs wrenched in pain. Smoke billowed downward from the ceiling. She unlocked the rear door and hurried through the enclosed patio. Glancing over her shoulder, she nearly lost her footing.

Unlocking the back door, Jenny reached behind her waist for the gun. "No," she shrieked. "God, no!" Both the gun and knife had disappeared. She must have lost them in the cellar.

She wiped the tears from her eyes and dashed toward the shed. A flickering orange hue illuminated the backyard. Everything around her spun. *Don't pass out! Keep going!* She focused all her energies on the shed. *Just a little further . . .*

Her ankle gave out; she plunged forward. She tried protecting herself with her hands, but her chin still struck the ground. What felt like a lightning bolt shot through her face. She cried and struggled to remain conscious. *Keep moving! You're close! Don't give up!*

Again the sensation of being watched overcame her. She looked over her shoulder toward the cabin. A figure half-cloaked within the smoke emerged. It was a man's silhouette, but it looked unnatural, ethereal – like a phantom lurking among the fringes of darkness. *He could have killed me by now . . . but he's just standing there . . . watching me.*

Jenny turned and crawled forward. The flames roared, the stench of smoke gagged her. As she neared the woodpile, she searched for the ax and hatchet, but like the elusive bullets, phones, and fireplace tools, they, too, had disappeared.

A sense of hopelessness besieged her. Cursing, she scrounged the base of the woodpile until she found a log small enough to fit her palm. She turned and faced the shadow flickering across the shed. The flames from the cabin seemed to give it a life of its own. *Why doesn't he end this? What is he waiting for?*

Rising to her feet, Jenny focused on how much she loved Katy and Nelson. Of how Maverick would nod whenever she asked him a question. She could not bear the thought of never seeing them again. She clenched her fists and shook with rage. No matter how much she suffered, no matter what it took, she would fight with everything inside her – and survive her attacker.

Jenny leaned against the shed and flung back the latch. The door creaked and quivered as it swung open. More anguish consumed her. *It opens outward! There's no way I can barricade it!*

Stepping inside, she turned toward the fully engulfed cabin. Even from across the yard, she could feel its blistering heat. Just before she closed the door, she searched in every direction, but once again, like a ghost, her attacker had vanished.

***

Jenny rummaged through the shed, hoping to find a more suitable weapon. The fire provided ample light from the two windows. A pair of rickety wooden shelves housed a gasoline can, a dozen ceramic pots, and at least six torn window screens. Along the walls hung a hacksaw, a shovel, a leaf blower, and a weed eater. An old, rusted barbecue grill stood at the far corner, covered in dust and cobwebs.

Setting the log aside, Jenny picked up the shovel. It felt too clumsy, too heavy. She checked the gas can. It was empty, but the scent of fumes remained potent. She shook her head, recalling the fiery rocks and bottle. *Guess the gasoline came from here.*

As she approached the window to her right, the floorboards creaked an eerie protest. She wiped a trace of blood from her chin and gazed out. Smoke filled the air. The yard lay vacant clear to the trail. She hurried to the left window and searched the area bordering the forest. Pine trees were huddled closely together, yet still her attacker remained unaccounted for. Since there were no front windows, she peered between the door and jamb. Smoke funneled upward into the sky; angry flames lashed from the cabin.

Someone will see the smoke. Firefighters will come and . . . she paused then frowned. *It's four miles to the nearest neighbor. How can anyone see smoke in this kind of darkness?*

She peered at the forest, searching for her attacker among the trees. So far the windless night had contained the fire. She brushed back her hair and wiped away a tear. With all those combustible belongings, the O'Dells had created the great-granddaddy of all firetraps.

Jenny eased down against a wall. She had to rest her ankle and decide who would want to kill her? Living in Iowa wouldn't necessarily hamper Chip. He knew where the O'Dells lived and even the whereabouts of their spare house key. Perhaps he had returned, murdered Arlene, and maybe even Joan and Marvin, then dumped their bodies in the freezer. After that he could have removed anything from the cabin that might be used against him. But if he wanted to murder her, why would he kill and dismember three innocent people?

Whoever her attacker was, he could force his way inside the shed at any time. A cynical grin spread across Jenny's face. *What's the fun in that?* He obviously wanted to prolong her pain and suffering. She thought most likely he would leave her alone for now, but if she ventured out, a bullet would certainly find her. She cringed and rubbed her eyes. *Whatever you do, stay awake, or you'll never see the light of day.*

Chip had already bled her dry, both emotionally and financially, so why would he try to kill her? Making herself reasonably comfortable, she grimly recalled the never-ending chaos surrounding their divorce.

***

Her IQ must have sunk by twenty notches. Why would she ever think in her naive, little mind, that she and Nelson could ever be free from the forces of corruption and evil? Her problems with Chip began almost immediately after his return from Iowa. Running late one afternoon, she hurried to pick up her son at school. When she arrived she couldn't find him.

"A tall man with a beard took your boy," Nelson's teacher explained. "He had a permission slip that matched your signature."

Jenny held her stomach and rushed away. The signature wasn't a forgery. She had written the note for Chip all right, last year, long before she left him.

She sped home and pulled into her driveway. Chip had parked his truck on her lawn with its front tires sitting in the middle of the flower garden. A frantic Nelson met Jenny at the door.

"I'm sorry, Mom," he cried. "He had a note."

She smiled and hugged the boy. "Why don't you start your homework and I'll go talk to him?"

Nelson nodded and hurried to his room. Jenny found her estranged husband sitting with his muddy boots propped on her kitchen table. Guzzling a can of beer, he turned toward her and shrugged. "The boy needed a lift. I hope you don't mind."

Jenny folded her arms across her chest and remained at the doorway. "What do you think you're doing?"

He removed his feet and sat up. "I just wanted to come by and wish you well."

She thought her jaw must have hit the floor. "You're putting me on, right?"

He rose to his feet, looking taller than ever. His mouth tightened and the crevices around his eyes deepened. "No, I'm serious." He gulped down the rest of his beer, crushed the empty can, and tossed it into the sink. "I wish you a happy ever after."

Jenny stepped aside as Chip swaggered by. Turning, he conjured up his most predatory grin. "Believe me, you're gonna need all the pleasantries you can get."

He walked out the front door, climbed into his truck, and raced away. Jenny watched from her living room window as his tires tore up her lawn and finished off the garden. She raced to the kitchen and stared at the clumps of dried mud on her table. "My God," she whispered, "we're in for a bloodbath."

The following week, Jenny had the sheriff's department deliver Chip's divorce summons. She knew anyone else would have been bullied and threatened. The next day, Nelson and his friends were playing in the backyard when Chip pulled up. Munchkin, her son's Pekinese, ran over to greet the man. Nelson watched in helpless bewilderment as his stepdad reached over the fence and picked up the small pet. Chip smiled, tossed the dog into his truck, and drove off. When a distraught Nelson told Jenny what had happened, she phoned the police. They labeled the episode as a "domestic dispute" and merely filled out a report.

For the next few days, the phone would ring, and when Jenny answered, no one responded. When these calls started keeping her awake at night, she changed phone numbers. A week later someone flung a rock through Nelson's bedroom window. The next night a rock shattered the living room window. Jenny had her lawyer push through a restraining order, but, unfortunately, Chip was right. It proved useless. A few nights later her tires were slashed. She never heard or saw a thing. Indeed, the man was like a phantom, prowling through the night, inflicting his own brand of vengeance.

Chip sold his house and moved to Iowa, at least officially, but Jenny knew otherwise. Like Dennis had mentioned, in order to keep his double life thriving, her ex could easily return whenever he wanted.

Acting as his own lawyer, Chip demanded alimony. "He just may get it," Jenny's attorney informed her. "He has no job, no traceable source of income, and is technically a disabled person. You, on the other hand, are a licensed veterinarian, with your own practice, earning a respectable living." She groaned and stewed in her anger. Chip had always claimed he would bankrupt her.

An average divorce in California takes about six months. Trenton verses Darnell – she had never bothered changing her name – lasted a full two years. Chip intentionally complicated the proceedings by asking for everything. He included both Maverick and Laramie, even though he had little use for them. His list of disputed property spiraled into the triple digits, including her gardening tools, chicken wire, a rusted lawn mower, and last but not least, a pooper scooper. The judge had a field day with that one.

Twice Chip failed to appear in court, citing his broken-down truck plus the hardship of traveling from Iowa. Incredibly, the judge tolerated every delay. Once, instead of showing up in person, he testified by telephone. Another time, he wore a neck brace and claimed he'd just been in an auto accident. When Jenny told Nelson about the brace, even he remarked, "He just wanted the judge to feel sorry for him!"

In the meantime her attorney's fees launched into the stratosphere. Even for a five minute phone call, or a brief memo, her lawyer charged her two hundred and fifty dollars an hour. Of course her estranged husband knew this. It was all part of his scheme. As long as the judge was willing to put up with his nonsense, Chip could well afford to draw things out.

Thankfully, the cad was not awarded alimony payments, but Jenny did have to pay him twenty-five thousand dollars, plus her lawyer took nearly twice that much. Strangely enough, however, she felt relieved. Her dealings with the king of pain were finally over with – or so she had thought.

A month after the settlement, Jenny's phone rang at two a.m. It was a Friday night and Fridays at the clinic were often brutal. She had euthanized two dogs and a cat. One of the dogs had been a toy poodle that eighty-year-old Estelle Compton had owned for sixteen years. Even though the animal had been critically ill, Estelle hadn't seen it coming. A longtime widow with no children, the dog was all she had. No matter what Jenny said, Estelle could not be comforted. She gave the elderly client the phone number to a local animal shelter, and encouraged the woman to adopt. Nevertheless, Estelle left the clinic in a most deplorable state. Thoughts of the matronly widow kept Jenny up for hours.

She had just drifted off to sleep when Arlene phoned. "You'd better get the hell over here," she demanded. "That damn, freaking Chip is stealing your horses!"

"I'll be right there. Have you called the police?"

"Sure, and by the time they get here, it'll be Christmas. Just hurry up! I'll fetch my shotgun and aim it seven inches below his belly!"

Jenny jumped out of bed. "No, just stay put. You hear me? Don't go near him!"

When Jenny finally arrived, her friend led her to the corrals. Laramie's pen stood empty, her beautiful Palomino had been stolen. But to her amazement, pacing back and forth in his corral, huffing and puffing, his eyes bulging in aggravation, Maverick was still very much around.

"Chip had no problems hauling Laramie into his trailer," Arlene explained. "But when it came down to Maverick, your cranky old horse stopped the bastard cold!" She burst out laughing. Jenny couldn't remember ever seeing her friend this worked up. "He found himself outmatched and outsmarted." Despite all the heartaches of that day, Jenny laughed as well.

"I've been around horses all my life and I've never seen one put up such a stink! He hollered his head off and reared so much, Chip couldn't get a halter near him. Hell, he knocked the moron on his ass . . . twice!"

Jenny laughed so hard, she broke into tears. When Maverick trotted over, she climbed into the pen and hugged him. Of course he was still panting and complaining, but the expression in his eyes said it all. They had become connected in both body and spirit. Still, it took him a while to settle down.

"It's okay, boy. I'm glad you hate him. Otherwise, I would have lost you, too."

It took an hour for the police to arrive. They wrote everything down in a report and, predictably, labeled the theft as another "domestic dispute." In other words, there was nothing they could do.

The incident, as bad as it was, had a bright side; it solidified Jenny's relationship with her mustang. He was a stinker for sure; her children could barely stand him. But he was family now and would always belong to her.

Later that weekend, after helping Estelle Compton adopt a beautiful Scottish Terrier, Jenny wrote a letter. She addressed it to Jackie Candle, Chip's unsuspecting prey in Iowa. Exercising some foresight, she had kept the woman's address. At first Jenny questioned her own motives, wondering if she was merely trying to settle the score. In the end she decided she should have written Jackie months ago. Her letter never veered from the facts and, for the most part, omitted any type of emotionality. Jenny summarized everything that had occurred between Chip and her. She enclosed copies of their property settlement, plus Munchkin and Laramie's theft reports. "At least you've been warned," she concluded. "I wish I'd had that luxury."

She mailed the letter the next day, but later on, feelings of doubt plagued her. How would Chip react? Would he stay away? Or would he return to seek even *more* revenge?

***

Jenny woke with a start. *My God, how could I have fallen asleep?* She glanced at the daylight shining through the windows then checked her watch. It was ten after six. *I was damn lucky. I could have been murdered!*

She used the log for leverage and struggled to her feet. Her ankle still felt tender but had improved considerably.

Rubbing her eyes, she looked out both windows. The odor of burnt wood filled her lungs, and a moderate haze hung in the air. She shook her head, braced herself, and peered through the space between the door and jamb.

The O'Dells' cabin had been destroyed beyond recognition. A blackened chimney and small portions of the front and rear walls were all that stood. Two narrow columns of smoke drifted upward from the living room area. *I hope you're happy . . . you son of a bitch.*

Jenny wiped away a tear and swallowed. Thoughts of Joan and Marvin drifted through her mind and she wondered if they had been butchered like Arlene. She ran a hand through her hair. There was only one way to find out.

Again, she peered between the door and jamb, searching for her attacker. There were just the towering pine trees and what remained of the cabin. She glanced at the log in her hand. It seemed so small, so insignificant. Perhaps she could find something better inside the ruins.

Jenny clenched her fists and nudged open the door. She inched forward, raised the log, and searched the area concealed by the shed's door. It seemed a likely place to hide. *Okay, no one's there. I might have a chance after all.*

She exhaled and glanced around. The sun had crept behind a cluster of clouds. Birds sang in the distance, and a northern breeze cooled her face. She gazed at the cabin; her stomach turned, then cramped. *The firefighters . . . they never came.*

She felt lost, isolated. Pushing forward, she steadied her breathing. *Keep looking. Don't let your guard down.*

Turning, she checked both sides of the shed. Again, her assailant remained unseen. *If he was back there, wouldn't he have already attacked me?*

Jenny hurried her pace. Every few feet she would look over her shoulder. She reached the remnants of the enclosed patio. The smell of burnt wood nauseated her. Ashes and debris appeared knee-deep in many places. Hardly anything in the interior seemed recognizable. There were a few scorched ceramic pots that had split apart and a singed refrigerator and stove.

Stepping over a mound of rubble, she made her way toward a broken pot. Its sharp edge could very well come in handy.

As Jenny bent forward her scalp suddenly burst with pain. Yanked backward by her hair, she screamed and thrashed about. An arm from behind quickly wrapped itself around her throat. The pressure on her scalp diminished – yet the force against her windpipe intensified.

Barely able to hold on to the log, she tried breaking the grip with her free hand. But her attacker proved too strong. As she was dragged from the cabin, her vision grew blurry.

Scream, Jenny! Scream!

But she couldn't. Her windpipe had been closed off. Her lungs strained for air. She grew lightheaded, nearly unconscious.

Remembering a self-defense technique she had learned from Arlene, she turned her head and tucked her chin into the crook of the arm. The pressure shifted from her throat to her chin. A surge of air inflated her lungs.

Out of the corner of her eye, she spotted a face. *Is it . . . Chip?*

Indeed, it was a man with a beard. She kept looking, trying to make him out. *Oh, God! How can this be?*

The man was not Chip. Her attacker was of medium build. His hair and beard were much too long. *It's the homeless man. The one I saw in the woods!*

Jenny was dragged closer toward the shed. She clawed at her assailant's arm, wrist, and hand. She kicked with her feet. *He's going to kill me. I have to break free!*

She swung the log over her head. A solid thud was followed by a cry of pain. She swung the log up again, as hard as she could. He screamed; they plunged backward together, slamming into the ground. Her elbows rammed into his body; her weapon flew from her grip. She broke free and rolled onto her side.

Pain rushed through Jenny as she stumbled to her feet. She staggered about, scanning the ground for the log. When she spotted it, she snatched it up and turned toward her attacker.

Dressed in a bulky jacket, baseball cap, and sunglasses, the man remained motionless. The hatchet that had turned up missing the night before, lay behind him. *He's wearing dark glasses . . . I can't see his eyes. If I can just get to the hatchet . . .*

She took a deep breath, inched left, then maneuvered around her attacker. As she neared the weapon, the man lunged forward and grabbed her wrist. She reacted immediately and bashed the log hard between his eyes. He shrieked, clutched his nose, and rolled back and forth, cursing and sobbing. Blood dripped from his nostrils. "You bitch!" he bellowed.

Jenny snatched up the hatchet. His voice sounded familiar. She spotted a fake beard lying on the ground next to the sunglasses. Raising the weapon, she tried to make out his features, but he kept thrashing around, clutching his face. "You broke my nose! Goddamn it! You broke it!"

Jenny's knees nearly buckled. She knew the voice well. The man squirming on the ground, the one who had been trying to murder her for two days, was Chip's business associate, Dennis Conway.

He kept cursing while more blood seeped from his nostrils. She positioned herself over him and raised the hatchet. Knowing the man didn't matter. She'd split his skull straight down the middle if she had to. "You damn asshole! W-why are you trying to kill me?"

Dennis removed his hands from his nose. His face looked bloodied, haggard, and sweaty. Glaring at her, his mouth twisted into a snarl. "None of your fucking business!"

He quickly swung his legs left, knocking Jenny to the ground. Landing hard on her back, again her lungs were purged of air. She rolled onto her side and, struggling for a breath, crawled toward the cabin.

Dennis stumbled to his feet then fought to steady himself. He cursed and wiped the blood from his face. He lunged forward, grabbed the hatchet, then thrust its handle against Jenny's throat.

"S-sorry," he gasped. The stench of gin hung on his breath. He coughed and spat out blood. "Believe me, I got no choice . . ."

A deafening boom echoed through the canyon. Something splattered onto the back of Jenny's head. The pressure halted and Dennis crumpled forward, pinning her to the ground. Her body tensed, her mind swarmed with confusion. She squirmed out from beneath him, rose to her feet, and realized she was covered in blood.

Dennis had fallen on to his side, facing her, his arms and legs twitching. He had urinated himself. Blood and saliva gushed from his mouth.

Unable to tear her eyes away, Jenny stood frozen. An opening the size of a chestnut had breached the back of Dennis' head. A larger hole had completely obliterated his right eye. Blood poured onto the ground; bits of flesh and brain had spewed everywhere. As her stomach shriveled, his twitching ceased.

Jenny picked up the hatchet and inched away. Her confusion ran rampant. She gagged and nearly lost her balance. The bullet had missed her by inches. *It's the sharpshooter . . . the one who shot the crow.*

She gazed toward the rear of the property. A tall, burly man wearing a black ski mask stepped out of the woods. Cradled within his arms he held an enormous telescopic rifle. As she watched in stunned disbelief, he stopped then stood motionless. He tilted his head and stared in her direction.

Jenny's trembling grew beyond control. Her heart pounded ice through her veins. When she stepped back, the man raised the rifle. She took a breath, turned, and ran as fast as she could. Her injured ankle shot pain through her. She bore left, using the remainder of the cabin as cover. A sharp cracking sound pierced the air as a bullet struck the front wall. Jenny stumbled but regained her balance. *Don't fall, damn it! Keep moving!*

She raced across the O'Dells' front yard then hurried onto the dirt road. Her ankle held her speed to a modest jog. She maintained her breathing at full, even breaths. Her heart steadied. *You can't outrun bullets, Jenny. Think! What else can you do?*

The road ran straight, flat, providing no cover. She knew she would never make the four miles to Longhorn Drive. The sharpshooter would have a clear view once he rounded the cabin. There was nothing else she could do but seek the shelter of the trees.

Jenny veered right and entered the forest. As she turned she heard another cracking sound and a bullet pierced the tree beside her. *He's gaining! Keep going!*

The proximity of the trees and her throbbing ankle forced her to slow down. *As long as I'm moving he'll have trouble aligning his sights.* She zigzagged through the woods, and after a few moments, discovered how rapidly the forest had thinned.

A large tree root seemed to come out of nowhere. She stumbled then resumed her flight. She focused first on the trees, then the ground. The dirt felt soft, uneven, covered in pine needles. *Don't fall! Watch where you're going!*

She pushed harder. The woods grew dangerously sparse. The sharpshooter now had a clear view. More terror claimed her. Eighty feet to her front, the forest suddenly vanished before an endless sky. *Oh dear God, what is that?*

Gasping, Jenny came to a halt. She bent forward and wiped the perspiration from her face. It didn't seem possible, but she was standing in a narrow clearing facing the edge of a cliff. She held the hatchet against her chest and peered downward. It was too steep, especially in the immediate area. She searched left. The clearing led to an extremely steep, rocky hill. She searched right. The cliff yielded to a thick crop of trees. She swallowed and pushed right. Perhaps further along the cliff she would find a better place to descend. If not she could always duck into the woods.

She stumbled onward; her ankle throbbed and threatened. She peered over her shoulder; her heart all but leaped into her throat.

The sharpshooter had advanced through the woods and was entering the clearing. There was no time to climb down the cliff. She had to push toward the forest.

Another shot rang out. A shearing pain pierced Jenny's leg. She collapsed to the ground and the hatchet cart wheeled away from her. The bullet had grazed her outer right calf, and blood soaked through her jeans. *Get up, Jenny! Get up . . . and run!*

Bearing her weight on her left leg, she rose and struggled onward. After three steps she tumbled to the ground. *Don't give up, damn it! Don't you dare!*

She stretched forward and grabbed the hatchet. The rifle sounded and she heard the bullet zip past her left ear. The projectile struck the hatchet's handle, stinging her hand; the weapon flew from her grip. Tears came to her eyes as the most dismal, terrifying reality swept through her.

Uncertain of what to do, she rose to her knees and raised her left arm while keeping her right hand on the ground. *I can't go on running. I have to find another way.* She struggled to her feet, took a breath, and recognized the sound of footsteps.

Jenny swallowed, took another weary breath, and turned. Still wearing the ski mask and holding the rifle by his side, a figure clad in black stepped closer.

What is he waiting for? Why doesn't he just finish me?

She remembered the hatchet. It was behind her, just a few yards away. If only she could distract him . . .

The man halted approximately ten feet before her. He remained stationary for what seemed forever, staring at her through the eye slits in the mask. He lowered the rifle and glanced toward the forest. When he appeared satisfied, he yanked off the mask.

Chip's eyes blazed with contempt as he flaunted that arrogant grin of his. "Hi, honey. I'm back."

Jenny felt the corners of her mouth creep up. She hated being right. "What's the matter, jerk-off? Didn't you torment me enough the first time around?"

His grin faltered, his eyes narrowed. Dropping the mask, he placed his left hand beneath the rifle barrel. "Yeah, something like that." Working the bolt, he ejected the spent casing. He raised the weapon to his shoulder and peered through the sight beneath the scope.

Petrified, Jenny stared into the barrel. *He's going to kill me . . . I'm out of time.*

As her breath caught in her throat, she spotted movement over Chip's right shoulder. Something had just charged out of the woods. The object looked blurry, out of focus, but as it closed in, her mind registered the impossible. Still saddled, still very much wide-eyed and indignant, her mustang barreled toward them. "Good God," she screamed, "Maverick, get out of here!"

Chip whirled toward the horse. Jenny froze as her former husband aimed the rifle. *Do something, damn it! He's going to shoot him!* She threw herself down and grabbed the hatchet.

Maverick halted twelve feet away, reared, and hollered. Everything about him appeared enraged.

Chip sneered and placed his index finger on the trigger. Jenny jumped to her feet and threw the hatchet. It struck her former husband's right boot, piercing the heel. He screamed and dropped to his knees. Again Maverick hollered then galloped away.

Cursing, screaming, Chip wringed out the hatchet, then lurched toward Jenny. "You piece of shit!" Wiping his mouth, he aimed the rifle. "Ya know something? I'm *really* gonna enjoy this." Easing the trigger back, he flaunted one of his more scathing winks. "Say hi to that bitch, Arlene, for me."

Jenny's heart nearly stopped. She covered her head and ducked. Then, just above Chip's cursing, there was an audible click. A moment of silence lingered as time stood still. There was another click, followed by a third. She lowered her arms while her ex-husband's face turned blazing red.

Reacting quickly, Jenny lunged for the hatchet. As she scooped it up, the rifle came down, striking the back of her head. Pain ripped through her. She threw her arms around herself as a second blow struck her left elbow. She screamed, curled up, and braced for more. There was a lengthy pause as the ground beneath her pounded in a familiar manner.

Through her arms, she caught a glimpse of Chip pulling back, struggling with his injured heel. Again, the impossible shocked her.

Oh God . . . it's Maverick!

The mustang was all over her former husband – rearing high in the air, kicking his legs – preventing Chip from swinging the rifle.

Jenny picked up the hatchet and rose to her feet. *Now's my chance . . .*

Chip stumbled backward, his face a mass of blood, sweat, and grime. The mustang maintained a vicious onslaught, forcing him toward the cliff.

Jenny rushed over and swung her weapon. Chip tried to deflect the blow with his rifle, but Maverick kept him off balance. The hatchet sank deep into her ex-husband's left shoulder, severing both flesh and bone. Clutching his wound, he screamed and dropped forward. Jenny paused, trying to catch her breath. She wiped the perspiration from her eyes then watched as Maverick galloped away.

Chip raised his head. Blood spurted from his shoulder. Dirt and saliva seeped from his mouth. He cursed, struggled to his knees, then halted. His outraged expression abruptly transformed into a mixture of shock and fear. When Jenny discovered the source of his reaction, her spirits sprouted wings. *My God, he's caught in the cliff's downward slope.* Gravity, it seemed, had taken over.

Chip's eyes bulged in horror. He collapsed to the ground and dug his fingers in the dirt, trying to stop his momentum. It was only as he slipped over the edge that he managed to seize a half-buried rock. His slide halted, but from the waist down his body dangled over the edge. He babbled incoherently while the sun glared in his eyes.

Jenny watched in silence. *He can't pull himself up because of his shoulder.*

Chip grunted and spat out a large chunk of dirt. "Fuck! Goddamn it!"

A sly grin spread across Jenny's face. Seeing him so utterly beaten and in such horrible danger uplifted every pore in her body. Raising the hatchet, she crept within striking distance.

Chip could barely squint. His beard and every crevice around his eyes had been drenched with sweat. The more he struggled, the weaker he became. "Okay, okay, you win! I'm history! You'll never see me again! Now, just give me a goddamn hand, would ya?"

Jenny hesitated for a long, perplexing moment. Her victory had come at a dreadful price. Her body reeled in pain, and she still didn't know the extent of Maverick's injuries. The bastard had murdered Arlene and perhaps the O'Dells as well.

An eternity seemed to pass. She stood frozen with the hatchet held high, her mind, body, and soul craving to finish this wretched, painful ordeal. The weapon grew heavier, her arms trembled, cold, stark reality worked its way through her. How could she possibly kill another human being? Or just stand by and do nothing – except watch him die? It would be sinking to Chip's pathological level – possibly sending her to prison for the rest of her existence. He wasn't worth it! Fighting back her hatred, instincts, everything inside her, she lowered the hatchet and held out her hand.

Chip flashed another one of his arrogant grins. She stopped and straightened. *What are you doing? How can you trust anything that comes out of that lying mouth of his?* She raised the hatchet with both hands. "Haven't you heard?" she murmured. "Killing a crow's bad luck."

She heaved the weapon down with every ounce of her strength. The blade plunged through Chip's wrist and struck the rock as a gut-wrenching scream burst from his throat. He slid backward, leaving a bloody trail in his wake. He dropped from the edge and she heard him scream all the way down until, at long last, there was the inevitable, bone-crunching thud.

Jenny shook her head and sighed. *God, that must have really hurt!*

It took her a moment to catch her breath. She reached down and picked up Chip's severed hand. Holding it by the thumb, she examined it. The cut looked exceptionally clean and straight, a remarkable accomplishment. *Hmm . . . guess the hatchet wasn't such a messy weapon after all.*

Peering down the cliff, she spotted her ex-husband's body lying in a pool of blood. She held her breath and flung the hand through the air. It spiraled downward until it landed mere inches from Chip's crushed head. Exhaling, she murmured, "How's that for a goddamn hand?"

She turned and spotted Maverick creeping toward her. He appeared shaken but his gait looked unhampered and sturdy. She laughed and her heart soared. She tossed the hatchet over the cliff and rushed toward him.

"Thank you," she whispered, holding the mustang by his reins. "You saved me. You're not a horse, are you?" She paused and forced back a flood of tears. "You were *never* anything like a horse. You're more like . . . what? A guardian angel?"

Maverick snorted and nodded.

She inspected his body from head to hoof. A bullet had grazed his right shoulder, but it wasn't deep. There were two significant scrapes on his front legs, no doubt from his fall the day before. She would treat his injuries using the emergency kit from her saddlebag then watch for signs of infection.

"It's a good thing Chip wasn't a better shot," Jenny declared. "Otherwise we'd both be pushing up daisies." She held Maverick's head and gazed into his eyes. "When we get home, I'm buying you a *huge* supply of carrots."

Pulling away, the mustang appeared aloof and unimpressed.

"Okay, let me rephrase that. I'm buying you a *lifetime* supply of carrots!"

This time he whinnied and nodded enthusiastically.

She gave him a hug then treated his wounds. After attending to her own injuries and downing a warm, but nevertheless thirst-quenching, bottle of water, she climbed into the saddle. Maverick turned and looked at her as if she'd just gone out of her mind.

"Relax, old-timer. We're just backtracking to the O'Dells'. We have to call the police, and if I remember right, Dennis Conway would never be caught dead without his cell phone."

The mustang nodded. A gentle breeze caressed Jenny's face as they made their way toward the woods. She smiled. *From now on, I'm going to follow Maverick's example . . . and listen to my instincts.* Smiling once again, she realized her recovery was at last complete.

***

The following is an excerpt from the novel, *Forty Years Behind the Badge* by Joseph K. Logan.

CHAPTER 17

November 11, 2007 – Case #0054677, code name, "Murder and Mayhem on the Shady Trail Express."

I transferred from Orange County to San Bernardino County five years before retiring and just three years after my promotion to captain. The second case after my transfer will always remain one for the record books. Gruesome, to say the least, it was a classic case of the obsessive nature of revenge and how sociopathic our fellow humans can be.

Two of my subordinates, Detectives John Farley and Ted Malcolm, had kept me posted on the progress of case #0054677 in the county of San Bernardino. I became significantly involved with this particular case because of several complexities that included a number of out-of-state interviews. Allegedly, Jenny Trenton of Bloomington, California, while riding her horse in the Wrightwood area, had been assaulted by her former husband, Norman "Chip" Darnell, of Anderson, Iowa, and a second man, Dennis Conway, of Colton, California. After interviewing seventeen individuals, including both Trenton and a Jacqueline Candle, I was able to piece together the events that led to the deaths of several people.

For two days suspects Darnell and Conway had stalked Trenton in the Wrightwood area. Trenton and Darnell were previously involved in a bitter divorce and property settlement. What probably triggered the attack was a letter that Trenton had written to Darnell's fiancée, Miss Candle, exposing him for being an especially corrupt, financial predator. This led to Candle booting Darnell out of her life, and out of her numerous monetary investments as well. That must have infuriated Darnell, who returned to California and masterminded a plot to hunt Trenton down and inflict as much pain and damage on her as possible. He even enlisted the aid of his former business associate and cohort, Conway. Apparently the two men had a falling out, as Conway had confided to Trenton about her husband's business indiscretions, plus his many extramarital affairs. Of course Darnell found out about this breach of confidentiality and, utilizing it, along with Conway's own illegal activities, blackmailed his ex-cohort into cooperating with him.

Five weeks prior to the assault on Trenton, Darnell murdered a Miss Lindsey Barnes of San Bernardino, an exotic dancer and part-time hooker. He dumped her dismembered body in the vicinity where his ex-wife often rode her horse. This otherwise senseless act was evidently carried out in hopes of making the murders appear like serial killings, thus diverting suspicion from the two suspects.

Darnell had been familiar with most aspects of Trenton's life, including her monthly horseback rides to Marvin and Joan O'Dell's cabin near Wrightwood. To arrange for Miss Trenton to be on the trail alone, the two men murdered Arlene Mott, a close friend of Jenny Trenton's. In order to terrorize the woman to the fullest extent, and remain consistent with a serial killer's methods, they dismembered Mott's body and bagged the parts. Knowing the whereabouts of a spare house key, the two men planted Mott's remains in the O'Dells' wine cellar while the elderly couple was away on vacation. They even left a note for Trenton, making sure she found the body. The suspects also removed the O'Dells' telephones and several other items that could be used as weapons. They even killed one of Mott's dogs that harassed them on the trail between Mott's ranch and the O'Dells'.

Jenny Trenton rode the trail unaware of any of the abovementioned events. By the time she arrived at the O'Dells' cabin, she had been shot at and thrown from her horse. By means of circumstantial evidence, I was able to determine that these shots were primarily intended to intimidate her. The suspects burned Trenton out of the cabin and she spent the night in a shed. The next morning, Conway attacked her and, in the struggle, Darnell blew his cohort's brains out with his Remington 700 model, bolt-action rifle. It was never determined if Darnell botched the shot or if it was an act of premeditated murder. In my opinion it was probably the latter, because Conway had extensive knowledge of Darnell's many fraudulent activities. By murdering Conway, Darnell could protect himself and eliminate both his problems in one convenient maneuver.

Darnell pursued Trenton to a cliff. Several more shots were fired and Remington bullet casings were found at the scene. Miraculously, Trenton's horse saved her by distracting Darnell long enough for her to overcome him. His body was recovered at the bottom of a gorge along with his rifle. It seemed that during the struggle, Trenton forced Darnell off the cliff by chopping through his right hand with a hatchet. A few miles west of the crime scene, a Ford Explorer that Darnell had rented with a fake ID was also recovered. Inside the vehicle were the O'Dells' missing telephones and other various items.

Trenton was greatly relieved to discover that the O'Dells had not been harmed. The elderly couple returned home from their vacation, only to find their house and all their belongings had been incinerated. During their many years together, the couple had acquired a lifetime of collectable items. After a yearlong battle with their insurance company, they received a settlement of well over a million dollars. They are currently residing in southern Florida, and for their sake, I hope they remain safe during the hurricane season.

The D.A.'s office of San Bernardino County took an unusual interest in this particular case. Since Trenton admitted that she *intentionally* killed Darnell, the district attorney, who I will refer to as Edward Foster, requested a highly detailed report. Our team included detectives Farley, Malcolm, and myself, and the investigation, conducted in various locations in California and Iowa, took eight weeks. My report included any relevant background on Trenton, Darnell, Conway, and the events that took place on November 10th through the 11th, 2007. Although I was aware there were several gambling pools going on within our department concerning the outcome of this particular case, I never took part in any of them. I have to admit, however, I was rooting for Trenton, but since she was the underdog, the odds were obviously stacked against her.

On February 3, 2008, I handed over my 150 page report to the district attorney. I sat in his office while he reviewed it. I had known

Foster for nearly thirty years. He had always been a stickler for carrying out the letter of the law and was an extremely aggressive prosecutor. He sat behind his desk and read my entire chronicle, page by page, which took him nearly four hours. Even though I went through great pains to make every detail clear, every now and then he wanted me to clarify a point. I drank seven cups of coffee during that time.

When Foster at last finished, he stood and handed me the file. I remained in my seat and prepared myself for Jenny Trenton's dismal fate.

The district attorney stepped away from his desk and stared out the office window. The wall clock ticked away the seconds. It became so quiet I could almost hear the man thinking. After what felt like hours, he turned and regarded me with those penetrating eyes of his. "Fuck Darnell," he murmured. "He got what he deserved."

In all my forty years on the force, there was never a case quite like "Murder and Mayhem on the Shady Trail Express." Even after all my experiences, this particular case taught me that justice can be served – but sometimes in ways you'd never expect.

PIZZA PAL

The following is an excerpt from the novel, *Forty Years Behind the Badge*, by Joseph K. Logan.

Chapter Four

After years of late night stakeouts and endless patrols in the city of Santa Ana, my transfer finally came through. My new beat was the swing shift in the beautiful community of Newport Beach, California. Even better, I was transferred from vice to homicide. My days of busting pimps, prostitutes, and drug addicts were over. Sure, Newport had its share of drunken beach parties, but considering the majority of the citizens were law bidding and respectable, the homicide rate barely existed. Compared to Santa Ana, I was certain that my new assignment would be a cinch. Six months later I found out differently. On a single night in July of 1975, everything I knew to be legit and rational blew up in my face.

It was a Monday afternoon and I reported to work twenty minutes early. The day was blistering and dayshift was about to pack it in. Some of the guys just looked at me and laughed. I suspected then something ugly was about to hit the fan.

Case #0030395: Code Name: Murder and Mayhem at Pizza Pal.

"Hey, Joe," my partner, Frank Romano, greeted. "Ahab wants to see us on the double."

Our captain's name was Gerald Anders, but because he limped from an old gunshot wound, the guys nicknamed him "Ahab." No one ever called him that to his face, however, because, when he lost his temper, his kisser would turn into a fireball. In fact, he would have made superintendent if he hadn't shattered some pimp's nose.

I glanced at my watch. "What are you doing here so early, Frank?"

My partner shrugged. "No reason. I just had one of those feelings . . ."

I groaned and rolled my eyes.

"I think tonight's gonna be a bad one, Joe. A real nasty, top-of-the-line, ball-buster."

That was Frank. Nearly every night he had a hunch about something. After seventeen years on the force, he considered himself a *bona fide* psychic.

As usual, Ahab's office looked a mess. You couldn't see his desk through all the file folders and candy wrappers. The guy was a chocolate freak and claimed eating lots of sugar actually calmed him down.

Captain Anders glanced up. In one hand he held a wanted poster, in the other a Hershey Bar. "You're early. Good. Rodriguez and Benson are babysitting a kid in I-3. Overtime's *kaput* and they have to knock off. They'll debrief you when you get there."

Feeling like a pair of yo-yos, Frank and I hurried off. I never even had a chance for a cup of coffee. Rodriguez and Benson were watching some guy through the one-way glass. Benson was munching on a donut; Rodriguez did all the talking.

"His name's Shawn Duncan and he was picked up on a disturbance over at Pizza Pal on Newport Boulevard. Claims his roommate, Donald Cappella, was murdered by the restaurant's owner, a Mister Nick Costello."

"Yeah, I know Nick," Frank offered. "He makes one hell of a pizza."

Rodriguez and Benson just stared at him.

"So where's the stiff?" I asked.

"There isn't one," Rodriguez fired back, "but Cappella's parents claim he's been missing for a couple of days."

Looking amused, they left. It was the same old thing – dayshift had just dumped another deadbeat case on us.

Frank and I scrutinized the kid. He wore collar-length hair and long sideburns. His clothes were wrinkled and there were blood stains on his shirt. He was fidgeting in his chair and kept looking our way. The guy was either on drugs, terrified – or both.

"What do you make of him, Joe?"

"I don't even know why we have to bother," I grumbled. "The roommate's probably shacked up someplace, stoned to the gills."

Frank shook his head. "I dunno know, Joe. I got a bad feeling about this . . ."

I took a long look at my partner. The lenses to his glasses were filthy, and he must have been gardening, because that humongous nose of his looked like a big, old, red chili pepper. "There you go again with those hunches of yours! Every day it's the same old thing."

"You just wait and see. As sure as that kid's gonna spill his guts, this time I'm right."

I rolled my eyes and left the room. We've only been partners for six months and already we're bickering like an old married couple.

While Frank watched through the one-way glass, I hurried to Interrogation Room Three, or as we call it, I-3. I've always hated those fluorescent lights in there. They make people look like they're half dead. I glanced at the kid sitting on the other side of the table, Shawn Duncan. He was probably around twenty-four, but to me he still looked like a kid, not to mention acting like something had just crept over his grave.

"I'm Sergeant Joe Logan." I sat down across from him. "I want to ask you a few questions."

He nodded. Sweat was already trickling down his face.

I hit the record button on the tape machine. "Did the other officers explain that whatever you say will be considered voluntary?"

He nodded again.

I shook my head. "You have to talk *out loud* because of the machine."

"Yes, they explained that."

"And anything you say may be held against you?"

His eyes widened and he leaned forward. "What for? I'm just trying to *report* a murder. It's not like I killed anyone."

I held back a grin. "Sure, kid, I understand. So, if you're okay, we'll proceed. Why don't you start at the beginning?"

"Aren't you gonna offer me a cigarette first?"

I shrugged and knew then it was going to be a long night. "What are ya talking about?"

"You know, like they do on television?"

"That's a load of crap, kid. We never do that stuff." I pulled out a pen to take notes with. "Now, let's get started."

The kid nodded and cleared his throat. "I just want to say one thing first."

I somehow managed not to roll my eyes. I tend to do that when I'm irritated. "Sure, why not? I've got all night."

"I know what I'm about to tell you will sound unbelievable, like some kind of fairy tale, or something, but if you don't take me seriously, then a lot *more* people are going to die. Do you understand?"

"Sure, I get it."

Fidgeting around some more, he wiped the sweat from his brow. "Okay, Sergeant, you'd better hold on to your seat, because what I'm about to tell you . . . will blow your ever-loving mind."

***

"My friend's name is Donnie Cappella – D.C. for short. He's my roommate and he's been missing since Friday night. We've been best friends since grammar school. He's a little goofy, but basically he's a good guy, and we've done everything together: double dating, all-you-can-eat buffets, you name it, we've done it. When I moved out of my parents' house, we rented the apartment where we're at now, a place called Paradise Cove on Newport Boulevard. Even though D.C. couldn't always help with the rent, things worked out okay.

"I'm an L.V.N. over at Harbor Hospital. Donnie used to have a job there, working as a janitor, but that ended when they caught him sleeping.

"A few months ago we started eating at Pizza Pal, a little hole-in-the-wall place just across the parking lot from our apartment. Even from a block away, the aroma from all that food hits you like a Mack truck, making you hungry, right then and there. They serve mind-boggling pizzas and all kinds of other Italian cooking. There's two separate entrances, front and back. At the front, there's just a little dining area with a few tables and chairs. In the back, there's an even smaller area for take-outs. The place always looks dirty, but the food's sensational. And I ought to know, I used to work in a pizza parlor back when I was a teenager.

"Donnie and me usually did the take-out thing. For a change of pace, we would alternate pizza with either spaghetti or lasagna. Almost every time while we were waiting for our meal, there would be someone in the kitchen yelling in Italian. We never actually saw the guy, so one day we asked about him.

"The kid behind the counter, whose name was Mario, looked over his shoulder. 'Oh, that's Nick Costello, the owner,' he told us.

"I shook my head and said, 'It seems like every time we're in here, he's chewing someone out.'

"Mario chuckled. 'Yeah, that's just the way he is.'

"A couple of days later we were back and there was a 'Help Wanted' sign in the window. Donnie noticed it and asked, 'Hey, what do ya think? Maybe I can cook pizzas for a living.'

"I shrugged my shoulders. 'I don't know, D.C. Every time we're in here, the owner's back there screaming his lungs out. Do you really want to deal with that?'

"Donnie smiled. 'I can take it. Besides, maybe I can bring home some freebies.'

"I nodded and smiled back. He had a point there.

"After we ordered our takeout, Donnie asked about the job. The kid behind the counter wasn't the same one as before. This guy's name was Felix. He said there was an opening because Mario hadn't shown up for work. Donnie filled out an application while we waited for our food.

"When our order came up, Felix took the form and ducked into the kitchen.

"A little while later Nick Costello came walking out. The man actually filled the doorway. He must have been about six foot seven and at least 275 pounds. He wore a chef's hat, had black hair and the darkest eyes I'd ever seen. Even his mustache was gigantic. He just stood behind the counter, stared at us, and never said a word. My blood temperature must have dropped by ten degrees. But it was all lost on Donnie. He just gazed at the guy and smiled.

"Nick returned to the back and we heard some mumbling. A few seconds later Felix popped out and asked D.C. if he could start the next day.

"Donnie jumped to his feet. 'Sure, what time?'

"The kid hesitated and glanced toward the kitchen. It looked to me like he wanted to say something, but couldn't. 'Come in around four,' he finally answered.

"We hurried out and that was the beginning of the end of my friend, Donnie Cappella."

* * *

I paused the tape recorder. "Just how long of a story is this?"

The kid shrugged. "Not real long. Why?"

"How about if we just cut to the chase?"

He frowned and snapped, "Do you want to know what happened or not?"

"Yeah, of course I do. But for God's sake, do we have to reinvent *Gone with the Wind*?"

That's when the kid got feisty. "Listen, Sergeant, either I tell it my way, or it's the highway."

I groaned and shook my head. Back then, patience was never one of my strong suits. "Yeah, all right, go ahead, but I was just joking about having all night."

The kid nodded and I released the pause button.

* * *

"Donnie started working at Pizza Pal mainly on weekends. He would work until midnight when they closed. Most nights I would be asleep when he came home, but the next morning there would be all kinds of Italian food in our refrigerator. It wasn't long before Donnie and me started putting on the pounds.

"D.C. would tell me all types of stories about Nick. The guy chewed out at least one employee every single night. He'd jump down some poor kid's throat over the most minor infraction. It didn't take us long to realize that Nick Costello, possibly the greatest chef in California, was, in reality, a closet Mussolini.

"On one of D.C.'s nights off, we took in a movie. I'd been hearing a lot of buzz about this flick called *Jaws*. The theater was right next door to Pizza Pal. During the middle of the movie when the shark was chasing after a guy who fell off a pier, we spotted Nick hurrying down the aisle. I guess he was looking for some jerk who had ducked out without paying his bill. As Nick turned and walked back up the aisle, Donnie and I yelled, 'Hey Nick, how's it going?'

"Without even slowing down, he glared at us and mumbled something that sounded *really* intimidating.

"As he passed by us, I almost melted into my seat. 'What the hell was that in his hand?' I asked D.C.

"Donnie stopped munching on his popcorn and answered, 'I think it mighta been his meat cleaver.'

"A couple of days later, I was in bed with my new girlfriend, Louise. We'd just finished having sex when Donnie knocked on my bedroom door, wanting me to come out.

"I got dressed and he handed me a newspaper article entitled, *PARENTS OF MISSING YOUTH ASK FOR HELP.* To my amazement, the story featured a photo of Mario Pinza, the same kid we knew from Pizza Pal.

"I sat the paper down. 'Holy shit, no wonder he never showed for work.'

"Donnie nodded. 'Yeah, and he's not the first person to disappear. Two other people from Garden Grove are missing.'

"A few more weeks rolled by and nothing ever surfaced about Mario. Then one Saturday night Louise asked me to take her to Pizza Pal for dinner. The place was packed, but for a change, it was pretty quiet in the kitchen. Donnie came over and greeted us. 'Hey, can't get enough Italian, huh?'

"I laughed and pointed at Louise. 'She's been dying to see the place.'

"Donnie glanced at Felix, who gave him the thumbs up sign. 'Well, then, how 'bout a little tour?'

"It turned out that Nick had taken off and left Felix in charge. As D.C. led us to the kitchen, I asked, 'Isn't it unusual for your boss to leave early, especially on a Saturday night?'

"Donnie laughed. 'Yeah, normally the guy's a real workaholic.'

"So Louise and I got the grand tour. The first thing we saw was a cast iron stove with huge pots of simmering sauce. There was a large, stainless steel pizza oven, a cutting table and take-out boxes stacked clear to the ceiling. Donnie showed us the huge blender that mixes the pizza dough and the rolling machine with the two metal cylinders that flatten it. Although I used to work in a pizza parlor, I still enjoyed myself and found it a great way to work up an appetite.

"Then I asked about a door near the kitchen that had a padlock on it.

"D.C. glanced over. 'Oh, that goes to Nick's apartment.'

"I was shocked. 'You mean the guy *lives* here?'

"Donnie shrugged his shoulders. 'No, Felix says he has a house over in Garden Grove. I think he just crashes here when he's too tired to drive home.'

"I glanced at Louise and smiled. 'Maybe he uses the place to lure chicks into, you know? For when he wants to play hide the salami.'

"Both Donnie and Louise turned red, but I just kept on talking. 'He probably seduces them by using his sauces as an aphrodisiac. The guy's probably the world's biggest pervert!'

"Donnie's bulging eyes kept staring over my shoulder. So I turned around and there was Nick Costello towering over me. Sweat was pouring down his face and his hands were clenched into huge fists. As I live and breathe, I thought I'd just bought the farm. He said something in Italian and Donnie took us back to our table.

"As we sat down, I apologized to D.C. for getting him into trouble. But he said not to worry. Then I asked Donnie if Nick was touchy about customers poking around in his kitchen.

"He chuckled and said, 'Hell, he's touchy about everything!'

"Then I asked him how he understood what Nick was saying. As far as I knew, Donnie didn't speak a word of Italian.

"Looking a bit confused, D.C. answered, 'I always understand him. I don't know how, but I just do.'

"That same night, Louise and I decided to wait up for Donnie. By the time he came home, it was a quarter past midnight. We were on the couch watching a movie called "The Seventh Voyage of Sinbad." We were at the part where the giant Cyclops tied one of the sailors to a spit and began to roast him alive. The monster just sat on a stool, turning the spit and licking his chops.

"When Donnie strolled in, I asked 'So, what's the verdict, *amigo*? Did Nick just chew you out . . . or did he fire you?'

"D.C. glanced at the TV and then stared a long time down the hallway. 'Why would he do that?'

"I kind of checked him out for a second. He looked different, like he was in a trance or something. 'Because of how he caught us in his kitchen, that's why, not to mention how I put him down . . . big time.'

"Donnie headed toward his room just like he was sleepwalking. Over his shoulder, he mumbled, 'He never mentioned it.'

"That was pretty much how it went for the next couple of days. Donnie seemed to be avoiding me whenever he could. He began working longer hours and when I asked him about it, he said Felix had quit and Nick needed the extra help. Even when I brought up that far-away look in his eyes, Donnie denied it. But later on, Louise came over with a newspaper article. This time it was about Felix. His parents had reported him missing.

"The next time I saw D.C., I showed him the article. He shrugged his shoulders and handed it back. He never even showed the slightest concern. I was worried about him, so I called Newport P.D. They transferred me to the Missing Persons Department. An Officer Jackson answered. He seemed skeptical, but I think he wrote down what I had to say about Mario and Felix. When I was done, I asked him what he thought. After a long pause, he said he didn't think the two cases were related. Just by his tone, I knew I had struck out. So I made a really lame decision, and started a little investigation of my own.

"The hospital where I work is right down the street from Pizza Pal. Last Thursday, I decided to have lunch there. I don't like eating anything heavy when I'm working, so for a change I was going to order a salad. I walked into the dining room and the little bell on the door jingled. Of course, the mouth-watering aroma clobbered me, so I thought . . . *the hell with it, I'm ordering a pizza!* I looked around. There were only two other customers – a pair of hippies sitting at a far table. Donnie was on his days off. In fact, he'd mentioned something about watching his parents' house while they were away on vacation.

"Apparently, Nick's employees weren't around, because when I approached the counter, the man himself walked out. In all the times I'd been there, I had never seen him wait on a single customer. He saw me and the most threatening leer stretched across his face.

"He tossed a towel on the counter and I felt like I was looking up at a sequoia. He barked at me in that gruff tone of his. I guess it was in Italian, but for some reason, I understood him. He'd just asked me what I wanted.

"I kept staring up at him. There was something red in his mustache, so I figured he'd been sampling some of his own sauce. 'One small pepperoni pizza and a Coke, please.' My voice sounded kind of weak and comical.

"Nick muttered in Italian and, completely beside myself, I answered, 'Yeah, it's for here.'

"He nodded and rung up my order on the cash register. I paid him and hurried to a table, but he kept staring at me. So I just sat there and realized that even if Nick was connected to the disappearances, he probably wouldn't be stupid enough to leave any evidence around.

"A few minutes later the two hippies left. Nick returned from the kitchen, gave me another one of his dirty looks, and dropped my lunch on the counter. I picked up my order while he poured me a Coke. He didn't say a word but stayed behind the register. I could tell he was suspicious . . . like he knew I was up to something . . . and he wasn't about to let me just sit there without being watched.

"Suddenly, Dominic, one of his employees, walked in and Nick waved him to the back. I overheard some muttering, and then Nick, giving me one last dirty look, rushed out the front door. Dominic stayed in the kitchen and turned on the rolling machine. But every few minutes he came out, gazed my way, then returned to the machine. I finished my pizza and headed to the cash register. Now that Nick had left, an idea finally hit me.

"When Dominic came out I asked him where the restrooms were. He looked at me as if I'd just flipped out and pointed to the sign over the hallway. I hurried to the men's room and counted to ten. I cracked the door open and sure enough, Dominic had returned to the back. I rushed down the hallway toward the door that led to Nick's apartment. The rear entrance to the kitchen was just around the corner, but I was pretty sure the rolling machine would be loud enough to drown out my activities.

"I thought it was strange, but the padlock on the door had been removed. I stepped inside and left the door open by a crack so I could hear the rolling machine. Inside there was just a single flight of steps. It was really dark and there were spider webs hanging off the ceiling. I started climbing and halfway up, one of the steps squeaked. Suddenly I was getting nervous and wondering what the hell I was doing. I was going to turn back when I saw the opened door at the top of the stairs, so I decided to keep going.

"I entered the apartment and, again, intentionally left the door open. I found myself standing in a dark, cramped living room with no phone and hardly any furniture – just a couch and TV.

"A butcher's block stood in the middle of the kitchen and what looked like blood was splattered all over it. I crept forward and another floorboard squeaked. Since it was so dark, I leaned over the sink and opened a blind. That was when I noticed a disgusting odor coming from the garbage disposal. It kind of smelled like something had died down there.

"I inched toward the refrigerator and there was some more blood on the handle. I worked up what was left of my courage and opened the door. Again, I noticed an odor, like the one coming from the disposal. No light came on, but sitting on the shelves were about twenty glass jars. All the labels had been removed and I couldn't make out the contents.

"I picked up the nearest jar and saw how badly my hands were shaking. The container felt heavy and there was something gross floating around inside it. I nearly gagged when I discovered the contents looked like a big old chunk of intestines.

"All of a sudden, I wasn't feeling so good. I returned the jar and pulled out another. When I held it to the light, a dozen eyeballs were staring at me. It caught me off guard and scared about ten years out of my life. I jumped so high I dropped the jar and it shattered on the floor.

"I nearly puked and passed out at the same time. Along with the liquid, and the broken glass, the eyeballs were scattered all over the place. Then I heard the rolling machine shut down and realized Dominic was on to me. I tried to kick the broken glass and eyeballs under the refrigerator, but there wasn't enough time to finish.

"From the base of the stairs, I heard Dominic shout, 'Hello?' Suddenly, my idea of leaving the stairwell doors open . . . seemed like a really stupid thing to do.

"I turned around and heard that same squeak in the middle of the staircase. I hurried out of the kitchen and began searching for a hiding place. I tried to avoid the loose floorboard but managed to step on it anyway. There was a loud squeak and, again caught off guard, I froze on the spot. But then the footsteps from the stairway also halted. *Stay still!* I told myself, *he'll hear me if I move.*

"I stood there for what seemed like a lot longer than it was . . . waiting for Dominic to start climbing again. As soon as he did, I rushed to the living room and looked around. There were two doors to the right – one to the bedroom and the other to the bathroom.

"Then, thank God, the bell that hung over the restaurant's door jingled, and a couple of seconds later, I heard Dominic's footsteps hurrying down the stairs. I took a breath and glanced at my watch. If I was careful, I could sneak out the back while the kid was busy with his customers. But when I reached the apartment's front door, I discovered Dominic had locked it!

"I got frantic and totally nuts. Not caring who heard me, I screamed and punched the refrigerator. I leaned over the sink, cursed, and tried to calm myself down. Then, as I gazed out the window, I saw a sight that chilled me like a cold blast from the North Pole. Nick Costello was hurrying back to Pizza Pal.

"I stumbled around, slipped on an eyeball, and crashed headfirst onto the floor. Knowing I could end up on Nick's butcher's block, I went crazy. I shot up and ran to the window by the sink, but no matter how hard I tried, I couldn't budge it. Then I heard Nick's voice all the way from the downstairs kitchen. I couldn't hear what Dominic was saying . . . but I didn't have to . . . because I knew the little creep was ratting me out.

"I hurried to another window and, using everything I had, managed to inch it up. As I struggled, I heard what sounded like a herd of buffalos rush up the stairs. I was sweating and my heart went ballistic . . . but I finally lifted the window.

"A set of keys jangled from the other side of the door. I glanced outside and, instead of a two-story drop, the roof to the dining room was just a few feet below. While I climbed through, I heard a key unlocking the door. Just as it flew open, I dropped out the window.

"The second I hit the roof top, I hurried over and jumped again. This time the drop was a lot farther down and my ankles took a beating.

"I hobbled off . . . glad to be alive. But being curious, I stopped and looked back. Nick was in the window staring down at me, and I swear his eyes were as big as baseballs. The pupils weren't even round! I know it's going to sound completely whacko, but they were shaped like black diamonds! I swear – you can strap me to a lie detector if you want – but there was nothing human about those eyes of his."

***

I paused the tape recorder and flipped on the intercom. "Frank, you there?"

"Yeah, Joe?"

"Get me some frickin coffee, would ya?" I glanced at Shawn Duncan. "You want some?"

He raised an eyebrow. "How about a soda?"

Holding back a chuckle, I answered, "Sorry, we're fresh out."

He sighed and leaned back. "You don't believe me, do you?"

I almost felt sorry for the kid. It was a good thing there was a state hospital over In Norwalk. Maybe *they* could help him out. "I dunno, kid. It's not for me to say."

"So what's the point of going on? We might as well call it quits right now."

"It's not up to you anymore," I said. "You've got blood on your shirt and you're telling me someone *else* murdered your roommate?"

Frank brought in a cup of coffee. I took a sip and asked him to join me in the hallway.

"So, what do ya think?" I asked.

He shrugged and his nose looked even redder than before. "I dunno. He's either scared, crazy, or both. Hell, I told ya this was gonna be a bad one."

I took another sip. "Ask Ahab to check which judge is on call, just in case we need a search warrant."

"Ya know, this whole thing's getting out of hand . . ."

"Yeah, but what bugs me is that this kid actually *believes* what he's saying."

My partner looked like he was about to step off a cliff. "Okay, Joe. You're doing fine. Just let the kid talk. Sooner or later he'll incriminate himself."

Frank took off and I returned to I-3. Looking like he hadn't slept in days, Shawn Duncan just stared at me.

I tilted my head and popped out a nasty crick in my neck "Okay," I said, "let's wrap this up."

***

"After that whole thing at Pizza Pal, I called my boss and told him something had come up, and I couldn't come back to work. Then I called you guys. I had no proof that Nick was killing and chopping people up . . . and, who knows, maybe even serving body parts in his customers' food, but if someone would just search that apartment, they would find plenty of evidence.

"No sooner than I got connected, Donnie walked in. I hung up the phone, which turned out to be a really stupid thing to do, sat D.C. down, and told him everything, *especially* about the eyeballs. Right away I noticed he was back to his old self. Then I remembered he'd been staying at his parents' house and hadn't been anywhere near Nick Costello.

"Donnie jumped up and headed toward the kitchen. 'The cops will think you're nuts without some kind of proof,' he said.

"I was really happy to see the change in D.C. and followed him into the kitchen. 'I don't know how we're going to do that, *amigo*. I'll be damned if I'm ever going back there again.'

"Then, blowing me away, he started dishing out Pizza Pal spaghetti from a carton. 'Hey, what the hell are you doing?'

"He just looked at me with those goofy eyes of his. 'I'm starving! You don't think there's anything . . . bad . . . in this, do ya?'

"That's when I lost my cool and punched the carton. Before I knew it, there's spaghetti everywhere, including the ceiling fan. Donnie yelled, 'Hey man, that cost me two-fifty!'

"I shook my head. 'If you really believed me, then why would you want to eat that crap?'

"D.C. stepped over the carton and began making a ham sandwich. 'You know, I could take a look around the place. I'm supposed to go back there tomorrow.'

"I nearly blew a gasket. 'Are you crazy? You can't do that!'

"Donnie sighed. 'First of all, we don't know if the stuff you saw was even human. If I can sneak into Nick's apartment and swipe an eyeball or something, then we can take it to the cops.'

"I rubbed my forehead. 'No, it's too risky. Just quit! You can call Nick right now and tell him you're history. I'll call the police. If they don't believe me, then that's *their* fault.'

"Donnie finished making his sandwich and took a huge bite. 'Just let me work tomorrow and I'll prove it one way or the other. If you're right, we'll be heroes. But if you're wrong, then I'll still have my job and you'll still have your rent money.'

"I found myself in a state of shock. For once, he was right.

"Donnie sat down and wiped a big glob of spaghetti off the kitchen table. 'I'm supposed to be in charge tomorrow, so that means Nick won't be around. Besides, I want to take a peek in that basement of his.'

"I had to make a huge effort not to stutter. 'There's a *basement* in that place?'

"D.C. smiled. A piece of ham was stuck on one of his front teeth. 'Yeah, and it's always locked, but I'll have the keys. If Nick's hiding anything, I'll bet ya a million bucks it'll be down there.'

***

"By the time I got home from work the next day, Donnie had already left. But I had phoned earlier to remind him not to take any chances.

"It was Friday night and Pizza Pal would be open until midnight. I tried to wait up for D.C. but nodded out while I was watching TV. By the time I woke up it was already 2:00 AM. There was a movie on, I think it was called "The Lost World." Just as I started watching it, some poor guy got eaten by a giant lizard. That was when I jumped off the couch.

"I rushed down the hallway to check Donnie's room, but he wasn't there. I broke into a sweat and didn't know what to do. He knew I was waiting for him, so I felt positive he'd come home right away. Although the thought of it scared me, I figured I'd better check out the restaurant anyway.

"I hurried through the parking lot that led to the outdoor mall where Pizza Pal's located. There were a few lights along the way, but other than that, it was pretty dark.

"The closer I came to the restaurant, the more nervous I became. After all the stuff that happened with Nick, I thought I'd never go near the place again.

"As I crept down the mall, I felt like I was in the middle of a ghost town. The store lights were turned off and the place looked completely isolated. As I approached, I began to shiver like it was ten below.

"Pizza Pal was quiet both inside and out. I glanced at the window where Nick had spotted me. It was so dark I couldn't even see the blind. I turned to the front entrance. A "Sorry We're Closed" sign hung on it. But what really floored me was the "Help Wanted" sign in the window. The last time I saw one of those, Mario turned up missing.

"Suddenly, from behind, a hand grabbed me. I jumped straight in the air and then found myself facing a shadowy figure. It was Dominic, Nick's employee, and he was obviously ticked off. 'H-hey, why are you always sneaking around?' he demanded.

"The beer on his breath nearly gagged me. 'I'm looking for Donnie,' I answered. 'Have you seen him?'

"Although it was dark, I could tell he was pretty wasted. 'We went out after c-closing and had a few beers. When he left, he said he was headed to F-Fountain Valley.'

"I was absolutely mortified. 'He went to his parents' house?'

"Dominic nodded. He could barely stand and I began wondering what he was doing here so late. 'Did Nick work tonight?' I asked.

"The kid waved his hand and belched. 'Yeah, he popped in. Why don't ya lay off the guy? He minds his own business and here ya are sneaking around.'

"I swallowed and promised to behave myself. Evidently, Dominic didn't have a clue about his boss's activities. I watched as he stumbled off, but then he halted and turned around. 'Oh, by the way, Nick wants to see ya.'

"It felt like he'd just punched me in the face. 'He does?'

"Dominic chuckled. 'Y-yeah, says he wants to *hack* things out.'

"And without another word, he turned and staggered away.

***

"I didn't sleep for the rest of the night. I tried, but my mind kept on the fast track. Did Nick really want to meet with me, or was it just a ploy to get me alone? And why didn't Donnie come home? Every time I closed my eyes I would see Nick's distorted face with those gigantic eyes of his. In fact, that entire weekend, I only slept for a couple of hours.

"My shift began at Harbor Hospital at 6:30 AM. On my morning break I tried calling Donnie's parents. In fact, I tried calling them three times from work, and several times later, but no one ever answered. When I came home, I found the apartment empty. I was beginning to think I would never see D.C. again.

"It turned out to be another lousy, miserable night. I called Louise and began telling her what was going on. I never even had the chance to finish. She said I was nuts and dumped me right then and there. I got totally plastered, thinking it would help me sleep, but it didn't.

"The next day I called the hospital, told my boss I was sick, and drove over to Donnie's parents' house. No one answered and I began wondering if they were still on vacation.

"I hurried back home and called the police. They transferred me to the Missing Persons Department again. I can't remember who I talked to, but it wasn't Officer Jackson. I told the guy everything except for the really weird stuff because I didn't think anyone who was even remotely sane would believe me. He said if Donnie hadn't shown up by tomorrow morning to come in and fill out a report.

"But tomorrow wasn't good enough. Donnie had been missing for nearly two days and I couldn't just sit around. So rather than go stir-crazy, I headed to Pizza Pal.

"It was about 6:30 PM and I knew on Sundays they close by 7:00. If I waited, maybe I could figure out a way to sneak into the basement. But the first thing I had to do was to see if Nick was there or not.

"I kept a safe distance and peeked around the corner of a clothing store across from the restaurant's front entrance. There were no signs of Nick or any of his employees. Thinking I'd better check the back, I hurried to the other side and peeked out from behind a parked car. Right away I spotted Nick and couldn't believe what I was seeing. He was just standing by the glass door hiding his hands behind his back, staring at me.

"I freaked out and ran all the way home. How the hell did he know I was coming? And what in blazes was he holding behind his back?

"Once I was inside my apartment, I locked the door and again called Donnie's parents. His mom finally answered. They had just returned from their vacation and she told me Donnie wasn't there. Of course, they knew their son had been around by all the empty pizza boxes he'd left behind. She then said 'He might be at his girlfriend's house.'

"I nearly had a cow. 'Donnie has a girlfriend?'

"'Yes,' she confirmed, 'at least I *think* he does.' She went on to say that D.C. had expressed some interest in a girl named Barbara Jean. I thanked Mrs. Cappella and hung up.

"I remembered there was a Barbara who worked at Pizza Pal. Donnie had mentioned her a couple of times. But I just couldn't believe he would forget our plan and shack up with her. Besides, no offense, Donnie was never much of a ladies' man.

"I began pacing back and forth and brainstorming. I was tempted to sneak back to Pizza Pal during the night to see if I could find a way in. If only I knew the whereabouts of that basement key.

"So I had another rotten night. I watched TV, flipped through some old photo albums, and took a stab at reading.

"Sometime after dawn, I woke up on the couch. I had dozed off and dreamed that Donnie had finally shown up. I was hoping to hear how he was over at Barbara Jean's, but he just sort of looked at me with those goofy, but sad, eyes of his. 'Nick killed me,' he cried. 'He cut me up into tiny pieces. He's a real monster, Shawn, the genuine article. Ya gotta stop him! He'll go after Barbara next, or maybe even you. Ya have to stop him . . . before it's too late!' That's when I forgot about the police department.

"So, this morning – my day off – I was so tired I could barely see straight, but I climbed into my car, and drove across the parking lot and pulled up by Pizza Pal's back entrance. I sat and waited. I had a perfect view of both front and back exits. Nick was probably upstairs and his employees would be showing up around 10:00. According to Donnie, on Mondays Nick would leave at 10:15 with a satchel of money and deposit it at the bank across the street. I wouldn't have much time, but while he was away, I could search the basement.

"At about 10:00, I saw Barbara knocking on the front door. I couldn't see who, but someone let her inside. Five minutes later, Dominic turned up, but there wasn't a sign of Nick. A little after 11:00 customers started coming in. I kept waiting, but by 2:00 I realized it was time to tell the police everything, right down to those eyeballs in that glass jar I'd dropped.

"Just as I was about to take off, I saw Nick leaving through the front entrance. In his hand was a satchel all right, just like Donnie had said.

"I hurried toward the back entrance and barged in. There was a little bell on that door, too. Dominic came out wearing that faraway look in his eyes, just like Donnie had a few days before. He approached me and murmured, 'We're not gonna serve you anymore.'

"I told him, 'Fine by me, but I'm here to search the basement.'

"Barbara came up behind Dominic. As far as I could see, her eyes looked perfectly normal. 'Why would you want to do that?' she asked.

"I swallowed and answered, 'Because three people are missing and Donnie's one of them. I don't know about you, but I'm pretty sure that basement has some answers.'

"Dominic simply muttered 'Take a hike, or we'll call the cops.'

"That was when I noticed a large set of keys clipped to his belt. I knew one of them had to be to the basement, so I stepped around the counter like I was going to sneak by them. Then as Dominic reached for my arm, I snatched the keys off his belt. When he tried to grab them back, I pushed him into Barbara and they both fell to the floor.

"I ran up the hallway and hung a right. There was a descending staircase that led to a door. There was no padlock, just a doorknob with a keyhole. When I reached it, I inserted one of the keys. Dominic hurried down, grabbed my shoulder and spun me around. I hauled off and slugged him a good one. He flew into the stairs and I saw his upper lip had split open. That's how I got these blood stains on my shirt. From Dominic . . . not Donnie.

"Barbara caught up and started hitting me with a broom. Then Dominic jumped to his feet and ran up the stairs. I hated to do it, but I grabbed the broom and shoved Barbara to the floor. I inserted another key, and when I turned it, there was a click. But Barbara grabbed me around my legs and was trying to topple me over. Just as I started to push the door open, I heard Dominic running back down the stairs. His eyes were no longer distant. In fact, they were glaring. He pointed a butcher's knife about two inches from my face. 'Hand over those goddamned keys and shut that door!' he shouted."

***

I popped out another crick in my neck, and turned off the tape machine. The kid's hair looked soaked and his eyelids were drooping. "Would you like some coffee, or a glass of water?" I asked.

He nodded. "Sure, some water would be great."

I picked up my coffee cup, opened the door, and strolled down the hallway. There was a window to my left and I could see it was already dark outside. The door to the observation room had been left open. Inside, Ahab had joined my partner and was sitting on top of the table with his arms crossed. Frank was leaning against a wall.

They were both staring at the one-way glass. I walked by them and grabbed a paper cup from the water cooler.

Ahab shook his head. "Christ, in all my years on the force, I've never heard such bullshit."

"Do we have any priors on Costello?" I asked.

My partner sighed. "Nope, he's clean."

"What about the kid's story? Does any of it check out?"

"Well, those two teenagers he mentioned, Mario and Felix, *are* missing." Frank shifted about, looking like his jockey shorts were cramping his style. "Both Jackson and Snyder over in Missing Person's did report phone calls from a Shawn Duncan."

"I'll get the warrant if you want." Ahab frowned and unwrapped a Snickers bar. "Whether this kid is telling the truth or not, either way someone's screwed. Missing Persons fouled up on those two teenagers, so if Duncan's story pans out, then their asses are in a sling." He shook his head and took a bite out of the candy bar. "But if his story doesn't pan out, then the three of us will look like a bunch of first-class morons."

I stepped away from the water cooler. "You seem to know Costello, Frank. What do you think?"

My partner shrugged. "Well, I've only seen him a couple of times. Other than liking his cooking, I don't actually *know* the guy."

Ahab chuckled. "What do you think of his cooking now?"

Frank turned a little green, but his nose still looked red. "If you don't mind, Captain, I'd rather not say."

Ahab grunted, slid off the table and gazed at me. "So, what do you wanna do, Logan?"

I stared into the one-way glass. Shawn Duncan was hunched over on top of the table, dead asleep. "Three kids are missing." I replied. "Let's get the warrant and check it out for ourselves."

***

Frank and I climbed into our vehicle, a 1974 Ford Galaxy. In my hand I held a search warrant all signed and ready to go. A pair of uniforms were already waiting for us at the pizza parlor, a mere ten minutes away. Eating a pastrami sandwich on rye, Frank nearly rear-ended a brand new Mercedes.

"Damn it!" I hollered. "Haven't I told you not to eat while you're driving?"

Frank set his dinner aside. "Sorry, Joe." He slowed down and pulled to the right lane. "So, what about that kid's story? Do you think it's on the level?"

I tilted my head and popped out another crick in my neck. "I sure hope not."

"I told ya this was gonna be a bad one, Joe. Three kids are missing and a local business owner just might be . . . a freaking cannibal." He stopped at a light and gaped at me. "And to top it off, I've eaten there more times than I can remember!"

I rolled my eyes. "Would you just drop it?"

"And didn't I take you there a couple of times, on our dinner breaks?"

My stomach dropped a load of acid. "Yeah, so what?"

The light turned green and Frank hit the gas. "And what do ya think about all that weird stuff? Like how Costello's eyes would get as big as baseballs?"

"How should I know?" I shot back. "I'm not a god-dammed head shrinker! Now watch where you're driving and quit bugging me!"

***

We pulled into the mall's parking lot at 2200. Two cruisers were already there, situated at the restaurant's back entrance. The lights were off and the place appeared to be closed. According to the kid, Costello was probably upstairs.

Frank and I climbed out of our vehicle. We were immediately joined by the two officers. Their names were Hodges and Jones.

Hodges looked over at the restaurant and then back at us. "What's up, Sergeant?"

"Just a routine search, guys." I lied, because briefing them would only make me sound like a lunatic. "No matter *what* happens," I emphasized, "cover the rear exit. If the suspect comes out, detain him. He's a big, burly guy with a mustache."

Hodges and Jones exchanged glances. "Yeah, we know," Jones answered. "His name's Nick. We eat here all the time."

I just smiled and tried not to cringe. The two officers proceeded to the rear entrance but remained out of sight. Frank and I headed toward the front. I banged on the glass door and Frank looked at me like it was for the last time.

"Would you relax?" I growled. "This whole thing's probably nothing but a snow job."

Frank shook his head. "I dunno, Joe. That awful feeling's still in my gut."

I chuckled. "It's probably something you ate."

Again, I banged on the door, harder this time. Frank took a step back and gazed at the sky. "Hey, Joe, look at this."

I glanced up. Directly over our heads were bands of all types of flickering lights that resembled a bunch of curtains flapping around in the wind.

"Those are northern lights, aren't they, Joe?"

"Yeah, guess so." I banged on the door again. "They're called aurora . . . something or other. I've never heard of them being this far south before."

A light came on at the back of the building. After a few seconds, Costello inched out of the shadows. He was wearing a white uniform – pants, shirt, and apron. There was a red substance splattered across his front.

"Jeez, he's even bigger than I remembered," Frank whispered.

Costello stopped midway in the dining room, tilted his head and stared at us. I placed my badge against the door. "We're Newport P.D., Mister Costello. Would you mind opening up? We'd like to ask you a few questions."

He nodded and pulled out a ring of keys. They were large enough to fit the kid's description. He unlocked the door and let us in. He never said a word, which was definitely unusual. His expression appeared inquisitive but not at all hostile.

I slipped my badge into my coat pocket. "Mister Costello, are you aware that three of your employees have disappeared?"

He smiled and nodded. I noticed how he was breathing through his mouth.

"There's Mario Pinza, Felix De Nero, and a Donald Cappella. Do you have any idea of their whereabouts?"

Costello just shrugged but, this time, I glared at him like I wouldn't accept that kind of answer. Finally, he muttered a few words. They sounded foreign all right, but to my surprise, I understood him just fine. "I don't know," he answered.

I glanced at Frank who was looking like he had fallen into some kind of trance. I started to feel a little weak and nauseous myself. I sized up Costello's arms. They could have passed for tree trunks. I handed him the search warrant. "We would like to look around, Mister Costello. How about if we start with the basement?"

He gazed at the warrant like it was a calculus exam. Finally, he said a few more words in that bizarre manner of his. Again, I understood him, word for word; he said, "Okay, come this way." I would never have believed it, but once again another aspect of the kid's interrogation had come true.

We started following Costello through the dining area. Over my shoulder I whispered to Frank, "Does that sound like Italian to you?"

I figured since Frank's second generation, he should know. "If that's Italian," he answered, "then I'm Florence Nightingale."

I turned around and Costello sucker-punched me square on the nose. He caught me off guard; there wasn't even time for me to blink. I shot through the air, bounced off a table, and landed on the floor. The pain was incredible and blood seeped out my nose.

"Put your hands in the air," Frank demanded.

Everything looked blurry, but I knew my partner had pulled his weapon.

"I said, put your hands in the air!"

Sliding around on the floor, I was knocked almost senseless and had trouble drawing my revolver. I turned toward my assailant. Costello stood in the middle of the room; his blistering red eyes were bulging out their sockets. Just like the Duncan kid had said, the pupils were diamond-shaped. When Costello's mouth opened in proportion to his eyes, a mind-numbing, high-pitched noise exploded through the room. The pressure inside my skull became so intense I thought every blood vessel would burst.

I turned to my partner. Frank remained in a firing stance but was struggling to hold onto his weapon. "Shoot the bastard!" I screamed. "Take him down!"

Frank fired off multiple rounds. Costello clutched his chest but, to my surprise, remained upright. Frank took aim again, but out of Costello's eyes came what appeared to be blue lightning bolts that blasted through the room in all directions. Frank was struck across a shoulder and sent flying through the front picture window. Glass shattered all over and I had to cover my eyes.

Finally, I drew my weapon and took cover behind the overturned table. Costello was still standing at the center of the room. The high-pitched noise had stopped, but his eyes and mouth remained enormous. Before I could take aim, out came another set of lightning bolts. Most of the impact was absorbed by the table, which slammed into my right elbow. A wrenching pain shot up my arm, and I had to switch my weapon to my left hand. I fired several rounds in rapid succession. Even left-handed I nailed Costello repeatedly. He staggered back, turned, and rushed toward the rear entrance.

I was stunned and nearly out of my head. I couldn't believe our suspect was still alive and taking flight. I forced myself to stand and stumbled toward Frank. He was lying on his back with his legs propped on the window ledge. His shirt, jacket, and pants were badly singed. There were a number of cuts on his face and his breathing appeared labored, but thank God his eyes were open.

"How bad are ya, Frank?"

"Never mind me . . ." he whispered ". . . just get that bastard."

I told him to hang on and started for the rear of the restaurant. As I stumbled around the counter, I heard glass shattering in the back. Obviously not having time to unlock the door, Costello must have crashed through the window. I heard the command, "Freeze!" from Officer Hodges. A burst of gunfire followed, very rapid, nine or ten rounds in all. I entered the take out area just in time to see Costello retaliate.

Hodges had taken cover behind a light fixture but was still hit with a lightning bolt and thrown into the side of his vehicle. Jones, who must have been heading toward the front of the building, was struck across his right leg. It all happened so fast it didn't seem possible. Both officers were down and for the moment, I could not help them. I became furious – totally pissed off. Come what may, I was going to take that son of a bitch, psychopathic freak down.

By the time I had a clear shot, Costello was hurrying south. I fired through the broken glass and hit him in the right shoulder. He barely flinched and rushed out of sight. I felt dizzy and out of breath, but I managed to climb through the busted window without cutting myself.

I hurried south and spotted Costello stumbling through the parking lot. Above us were the aurora lights that Frank had brought to my attention earlier. Although he should have been dead three times over, the bullets had obviously slowed Costello down. His movements looked sluggish, but I couldn't see a drop of blood anywhere.

I took aim and nailed him in the back of his left knee. The shot was more luck than skill. He went down, but to my disbelief, he was able to right himself and stagger off. I took my time and fired my last round. The bullet hit him in the back of the head, a definite "kill shot." This time he went down to his knees but remained upright. *This is nuts*, I told myself. *He's taken at least a dozen hits!*

I popped another clip into my weapon and inched forward.

Just as I thought the pursuit was over, something happened to Costello. He hadn't budged since he'd dropped to his knees, but as I approached, I detected movement on his person. Naturally, I thought it was him, but it wasn't. A bright, blue glow had begun to radiate from his body. It surrounded him from the ground up and started to rotate, counter-clockwise. It whirled around and broke into a thousand glowing particles. They rotated faster and formed into streaks of light that resembled laser beams. Incredibly, as they circled him, his body began disintegrating.

"Christ Almighty, what the *hell* is this?"

After a few more seconds, the streaks of light were all that remained of Costello. They kept whirling around and began circling upward. As I watched, they were absorbed into the aurora lights, and almost immediately, they exploded into a rainbow of colors. And then a moment later, all traces of the lights had vanished.

I stood motionless as a cold shudder swept through me. My mind couldn't understand any of what I'd just witnessed. Suddenly, everything turned black and I crumpled to the ground. When I came to, a paramedic was crouched over me, and there were ambulances all over the place.

I struggled to my feet and, without saying a word, made my way to the restaurant. I was determined to check on Frank. I had the feeling that I'd been out for some time. My legs were weak and I felt dizzy, but I knew I'd be okay. The paramedic chased after me with a gurney, but I told him I wasn't going anywhere.

Officer Jones was being loaded into the back of an ambulance. He was sitting upright and was wearing an oxygen mask. I spotted a covered body lying on the ground. I remembered how badly Hodges had been hit. "God," I whispered, "I hope Frank's all right."

As I hurried to the front of the restaurant, Ahab stepped out from the entrance. Just behind him there was a tall, lean guy who looked to be in his late twenties.

"Logan, what happened here?" my captain demanded.

I ignored his question and circled around them. There was another ambulance parked in the middle of the mall and they were loading Frank into the back. My partner was wearing an oxygen mask and appeared to be unconscious.

"Is he going to be all right?" I asked.

One of the paramedics glanced at me then slammed the ambulance door shut. "We don't know." He looked at the stranger and when the guy nodded, the paramedic answered, "He lost consciousness a few minutes ago and his vitals are low. We'll take him to Harbor Hospital and they'll do everything they can."

The paramedics took off and Ahab approached me. "Where's your suspect, Logan? Don't tell me he got away."

I turned and started for my vehicle. "I don't have time right now, Captain. I gotta check on Frank."

Ahab grabbed my arm. "Not right now, Joe. We've got four men down tonight – one dead and three injured. I need some details." He frowned and stared straight into my eyes. "By the way, are you okay? Your face doesn't look so hot."

"I think Costello might have broken my nose." I sized-up the stranger and smelled a shitload of trouble. "Who are you?" I asked.

The guy flipped out a badge. "I'm Special Agent Schofield, FBI, and you'd better come with me, Logan."

I popped another crick out of my neck and we followed Schofield into the pizza parlor. The dining room looked more busted up than I remembered. As we made our way down the stairs to the basement, a flash from a camera caught my attention.

As Ahab, Schofield, and me entered the room, the photographer left. The city coroner, an elderly gent by the name of Addison, appeared to be waiting for us. He was wearing plastic gloves and a disgusted look on his face.

I glanced around. There was a wooden table, a refrigerator, and a couple of bulging trash bags piled against a wall. There was a conspicuous odor in the air, not to mention the huge meat grinder bolted to the table. Of course, there was blood splattered all over the place.

Agent Schofield motioned to the trash bags. "They're stuffed with bones, Logan."

I felt my nose throb. "Human?"

"Yep."

I shook my head. "Christ . . . Almighty!"

"Doctor Addison took some samples. He believes the tissue in the grinder and the blood on the table are also human."

I started to feel worse. "I guess that Duncan kid knew what he was talking about."

Schofield gave me a condescending smirk then nodded at the coroner.

The elderly doctor opened the refrigerator door. Inside were several items wrapped in plastic. I couldn't make out what they were, but I could well imagine.

"Human heads," Schofield confirmed. "Six in all."

He motioned to Doctor Addison, who pulled out one of the heads. As he unwrapped it, my stomach did a remarkable imitation of a submarine dive. The bag's contents were starting to decompose, but I recognized the face right away.

"So who does this look like to you, Sergeant Logan?"

"Nick Costello," I shot back.

Schofield chuckled, but his eyes were fuming. "So if this poor slob is Costello, then who the hell murdered all these people?"

***

I finally made it to Harbor Hospital at 0030. I couldn't believe Ahab would let Schofield grill me like that. All I wanted to do was check on my partner. So, after nearly an hour, I told the fed to go stuff himself. Job or no job, like they say, sometimes "you gotta do what you gotta do."

By the time I arrived at the Intensive Care Unit, Sharon, Frank's wife, and their oldest son, Peter, were already by my partner's side. Sharon jumped up and hugged me. She gave me the lowdown between sobs. Frank was in a coma. His heart had stopped, but a team of doctors had revived him.

Sharon gazed right through me. Her eyes looked like she'd been crying for years. "For a few minutes there . . . Frank was dead!"

Reality hit me hard. I stood there speechless because all this life and death stuff had happened within the last thirty minutes.

The three of us huddled by Frank's bed for hours. Although my partner was still in a coma, his condition started to improve. The conversation between Sharon, Peter, and me remained limited. The feds must have already cornered them, because they never asked me any questions. A nurse came by and said it was too crowded and someone had to leave. Everyone wanted me to have my nose x-rayed, but until Frank came around, I wasn't interested. I relocated to the hallway, and a few hours later an exhausted Sharon and Peter came out. She still had kids to send off to summer school, so I told her I would keep them posted.

I sat next to my partner. The poor guy looked horrible. Twenty percent of his body had been burned, he was covered with IVs and other crap, and his eyes looked like black holes.

During the night, I asked about Officer Jones. I didn't think I could be shocked any further, but when I heard the news my guts were turned inside out. His right leg had been so mangled, the doctors had to amputate it. At the age of twenty-six, Jones would never work the streets again.

Sometime that morning, I was confronted by a hard-assed nurse who may have been half Doberman. "You have to leave," she informed me. She had one of those lazy eyes that kept wandering around. "Only family members are allowed in here, Sergeant. We do have our rules."

I lied and told her I was Frank's brother, but she didn't buy it. Just as I started to leave, someone walked up from behind.

"That's okay, Nurse Phelps. Doctor Hollinger said Sergeant Logan could stay."

Shawn Duncan stood beside me dressed in a white uniform. He handed me a cup of coffee and a jelly donut. "Besides, we always accommodate members of our police force."

I put the coffee down and shook his hand. Minus her broom and flying monkeys, the frumpy nurse took off. Strange as it may seem, I found myself glad to see the kid. "I didn't think you'd be around today."

"I can't afford to miss any more work," he said. "I'm sorry to hear about your partner, Sergeant. I hope he pulls through."

"Thanks, I appreciate it."

"What happened with Nick?"

I sipped my coffee. "Let's put it this way: he's gone, but there won't be a word about him in any of the newspapers."

"Why not?"

"The feds put a lid on it. In fact, they'll be paying you a visit any minute now."

The kid seemed to brace himself. "What about Donnie? Can you at least tell me about him?"

I nodded. "I'm sorry, but he didn't make it. There were some others, too, but I can't divulge any more information."

The expression on Shawn Duncan's face tore my guts to shreds. But what could I do? The feds would have my ass in a sling for mentioning a word of this.

"Well, thanks for trying to help Donnie, Sergeant Logan, and for taking care of Nick, too. I'm sure he would have killed me if you hadn't believed my story."

I stopped about a hair short from rolling my eyes. "It wasn't a matter of believing you, kid. It was a matter of not taking any chances."

We talked for a while. He suggested to stay away from the vending machines, but said the cafeteria food was decent enough.

"I'll check on you from time to time," he promised.

As a matter of fact, we kept in touch for at least twenty years. You might say I'm a sucker for people who buy me coffee.

***

All that day Frank's condition slowly improved. His breathing and vital signs were okay, but he couldn't seem to wake up. Sharon came in around 0900 and stayed well into the night. While she was there, I headed for the cafeteria. Except for that donut Shawn Duncan had given me, I hadn't eaten a thing for quite some time.

Doctor Hollinger checked on Frank every couple of hours. Around midnight, after Sharon had left, he informed me, "Your friend might be coming around. His vitals and reflexes are good and his pupils are equal and reactive to light."

Just after 0300, my partner opened his eyes. He gazed at me and whispered, "I told ya it was gonna be a bad one . . ."

I leaned over him. "Well, it's about time." I took a breath and cracked a smile. "What do you think you're doing, anyway? Trying to give me an ulcer?"

He chuckled and tried to sit up. I pushed the button on the side of his bed and raised him to a sitting position. I handed him a plastic water cup and he drank through the straw.

"Thanks for sticking around," he croaked. "God, Joe. You look awful."

"Yeah, people keep telling me I look like a raccoon."

He nodded. "Maybe ya better get an x-ray."

"Yeah, sure. As soon as Sharon gets here."

"How long was I out?"

"Twenty-eight hours and twelve minutes, give or take. Aren't you gonna ask me about Costello?"

"I already know. You shot him and he disappeared into the lights."

The expression on my face must have looked hilarious.

"And then the feds took over. Shut the whole thing down."

"Hell, Frank, how can you possibly know that?"

He asked for some more water and I handed him the cup. "I was dead, wasn't I, Joe?"

"Yeah, you were, Frank. For a couple of minutes there."

"Well, right about then, I sat up and saw myself lying on a bed. The doctors were working on me, trying to bring me back to life. Then before I knew it, I was floating in the air . . . without even trying. It was the strangest thing."

I eased back into my chair. "Christ, Frank. You're bullshitting me, aren't ya?"

He shook his head. "A few seconds later, I was somewhere else. I don't know if it was heaven or not, but it was beautiful, like floating in the sky." He paused and took a breath. "There were these . . . people . . . I guess you could call them people. They were white all over and every one of them looked the same. The only way I could tell them apart was by their voices."

"Frank, maybe . . ."

"One of them told me what happened to Costello." He paused again and I was afraid he'd conk out before he finished. "But then this guy told me it was not my time and I had to go back."

"But did he say anything else about Costello? Like who he was or where the hell he came from?"

Frank nodded. He seemed to be straining to remember. "Yeah, he said it *wasn't* Costello. He told me it was some kind of rogue . . . a sort of . . . impostor . . . like a chameleon or something . . . and *not* of our world."

"Okay, Frank, I'm glad ya told me." I shook my head. Even though I didn't know what to make of his strange little experience, I still wanted to protect him. "Psych evals can be real pissers. So why don't we just keep this to ourselves . . . okay?"

He smiled and looked like he was ready to take the snooze of a lifetime.

"You'd better get some rest and I'll call Sharon." But as I approached the door, I turned and asked, "Hey, did that guy ever say who he was?"

"What guy?"

"The one you talked to while you were a stiff."

"Yeah, he told me."

"So who was he?"

"Francisco Romano."

I popped another creak out of my neck. I felt tired and didn't know what the hell my partner was talking about. "I don't get ya, Frank. Who's Francisco Romano?"

He grinned and murmured, "My great-great grandfather."

***

So ended case #0030395, code name, "Murder and Mayhem at Pizza Pal." It's been over thirty-four years now, so if the feds want to bust me for spilling the beans, then let them. This was Frank's last case. He was reassigned to desk duty, but we remained friends to the very end. In fact, he lived long enough to enjoy his retirement. Captain Anders came down with diabetes, probably from all those candy bars, and passed on awhile back. Officer Jones died of cancer in '07. Shawn Duncan moved to England about fourteen years ago. So, basically, I'm the only one left, and I don't give a rat's ass. I think the public should know about this case, and besides, it's pretty strange to say the least.

To be honest, I'm not the kind of guy who believes in this sort of stuff. I don't buy into ghosts, demons, aliens, Sasquatch, or any of that. But for the last thirty-four years, I've been trying to figure out a rational explanation for what happened on that night in July of 1975. So far, I haven't come up with a damn thing.

SCARE TACTICS

CROFT INTERNATIONAL TOWERS, DOWNTOWN LOS ANGELES - OCTOBER 29, 2017

Room 669

Miranda Howell clenched her fists and approached the door to the mailroom. Her hair appeared ruffled, her eyes red and watery. Perspiration had soaked through her blouse, her nylons were torn, and a black purse hung from her shoulder. She wore what resembled a Bluetooth phone in her right ear. Taking a breath, she gazed at the business card clutched in her hand. "Last one . . . almost there." She shook her head. "Brahman . . . I hope you're wrong."

She shuddered then wiped her forehead. The card slipped from her hand and drifted to the floor. She glanced at her watch. It was midnight, exactly. "Howell 7167," she whispered.

The door opened and a blinding light flashed. Miranda shielded her eyes, inched inside, and the door closed without a sound. The ceiling lights flickered as the corridor remained hushed. Then, after a long, lingering moment, a single scream erupted.

CROFT TOWERS - OCTOBER 30, 2017

Stuart Collier stepped inside the elevator, murmured "Eighteen," and the doors closed. Miranda Howell was standing in a back corner. She nodded hello but avoided his eyes. To think he used to consider her an ongoing threat — his primary adversary. He looked her up and down from her stiletto-heeled shoes to her short, black hair. *She's a ball-buster, all right, sharp as they come.* As far as he was concerned, her only downfall was refusing to sleep around.

While they raced upward, the song "Don't Walk Away Renee" resonated through the speakers. Stuart cringed. He didn't know what he hated more, the song or the uncomfortable memories it brought to mind.

Built into the upper portions of the walls were eighteen, twelve by twelve inch screens. Imagine that? Monitors in an elevator. Danton McCray, Croft's number-one, right-hand stooge, had them installed. The images on the screens included the main lobby, with its elaborate water fountains and metal sculptures, and the various hallways throughout the building. Ironically, the employees' parking garage, located in the basement, the one area where precautions were sorely needed, lacked a single security camera. Since it was after hours, the monitors merely displayed empty lobbies and hallways. Stuart sighed. *A total waste of the old man's money, if you ask me.*

Miranda stepped out at the eleventh floor. *She's heading for her office,* he concluded. *Probably forgot her damn chastity belt.* The doors closed and he grinned. *Poor baby, she looks traumatized . . . must have tanked on her U.S.D. interview. What a shame!* He smiled all the more. *Well, that's one less shark to worry about.*

The elevator reached the eighteenth floor, a chime sounded, the doors opened. In the middle of the lobby stood the oval-shaped security desk. As of last month, there was no need for a security guard, at least not on eighteen. Danton McCray had Al Ballantine canned and replaced with a computer. CPUs never needed a lunch break or a trip to the head. They had no unions and never demanded a raise. Chalk up another victory for technology. Too bad. Ballantine was one of the few people Stuart actually liked. Perhaps one day everyone would be replaced. Wouldn't that be a kick in the head? Maybe the old man would even swap Danton McCray for a more cost-effective counterpart.

Stuart approached the security desk and cleared his throat. "Stuart Collier to see Mister Croft."

Across the counter sat the MPR 2017. No larger than a table fan, it was encased in a thick, clear-glass enclosure. There were tiny holes in the center for communication and ventilation purposes. It was shiny, black, and if you were close enough, you could see your reflection in the glass. "Mister Croft does not receive visitors," it replied.

Stuart rolled his eyes. The computer's calm, distinctive voice reminded him of a snobby English butler. He had to restrain himself from calling it a shit can or something worse. "Check your records, please. I'm here for the U.S. Director's interview."

Its blinking green light sped up. "Prepare for a scan, Mister Collier."

Stuart nodded and stepped to the designated area. He could hear the hum from the ceiling cone as it scanned him. *Do I look like a terrorist? Maybe it thinks I'm a suicide bomber?* He shook his head. Life had been much easier when Al Ballantine was around.

The blinking green light slowed to halt. "You may proceed, and have a productive interview, Mister Collier."

Stuart turned and whispered just low enough so the computer couldn't hear, "Up your motherboard, shit can."

He swung around the security desk and hurried down the hallway. There were no windows on this floor, just the old man's office plus plenty of conference rooms along both sides of the hallway. Stuart gazed at the far end toward the double doors. They appeared to be made of solid mahogany and looked oddly out of place in a building constructed of concrete, metal, and glass. When he came within eight feet, the doors swung open. A lone secretary sat at her desk on the right, dictating into an MPR 2015 computer. When she spotted Stuart, she logged off.

"Welcome, Mister Collier."

Her name plate read Alice Baxter, which to him sounded like a rather conservative name for such a beautiful young woman. *God*, he wondered, *what in hell could she have possibly done to get such a cushy, high-profile job?*

"Mister Croft will see you now," she stated in a rather detached manner.

He smiled and turned toward a second mahogany door. Just as he approached, it slid open. Danton McCray stood in the entryway, grinning like a boa constrictor.

"Stuart, come in and have a seat." Of course they didn't shake hands. McCray never did. And, supposedly, Croft would fire anyone who tried to touch him.

Stuart unbuttoned his suit coat and eased into a black, leather swivel chair. The largest desk on the North American continent stretched before him. His boss sat on the opposite side with his back turned toward Stuart. He waited as the man studied the international stock market results as they raced across a twenty by ten foot screen. When the screen turned black, the man swung around. It was the first time Stuart had ever seen Mister Croft. He wasn't sure what to expect, as there wasn't a single photo of him in the entire building. And it seemed strange, but he didn't know hardly anything about this elusive billionaire, if he was married, had kids, or if he was a bachelor.

"Greetings and salutations, my boy," Croft greeted with a slight British, or perhaps South African accent. "Are you ready to achieve the dream of a lifetime?"

Stuart had never cared for surprises. He had pictured an older guy with bad teeth or long fingernails, but Marcus Croft could not have been more than forty-five-years-old. He was of medium build and dressed in a flawless three-piece suit, probably Italian. He possessed a full head of dark brown hair, combed straight back, with a touch of gray at the temples. His eyes appeared incredibly sharp and seemed to scrutinize everything around him.

Stuart smiled and answered, "Yes, sir, I'm ready for anything."

Croft grinned and glanced at McCray, who had withdrawn to a far, dimly lit corner. "Well, I'm *very* happy to hear that, Stuart, because that's *exactly* the attitude we're looking for. So, let's get cracking, shall we? Computer, file 7187."

An auxiliary screen built into the wall at the rear of the office came to life. With meticulous intensity, Croft examined the data flooding onto both front and rear screens – detailed records from the five states Stuart had supervised over the last six years. California posted a 5,587,000 fiscal gain, Oregon 3,866,000 gain, Washington 2,792,000 gain, Nevada 4,477,000 gain, and Arizona 1,411,000 gain.

Croft calculated the total nearly as fast as his computer, a MPR 5000, no less. "Well, that's one billion, six hundred and eighty million in all, not bad, Stuart. Your districts have accumulated some respectable profits, although Arizona might have been better. But in this overall fucked-up economy, I dare say you've done quite well."

"Thank you, sir." Stuart flashed his brightest grin. And why not? He had paid a month's salary for those pearly whites of his.

Croft peered at McCray. "What do you think, Danton?"

Stuart turned toward Croft's longtime associate. Partially concealed within the shadows, McCray leaned against the back wall, just below the screen. "Not bad," he murmured. "But why move him when he's done so well?"

Croft waved a hand. "Nonsense, Danton. Just imagine what Stuart could do as our U.S. Director! Why I can just *smell* the profits! Computer, carry on."

A photo of Stuart's parents appeared on the screen.

"You were born in Madison, Wisconsin, to Sylvia and Fredrick Collier in 1977. Your mother was killed when you were twelve, is that right?"

Taken by surprise, Stuart gasped, "Yes, but . . ."

Croft raised a hand. "Bear with me, Stuart. Your father was a worthless alcoholic, and after the accident you lived with your grandparents. You graduated from Northwestern University at the top of your class, a Bachelor in business; however, it seems as though you cheated on some of your exams."

Stuart slouched forward. An uneasy feeling meandered through him. "Mister Croft, with all due respect . . ."

"No, no, don't be modest, Stuart! You paid good money for those answers, now didn't you? That demonstrates *initiative* and a strong desire to succeed. Very impressive!" He gazed back at the screen. "You began working for Bank of Chicago in '98, the year you graduated."

A photo of Renee appeared on the screen and Stuart's breath caught in his throat.

"While working there you met Renee Newman, a coworker, and, against company policy, started banging the life out of her. Due to your distaste for condoms, you knocked her up after a year." Croft arched an eyebrow. "Really? It took that long?"

"Sir, I can't see . . ."

"She had to quit work, and after she refused an abortion, you felt obligated to marry her. She gave up her career, raised your son, and took to the bottle – just like your dear, old father."

Stuart grew so agitated, he could barely contain himself. "Sir, really, what kind of interview is this?"

Croft paused and sighed. "We're just trying to ascertain if you're qualified for the position, Stuart. Now quit being so defensive. This is great stuff! The more dirt, the *better* your chances. Just think about raising your annual income to one point five million. Why, that's ten times as much as you're making now! Isn't a thorough review of your life worth that kind of wealth?"

Stuart shook his head. He had to calm down and persuade one of the most powerful men in the world to stay out of his private life. "Please, don't get me wrong, sir. I'm the first to admit, the money would come in handy . . ."

Peering at the screen, Croft snickered. "Yes, I can see you like the ponies, and your credit card debt is enough to negate the federal deficit."

"Yes, but I don't see the need to dig into such *personal* matters, sir."

Croft again glanced at McCray. "Danton, would you care to enlighten our candidate in regards to our interviewing techniques? I seem to be falling short."

Stuart turned to face McCray. Of course it had to be his imagination, but to him, the guy looked like a Nazi bureaucrat who had just aged ten years in the last ten minutes. "What Mister Croft is trying to tell you is we need a tough ball-buster who will stop at nothing to make a killing."

Shifting about, Stuart swallowed and nodded. *Great! Looks like I'm screwed.*

"Well done, Danton! Now let's continue, shall we? You scrambled up the corporate ladder while working for Bank of Chicago where you used inside Intel to make a small fortune. You moved your family to L.A. against your wife's wishes and accepted a position over at Mutual of California, our former competitor. You hired on as a bank manager and were quickly promoted to district manager."

Dozens of photographs of female employees flashed across the screen. "This is when you started banging every woman with a functioning vagina. During this time your wife became pregnant again and lost the baby during the first trimester. She blamed the miscarriage on the stress you gave her, especially from all your . . . extramarital affairs." Croft's eyes grew huge with indignation. "Why that arrogant bitch! How dare she!"

Stuart shrank in his seat. *How the fuck could he possibly find all this out?*

"You were involved in several petty frauds while at Mutual of California." Croft shook his head. "Now that's disappointing! You should have bankrupted those assholes! But you were never indicted for any of your indiscretions . . . well, that's a relief. After your *mandatory* resignation . . . you hired on with us in '04 as Director of Operations for Southern California."

Page after page of facts and photos filled both screens. Stuart couldn't believe how Croft managed to keep up with it.

"You haven't participated in any fraudulent behaviors while working for *our* company." Sheer exuberance gushed from Croft's eyes. "Now that's what I like, good, old-fashioned loyalty.

"Your districts were all in the black each quarter. You fought against the union and employee benefits during your tenure. You coerced many of your subordinates into working long hours and on holidays." He paused and gave Stuart an appreciative wink. "How marvelous! The day *after* you divorced Renee in '07, you married Evelyn Patterson, one of your bank managers. Now that's brilliant! No sense in putting things off, hey, my boy?"

Stuart sighed. *Maybe I ought to play along with him. Like he said, the more dirt, the better.* "Yes, that's right, sir. No sense in putting *anything* off."

"Renee's now a slobbering alcoholic living in the slums of San Francisco and your only son, Stephen, resides in . . ." he hesitated briefly, then lowered his voice ". . . a state hospital?"

Stuart's eyes glazed over. He coughed and cleared his throat. "Y-Yes, he was in a car accident . . . some time ago."

Croft leaned back in his chair and sighed. "Now that's too bad. What a pity. Well, we probably could go on for hours, but why bother? Stuart, I like you. You're my type of employee! I think we can safely say you've passed the interview!"

Stuart shot to his feet and had to fight the urge to shake hands. He glanced over at McCray then back to Croft. "Really? You mean it?"

His boss nodded. "Why, yes. I *never* kid around when it comes to profits."

"But sir, you haven't even asked me a single question."

"It doesn't matter, my boy. Everything I need to know is right here in the computer."

Stuart wanted to jump on top of Croft's desk, kick up his heels and scream like a maniac. He could not believe what he was hearing. "Man, oh man! I never thought I'd ace an interview for being an asshole!"

McCray stepped out of the shadows. His eyes appeared unnaturally clear and bright. "Are you going to tell him about the *second* half of the interview, sir?"

The boss nodded and walked around his desk. "Yes, that's right. Now would *certainly* be a good time."

Stuart's mouth dropped open. "You mean there's more?"

"Of course, there is! You didn't think it would be that easy, now did you?"

Stuart flopped into his chair. "Who do I have to kill to nail this promotion?"

Croft chuckled, stepped over and, to Stuart's surprise, slapped him on a shoulder. According to the rumor mill, it was something he would never do. "No, no, it's nothing like that. The second half of your interview is just a contemporary approach, that's all. Come to think of it . . . I invented it."

McCray slowly crept forward. For the first time in all the years Stuart had known him, the guy actually cracked what looked like a genuine smile. "That's right, Mister Croft. You invented the *entire* procedure."

"Would you kindly alert Angel, Danton? Tell him we're nearly ready."

A ghoulish expression lingered on McCray's face before he turned and left the room. A perplexed Stuart peered at Croft. "Who's Angel?"

"Oh, he's just a referee of sorts, a monitor who'll be keeping tabs on your progress." Croft peered at Stuart. "Don't look so glum, my boy! You're practically one of the family now."

"So what do I have to do, sir?"

"Just go downstairs, visit a few offices, make your observations and, presto, you're done. Now is that so bad?"

"Can you at least tell me what I should expect in these offices?"

Croft shrugged and leaned against his desk. "Well, if I told you, then it wouldn't be much of a test, now would it?"

"So it's a *test*?"

"Yes. Just think of it as a mental agility test, or a stress test, if you prefer. It's just my way of ascertaining if you have the capabilities to give us your all. You look physically fit, Stuart. Do you work out?"

"Yes, at least an hour every day. Why? Is that going to help?"

Croft smiled. "Actually, no. But it won't hurt, either. Your stamina will be tested more on an emotional level." He reached into his coat pocket and pulled out a handful of business cards. "Just take these handy little items and place them in your pocket. No fair peeking! Remember, we have the entire building monitored, except for the restrooms, of course."

Stuart stood and slipped the cards into his shirt pocket.

"When you enter the elevator, take the first card out. Written on the back is the office number you report to. Simple, right? Visit all seven offices and when it's over, the position is yours."

A hint of concern suddenly crept into Croft's eyes. "I'm sure it will never happen, but if for any reason you find yourself becoming overly stressed, or heaven forbid . . . scared . . ."

"Scared?"

"Well, you never know. We want people with *courage,* with the balls and guts to make millions, even *billions* for our company. We live in an age of pussies, chickenshits, and bleeding hearts who are afraid to *crush* a few toes or *kick* some ass to make things happen."

"I may be a lot of things, sir, but I'm not a pussy."

Croft chuckled and stepped away from his desk. "I already know that, my boy, but I just wanted to mention you can quit at any time." He sighed and shook his head. "But unfortunately, if it comes to that, then your chances for the USD position are *nullified* . . . permanently." He crossed his arms over his chest and regarded him sternly. "Do you understand, my boy?"

Stuart nodded. "Sure, I understand. You don't have to worry about me, Mister Croft. I'll be in this for the long haul."

His boss grinned and again slapped him on the shoulder. "I'm *very* happy to hear that, Stuart." Croft reached into his coat pocket and removed a black velvet jewelry case. He opened it; inside was a large gray and yellow capsule. "But, first of all, you're going to have to swallow this."

Stuart groaned. "What is it?"

"Just a mild steroid, a sort of energizer to enhance your performance."

Taking a jittery breath, something inside Stuart gridlocked. "What if I refuse?"

Croft shrugged. "Sorry, rules are rules. Besides, you're no stranger to steroids, now are you?"

Stuart studied the capsule. He had taken plenty of steroids before, but none of them had ever looked like this. "So what kind of enhancer is it?"

Croft rushed over and before Stuart could react, they were standing face to face. His boss's eyes flared with rage. Scotch whiskey fumed his breath. "It's something new! What difference does it make? If you want to piss away your promotion over a lousy pill, then fuck it! We'll call it quits right now and you can stay a slave to your credit cards for the rest of your debt-ridden life!"

Stuart stepped back and scrutinized the capsule. *Damn, what am I getting into? For all I know, this could be cyanide.* He shook his head. One point five million dollars flashed in his mind like a neon sign. Orchards of money trees, as far as the eye could see, with hundred dollar bills dangling from their branches, populated his fertile imagination. *Shit, reality sucks. It really does!* He raised the capsule. "Can I at least have something to drink with this?"

The rage in Croft's eyes instantly disappeared. He smiled, nodded graciously, and handed Stuart a glass of water that was sitting on his desk. "To your health and, might I add, good fortune."

Stuart paused and took a deep breath. "Where did this water come from? It wasn't on your desk a second ago."

"Oh, for chrissake! Are you going to take the fucking thing or not? One minute you claim you're in this for the long haul, then the next your ass is on the fence!"

Stuart quickly placed the capsule in his mouth and swallowed the water.

His boss turned and peered at the VDT. "Computer, camera fifty-four."

The screen lit up and exhibited a live video of Stuart. It then scrambled to what appeared to be a high definition x-ray of his skull.

To his astonishment, the entire screen was filled with the unmistakable image of the capsule neatly wedged beneath his tongue.

Croft frowned and his eyes narrowed. "Just swallow the fucking thing!"

Stuart grunted and gulped down the capsule. *God,* he thought, *nothing gets past this guy.*

"Good, now wear this." Croft handed him what appeared to be some type of sophisticated hearing aid. "It's called the *E Drum,* the latest in technology. It's far more advanced than a Bluetooth and features an ultra-sensitive receiver, microphone, and camera. Just attach it to your right ear and we're good to go."

Danton McCray returned, nodded at his boss, then gazed indifferently at Stuart.

"Well, we're all set," announced Croft. "Any questions?"

Stuart flashed his most confident grin. "No questions, sir. All I can say is I'm ready, willing, and able to kick whatever ass you tell me to!"

"Splendid! I'm sure by tomorrow you'll be settled into your new position . . . as the U.S Director of Croft International!" Then amazingly enough, his boss held out his hand.

Stuart hesitated then reluctantly reached forward. They shook hands . . . and something repulsively offensive about Croft's touch overwhelmed Stuart. His stomach shrank and a vicious shudder raced down his spine. He didn't know what to think or how to feel. All he could do was pull his hand away and inch toward the door.

Croft appeared to be scrutinizing him, perhaps even worming his way into Stuart's mind. A cynical glimmer crept into the man's eyes. "And don't forget, if you start feeling *scared* for any reason . . . you can always wimp out." He chuckled, glanced at McCray, then back at Stuart. "Sorry, what I meant to say is you can always back out."

Stuart peered over his shoulder and forced a grin. "Thanks, Mister Croft, but to tell you the truth, with me there's no backing out."

***

Storming into the lobby, Stuart roared "Down" to the elevator. His stomach hadn't felt this queasy since he quit eating meat. He shook his head and clenched his fists. He knew Marcus Croft was supposed to be a greedy, eccentric egomaniac, but no one had ever mentioned anything about him being a lunatic.

Stuart took a long, deep breath. What a load of bullshit! The promotion should have been his. The whole second half of this interview sounded like nothing more than a bunch of cheap, underhanded scare tactics, designed to sabotage the morale of hardworking, industrious employees such as himself.

The chime sounded and the elevator doors opened. Stuart stepped inside and removed the first business card from his shirt pocket. He glanced at it, blinked, then looked again. It was one of his mother's cards, except it looked brand new. In a fancy font it read, "Sylvia Collier, Accountant, Jorgensen's Publishing Company, Madison, Wisconsin."

How in God's name did Croft come up with this?

The elevator doors closed and Stuart flipped the card over. "1220" had been handwritten in black, bold ink. Hell, weren't there a dozen accountants sharing that office? So what was he supposed to do? Audit the books? He groaned and muttered, "Twelfth floor."

Just as the elevator started to descend, static blasted into Stuart's head. He jumped backward and clutched his right ear. He was about to rip out the *E Drum* when the static halted.

"Testing, one, two, three!" bellowed Croft. "Stuart, you there, my boy?"

"Yes, hello, sir. Would you mind turning the volume down?"

"No, not at all. There . . . is that better?"

"Yes, much better."

"We're receiving some great audio and a wonderful video on this end, Stuart. I must say, you're *very* photogenic."

"Thank you, sir."

The elevator stopped at the twelfth floor.

"Okay, here we go. I'll check back with you in a minute. I'm sure you'll breeze through this first test in no time. Bon voyage, my boy! Croft, over and out."

When the doors opened, Stuart stepped out, turned right, then made another right down the hallway. His objective was the third door on the left. Sure enough, the brass plate next to the entrance read "Accounting." He wiped his forehead and murmured, "Collier 7187." The door opened and Stuart stepped inside.

ROOM 1220

For a moment the office remained dark, and Stuart could not see a thing. When the lights clicked on, they were so blinding he had to shade his eyes. As the door closed, the lights softened and his surroundings came into focus.

Stuart glanced around in stunned amazement. *What the fuck is this?*

He was standing in the living room of his parent's former house on Birch Street in Madison, Wisconsin. The television stood against the wall to his immediate left. In front of him were the oak coffee table and vinyl couch he remembered from years ago. Sacked out on the couch was his father. Of course, he was snoring; his hair appeared uncombed and his face unshaven. *He's been on another one of his fucking benders*, Stuart concluded. *Sure hope I won't have to deal with any of his crap.*

On the far left he noticed someone sitting at the nook table. He shook his head and looked again. *No, no, this can't be!*

Eating a bowl of cereal was a boy – a very young Stuart Collier. Dressed in his grammar school uniform, complete with tan shirt, maroon tie, and dark pants, he appeared exceptionally happy, naive, and innocent.

What the hell is this? How did I get here? Did I go back in time?

Static crackled in Stuart's ear, followed by Croft's voice. "Stuart, are you there?"

"What is this, Mister Croft? Where am I?"

"How would I know? You tell me."

"How could you *not* know, sir? You sent me here."

"All I'm doing is monitoring from my office. The computer's programming everything. So can you tell me where you're at?"

Stuart glanced around some more. As far as he could tell, everything was the same as when he was a boy. There were two green window drapes that were drawn open, and it was dark and snowing outside. The painting over the couch featured a narrow creek meandering through a grassy field with a red barn nestled in the background. It was his grandparents' farm just outside Campbellsport. His mother had painted it from her childhood memories. "I'm at my parents' house in Wisconsin, back around . . . 1989, I think."

"The boy at the table, is that you?"

Stuart had to swallow. "Yeah, it sure is."

"Terrific! Who's the slob on the couch?"

"That's my old man."

"Tough luck, my boy. Looks like he's had one too many."

"Yeah, that's nothing new . . . but this whole thing's . . . ancient history. H-how did you do this, Mister Croft?"

"I told you, Stuart, I'm not doing anything. It's the computer. I'm no genius when it comes to this type of technology, but it has something to do with programming three-dimensional holograms."

There was a bark from the kitchen. Foxy, the Colliers' Cairn Terrier, came running up to Stuart, wagging her tail. When he bent down and tried to pet his former dog, his hand swept straight through her. "What the hell is this?"

"Oh, you won't be able to touch anything," Croft interjected, "or communicate, either. For all seven tests you'll be like a ghost. No one can see or hear you. In fact, I'm surprised by that dog's reaction. It must possess some highly developed senses that can detect your presence."

Stuart turned toward the kitchen. He could smell one of his mother's apple pies baking in the oven. During the long, bitter winters, she would bake one of her specialties early on Friday mornings. The heat from the oven would help warm their house.

"Honey, did you take Foxy out?" came his mother's voice from a bedroom down the hallway.

Stuart whirled to his right. *No, I don't believe this! It's not possible!*

"Not yet, Mom," answered the boy.

Foxy bolted toward the young Stuart as he pushed away from the table.

Glancing at her wristwatch, Sylvia Collier entered the room. She looked exactly how Stuart had always remembered her: green eyes, high cheekbones, and dark, wavy hair. Feeling his legs about to melt beneath him, Stuart held his arms out toward her, and to his shock, Sylvia walked straight through him. He shuddered and staggered backward. It felt as if an icy wind had penetrated his body, leaving him feeling appalled and strangely violated.

Apparently, his mother never felt a thing. "That's all right," she said to the boy. "I'll take her out while you're finishing breakfast."

Suddenly, the most horrible realization hit Stuart. "No, no! You can't go outside!"

Sylvia hurried to the coat closet and removed her jacket along with the dog's leash. As she slipped her coat on, she called to Foxy.

"Don't go out there!" Stuart hollered. "It's not safe!"

"You can yell all you like," insisted Croft, "but she still can't hear you."

Foxy ran up and Sylvia fastened the leash to the dog's collar.

Stuart raced over to the boy. "Hey, stupid, do something! You have to stop her!"

"It's no use," Croft urged. "You're like a ghost, remember?"

Sylvia hurried out the door. Stuart approached his father sleeping on the couch. He gritted his teeth and hurled his fist through the man's face. "Get up, you drunken bastard! Don't you know what's going to happen?"

"Talk to me, my boy," pleaded Croft. "Tell me what's going on."

Stuart was too flustered to answer. "There's gotta be something I can do!" He rushed to the front door, but when he tried to turn the knob, his hand swept through it. "Goddamn it! How am I supposed to get around?"

"Just step through it," Croft advised. "You'll find it easy and, might I add, quite helpful."

Stuart held his breath and barreled through the door. Once again it felt as if an icy breeze had pierced his body. He shuddered and peered toward the street. It was snowing heavily and visibility seemed nonexistent. Then he heard what devastated him — a muffled thud, followed by a dog yelping.

Struggling through ankle-deep snow, Stuart caught a glimpse of Foxy racing home. He shielded his eyes, turned right, and lost his footing. He fell face first, landing on the street.

"Goddamn it!" He spat out a mouthful of snow, turned to his side, and spotted something which would haunt him from that moment on – a thin, winding trail of blood. He jumped to his feet and followed it. "Croft, you fucker! Why of all days did it have to be today?"

Stuart followed the bloody trail down Birch Street for two city blocks. When he approached Harrington Avenue, a major thoroughfare, he discovered the trail had veered left. He followed it for another block and it ended just behind a parked Volkswagen van. He raced toward the driver's side, dropped to his knees and peered under the vehicle. His mother's broken and mangled body had been dragged beneath it. Her eyes were staring vacantly at him. Her skull had been crushed.

It felt as if every drop of Stuart's blood had turned to ice. "Damn it! Why? Why?"

The police would later claim it had been snowing so hard that the driver of the van had not seen his mother. When the woman felt the impact, she looked in her rearview mirror and only spotted a dog running away. She thought she had hit the animal but, obviously, it was still alive.

"How could that be? How could anyone not know?"

Stuart rose, took a breath, and wiped the snow from his pants. It seemed strange, but he could not feel the cold, the dampness, or even the wind. Nor could he remove the image of his mother's battered face, which would be cemented in his mind for the rest of his life. *Someday I'll get that fucking Croft for putting me though this. I'll pay him back and then some . . . so help me!*

As Stuart turned, a young boy rushed toward him. It was his younger self following the bloody trail – just as he had some twenty-eight years earlier.

"No, go back!" he shouted. "You don't want to see this!"

The boy raced through Stuart's body and again there was that horrible sensation. The twelve-year-old bent down and looked under the van. There was an agonizing moment of silence, then the most heart-wrenching scream shattered the early morning darkness.

"Goddamn it! Why the hell did it have to be like this?"

A blinding light suddenly engulfed Stuart and he had to cover his eyes. When he removed his hand, he found himself surrounded by small office cubicles. *I'm back*, he realized. *Back in 1220.*

From the *E Drum* Croft murmured, "Sorry, Stuart, but it wasn't me. The computer's choosing random subjects on its own. I have no idea of any of the programs. But still, I'm sorry you had to go through such a horrible ordeal . . . especially for a second time."

Stuart nodded. He was still trying to catch his breath. He had to pull himself together, stuff his rage, and somehow come across as sincere. "It's okay, sir. No apology necessary."

"Are you all right?"

"Never better."

Croft chuckled. "You were pretty upset with me, now weren't you?"

Stuart shook his head. "No, I was just taken off guard, that's all. I didn't mean any of it."

"I understand. Well, I'm happy to report that you've aced your first test!"

"That's good. Thank you, sir."

"Are you ready for your next go 'round?"

"Absolutely," Stuart returned.

"Wonderful! Just jump on the elevator and I'll be in touch. *Arrivederci,* my boy! Croft, over and out."

***

Stuart stepped out of the elevator on the ninth floor. He turned right then made a left. He wasn't familiar with the next room, as Croft leased most of the offices on nine to other firms. Good old fucking Croft. Stuart had no idea how he managed to send him back to 1989 and he didn't buy a word of how it was all just holograms. He couldn't feel the cold, but since he caught wind of his mother's apple pie, that meant his boss was one conniving, pathological liar. Hopefully, whatever was in 970 would be a cinch compared to 1220.

Nearing his destination, Stuart reached into his pocket and took a long look at the next business card. Who the hell was Abdul Hassan? Apparently he owned "Fairway Garments," a clothing outlet in Chicago. Now why would anyone bother having such an elaborate business card for a clothing store?

Stuart turned and peered down the corridor. He could have sworn that someone had just been following him. Other than an occasional janitor, he didn't expect to see anyone at this late hour. Then again, what about that Angel guy? Croft had mentioned he would be involved in this travesty, but so far, nothing. He grimaced. With all the video surveillance and the pain-in-the-ass *E Drum,* he didn't need one of Croft's flunkies sniffing around.

The sign next to 970 read "McCormick & Sons," one of the many law firms on nine.

Stuart belched. Ever since he shook hands with Croft, his insides had turned to garbage. He paused, rolled his eyes and groaned. His adverse symptoms weren't from touching Croft, they were from the capsule. Since he'd been bullied into taking the damn thing, he would just have to deal with it. He took a breath, cleared his throat, and whispered, "Collier 7187."

ROOM 970

Again there was a blinding light, and when Stuart was finally able to see, he was standing in the lobby of a bank. Customers were scurrying about and there was a line in front of the tellers. A lengthy hallway to his right led to the usual number of offices. It all looked a little too familiar. In thin, silver calligraphy, the chrome logo on a far wall read "Bank of Chicago."

"Greetings, Stu," Croft hailed from the *E Drum*. "Looks like you're back at your old stomping grounds."

"Yes, sir, where I first started."

"Computers! Don't you just love them? Hey, look to your left. Now doesn't *she* look inviting?"

Stuart's mouth dropped open. Of all people, Renee stepped out of the file room. She was young again, not quite twenty-four. She walked with all the confidence of someone who was about to hop on a magic carpet ride, seeking untold adventure and wealth.

"Wow, I wouldn't mind banging her myself!" raved Croft. "And to think, after you sucked her dry, she drank herself into a skid-row slut."

Stuart had to clench his fists. *Stuff it, man, stuff it. Don't let him goad you.* He cleared his throat and took a soothing breath. "Yes, she was quite the looker, that's for sure."

"She's heading for one of the offices. Why don't you see what she's up to?"

Nodding, Stuart followed Renee down the corridor. His body ached as her hips swayed back and forth. He could not tear his eyes away from her long, shapely legs and her tight, leather skirt. *Damn! Why did I ever let her go?*

Renee turned left and entered the doorway at the very end of the hallway.

Whoa! That was my office back then in Chicago!

Stuart stepped into the room just as his former wife delivered a file folder. The imposing figure sitting behind the desk was the twenty-three-year-old version of Stuart. His suit, shirt, tie, everything appeared perfectly tailored. He looked every bit the personification of a rising young executive. Sitting before him was a dark-haired man with a beard, probably in his late thirties. He was fidgeting about and wiping his face with a large, dingy handkerchief.

"Damn, Stu!" shouted Croft. "Look at you! What a stud! And bank manager, too!"

Renee turned and hurried toward the door. Although Stuart tried to step aside, she still managed to walk straight through him. He closed his eyes and cringed. *God, I hate that!*

"It must be 1999 and you've been banging Renee for just over a year," Croft elaborated. "Pretty soon now she'll have a nice little bun toasting in her oven. By the way, who's that nervous fellow sitting over there?"

Stuart could not help but gawk at his younger self. Even back then he was full of confidence, bravado, and determination. "I dunno. Just some client, I guess."

His younger self glanced through the file, sorted the papers into a tidy stack, then stared at the stranger. "Well, Mister Hassan . . ."

"Please, call me Abdul."

There was a trace of anger in the younger Stuart's eyes. "No, that wouldn't be appropriate. Now, Mister Hassan, as I was saying, you lack sufficient credit for a business loan."

Jittering about, Abdul wiped his face. "But, sir, how can I obtain credit if no one will give me a chance?"

"Well, have you tried City Finance? They're just down the street."

Abdul leaned forward. "Yes, I've tried everyone!" His voice had grown louder; his face turned red.

The twenty-three-year-old Stuart closed the file. The right-hand corner of his mouth curled upward. "Well, that's too bad, but your lack of credit is simply unacceptable."

Abdul stood. His hands were trembling. "Please, sir, if you don't help me, my business will fail!"

The younger Stuart pressed a button on his intercom then glared at the man. "Look, don't you get it? I'm not about to stick my neck out for some fucking camel-jockey who doesn't have credit!"

Croft howled with laughter. "Damn, Stu, now that's telling him!"

Abdul leaned forward and grabbed Stuart's arm. "Please, sir. Yell at me! Curse at me! But my wife, my children, we need that loan!"

The younger Stuart gritted his teeth. "You touch me again and I'll fuck you up royally."

Two security guards rushed in and seized Abdul by his arms. Without a word they dragged him out of the office and down the hallway. "Please, sir, please!" Abdul begged. "You're condemning my business!" He pleaded all the way to the bank's entrance.

The twenty-three-year-old Stuart grinned and flung the Hassan file into his shredding basket.

Croft ranted breathlessly from the *E Drum*. "You're one cold-hearted mercenary, you know that? I could use a thousand like you!"

Stuart smiled as he swelled with pride. "Thank you, sir."

The light appeared and Stuart breathed a sigh of relief. *Hell, that wasn't so bad. Nothing like before.* He would be back at McCormick & Sons in no time and then onto the next test. But when the light dissipated, he found himself standing in an aisle between two rows of people. "What's this? A funeral parlor?"

"Oh, oh!" Croft cried out. "Looks like the proverbial worm has turned."

Dozens of people filled the room, many of them moaning and sobbing. Stuart turned toward the front. Three closed caskets stood before him, each with a photograph on top. A metal sign beside one of the caskets read "Abdul Hassan and family."

"What the hell is this?"

"Well, my boy," sighed Croft, "the computer's informing me that after you blew off Abdul, his business bellied up. Apparently, he went ape-shit and whacked his wife and teenage son, then offed himself as well."

Stuart felt something nibbling away at his nerves. "You're kidding?"

"No, not at all. Guess you don't read newspapers much, now do you?"

Stuart's heart sank and the burning inside his stomach cranked up a notch.

"Tough luck, my boy. But look at it this way, now you have three less *camel-jockeys* to fret about. Besides, it could have been worse. Abdul never had the chance to waste his daughters. Now that's something positive, isn't it?"

Stuart could barely function. He stumbled toward the caskets and nearly lost his balance.

"But, never fear, this doesn't change a thing! In this line of business, you have to have balls of steel! Shit happens, but the strong not only survive . . . they thrive!"

Stuart wanted to tell Croft to go fuck himself, and although he tried repeatedly, every time he opened his mouth, nothing but gibberish came out.

"Well, time marches on. We still have five more tests to go, so I'll be seeing you faster than you can say . . . 'I'll fuck you up royally!' *Adios, amigo!* Croft, over and out."

***

Stuart stared at the wall clock from a cafeteria table. It was just after 11:00. He shook his head and mumbled a long stream of obscenities. This brutal night seemed endless. His stomach had finally settled down, so he grabbed some coffee from a vending machine. He usually avoided caffeine, but tonight he needed it. His head throbbed and every now and then he became dizzy and started seeing things. Glimpses of murky shadows racing across the walls, floors, and even the ceiling, sporadically appeared. Every time he spotted one it would vanish, probably to whatever hellhole it had come from.

I wonder what was really in that fucking capsule? Stuart took another gulp of coffee. Five offices down, two more to go. After the last one, Croft claimed he had some urgent business and called for a thirty-minute break.

The last three offices had been just as bad as the first two – maybe even worse. The third business card belonged to David Malden of all people. Stuart might have fouled up on not remembering Abdul Hassan, but he sure as hell remembered that crazy bastard Malden. So he stepped into 790 and, after dealing with the light, found himself standing in front of his former work site, Mutual of California. It was just after closing and several employees were leaving the building. He watched his younger self exit through the front entrance. He was older now but had recently become a competitor at power-lifting. In a matter of months, Stuart had grown muscular and physically fit.

As his younger version rounded the corner toward the employee parking lot, Stuart followed along. He knew exactly what was about to happen. Just as the younger Stuart approached his Silverado, Malden stepped out of the alleyway. The guy's face looked red, his fists were clenched, and a murderous glint flashed across his eyes.

With his timing as abrasive as ever, Croft butted in via the *E Drum*. "The computer's informing me that this is Victoria Malden's husband, the woman you've been banging during Renee's second pregnancy. Is that correct, my boy?"

Stuart sighed. "Yes, I guess so, sir."

"The very pregnancy that resulted in a miscarriage that Renee blamed on you and all your fooling around?"

Stuart cleared his throat. "Ah, yes to that, too, sir."

Malden confronted the younger Stuart. "You're an arrogant piece of shit, you know that? Who do you think you are, sleeping with my wife? You asshole!"

The twenty-eight-year-old Stuart burst out laughing. "So what do you want to do about it, pencil-dick? Are ya just gonna stand there and call me names? What good is that going to do? Wouldn't you rather rip my head off? Or kick me in the nuts? Or pound my face in?"

Malden scoffed. "Oh, yeah, what chance do I have? You're twice my size!"

The younger Stuart shook his head. "Come on, be a man, defend your marriage. Beat me senseless and I'll let you have Victoria all to yourself!"

Malden turned and motioned toward the alleyway. The twenty-eight-year-old Stuart set his briefcase down, caught up to the smaller man, and punched him in his left kidney. Malden clutched his back and crumbled to the ground. The younger Stuart then kicked him in the ribs, spine, and face. Every time Malden tried to stand, he was beaten back down.

"Damn, Stu! You should have been a professional kickboxer!" exclaimed Croft. "The poor bastard never saw it coming!"

Stuart watched as Malden's blood splattered across the pavement. "Like I always used to say, sir . . . why take chances?"

"Now that's what I call stacking the deck! Bravo, my boy! That's the kind of initiative I've been searching for! But why all the kicking? Why not use your fists more?"

Stuart shrugged. "Maybe because I didn't want to hurt my hands."

Croft chuckled. "Yes, scraped knuckles would certainly make you look like a thug, now wouldn't it? So you gave the guy a broken nose, three broken ribs, and a shattered hand?"

Stuart shook off a touch of remorse. After all, Malden had approached and challenged him, more or less. "Sounds about right."

"Well, it looks like your little love affair broke up the entire Malden family. Their children had a lot of emotional problems after the divorce and have been in psychiatric treatment for years."

Stuart nodded. He was beyond humiliation. Croft went on to explain that the "fight" was the start of a downhill slide for Malden. He moved out of Los Angeles and ended up working nights at a 7-Eleven in Pico Rivera. During a robbery, he took a bullet over a measly hundred dollars. According to the computer, he'd been on life support for over a month now.

"And to top it off, you dumped Victoria as soon as she filed for divorce! Now that's brilliant, my boy, absolutely brilliant!"

While Croft sang Stuart's praises, the light returned him to 790.

***

Stuart gulped down another cup of coffee. It tasted like burnt liver, but it was doing its job. He kept watching the clock; just ten more minutes and he should be hearing from Croft.

Office 1421 proved to be a total disaster. The name printed on the fourth business card had been Doctor Richard Moore. It was *déjà vu* all over again. Who the hell was Richard Moore? Could he be Renee's psychologist, gynecologist, or what? But the name of the hospital printed beneath Moore's phone number sounded familiar.

When the door to 1421 opened, Stuart found himself at the corner of Leman and Adams, a very swanky district. He smiled and exhaled. *Good old Beverly Hills, now that's more like it!*

A 2005 silver Porsche Boxster swerved out of a hotel parking lot and cut off a black Silverado. The Porsche came within inches of colliding with the larger vehicle.

Stuart groaned and felt his stomach bottom out. "No, not this! Anything but this!"

Sure enough, the younger Stuart climbed out of the Silverado. "What the fuck's wrong with you, asshole?"

The driver of the Porsche sat at the nearby light with his window rolled down. He sported a Mohawk haircut, facial tattoos, and a nose ring. He gazed at the younger Stuart as if he was a babbling lunatic, then leaned out the window, blew him a kiss, and for the ultimate *piece de resistance*, flaunted his middle finger.

The driver's gestures were more than the younger Stuart could bear. "I'll kill ya, you son of a bitch!" He charged at the Porsche and the kid raised his window just in time.

"My, oh, my!" Croft hollered from the *E Drum*. "What a nasty temper you have!"

"Why did it have to be *this* day, Mister Croft? Why not when I pushed my father through that plate glass window? Or when I dropped a cherry bomb down that rabbit hole? Why, of all days, did it have to be *this* day?"

Of course Croft ignored his questions. "Hey, isn't that Renee in your passenger seat? And your son – what's his name – sitting in the back?"

As Stuart watched in dumbstruck horror, it felt as if the tentacles of disaster had just dragged him into its jaws.

His younger self pounded on the Porsche's roof. The driver laughed and kept flicking his tongue. When the light turned green, the vehicle sped off, leaving a coughing Stuart in a cloud of exhaust.

Croft's voice suddenly shot up a decibel. "Oh, no, Stuart! What have you done?"

Ever so slowly, the Silverado crept down the sloping street. Renee screamed and banged on the window, trying to get her husband's attention. Even their son yelled and pounded his fists on the glass. But the younger Stuart, still waving his fists and shouting at the Porsche, remained oblivious. By the time he spotted the Silverado, it was forty feet away. "Renee!" he shrieked. "Hit the brake!"

His wife fumbled with her seatbelt. The vehicle picked up speed, jumped a curb, and demolished a fire hydrant. Water shot ten feet in the air, drenching the Silverado and everything around it.

Croft groaned. "Didn't you shift your truck into park?"

Stuart swallowed. He had to pull himself together and answer without revealing all the devastation raging around inside him. *Can't let Croft see me sweat. He'll take it as a sign of weakness.* "I-I just thought . . ."

The air bags deployed, the Silverado halted, and Renee had to struggle to turn in her seat. Stuart would never forget what followed. The intensity of his wife's screams unleashed what felt like razor blades inside his stomach.

The younger Stuart had to race through the deluge from the hydrant to reach his vehicle. "Stephen! Stephen!"

"Oh, shit!" blurted Croft. "Wasn't your son wearing a seat belt?"

Stuart lowered his eyes. "N-no . . . he took it off."

Croft sighed, "Oh, that's a pity. I'm sorry, but our computer seems to be on a particularly nasty roll tonight. Are you okay? Do you need a break?"

The light appeared and Stuart shielded his eyes. "No, I'm all right." He thought the ordeal had ended, but when the light faded, he found himself standing in what was obviously a hospital waiting room. *No, no! Croft, you sick bastard!*

Renee and the younger Stuart sat against a far wall. She had her back turned toward him and was continually wiping her eyes. He was slumped over and appeared to be lost in a stupor.

Croft jumped in. "Well, my boy, you're in for some serious shit now. Guess you'll be in the proverbial dog house for the rest of your pathetic life."

Everything inside Stuart seemed to be crumbling. He felt out of breath, light-headed, and his stomach shriveled. "Is there any way we can skip this part, sir?"

"I'm afraid not. Once the computer takes control, we have to ride things out."

A physician entered the room. He wore black-rimmed glasses and was dressed in green scrubs. The expression on his face spoke volumes of doom and sorrow. "Hello, I'm Doctor Richard Moore."

Renee and the younger Stuart shot to their feet.

"I'm sorry to tell you this, but your son has suffered a fractured neck."

Renee clutched her stomach and collapsed into a chair. The younger Stuart looked as if he'd just been delivered the death sentence.

"But he's a strong boy and will most likely survive." The physician paused and cleared his throat. "But as far as living a normal life . . . I'd say his chances are extremely slim."

"So that's how your son ended up in a state hospital," whispered Croft, "confined to a bed and unable to walk or feed himself. What a waste. A real *senseless* waste!"

Stuart felt his eyes watering. His voice sounded as if he'd just been buried alive. "W-we did what we could." He took an anxious breath. "There was . . . neurological damage."

Croft remained silent for what seemed forever.

Renee leaped to her feet and grabbed the younger Stuart by his collar. "You fucking bastard! You stupid, goddamn, miserable asshole! You did this to our son! You and your temper! You just had to chase that car! Not a thought for our safety! It's all about you and your fucking ego!"

And then, at long last, everything turned white.

* * *

As Stuart finished his coffee, he turned and stared at the cafeteria's entrance. It had just happened again. He could have sworn that something dark and indistinct had just glided into the room. Yet, when he turned around, there was only an emptiness surrounding him – a strange, unsettling emptiness that made him feel as if he was the last person on the planet.

He groaned and crushed the empty coffee cup. *Just another illusion courtesy of Croft and his fucking capsule.*

And now, on top of everything else, a fly seemed to be going out of its way to pester him. The thing was persistent; he had to give it that. Tried its best to get inside his ear and he nearly nailed it that time. Come to think of it, he had never seen a fly in this building before, but like the saying goes, "there's always a first time for everything."

Stuart mangled the coffee cup into a tight little ball and tossed it at the trash container. It bounced off the rim and landed on the floor. The fifth room had actually been easier than the fourth, but unfortunately, that wasn't saying much.

Once again Croft and his handy computer had Stuart completely stumped. The next business card belonged to an Officer James Perez, San Francisco P.D. *Here we go again. Who's Officer Perez? I don't know any cops. What did I do this time? Rob a doughnut shop?*

Stuart flipped the card over. His next destination would be 513, which turned out to be an office supply room – at least that's what it was before the light turned on.

When Stuart was finally able to see, he observed his younger self sitting behind his office desk, engrossed in paperwork, at the Croft Tower, San Francisco. A framed picture of his wife sat at a far corner of the desk, surrounded by stacks of file folders. The photo wasn't Renee's. That marriage was as dead as James Dean and Elvis Presley combined. It was a photo of Evelyn and Stuart's twelve-year-old stepdaughter, Brianna. The date on the desk calendar read November 23, 2011.

What happened then? It was only six years ago.

"Well, Stu, it looks like you're back at your old office." It sounded as if Croft was shuffling some papers around. "By now we've promoted you to Executive Director of the California Branch, and you've been married to the former Evelyn Dexter for nearly four years."

Stuart murmured, "Sir, I think the computer made a mistake. I've never met an Officer Perez."

"Well, who knows, my boy. Let's just wait and see what happens."

The intercom buzzed and Stuart nearly jumped out of his skin. Still engrossed with his paperwork, the younger Stuart shouted, "What is it, Mary?"

"Jerry Bradley would like to see you, sir."

The young Stuart rolled his eyes. "Okay, send the little do-gooder in."

Croft asked, "So, you *do* remember sweet, kind-hearted Jerry, now don't you?"

"Of course, he was my assistant for three years before I canned him for being such a useless bleeding heart."

Jerry entered the office carrying a file folder. He looked a lot older than Stuart remembered. *Yeah, working for me would age just about anybody.*

The younger Stuart never bothered to glance up. "What is it, Bradley?"

Jerry set the folder in front of his boss. "Sir, would you please review the Randolph file just once more? With six children, they're an awful large family to simply toss into the street."

"For God's sake, Bradley, quit whining and have some balls for a change!"

"Sir, Mister Randolph's doing his best to find employment. It wouldn't hurt to wait a little while longer. We could always send them another notice . . ."

"They're six months behind in their mortgage already! Either foreclose, or I'll crush your wimpy little nuts in a vice."

Bradley's face turned a vivid red. He left the office without uttering another word.

Croft wailed with laughter. "Well done, Stuart! I especially like your *colorful* candor."

"So I had the Randolphs evicted, sir. I don't see what that has to do with this Perez guy."

Out of nowhere, a rolled-up newspaper appeared at Stuart's feet. *Where the hell did that come from?*

"Go ahead, my illustrious protégé, take a peek."

Stuart bent down and, to his surprise, was able to pick up the newspaper. "Hey, how come I can touch this? You said I wouldn't be able to touch anything, remember? That I was like a ghost."

"That's because the computer sent it over. It's a loophole, in a round-about way."

Stuart removed the rubber band from the paper. "It's from October 8, 2012."

"That's right, now turn to section A, page 5."

Stuart turned to the page. There was a brief article entitled "Off-Duty Police Officer Fatally Shot." He read the first few lines then dropped the paper.

Croft cleared his throat. "So, how about that, my boy? You *do* have a connection to Officer Perez."

"I-I can't believe this. It's just not possible."

"No, it's true. After you evicted them, things became rather desperate for the Randolphs. The father ended up robbing a pawn shop. Officer Perez tried to intervene, and now he's rotting in a cozy little grave across the bay. Wayne Randolph is serving a life sentence and his wife and kids — well, let's just say they're up shit creek in a leaky canoe . . . or without a paddle, or however the saying goes."

"Why are you telling me this, Mister Croft? I was just doing my job, that's all. In fact, I was working for you at the time."

"Well, like I said, I'm just making sure you have what it takes. A lesser candidate would get all *mushy* over something like this, now wouldn't they?"

Stuart nodded. "Yeah, guess so."

"So tell me. Just *how* are you feeling inside, my boy? Are things getting all *mushy* deep down in the pit of your stomach?"

Stuart responded like a pumped-up draftee at boot camp. "Hell no, sir! Not one bit!"

"Good, I must say, you're doing fantastic! But you still have two more tests to go, now don't you?"

Once again the light flashed and Stuart had to shade his eyes. All this humiliation felt exhausting and, more importantly, ate away at his dwindling nerves. Sure, most of these scenarios made him feel like a bloodsucking fiend, but he was not about to take the blame for anyone's death or misfortune. So what if he took his job seriously and performed it better than anyone else? Denying loans and initiating foreclosures were all part of the corporate ladder. And even though Croft was rubbing his nose in it, he obviously agreed. So no matter how horrible his actions looked, they were still helping him ace an enormous promotion.

Stuart could hear Croft talking to Danton McCray. For once the billionaire sounded rather annoyed with his right-hand stooge.

"Stuart, I have to take a break. It may be after hours in L.A., but right now things are really heating up in good old Singapore. I shouldn't be more than thirty minutes. I'll contact you when I'm ready. In the meantime, *au revoir, mon ami!* Croft, over and out."

***

Stuart glanced at his watch. It was nearly 11:30 and still no word from Croft. The fly had returned. The little turd-lover seemed determined to torment him to the brink of insanity. Stuart coughed and shook his head. He'd better take a leak while he still had the chance.

Just as he stood, the tiny pest landed on his forearm.

Stuart smiled. *Okay, sucker, time to die!*

When he inched his arm closer, the insect reared up on its hind legs. *What the . . . ?*

There was something different about this particular fly. It fact, it looked like an image straight out of a nightmare. In exact proportion to its size, it possessed a human's head.

Oh, shit! This can't be!

"You're an asshole," it shrieked in a distant, high-pitched voice. "A real fucking asshole!"

Stuart's mouth dried out and his legs grew weak. *I'm hallucinating. This can't be real!*

The fly seemed to be enjoying itself by scurrying back and forth on Stuart's arm, ranting and raving. "I only land on shit, and you're the biggest pile I could find!"

Stuart cringed. The fly's face was too small to make out, but the creature's voice sounded disturbingly familiar. *I gotta be crazy! Completely nuts! It sounds like . . . Danton McCray!*

The creature kept occupied by rubbing its forelegs together. "You're a real prick, you know that? Don't worry. You'll get fucked sooner or later!"

Stuart took a breath and swatted the thing with his free hand. To his surprise, it made no attempt to escape. "What do ya know? Looks like you got *fucked* yourself."

When he raised his hand, there was nothing left of the fly but a single spot of blood. "Goodbye, McCray, you snake. Can't say I'll . . ."

Before Stuart could say another word, he began coughing and could not stop. Everything around him started to spin and his throat erupted into what felt like an inferno. He shook his head, clutched his throat, and rushed toward the men's room.

***

Stuart hurried into the restroom. His coughing had subsided, but the smartass fly with McCray's distinctive voice had rattled him deeply. *Croft, you bastard! You drugged me! I know you did!*

After Stuart cleaned the stain off his coat sleeve, he used the urinal. He washed and dried his hands and tossed the paper towel at the trash container. It bounced off the wall and landed on the floor. He ran a hand through his hair and stared in the mirror. *Damn! I look like a mortician's worst nightmare!*

Again, Stuart's coughing erupted. His windpipe tightened and his lungs strained for air. His face turned dark and blurred vision overwhelmed him. He doubled over, grabbed the counter, and realized something was crawling up his throat. When it neared his mouth, he gagged, and the object flew into the sink. *Holy shit! What the fuck's that?*

Stuart's coughing halted and his breathing stabilized. He wiped the tears from his eyes and took a heavy breath. Leaning against the counter, he peered into the sink.

A dark creature the size of a quarter floated around in a pool of green mucus. Stuart watched in astonishment as it struggled out of the fluid and rose to its feet. Eight slender legs protruded from an oval-shaped body. As it crawled, it started to grow – at an incredible rate. Stuart thought it resembled a spider or a scorpion, or maybe both.

What the hell is that? Stuart didn't know what to distrust – his eyes or his sanity. The creature's movements began to escalate. Its snapping, reddish mandibles were in constant motion. As he watched, its body enlarged to the size of a fist.

This is crazy! How can that thing be real!

The creature sped around in a tight circle. It halted, looked up, then raced forward. Stuart reacted decisively and slammed his hand down. Green, black, and red slime splattered on his palm, the sink, mirror, and counter. Disgusted, he wiped his hand with a paper towel.

That fucking Croft! I'm still hallucinating! It's from that capsule. It has to be!

A low, creaking emerged from the hallway. Stuart turned and glared at the door. *Now what? Another disappearing shadow? Or maybe it's that Angel guy finally showing up.*

As the door eased open, Stuart was surprised to see a lone janitor dressed in a faded blue uniform. The man struggled through the doorway while pushing a plastic utility cart. Stuart had seen the custodian before. He was an older black guy, probably around seventy. His name badge simply read "Brahman."

The janitor spotted the paper towel lying on the floor. Glancing at Stuart, he held the small of his back, bent down, and picked it up. "Working late, I see."

Stuart stepped over to a clean sink and rinsed his face. "Yeah, someone's gotta bring home the bacon."

Brahman tossed the paper towel in the trash and noticed the bizarre substance splattered across the counter, sink, and mirror. He turned and gazed curiously at Stuart. "Something didn't agree with you?"

A cynical grin spread across Stuart's face. "Yeah, you can say that again!"

"So I presume by now you've met your boss, the mysterious Mister Croft?"

Stuart belched. His stomach couldn't seem to make up its mind. One minute it was okay, then the next it grew nauseous. "Yep, today for the first time."

Brahman removed a bottle of glass cleaner from his cart. "Too bad. He's evil, you know."

Stuart glared at him briefly then dried his face with a fresh paper towel. "Oh, yeah? Let me get this straight. You're saying you actually *know* him?"

The custodian shook his head. "Nope, and I wouldn't want to, either."

"Then how the fuck can you say he's evil?"

Brahman sprayed some cleaner on the mirror. "Next time you see him, take a good look. He's not that hard to figure out."

Stuart gazed at his reflection as he straightened his tie. "So what did you hear? That he's a shrewd capitalist, a brilliant banker, or an outright asshole?"

The janitor turned and looked at Stuart as if he was a condemned man. "He covets money and makes people do horrible things. Like I said . . . he's evil."

Stuart turned toward the exit, removed a dime from his pants pocket, and slapped it on the counter. "Thanks, I'll keep that in mind."

ROOM 317

After stowing his coat and tie in his office, Stuart approached the sixth room. *Just two more to go,* he reminded himself. He took a deep breath and murmured, "Collier 7187."

The door opened, Stuart stepped inside, the light appeared, then quickly faded. He found himself in the middle of an unfamiliar bedroom. The carpet appeared worn and the walls needed painting. The bed had been left unmade, and along with an ice bucket and a smudged water glass, an opened bottle of Jack Daniels stood on the nightstand. A talk show played on a small television set perched on top of an old, battered dresser.

"Hey, that dresser looks familiar."

"Stuart, I admire your powers of observation," chimed Croft from the *E Drum*. "Indeed, you *were* once the proud owner of that very relic."

A water faucet sounded from behind the adjacent bathroom door. Stuart glanced at a nearby wall calendar. Each day of October 2017, had been crossed off right up to the 30th. "Well, what do you know? It's today," Stuart whispered.

"Yes, just eleven hours ago, as a matter of fact."

"So who lives here, sir?"

"I believe . . . we're about to find out."

The sound from the water faucet halted and then the bathroom door creaked open. Stuart's stomach plunged and his heart pounded. Renee staggered out and flopped onto the bed. She wore a long, wrinkled T-shirt and her uncombed hair appeared oily. She seemed thinner, much older, and her face looked pale and gaunt.

Stuart stepped back and recalled how Croft had said earlier "After you sucked her dry, she drank herself into a skid-row slut." He rubbed his eyes and barely collected himself. *So much for the magic carpet ride.*

"You cheated, Mister Croft. The business card said Mason's Furniture."

"I didn't cheat. That *was* her employer and the card belonged to her."

Renee poured some Jack Daniels into the glass and took a sip. She reached over to the nightstand and picked up a crumpled pack of cigarettes.

Stuart's downtrodden expression transformed to one of complete exasperation. "Hell! I knew about the drinking, but when did she start smoking?"

"The computer's telling me she began after your divorce, Stu. It seems all the cheating and grief you put her through sent her down a bitter path."

"Well, Mister Croft, her being a lush is no surprise to me, so why don't we just flush this toilet and move on? You can blame me all you like, but Renee's the one who's responsible for her situation, not me."

"Bravo, my boy. I couldn't have said it better myself! But let's just wait and see what happens, shall we?"

Stuart gazed apprehensively at his ex-wife. She inhaled a long, leisurely drag from her cigarette then took another sip of Jack Daniels. Her face remained expressionless and her eyelids started drooping.

"Shit, she's falling asleep!"

"Precisely!" Croft confirmed.

Before long, Renee's eyes closed and the cigarette began to slip from her fingers.

"Hey, wake up, you stupid idiot!" yelled Stuart. "You're gonna set yourself on fire!"

"You're a ghost, remember? She can't see or hear you."

The cigarette dropped from Renee's hand and rolled onto the bedding. As Stuart watched in anguish, it began to smolder. Swearing, he rushed over and tried to scoop up the cigarette, but his hand merely swept through it.

"Come on, Mister Croft! We just can't stand around and watch her die!"

"We don't have a choice, Stu. It's already a done deal, remember? What's happening at this very moment . . . actually occurred eleven hours ago."

The smoldering grew more intense and smoke drifted through the room. Renee's glass of Jack Daniels tilted downward, spilling the contents onto the sheets.

Stuart wrestled with his emotions. He had to remain calm, look as though he could care less. Concern, remorse – any display of sentiment – would certainly sabotage his promotion.

The alcohol fueled the smoldering bed sheet and a moment later a flame appeared. Stuart grew lightheaded and his stomach churned acid. He battled back tears and had to clench his mouth shut. Inch by inch, Renee and her bed were consumed by a fiery blaze. By the time she screamed and sprang up, her destiny was only a matter of a heartbeat away.

"You stupid bitch! Why the hell would you do this to yourself?"

At first Stuart thought it was the fire blinding him, but it was the light. Once again it had come to whisk him away. This time he couldn't have been more relieved. Trembling, he shielded his eyes. *Why should I care about her? Croft is screwing with my head, that's all! Trying to lay a shitload of guilt on me!*

When Stuart found himself in the middle of Room 317, however, the stench of burning flesh still filled the air. He doubled over, gagged, and threw up a mixture of coffee and black bile.

That's it! Screw it. I'm quitting. All I want to do is go home, get shitfaced, and put all this grief behind me.

A familiar humming resonated from the *E Drum*. "Are you okay, my boy?"

Stuart wiped his mouth and headed for the door. "I'm out of here, Mister Croft. I don't know what you're trying to do, but a person can take only so much!"

"Nonsense! You want to stop now with just one more test to go? That's exactly what Miranda Howell did. Started pissing her panties and blowing off her promotion at the very *brink* of success! Is that what you're going to do, my boy? Be a quitter *and* a coward?"

The door opened and Stuart hurried down the hallway. "So, did Miranda have to watch someone *die* like I just did?"

Croft's voice sounded offended. "Of course not. These tests are programmed on an *individual* basis."

"You drugged me, didn't you, sir? What the hell was in that capsule, anyway?"

Croft snickered. "It's a little late to worry about that . . . now isn't it?"

Stuart came to a halt. Out the corner of his eye, he caught a glimpse of something moving behind him. He took a breath and turned around. A murky shadow, roughly six feet in length, zigzagged across the ceiling at the far end of the hallway. It traveled at an incredible speed and vanished around a corner.

"What's following me, Mister Croft?"

There was a brief pause before his boss answered. "Angel has been observing you from the video monitors, but that's it." He hesitated again. "Does congenital paranoia run in your family, my boy?"

Stuart resumed his way. "Forgive me for saying so, sir, but your tests suck!"

"I told you, they're designed to weed out the weaklings . . . individuals who don't have the balls to handle such enormous responsibilities."

Stuart turned the corner and approached the elevator. "Lobby!" he snarled.

"So, is that *who* you are, Stu? Someone who wimps out when they're minutes away from making millions of dollars?"

The chime sounded and the elevator opened. Stuart paused before stepping inside. A lifetime of bitterness swept through him. Bit by bit, his resistance crumbled. He held his breath and shuddered. *A million and a half a year with one last test to go!*

He cleared his throat and stepped into the elevator. "No one calls me a quitter or a coward, Mister Croft." He removed the last business card from his shirt pocket. "I'll take that dare of yours. But I'm warning you, I'm gonna *trounce* the hell out of your last fucking test."

ROOM 669

Stuart approached the door and glanced at the sign. He suspected as much. *It's the mail room. Just an ordinary, lousy mail room.*

He carefully gazed at the last business card. It belonged to his current wife, Evelyn. He moaned and returned it to his coat pocket. *What's it going to be this time? My latest affair? Cheating on my income taxes? After what I've been through, nothing can touch me.*

"Collier 7187." His voice sounded distant and feeble. The door opened and Stuart covered his eyes. *This is it. I'm going to be so fucking rich! And after a few years, I'll tell Croft to kiss my ass goodbye.*

As the light faded, Stuart glanced around.

"Well, my boy," greeted Croft from the *E Drum*, "welcome to your humble abode."

"Yeah, guess so." He sighed and rubbed his eyes. Stomach aches, headaches, smartass flies with human heads, and a spider-like creature that barfs out of your mouth. What could possibly be next? "It's my house in Woodland Hills," he answered. "The one we owe two mortgages on."

"Oh, and what a lovely layout! You've done quite well, now haven't you? Crystal chandeliers, European furniture, and that naked lady statue by the terrace, the one with the gigantic tits. How *tastefully* divine!"

Stuart managed to restrain a groan. "Yes, Evelyn has expensive taste."

"And so do you, with a Ferrari Enzo and a Mercedes McLaren parked in your garage."

To his surprise Stuart found himself grinning. "You forgot my Jeep Cherokee."

"Yes, and that, too. No wonder you're wallowing around in debt. But never fear, I believe that's about to change."

The Colliers' front door flew open. Evelyn, Brianna, and the future Stuart walked in. Lugging a pair of suitcases, the newest Stuart looked tired, disgusted and surprisingly older.

"Sir, what day is this?"

"A month and a half from now. Why?"

"I guess it's the day Brianna comes home for Christmas. She's a freshman at Berkeley."

"I see. A reunion! How quaint!"

Stuart's step-daughter flopped onto the couch. She sported a black leather skirt that rose well above her knees. As usual she wore a lavish amount of mascara and her dark roots flourished abundantly. She chomped on her gum, fidgeted, and watched intently as the other Stuart hauled the suitcases to her room.

Evelyn tossed her purse on a chair and hurried to the bathroom. When the other Stuart returned, Brianna gradually lifted her skirt and tantalized her stepfather with a most provocative smirk.

"Oh, my!" exclaimed Croft. "What, pray tell, is this?"

The future Stuart shot the teenager a furious scowl. Just before her mother returned, Brianna slid her skirt back down.

"I have to finish my Christmas shopping," Evelyn announced. "Can I leave the two of you alone for a few hours without your usual bickering?"

The future Stuart turned and headed toward the front door. "Probably not. I'll tag along, if you don't mind."

Evelyn rolled her eyes. "Then how can I shop for your presents? Just relax and get reacquainted with your stepdaughter. I won't be long."

She hurried out the door, her spike heels clattering on the imported ceramic tile. Brianna jumped up as soon as the door shut.

"You heard my mom, we have to get reacquainted."

Croft burst out laughing. "This is so unbelievable! I would have never guessed you for a pedophile, my boy."

"I'm not a pedophile!" hollered Stuart. "She's eighteen and has been trying to nail me for years!"

He could not believe it, but Croft actually giggled. "Yeah, okay, sure. Whatever you say!"

As Brianna advanced, the future Stuart kept backing away, until he reached the fireplace. "You fucking slut! I told you to knock it off!"

"Oh, I love it when you talk dirty!" She slinked over and caressed his chest. "Stop being so difficult. I know how much you like it." She lowered her hand to his stomach. "It's Christmas and I just wanna unwrap my present."

Croft grew hysterical. His laughter no longer sounded human — more like a rampaging hyena out of an old Tarzan movie.

Stuart looked away, his expression riddled with shame. *Is nothing secret? And the worse it gets, the more Croft enjoys it.*

As Brianna reached lower, the light at long last made its appearance.

"Well, let's give the two lovebirds a little privacy, shall we?"

Stuart wiped his forehead. *This is it. It's finally over! I'm going to be so fucking rich!*

Then, as if Croft knew exactly what Stuart was thinking, he cleared his throat and murmured, "So why don't we see what your dear little wife is *really* up to?"

When the light dissipated, Stuart found himself in what appeared to be an extremely upscale hotel suite. A voluptuous blonde was propped against the headboard of a king-sized bed. The surroundings remained dimly lit, but from what he could see, she was dressed in a black, see-through negligee and was casually filing her fingernails.

"W-where are we, Mister Croft?"

"We're at the Beverly-Wilshire Grand Hotel, Stuart. A lavish enough accommodation for the rich and famous, but I would never be caught *dead* in this place."

"But what about Evelyn, sir?"

"Be patient, my boy. Time will tell."

The bathroom door opened and to Stuart's bewilderment, Evelyn stepped out. With her hair sopping wet and her face sprinkled with moisture, she wore a white terrycloth bathrobe.

Once again Croft burst out laughing. "Man, oh man! The look on your face tells it all! You had no idea she was playing around on you, now did you? And with a woman, at that!"

For a long, agonizing moment, Stuart found himself unable to speak. He wanted to deny this latest disaster, but deep down he knew Evelyn was capable of just about anything.

"So how does it feel to be on the receiving end, my boy?"

Stuart shook with rage and thought his stomach would explode. The urge to tell Croft to go fuck himself had reached a new breaking point. He could barely swallow and had to force himself to speak. "I'm pissed . . . totally pissed! That's how I feel!"

Evelyn sauntered toward the bed and the blonde tossed the nail file onto the nightstand.

"You're *banging* her teenage daughter, but when she cheats on you, you're pissed?" Croft sighed and chuckled. "Bravo, my boy! How chivalrous of you!"

Evelyn untied the sash to the bathrobe and it dropped to the floor. She stood naked with her skin glistening with moisture. The blonde grinned and slid toward her.

Stuart could barely breathe. "It doesn't matter. This is so outrageous . . . it's . . . it's . . . ."

"I bet you're so pissed, you could *kill* them . . . now couldn't you?"

The blonde pulled Evelyn into her arms and kissed her.

"Yeah, I could kill them! I could kill them both!"

Croft paused briefly. "Well, what do you know? Take a look behind you."

Stuart turned and had to wipe the tears from his eyes. On the dresser in an opened stainless steel case, he spotted a semi-automatic handgun. "W-where did that come from?"

"Smith and Wesson, I believe. A nice, handy problem solver, if you ask me. So what are you waiting for? Go ahead, let them have it!"

Stuart crept over and, to his surprise, was able to pick up the weapon. "What's going on, sir? You said I was like a ghost. That I couldn't touch anything."

"Yes, but we're in the future now and the rules have changed. Damn! Would you look at those two? They're really getting it on!"

Stuart staggered toward the bed. Evelyn had slipped under the covers and was locked in a fiery embrace with the blonde.

"You can just stand there and watch," murmured Croft, "if you're into that sort of thing. But she and her little girlfriend are making you look like a . . . first-class loser!"

Stuart swallowed and raised the gun. It wasn't heavy, but his trembling prevented him from holding it steady.

"Do it, my boy! Blow their brains out! Stop them before it's too late!"

Perspiration trickled down Stuart's face as he aimed for the back of Evelyn's head. His hands were clammy. His heart raced. His insides had reached a boiling point. Placing his index finger on the trigger, he tightened it.

"Hurry, Stuart! Waste those degenerates!"

He pulled the trigger, blinked, and waited. There was no discharge, no recoil, just a pathetic click. He took a quick breath and pulled the trigger three more times. *Empty! It's not even loaded!*

Stuart cringed and lowered the weapon. A lone tear trickled down his cheek. He expected another burst of laughter from Croft, but there was only a disturbing silence.

Finally, as the light appeared, his boss cleared his throat. "Well done, my boy. Now I know just how . . . *far* . . . you will go. Indeed, you *do* have what it takes."

Stuart found himself hunched over a stack of empty mailbags. Exhaustion sapped his strength. Sensations of betrayal and mortification burned inside him. "I'm still going to kill that bitch, Mister Croft. She's not getting away with this."

"My, aren't you the psychopath? But let's move on to more pleasant subjects, shall we? How about joining me for a little champagne? Because, as of now, you're officially my U.S Director! And I must say, you genuinely *deserve* what's coming to you."

"Thank you, sir," Stuart replied. *It's about fucking time,* he mused, *you son of a bitch!* He took a breath, turned, and stepped out the door. No sooner had he entered the hallway than the lights dimmed.

"Hey, what's going on?"

"Oh, the hallway lights always turn down at midnight. No sense in wasting energy."

Even though it was dark, there was enough light for Stuart to make his way. The lobby at the end of the hall appeared brighter and about forty yards to his left. *Hell, Croft's worth billions and suddenly he's trying to save a few bucks on energy?* Stuart shook his head as a weary grin crept across his face. *Evelyn had me so pissed . . . I almost forgot how rich I'm going to be!*

Advancing cautiously down the hallway, Stuart halted after a few yards. Something behind him sounded as if a distant train had just barreled through a tunnel. When he turned around, there was only the surrounding gloom.

"Ah, Stuart," Croft murmured from the *E Drum*, "Why don't you hurry? The computer's informing me there's a malfunction occurring which may prove harmful. So let's get cracking, shall we?"

Stuart rolled his eyes and resumed his way. "What kind of malfunction are you talking about, sir?"

Croft hesitated before answering. "Well, let's just say you're better off . . . not knowing."

When Stuart again heard the sound, he whirled around. What he perceived through the darkness sent an icy shudder through him. *What the fuck is that?*

It had to be the same shadowy figure he'd spotted earlier. Its general shape appeared human, but its movements looked bizarre and outlandish. In just a few brief moments it shot through a wall, the ceiling, and dove into the floor – disappearing temporarily – but all the while advancing toward Stuart.

No, this can't be real! It's another hallucination! It has to be!

He turned and hurried toward the lobby. No matter how much it unnerved him, he kept glancing over his shoulder, trying to determine what was chasing him.

"Hurry, my boy!" Croft's voice possessed an unmistakable urgency. "Get to the elevator, fast!"

Stuart broke into a full run. His thoughts had become scattered, and for the first time in his life, stark terror rushed through him. "What is that thing, Mister Croft?"

"You're almost there. Hurry!"

He pushed himself harder as he neared the lobby. The closer he came, the brighter the lights grew. As the sound heightened, he slid across a freshly mopped floor and collided into a wall. Recognizing a janitor's cart just beyond the murkiness, he pushed forward. *Damn it, Brahman! What are you trying to do? Kill me?*

Stuart raced into the lobby shouting, "Eighteen!" Listening for the approaching elevator, he waited for what seemed forever.

"Eighteen! Damn it! Eighteen!" The bell chimed. The doors opened. He hurried inside just as an enormous, billowing darkness stormed into the lobby. The doors shut, and wheezing frantically, a bewildered Stuart gasped, "W-what was that, M-Mister Croft?"

The elevator jolted, and to Stuart's horror, the digital display flashed downward. A metallic and indifferent voice crackled through the speakers. "Minus one . . . minus five . . ."

That voice. It's Renee's. I'd know it anywhere. The lights dimmed and the stench of alcohol infected the air.

Burning sweat ran down Stuart's face as he realized he was not alone. He jumped backward and struck the safety rail. His eyes bulged. *What the hell is that?*

"Stuart, I want you to meet one of my most gifted associates. We call him Angel. Of course, that's not his *real* name, but since he's been observing you, we thought the term sounded ironic . . . not to mention quite endearing."

The shadowy figure seemed to occupy the entire elevator. It possessed no distinct details — no facial features, hands, or legs, just a murky silhouette swirling in constant motion.

Stuart punched the emergency knob repeatedly but the elevator continued its descent. More euphoric than ever, Croft appeared on all eighteen video screens. Grinning triumphantly, he flaunted a bottle of champagne. "Congratulations, Stu! What a joyous occasion!"

"Mister Croft, I-I don't understand."

"Well, my boy, the truth is, you've done such an *incredible* job, that I've decided to make you my junior partner. You'll be running the entire organization. Not the one you've been acquainted with but my *actual*, legitimate enterprise!"

The shadowy figure appeared to be glaring at Stuart, scrutinizing him with intense interest.

"Minus ninety-eight . . . minus one hundred and ten . . ." The elevator's descent accelerated. The sound just beyond the walls roared at a deafening pitch.

"Of course, the job doesn't pay well. In fact, it doesn't pay anything! But the good news is you'll be performing the same precise functions as you've been performing all your life . . . making people *exceptionally* miserable. Now, is that job satisfaction or what?"

The heat progressed from stifling to unbearable. Stuart could scarcely breathe. The elevator rattled and lurched, hurling him to the floor. He shifted to the left corner and clutched the safety rail. "B-but why am I . . ."

Something was happening to the shadowy figure. Its face appeared to be evolving.

"The elevator's taking you to the bottom level, my boy. That's where you'll be working."

Perspiration drenched Stuart's face. Scorching heat ravaged his throat. The details of the figure's face grew clearer.

"I have to confess, my dear boy, I don't actually own a computer that creates holograms and I was never keen on making you my U.S. Director. Hell, to tell you the truth . . . I'm not even human."

The shadowy being's features came into focus. Tears streamed down Stuart's face. He could not stop trembling. *Oh, God! No! No! Not him!*

"Surprise, surprise! Yes, my boy, your dear old daddy has come to whisk you away to your new profession!"

No! This can't be! I'm still hallucinating!

It grew sweltering. Stuart's body felt as if it had wasted away. As his lungs strained for air, his father's face transformed. Looming over him was something outrageously fiendish with reddish skin, twisted horns, and reptilian eyes.

No! No! Please, not that!

The elevator quickly decelerated. Renee's indifferent tone took on a vengeful edge. "Minus six hundred and fifty . . . minus six hundred and sixty . . ."

Croft's face also transformed. Horns, fangs, and yellow-green eyes materialized. Snorting, he lapped up his champagne with a long, narrow tongue. "Congratulations, my boy." His voice deepened to a menacing tone. "I'm sure you'll perform an exceptional job! And, incidentally, that capsule you swallowed, the one you thought caused hallucinations . . . was simply a mixture of sugar and caffeine."

"Minus six hundred and sixty-six," announced Renee, "bottom level."

The elevator halted, the chime sounded, the doors opened. A single scream erupted.

"Oh, and by the way, my dear *industrious* protégé . . . have an illuminating Halloween. *Gute Nacht!* Croft, over and out."

About the Author

Michael Raff was born and raised in Chicago, Illinois. He discovered his love for writing at the age of thirteen while still in grammar school. He moved to California in 1968 and attended creative writing courses at Cypress College. He became a psychiatric technician in 1974, working for the state of California until retiring in 2007.

Michael discovered he had a flair for writing horror in 1983 when he wrote "The Door," the first of his many short stories. Currently, he is a member of the High Desert Branch of the California Writers Club. His nonfictional, romantic, coming-of-age book, *Special,* was published in 2011. Additionally, *Seven: Tales of Terror,* his first horror anthology, was published in 2013, followed by his second horror anthology, *Scare Tactics,* in 2014. His current writing projects include *Stalkers* and *Skeleton Man*, both non-anthologies. He and his wife, Joyce, live in Hesperia, California, along with their amazing assortment of dogs, cats, a horse, and a pigmy goat named Toby.

Made in the USA
Columbia, SC
19 June 2024

36949435R00195